THE BASILEIA LETTERS
Volumes 1 & 2

by
Ron McGatlin
(Brother Ron)

I

THE
BASILEIA LETTERS
Volumes 1 & 2

Copyright 2001
Ron McGatlin
all rights reserved

ISBN 0-9654546-4-9

All Scripture Quotations Are From the
"New King James Version".
Copyright 1983 by Thomas Nelson, Inc.

Published by
BASILEIA PUBLISHING
107 W. Independence Blvd.
Mt. Airy, NC 27030

http://www.basileiapublishing.com

Printed in the USA by

MORRIS PUBLISHING

3212 East Highway 30 • Kearney, NE 68847 • 1-800-650-7888

Contents

"THE BASILEIA LETTERS, Volumes 1 & 2" is a compilation of teaching letters written by Ron McGatlin in the years 1997-2000, just prior to and at the turn of the century, the end of the second millennium and the beginning of the third since Christ, and the beginning of the seventh millennium of Biblical history of mankind.

****

Brother Ron's Life Verse

Mat 6:33 "But seek first the kingdom of God and His righteousness, and all these things shall be added to you.

****

Brother Ron's Prayer, in 1997 untill the end. Psalm 71:15 -18:

My mouth shall tell of Your righteousness
And Your salvation all the day,
For I do not know their limits.
I will go in the strength of the Lord God.
I will make mention of Your righteousness,
of Yours only. O God,
You have taught me from my youth;
And to this day I declare Your wondrous works.
Now also when I am old and grayheaded,
O God, do not forsake me,
Until I declare Your strength to this generation,
Your power to everyone who is to come.

****

BASILEIA LETTER

Number 1

What is a Basileia Letter? & What does Basileia have to do with me?

Jesus said, "But seek first the "basileia" of God and His righteousness, and all these things shall be added to you." *(Mat 6:33)* Basileia is the Greek word translated "kingdom" in the New Testament. Basileia is used 164 times in the New Testament, over 100 times by our Lord Jesus the Christ. Basileia or kingdom has a prominent role in the teachings of Jesus. Most of His teachings had to do with the concept of this significant word. He began many of the parables with this statement: "*(the basileia of Theos is like),* the kingdom of God is like; " and then he would give an illustration teaching hidden wisdom of the kingdom of God. Or, interchangeably, He would start the parable with, "*(the basileia of ouranos is like),* the kingdom of heaven is like," and then tell the parable of hidden "basileia" wisdom.

Most people don't realize that Greek words are often used as names of products and companies today. For example "nike" is a Greek word meaning conquest, or means of success.

Basileia is defined in the Strongs as: "G932: basileia, bas-il-i'-ah; prop. **royalty**, i.e. (abstr.) **rule**, or (concr.) **a realm** (lit. or fig.):--kingdom, + reign." From G935: basileus, bas-il-yooce'; **a sovereign** (abs., rel. or fig.):--king. Prob. from G939 (through the notion of a foundation of power): basis, bas'-ece; from baino (**to walk**); **a pace** ("base"), i.e. (by impl.) the foot:--foot.

Jesus taught more about the basileia (kingdom) of God/heaven than any other thing. He made it clear that man's first priority was, and is to seek the basileia of God/heaven. He also taught that all the other things man needed would be added to him if he would seek the

6

basileia of God and His righteousness, as his top priority. Does this mean that Christians are to be seeking the basileia of God instead of seeking to get money to meet their needs, or instead of seeking pleasure, or prosperity, or position, or anything else? Matthew 6:33, does say, *"and all these things will be **added** to you."* It does not say go out and seek money for food, clothing, etc. *(Luke 12:29)*

Is this beginning to sound like a super cop-out? Is one not required to try to get things any more? Does one need only stay home and seek the basileia of God? It is not exactly like that! It might be important for Christians to find out what exactly it really means to seek the basileia (kingdom) of God and His righteousness. Christians have a tendency to see everything about the kingdom of God/ heaven as religious and church related. Is seeking the kingdom of God more than receiving Jesus as saviour, reading the Bible, and praying? These things are certainly primary to seeking the kingdom, but the kingdom involves one's entire life.

Attending church services one day a week and tithing ten percent of one's income is not the whole thing. God wants the other six days and the other ninety percent to seek Him as well. God is more concerned about the six days and the ninety percent than the one day and the ten percent.

Seeking the basileia of God means, in part, ordering one's entire life by the sovereign rule of God. It means walking in the Spirit of God, and dieing to one's self life to the extent that Jesus can live within and rule every aspect of one's life. It means allowing the grace of God to empower one to overcome sin and weaknesses in one's life. It means to be so in tune with the love of God that serving God by serving Jesus in others, is a natural result. It means being so filled with the life of God by His Spirit that power and enthusiasm naturally flow from the life. It means feeling the pain of others needs and becoming a part of the solution to meet their needs.

7

It means that there is nothing that even comes close to God in our lives. It means that without Him we would have no life. But with Him we have abundant life, overflowing life. Life flowing to others and the world around us, as rivers of living water. It means we will become very active and busy serving God by serving others. Seeking the kingdom of God will probably result in our getting up earlier, and being more active in doing whatever God has given us to do. It may result in one becoming so active serving God by serving others, that one has neither time nor desire to watch hours of mindless TV, or play hours of useless video games.

Spectator sports may no longer be the focus of one's life. Seeking the basileia may mean getting up from one's seat in the grandstands and getting out on the playing field of real life. Involvement in the all consuming adventure of truly seeking the basileia of God and His righteous way of doing and being, in the real world, is far more exciting than watching any sports team, TV program, or video game, in the fantasy world.

Seeking the basileia of heaven does not mean seeking God and religion as a part of one's life. *(Jer 29:13)* It means seeking the kingdom of God to come forth in one's daily living, and the will of God to be done in one's entire life. *(Mat 6:10)* It means seeking God's direction for one's life activities such as: education, vocation, avocations, relations and recreations; and it means seeking His power to do the things He directs one to do. *(Prov 3:6) (Zec 4:6) (Phil 4:13)*

To repent means to change one's way of thinking, to turn to a different way. John the Baptist the forerunner of Jesus the Christ, called for people to repent because the basileia (kingdom) had arrived.Then Jesus came after him preaching the same message, "repent for the kingdom of God is at hand". They were saying change your way of thinking and doing because there is now a much better way, the basileia of heaven way. Now you can have a better life and

8

the world can be a better place. It can now be ruled by the ways of
God as it is in heaven.

*Mat 3:1-2: In those days John the Baptist came preaching
in the wilderness of Judea, and saying, **"Repent, for the kingdom
of heaven is at hand!"***

*Mat 4:17: From that time Jesus began to preach and to say,
"Repent, for the kingdom of heaven is at hand."*

Jesus taught the foundational principles of the basileia of God
as heaven's way to live life now on earth. He preached the gospel
(good news) of the basileia (kingdom) of God. Jesus went about
proclaiming the good news message, that the basileia of God was
now at hand and available to change life for the better. Jesus called
upon the people to change their way of life and come to the basileia
(kingdom) of God way. Jesus preached the gospel of the sovereign
ruler/dominion of God from heaven, on earth, the gospel of the kingdom.

*Mat 4:23: And Jesus went about all Galilee, teaching in
their synagogues, preaching the **gospel of the kingdom**, and healing all kinds of sickness and all kinds of disease among the people.*

*Mat 9:35: Then Jesus went about all the cities and villages,
teaching in their synagogues, preaching the **gospel of the kingdom**, and healing every sickness and every disease among the
people.*

*Mark 1:14-15: Now after John was put in prison, Jesus came
to Galilee, preaching the **gospel of the kingdom of God**, and saying, **"The time is fulfilled, and the kingdom of God is at hand.
Repent, and believe in the gospel."***

9

No one can deny that the world has been more greatly affected for the better, by Jesus' life and message, than by any other thing in the history of the world. The great hope for the world is that more and more people will receive the life and message of Jesus the Christ, and that His life and message flowing through them will impact the world. As one by one, multitudes seek the kingdom of God with their whole heart, and really hear the gospel of the kingdom, the way Jesus taught it, the world will be a better place; fewer and fewer people will continue under the curses of judgments. There is no cause or project on earth more worthy than seeking the basileia of God. There is no greater message than the gospel of the basileia of heaven.

The gospel of the kingdom focuses on the resurrected life of Jesus the Christ returning to earth in the Holy Spirit to dwell within believers and bring forth the life of Christ to change individuals and the world. Jesus spoke of His death on the cross that forever paid the penalty for all sin. By His death at the cross the curse of sin and judgment is broken for all who believe and receive the living Jesus, by the Holy Spirit. His resurrected life within, empowers believers to live righteously.

*John 1:12 KJV: But as many as received him, **to them gave he power to become the sons of God,** even to them that believe on his name.*

*Gal 5:16: I say then: **Walk in the Spirit**, and you shall not fulfill the lust of the flesh.*

*Rom 5:10: For if when we were enemies **we were** reconciled to God through the **death** of His Son, much more, having been reconciled, **we shall be** saved by His **life**.*

Col 1:27: To them God willed to make known what are the riches of the glory of this mystery among the Gentiles: which is **Christ in you**, *the hope of glory.*

Rom 8:9: But you are not in the flesh but in the Spirit, if indeed the Spirit of God dwells in you. **Now if anyone does not have the Spirit of Christ, he is not His.**

Rom 14:17: the kingdom of God is not eating and drinking, but righteousness and peace and joy **in the Holy Spirit.**

John the Baptist first announced the at hand kingdom. Then Jesus preached and taught the gospel of the basileia (kingdom) of God. Later, when Jesus sent His disciples out, He instructed them also to preach the basileia. He told the twelve to preach, "the kingdom of heaven is at hand." He also told them to demonstrate the basileia of God by meeting the needs of the people with basileia power.

Mat 10:7-8: And as you go, **preach, saying, "The kingdom of heaven is at hand.** *Heal the sick, cleanse the lepers, raise the dead, cast out demons. Freely you have received, freely give."*

Jesus sent out seventy other disciples two by two and gave them similar instruction.

*Luke 10:9: And heal the sick there, and say to them, "****The kingdom of God has come near to you.****"*

He also added an instruction to the seventy disciples regarding those who would not receive them. They were to tell them that the basileia was near them.

11

*Luke 10:11: The very dust of your city which clings to us we wipe off against you. Nevertheless know this, that **the kingdom of God has come near you.***

Jesus also told them about very strong judgment for those who would not receive them and the message of the basileia of God they brought.

Luke 10:12: "But I say to you that it will be more tolerable in that Day for Sodom than for that city.

Jesus later instructed all believers to preach the gospel (good news). He went on to tell the believers to demonstrate the power of the gospel by healing the sick, and with other powerful works. What gospel was He instructing to be preached? You guessed it! The gospel of the basileia of God.

Mark 16:15: And He said to them, "Go into all the world and preach the gospel to every creature.

Jesus said the Gospel of the basileia of God is to be preached to all the world.

*Mat 24:14: And this **gospel of the kingdom** will be preached in all the world as a witness to all the nations, and then the end will come.*

Christians need a greater revelation of the gospel of the kingdom.

As mankind completes six thousand years of history, and the seventh millennium is beginning, God's dealings with man and the world are intensifying. Christians must have a greater revelation of the gospel of the kingdom, and the kingdom power available to carry out the work of God in this age. The ungodly are now rapidly becoming increasingly evil in their openly satanic and demonic ways. The godly must become increasingly intense in the manifestation of the love and power of the kingdom of God way. Halfway is not far enough. Part time faith is not good enough. Sunday only Christianity will not get the job done in this age. God is revealing more of the deeper mysteries of the basileia of God from His Word, by His Spirit.

Personally, for many years I read and studied the Bible. It was the focal point of my life, my guide and source of direction. The living Word continued to amaze me day by day as old familiar passages continued to yield new light and meaning. To some degree I was accustomed to this wonderful phenomenon.

From time to time, as fresh revelation shed new light on the Word, it seemed that my whole Bible became new. When I was born again, the Bible suddenly spoke clearly of salvation by grace through faith in the cross of Jesus Christ. Later when a deeper experience occurred in my life, suddenly passages became alive to me that I'd some way not even noticed before. Many scriptures about healing, miracles, powers of darkness, casting out demons, healing the heart, and the baptism of the Spirit, "appeared" in my Bible.

These and other experiences, as great as they were, had not fully prepared me for what happened to me in January of 1986. I had left the ministry where I'd been serving and had no other occupation at the time. My days were spent in a nice quiet travel trailer beside the house praying and studying the Word. I'd begun again to read the book of Matthew. This time one word seemed to be on almost every page—and again and again came from the lips of Jesus

13

as He seemed to preface many of His teaching with this word. I knew I'd read it hundreds of times, but it had never really "been there" before. It had always just seemed to flow "under" or "behind" what was being said without adding meaning to the passage.

Because this word had suddenly "appeared," and because I knew little or nothing about it, I became curious. So I prayed a simple prayer. The answer to that prayer changed my entire life forever. Suddenly in a moment of time, it seemed everything I had ever known was shaken and began to take on a whole new light, a new meaning. Mysteries began to clear up about things I'd wondered about for years. Pieces began to fit together that I could never get to fit before. A deep satisfaction began to come into my heart as things began to become real and make practical sense for the present instead of religious ideas and doctrinal systems from the past or for the future.

I had simply prayed, "God, what does this word "kingdom" mean? What is the kingdom of God—kingdom of Heaven—Why did Jesus talk about it so much? That simple phrase, "kingdom of God", that did not even appear to be there before, has become the focal point of my life as it was with Jesus. In the days that followed this prayer, the heavens were opened to me. God was closer to me than ever before. Every question that I asked was instantly answered with staggering impact and clarity. I was amazed again and again and often overwhelmed, my mind reeling as God poured simple profound revelation of His kingdom into my heart. I became very careful about the questions I asked.

One of my reactions to all of this was that of thinking that people would surely come against me because many of the things God was revealing to me were different from the way my church had taught them. I'd never before heard a word of the kingdom message like God was giving it to me. I was afraid I'd be the only person with this radical message. Then God told me He was giving this message to certain men around the world and that it would eventually just seem to come up from everywhere like the grass in a field. In the years that followed, He allowed me to receive tapes from men in various parts of the world who had received the same message. Now, there are many churches preaching the gospel of the kingdom that Jesus preached. Praise the Lord!

All of the men that I know of personally who first began to receive the gospel of the kingdom were over fifty years old and some over seventy. They were all men who had experienced the moves of God over the past forty to fifty years. All were apostolic in the nature of their ministry. Some had planted hundreds of churches. Others had started Bible colleges. Some were prominent Christian educators in the secular educational systems of their nations. Some were Christian businessmen who had started many businesses. All were still actively involved in serving the Lord. They all seemed to be men with pure hearts toward God and no motives left except to serve Him. All of these men speak of a deep inner satisfaction as they received the kingdom of God revelation. Their souls were satisfied as different words and moves of God began to fit together in their minds. They seemed to have a more well-defined understanding of the purpose of man and our planet.

When Jesus preached the gospel of the kingdom, many religious people had a hard time receiving it. The message he preached didn't fit their system of theology. Jesus warned them not to try to fit the new revelation into their old system.

Luke 5:36-39: Then He spoke a parable to them: "No one puts a piece from a new garment on an old one; otherwise the new makes a tear, and also the piece that was taken out of the new does not match the old. And no one puts new wine into old wineskins; or else the new wine will burst the wineskins and be spilled,

15

and the wineskins will be ruined. But new wine must be put into new wineskins, and both are preserved. And no one having drunk old wine immediately desires new; for he says, 'The old is better.'

Our wineskin is like a filing system. We each have within us a theological filing system, a system of mental file folders with headings and sub-headings. As an example, some of our headings might be something like: salvation, the cross, resurrection, Pentecost, Holy Spirit, baptism, healing, deliverance, second coming, and many more. Each piece of new theological data, when received, is analyzed, compared to the data in the system, and then filed under the proper heading.

The new wine of the gospel of the kingdom will not fit the old file system. We don't have a folder for it. And the revelation of the kingdom will not fit under any of our headings. We cannot simply make a new folder and stick it in somewhere. It will not fit under any other heading. The gospel of the kingdom becomes the system into which all other revelation and truth of God will fit. The kingdom that Jesus preached is the major heading under which all other God-given doctrine can be filed. We must have a new wineskin. If we try to patch in the gospel of the kingdom, we may become frustrated and burst our old wineskin, spilling out the contents with a splatter.

What is the *kingdom* of God we are told to seek? *"King"* means "ruler or sovereign", and *"dom"* is the root from which we get words like "dominion, dominant, domain and dome". Thus the kingdom of God means the "sovereign ruler/dominion of God, the ruler/dom of God".

The kingdom of God is a realm , a lifestyle, sovereignly ruled by the foundational power of God, through which God's ruler/dominion is brought forth on earth.

The kingdom walk or lifestyle is produced by the appearing or manifesting of Jesus through the Holy Spirit within God's people. When the character and nature of Christ is developed in the hearts of God's people, they become the purified bride of Christ. God's love flowing in and through His bride produces obedience, and righteousness prevails. Righteousness always leads to peace and joy. The bride or wife of Christ carries out her part as pictured in *Proverbs 31:10-31*, and the ruler/dominion (basileia) of God is functioning in the world.

The secrets of how to rule our planet God's way are locked up in the revelation and understanding of the basileia (kingdom) of God. They are extremely potent and can indeed produce the overcoming of any negative force in the world. There is nothing impossible to those who possess the understanding of the practical working of God's basileia on Planet Earth. This powerful understanding could be very dangerous in the hands of impure men who would seek to use it to establish their own kingdom, plan, or government. That is why God's kingdom ways will be revealed only to the purified bride. The revelation of the kingdom of God begins with the purification of the motives of our heart.

Only a pure heart can hear the secrets of God's kingdom. This means a heart free from all other allegiances, a heart healed from all the enemy's wounds—a heart that not only intends to serve God only but also has the freedom to actually do it.

For about two years before I began to hear the word of the kingdom, the Lord dealt with me extensively in what I call the personal ministry of Jesus. He led me to people who had gifts and anointings to assist in appropriating the ministry of Jesus to heal my broken-heartedness and bring about my deliverance. For many years I had sought to serve the Lord with great zealousness and commitment. Yet, areas of serious lack and defeat were in my own life.

17

It took a bold, fresh revelation from God to loose my bonds and set me on a road to restoration and greater heights than I'd ever before known. I will ever be indebted to those who have given of themselves to bring the personal ministry of Jesus to me—the ministry of healing the brokenhearted and setting the captives free. It's been my great pleasure and my means of repayment to those who ministered to me, to give of myself to carry the ministry of Jesus to others.

"BASILEIA LETTER" is a part of that effort. We do not have all the light, all the understanding and revelation of God from His Word. But we do have a part. Our heart's desire is to bless you by sharing with you the part God has given into our hand.

And this gospel of the kingdom will be preached in all the world as a witness to all the nations, and then the end will come. (Mat 24:14)

18

BASILEIA LETTER

Number 2

In modern Babylonian culture, Riches are often The number one priority.

Jesus said, "How difficult it is for those who have riches to enter the kingdom of God." This statement shocked His closest disciples, who knew that Jesus spoke of a broader sense of riches than just a lot of money. Riches were measured in that day, as by many today, in terms of possessions, such as lands, houses, livestock, servants, and family. Yes, family! Brothers, sisters, children and wives were considered as part of the riches of a wealthy man. All of these items were noble in the eyes of the disciples, as they are in our own. It was a noble man who acquired and cared for all these things.

The disciples also were aware that the kingdom of God Jesus was teaching them about was in part, a lifestyle; a way of living God's way with all its benefits. *(Rom 14:17)* In their thinking, the noble man who had acquired all these quality things was surely closer to the kingdom of God lifestyle than anyone else.

Mark 10:17-22: Now as He was going out on the road, one came running, knelt before Him, and asked Him, "Good Teacher, what shall I do that I may inherit eternal life?" So Jesus said to him, "Why do you call Me good? No one is good but One, that is, God. You know the commandments: 'Do not commit adultery,' 'Do not murder,' 'Do not steal,' 'Do not bear false witness,' 'Do not defraud,' 'Honor your father and your mother.'" And he answered and said to Him, "Teacher, all these things I have kept from my youth." Then Jesus, looking at him, loved him, and said to him, "One thing you lack: Go your way, sell whatever you have and give to the poor, and you will have treasure in heaven; and come, take up the cross, and follow Me." But he was sad at this word, and went away sorrowful, for he had great possessions.

Indeed, this was a noble and good man who had lived righteously and prospered. Yet he had not yet entered into the "eternal life" quality of life, the kingdom of God lifestyle. Jesus saw his heart and knew that his noble life and possessions were very important to him.

Is it possible that many good Christians are failing to enter the kingdom of God lifestyle because too many other things are too important to them?

Is it possible that many who are poor, and in prison, and of no reputation, can enter the kingdom more readily than many noble and rich people. Perhaps God so desires for His people to enter life that He may allow some to loose their noble reputation and quality possessions. *(1 Cor 1:26)*

*Mark 10:23-31: Then Jesus looked around and said to His disciples, "**How hard it is for those who have riches to enter the kingdom of God!**" And the disciples were astonished at His words. But Jesus answered again and said to them, "Children, how hard it is for those who trust in riches to enter the kingdom of God! It is easier for a camel to go through the eye of a needle than for a rich man to enter the kingdom of God." And they were greatly astonished, saying among themselves, "Who then can be saved?" But Jesus looked at them and said, "With men it is impossible, but not with God; for with God all things are possible." **Then Peter began***

---

*to say to Him, "See, we have left all and followed You." So Jesus answered and said, "Assuredly, I say to you, there is no one who has left **house** or **brothers** or **sisters** or **father** or **mother** or **wife** or **children** or **lands**, for My sake and the gospel's, who shall not receive a **hundredfold now in this time; houses** and **brothers** and **sisters** and **mothers** and **children** and **lands**, with **persecutions;** and in the age to come, eternal life. But many who are first will be last, and the last first."*

    Peter apparently wanted to be sure that the Lord remembered that they had left their noble life and possessions to follow the Lord, as He had asked them to do. The Lord then assured them that their sacrifices had not been in vain, but they would enter into the kingdom lifestyle now in this life, with many times the noble possessions they previously had, and eternal life in the age to come. Entering the kingdom of God seemed such a mystery to the disciples at that time.

Many today are still puzzled by what it really means to enter the kingdom of God.

    We need to remember that even though the Word of God was being spoken in the disciple's presence, they had not yet received the indwelling Holy Spirit and therefore lacked the potential for the revelation of the Word by the Holy Spirit that believers have today.
    In Mark Chapter 9, Jesus speaks of making severe personal sacrifices in order to enter into "life" "the kingdom of God".

*Mark 9:43-48: "If your hand causes you to sin, cut it off. It is better for you to **enter into life** maimed, rather than having two hands, to go to **hell**, into the **fire** that shall never be quenched;*

21

*where 'Their worm does not die, And the fire is not quenched.' And if your foot causes you to sin, cut it off. It is better for you to **enter life** lame, rather than having two feet, to be cast into **hell**, into the **fire** that shall never be quenched; where 'Their worm does not die, And the fire is not quenched.' And if your eye causes you to sin, pluck it out. It is better for you to **enter the kingdom of God** with one eye, rather than having two eyes, to be cast into **hell fire**; where 'Their worm does not die, And the fire is not quenched.'"*

The choices in these verses are, either to make the necessary severe sacrifice of whatever causes one to sin, and enter into life, abundant life, eternal life, kingdom of God life, now. Or, to not make the sacrifice and be cast into a hell fire lifestyle, now. This is not just hell fire after one dies. It is a very present purification judgmental burning and wasting now, that never is quenched but is constantly burning one's sinful life. No Christian is exempt from the purification fire of God. But every sacrifice that one makes toward the righteousness of the kingdom of God lifestyle, will provide the seasoning and preserving of the presence of God in the life. This is what makes life good. As salt brings out the flavor of food, the anointing of God brings out the great and wonderful flavor of life, the kingdom of God lifestyle.

*Mark 9:49-50: "For **everyone** will be seasoned with fire, and every sacrifice will be seasoned with salt. "**Salt is good**, but if the salt loses its flavor, how will you season it? Have salt in yourselves, and have peace with one another."*

One must enter the kingdom of God as a child enters life.

Mark 10:14b-15: "Let the little children come to Me, and do not forbid them; for of such is the kingdom of God. Assuredly, I say *to you, whoever does not receive the kingdom of God **as a little child** will by no means enter it."*

A child is born into the world naked and without any posses-sions. Yet the child has a whole lifetime ahead. A lifetime in which the child will be clothed, mature, acquire possessions, and experi-ence life. As it is in the natural realm, so it is in the spiritual realm. A child's life is uncluttered by the responsibility of possessions. The simplicity of a child's life provides an atmosphere in which trusting by simple faith is easier than it is for a person with much responsi-bility, of many possessions. *(John 3:3-7)*

A child must be born into natural life. In a similar way one must be born in the spiritual realm. *(1 Pet 1:23)* Spiritual birth comes from the original coming together of one's spirit with the spirit of Christ Jesus the Saviour. And then receiving Him as Lord of one's life, means putting every thing one possesses into His hands, allow-ing God to be in complete control of everything about one's life. *(Luke 14:33)* It means returning to the state of being naked and without possessions to begin a new life in which God will clothe and provide for one's every need. *(Luke 12:28) (Mat 6:30-33)*

The kingdom of God, kingdom of heaven, lifestyle is one that is free from owning riches, but not free from enjoying wealth and noble life as God becomes the provider, and the disciple becomes His servant. In the kingdom of God one is always aware that God owns all the noble wealth. As God's servant, one becomes a man-ager of God's wealth and not an owner.*(Eccl 5:19)(Mat 25:14-28)*

A man or woman never owns their family, their ser-vants, their bank accounts, houses, lands, businesses, ministry, nor any other riches.

23

A person who attempts to own their spouse, children, or any other wealth, will create many problems and will **not enter the kingdom of God lifestyle.** *(James 5:1-3) (1 Tim 6:10-11)* Therefore one who has assumed ownership of many riches, and feels some degree of security in them, must give them to Jesus. *(Luke 14:26-27,33)* From the spouse and the children, to the last penny, everything must be given into the hand of God, in order to enter the kingdom of God lifestyle. This may become easier to do when one has very little; but, it may be hard for one who has acquired much possessions.

Jesus has not told **everyone** to go and sell all their possessions and give it all to the poor. God may at some point give such an instruction to any individual, personally, as He did with the noble rich man who was trusting in his riches. The Word of God does, however, clearly teach that one is to be a steward of God's goods and not an owner. *(Luke 19:13-26) (Mat 24:45-47)* This means all we possess is available at all times to be used or managed as God directs. One must hear God's plan and purpose for all his life, including all possessions. *(Isa 55:2-3)*

There is no merit in being naked and poor. There is nothing spiritual about poverty. Often poor Christians are among the most covetous and materialistic people. Giving to God all that we have is a part of the process of entering the kingdom of God lifestyle. Poverty is not the kingdom of God way of life. On the contrary the person walking in the kingdom of God lifestyle will find that there is always enough to complete God's plan for him at that time. One walking in the kingdom way will be adequately supplied in the kingdom of heaven, on earth, now, to accomplish all of God's plan.

The wonderful faith principles of the prosperity message being taught today, are a pendulum swing from the old message that poverty was godliness. Probably most men of God teaching the won-

derful faith principles are stewards who realize that they own nothing, but serve God by managing His goods according to His direction.

Yet the emphasis of the prosperity message has caused
some to believe that faith is a means of getting riches
to meet one's needs and wants.

Faith is the second greatest principle in the kingdom of God.
Love is the first and greatest principle. *(1 Cor 13:13)* Love leads us
to first give up our self life with its needs and desires, in favor of the
resurrected life of Jesus Christ living within by the Holy Spirit. Then
the faith principles working by love are very important to accom-
plishing God's purpose. *(Gal 5:6)* God will supply one's needs and
wants (as our wants become only His wants). *(Psa 37:4) (John
15:7)* Faith principles are tools which will help bring forth the plans
and proposes of God. If one should acquire true and noble riches,
he is to manage them for God, and not own them. One must haveaith
in God, not faith in his own faith. *(Mark 11:22)*

We must not reject the message
of faith and prosperity.
We must know and use the principles of faith,
in the proper order and place.

When God begins to bless one's life and gives to him noble
riches in the kingdom of God, the temptation will always come to
hold on to, or use in one's own way some of what God has given.
One must seek God's direction and plan at all times. God will give
the servant his own portion to enjoy after the servant has been faithful with another's (God's) goods. Money is the least commodity in

25

BASILEIA LETTER
Number 2

the kingdom of God. If one is faithful with what is least in the kingdom, God will give him true riches. *(Luke 16:10-12)*

To employ faith principles to get noble riches that one wants for himself, apart from God's specific direction, can become a form of sorcery. Seeking to get the things one needs or wants by any means, including appropriating faith principles, is not God's plan for His children and will never lead to the kingdom of God lifestyle.

God's children are instructed to not seek riches, nor even to seek to meet their own needs. The instruction is to seek the kingdom of God and all the things one needs will be added to him.

*Luke 12:29 -32: "And **do not seek what you should eat or what you should drink,** nor have an anxious mind. For all these things the nations of the world seek after, and your Father knows that you need these things. **But seek the kingdom of God, and all these things shall be added to you.** Do not fear, little flock, for it is your Father's good pleasure to give you the kingdom."*

*Mat 6:33 "But seek first the kingdom of God and His righteousness, and all these things **shall be added to you.**"*

The first and number one priority for God's children is to seek the kingdom of God.

Yet, most are not sure what seeking the kingdom of God really means. Many have a generic view of seeking the kingdom of God as in some general way seeking to be more involved with church, or praying more often, or reading the Bible more, or memorizing Scripture, or giving more to the church, or some other worthy activity. Some think that seeking the kingdom means seeking to be born again. Others would include seeking to be filled with the Holy Spirit.

Some others would think that seeking the kingdom of God is trying to stop doing drugs, or stop drinking alcohol, or stopping some immoral habit, or staying out of prison, or quitting their life of crime, or working on their bad temper that leads to others getting hurt, or quitting many other sinful practices.

All these things may have some part in the process of cleansing ones life and moving toward the kingdom of God. But none of these things define the kingdom clearly. How can we seek something if we do not know what it really is, and exactly what it looks like.

Suppose your employer instructed you to go into the city and seek out a "zeldiphruxet". And suppose he further promised that you would receive a very good promotion when you returned with the "zeldiphruxet". But if you could not find one and bring it back you would lose your opportunity to enter into the management level of the company. Where would you go, and in what area would you begin to search? Would you look for something small or large, alive or inanimate, something beautiful or ugly? What color would you look for? What shape would it be? What is it used for? Is it something to eat, something to wear, something to read, or a tool for the shop?

The first step in seeking for a "zeldiphruxet" is to find out what it is, what it looks like, and all that you can know about it. Otherwise, you might spend a lot of time and effort searching diligently for something and not finding it, because you don't know what it is, or what it is like.

Many search for the kingdom of God, without really knowing for what they are looking.

27

Is this why Jesus spent most of His brief time of ministry on earth teaching about the kingdom of God, kingdom of Heaven? He taught what the kingdom is like, how it works, how to enter it, and he compared it to the other system. He began much of his teaching with, "The kingdom of God is like-". And then He would give vital information about how to understand and live in the kingdom of God, on earth, from heaven, now. All you will ever need to know to seek the kingdom, enter into the kingdom of God lifestyle, and walk in the kingdom from heaven on earth, now, can be revealed by the Spirit from the Bible. The four Gospels and the book of Acts which cover the life and ministry of Jesus are especially rich in kingdom of God understanding. If you sincerely seek the kingdom of God, you must search out the revelation of the teachings of Jesus in the Scripture.

You are very blessed to be a part of this generation. A generation entering the seventh millennium of the history of man. A generation in which the Gospel of the kingdom is again being preached and many are entering in. Jesus preached the Gospel of the kingdom. *(Mat 9:35)* His disciples preached the Gospel of the kingdom. *(Luke 9:1-2)* But, the great Gospel that Jesus and His disciples preached was lost from the church during the darkness of the ages past. Now in this time God is returning the great Gospel of the kingdom to His people. *(Mat 24:14)*

Do not be tricked into believing that the Gospel of being born again is the whole thing. It is the first thing, not the whole thing. The Gospel of salvation includes much more than just being born. It includes growing up into the spiritual kingdom of God. The Gospel of Jesus includes the resurrected life of Jesus living now in the believer to bring forth His kingdom, from heaven, on earth, now. *(Col 1:27) (John 14:18-20)*

28

Would you be free from the burden of sinful living? Seek the kingdom of God.

Would you be free from painful poverty? Seek the kingdom of God. Would you be free from depressing boredom in your life? Seek the kingdom of God. Would you be free from fear, worry, and doubt? Seek the kingdom of God. Would you be free from the burden of the responsibility of wealth? Seek the kingdom of God. Stop seeking to fix yourself by seeking to meet your own need, and seek the kingdom of God. Stop seeking to legalistically, in your own strength, keep Gods laws, and instead seek the kingdom of God, and have all the power of Jesus within you to live righteously. Stop seeking to get money to overcome your poverty and instead seek the kingdom of God, and all these things shall be added to you. Stop seeking to entertain yourself to alleviate boredom, and instead seek the kingdom of God, with its exciting adventures and opportunities to be productive by serving others. Stop trying to battle your way through fears, phobias, worries, and doubts, and seek the kingdom of God, and have the indwelling powerful faith of Jesus Christ within. *(Gal 2:20)*

"The kingdom of God is within you." *"Christ in you, the hope of glory."*

The grace of God is the unmerited favor of the gift of the powerful resurrected Christ living within the believer, by the indwelling Holy Spirit, to produce the life of Jesus the Christ, the kingdom of God lifestyle. The Grace of God is not a whitewash covering for one's continued sinful and powerless living. The mercy of God will forgive one's every failure, if there is repentance and no attempt to justify one's sin. But the grace of God can empower one to live righteously, as Christ lives within.*(Acts 4:33)*

Are you ready to further give up trying to fix things and seek the kingdom of God in a greater fashion? Multitudes are ready for more of the kingdom than they have known and experienced in the past. This is the time for believers every where to look to God for the next step. Truly this is one of the most exciting spiritual times in all of history. Christ coming to earth, dieing on the cross, and being resurrected to be seated at the right hand of the Father, and returning to earth in the Holy Spirit at Pentecost, is the paramount event of all history.

And now is the time for the fruit of this magnificent event to become evident in your life and mine. It is the time of the purification of God's people into his jewels. *(Mal 3:17)* And the time to become the glorious Bride of Christ, without spot or wrinkle. *(Eph 5:27)* It is a time charged with the presence of God. A time of greater power than the charismatic renewal of the past. A time of the powerful peaceful anointing of God's love flowing to cleanse and renew the vilest sinner and the weakest church member. A time of overflowing inner joy and praise. A time of reality of God flowing into all walks of life. A time of quiet victory over the meanest strongholds of the enemy. The victory of the power and presence of God is flowing toward God's children on earth. Give up your self life and open your heart to the greatest move and work of God since the first century.

This is not a time of great charismatic leaders. It is time for all big shots in the kingdom to become nobodies; to step down from their pedestal and join equally with the throngs of nobodies filled with Christ, lifting their hearts in praise toward the one leader, Jesus the Christ. It is a time for all to seek more of His kingdom. It is the time to let the King rule His kingdom, first in every heart, and from there into the world.

This is the time looked forward to by all of the saints and patriarchs of the Old and New Testaments. The time not even dreamed about by some saints of the dark ages. The kingdom of God is not just going to happen, it is happening. Will you fully get in on it? Decide now to renew seeking the kingdom of God with your whole heart. Begin studying the teachings of Jesus in the Gospels and the book of Acts. Ask the Spirit of God to reveal to you clearly just what the kingdom of God is, and what it is not.

Eph 5:17-18: Therefore do not be unwise, but understand what the will of the Lord is. And do not be drunk with wine, in which is dissipation; but be filled with the Spirit,

BASILEIA LETTER

Number 3

Who do men say that I am?
Who do you say that I am?

𝕵esus asked these questions of His disciples, and they apparently answered the first question collectively. But, the outspoken Simon Bar-Jonah answered the second question.

*Mat 16:13-16: When Jesus came into the region of Caesarea Philippi, He asked His disciples, saying, "**Who do men say that I, the Son of Man, am?**" So they said, "Some say John the Baptist, some Elijah, and others Jeremiah or one of the prophets." He said to them, "**But who do you say that I am?**" Simon Peter answered and said, "**You are the Christ, the Son of the living God.**"*

Jesus asked these questions in the context of a discussion about the need for the disciples to beware of the leaven of the religious Pharisees and Sadducees.

*Mat 16:12: Then they understood that He did not tell them to beware of the leaven of bread, but of the **doctrine** of the Pharisees and Sadducees.*

Men, who were intensely religious and Old Testament scholars, believed Jesus to be someone of some spiritual importance. They supposed that He was a reborn prophet. Some thought maybe John the Baptist, or Elijah, or Jeremiah, or one of the other prophets. They were confused and very wrong in their evaluation of Jesus. This resulted in their developing wrong doctrines and actions. Not

32

only did they miss out on the kingdom of God life, because of what they believed about Jesus, but they also had an effect on many other people. They made it difficult for others to believe who Jesus really was, and to respond to Him as the Christ (the anointed one), the Son of the living God. *(Mat 23:13)*

The potential was there for them to have caused doubts in the minds of the disciples as well. That is why Jesus was warning them to beware of their doctrine.

Jesus, however, knew who He was and was not affected by men's evaluation of Himself.

Imagine with me for just a moment. What would have happened if Jesus, the anointed of God, had listened to the religious men and believed even a little of what they were saying about who He was? I know this is a very unreasonable imagination, but what would have been the result of doubts in the mind and heart of Jesus about who He really was? What would have happened if He had allowed men to shape His beliefs, instead of listening to God? I believe it is safe to say that if Jesus had listened to men, and allowed men to shape his self image and affect his faith about who he was, there would have been no miracles, no powerful ministry, no salvation for the lost, no healing for the lepers, no one raised from the dead, and no demons cast out. **Jesus would have accomplished no mighty works of God if He had accepted what others said about Himself.** Thank God! Jesus listened to the Father and not to men.

Is it any different for you and me? Our Lord is dealing with me at this time as these things are being written. The Holy Spirit is stirring within my own heart, convicting me of allowing men to shape who I am, or, more accurately who I am not, by their evaluations. The negative reports, misunderstandings, and underrating, cheapening, devaluations of men are most damaging to the servant of God, when they are received within the individual.

Unlike Jesus, many of us may have allowed the critical devaluation of men to affect who we are.

Perhaps being born in sin, in a sinful world, has caused us to be more vulnerable. *(Rom 5:19)* Patterns developed early may be reinforced later in life. Even after receiving Jesus the Christ (the anointed one) into our hearts and lives to rule and reign, the old limiting patterns of inability and spiritual impotency may block or hinder the work of God in and through our lives. Our minds may have been so impressed over and over again with our perceived limitations, faults, and inabilities, that we have come to believe that this is just the way God made us. This is just the way things are for us. We expect to mess up in one way or another and be rejected again.

We may subconsciously begin to harbor serious doubts, and fears of rejections and persecutions. We may even begin to imagine negative scenarios of rejection, persecution, and failure.

The negative limiting words of men imprison our soul when we receive them and believe them. Each limiting negative word, when planted in our hearts, is like a bad seed growing into prison bars.

We are restrained and limited on all sides. It is like being in an invisible enclosure. We cannot straighten up and stand tall because our head will hit the ceiling of the enclosure. We cannot move in this direction or that because we will bump into the wall. We may see others that are free and open, who are able to move in spiritual love and power and are not seriously restrained by fears of rejections and persecutions. We may wish we could be that way, but we feel certain that if we tried, we would only encounter more rejection and persecution. This cripples our ability to function in the spiritual realm, and our ability to relate to others.

With our heads we may know that Jesus, the anointed one of God and His anointing abides within us; the same Jesus that does not receive men's evaluation, because He listens to the Father and not to men; the same Jesus who does mighty miracles and marvelous works of God. Yet because of the continuing restraint of the prison bars of inner beliefs planted by men's negative, degrading words, we may fail to fully experience Christ within. The mighty rivers of the living water of the love and power of God greatly desire to flow from the Christ within us. Yet our restraints and limitations planted by the debasing evaluations of men may prevent all but a small trickle of flow. Those around us who thirst for the love and power of Christ are defrauded by our perceived limitations, faults, and spiritual inabilities.

"But who do you say that I am?"
"You are the Christ, the Son of the living God."

Who do you say Christ is within you?

Does your lifestyle say, "He is like John the Baptist, or one of the prophets," men of spiritual merit and power, but men who all pointed toward Jesus and said, "I am not the one"? Or, is He **the Christ (the anointed one), the Son of the living God**, living within your body to do all the works that He did when He lived in His natural body. Works of salvation, healing , and deliverance; works to alleviate suffering, pain, and poverty of spirit, soul, and body; works that bring peace and goodwill to our world. What might happen to benefit the lost and dying if you and I would break through our enclosure and allow the rivers of living waters to flow to the thirsty people around us. What would happen to our world if everyone in whom Christ dwells broke their self imposed restraints and let the power of the faith of Christ destroy their invisible enclosures, pouring out a flood of the living waters of the Word, love, and power of God?

When Simon Bar-Jonah answered Jesus' question, "But who do you say that I am?", with the reply, "You are the Christ, the Son of the living God.", then Jesus began to tell him something about who he was, and what kind of life he would live because it had been revealed to him who Jesus really was.

*Mat 16:17-19: Jesus answered and said to him, "Blessed are you, Simon Bar-Jonah, for flesh and blood has not revealed this to you, but My Father who is in heaven. "And I also say to you that you are Peter, and **on this rock I will build My church**, and **the gates of Hades shall not prevail against it**. "And I will give you the **keys of the kingdom** of heaven, and **whatever you bind** on earth will be bound in heaven, and **whatever you loose** on earth will be loosed in heaven."*

The name Peter means a piece of rock. Peter was previously referred to as, "Simon called Peter".

The word "church" means called out ones. This is the only recorded occasion of Jesus saying the words, "My church". He did use the word church on one other recorded occasion.

The word "build" is also translated "builder", "edify", and "embolden". Embolden is an old word that means to make bold or encourage.

Jesus was saying, Just as your name is rock,

I will use this rock of the revelation of who I really am to build up, edify, and make bold my called out ones.

He goes on to tell Peter of the great power of this rock to His called out ones. The gates of Hades refer to the power of the enemy to control movement by restraining, such as the invisible enclosure we've been talking about. Gates are also used as a defense to keep out attackers. Those who truly have a revelation that the Jesus talking to Peter in this verse, is the same Jesus now living within the "called out ones"; and that **He is the Christ, the Son of the living God,** will not be restrained from breaking out of their enclosure to powerfully and boldly do the works of Christ. Jesus goes on to make it clear that He will give the power of the kingdom of heaven to bind and loose on the earth to anyone with the rock (the revelation of Jesus as the Christ the Son of the living God).

Who do men say you are?
Who does Jesus say you are?
Which one will you choose to hear and believe?

Will you listen to what men say and continue to be restrained from presenting the powerful love of the grace of Christ to the world around you? Or will you hear what Jesus says about you and flow the spiritual power of the living God by the anointing of the Anointed One, Christ Jesus within? Will you listen to men and allow only a trickle of the rivers of living water to flow from your inner being?

37

Or, will you hear the Word of the Lord and allow unrestrained rivers of living water to flow to the dry and thirsty land around you?

*John 7:38-39a: "He who believes in Me, as the Scripture has said, **out of his heart will flow rivers of living water.**"*

But this He spoke concerning the Spirit, whom those believing in Him would receive.

Now is the time! The time is now! God is abundantly flowing His grace, His love, His power, to and through His people. The Word of the kingdom, the gospel of the kingdom of God is coming forth now on our small planet. Please do not assume that it will always be this way, or that you will have plenty of time to do the works of God later. It is not wise to say within our heart, "let me finish this or that", *(Luke 14:16-20),* or "let me get a little more prepared". Many reading this have enough preparation to do many times more than they have done to this point. Perhaps we should use more of what we already have, rather than seeking to get more before becoming active in the kingdom of God.

If you have studied the teachings of Jesus in the Gospels and perhaps read "Overcoming Life On A Small Planet", you know that the kingdom of God, kingdom of heaven is not just the church or something religious. The kingdom of God from heaven encompasses all of life. The powerful principles and anointing of Christ are the foundation and power for real success in every area of living. No business will succeed like a Christ directed and empowered business. No teacher will teach children reading, writing, and arithmetic better than one anointed of Christ. Every job, work, or service will be performed better by the Christ directed and empowered servant of God.

The disciples had been fishing hard all night and caught nothing, until Jesus gave them instruction.

Luke 5:4-6: When He had stopped speaking, He said to Simon, "Launch out into the deep and let down your nets for a catch." But Simon answered and said to Him, "Master, we have toiled all night and caught nothing; nevertheless at Your word I will let down the net." And when they had done this, they caught a great number of fish, and their net was breaking.

In John 21, the disciples had again fished all night and caught nothing. But when they heard and obeyed the instruction of the Lord to cast the net on the right side of the boat instead of the traditional left side, they were very successful.

John 21:3-6: Simon Peter said to them, "I am going fishing." They said to him, "We are going with you also." They went out and immediately got into the boat, and that night they caught nothing. But when the morning had now come, Jesus stood on the shore; yet the disciples did not know that it was Jesus. Then Jesus said to them, "Children, have you any food?" They answered Him, "No." And He said to them, "Cast the net on the right side of the boat, and you will find some." So they cast, and now they were not able to draw it in because of the multitude of fish.

What if the disciples had not heard and obeyed the word to launch out into the deep and let down their nets? What if they had thought within themselves, "we have tried hard and it did not work, it is foolish to try now," and did not go? What if they had rejected the word to break with tradition and cast their net on the right side of the boat?

What if you and I do not hear, or do not obey the word to launch out into the deep? What if we are afraid of the deep waters because of the limiting doubts planted in our hearts? What if our traditions are more important to us than the words of Jesus the Christ? Will we continue to cast our nets fruitlessly on the traditional side? Or, will we cast our net on the other side when Jesus, the Anointed One within, tells us to?

Will we continue to be just a trickle in a dried up river bed? A river bed that should be flowing full of the crystal clear life giving, cleansing, water from the throne of God, through the Anointed One, the Christ within us?

Rev 22:1: And he showed me a pure river of water of life, clear as crystal, proceeding from the throne of God and of the Lamb.

Do we dare stand before God and tell Him how bad His world is; tell Him how dry and barren the world and its people are; while we are the only thing limiting the flow of rivers of living water? Do we dare to continue our "trickle down" spiritual living?

Thank God for those who are now flowing rivers of living waters and are heartily serving God, in ministry, in business, in education, and every area of the kingdom of God. If you are one of those and you know that your river is flowing full, please pray for the many of us "trickle down" servants.

Today is the right time for us to sever the bonds and prison bars of what others have said about who we are. This is the time to cast off our self imposed limitations and believe God. What do we have to lose? Our trickle is not doing much good for the world or ourselves.

Did Jesus open the prison doors? Can He remove our spiritual blinders? Has Jesus provided for the healing of our broken heart? **Is the resurrected Christ now within us** to remove all of our restraints and set us free, to flow His abundant life, rivers of living water?

*Luke 4:18: "The Spirit of the LORD is upon Me, Because He has anointed Me To **preach the gospel** to the poor; He has sent Me to **heal the brokenhearted**, To **proclaim liberty** to the captives And **recovery of sight** to the blind, To **set at liberty** those who are oppressed.*

*Isa 61:1b: He has sent Me to **heal the brokenhearted, To proclaim liberty** to the captives, And the **opening of the prison** to those who are bound.*

Yes! Beyond any doubt, Jesus has provided everything we need; and **the Spirit of the resurrected Christ** is now within us to complete the work.

All of the power of heaven is ready to set us free.

Everything that needs to be done, has been done. But it all waits on us. We must decide. Will we continue to decide to believe what men's words and actions have planted in us? Or, will we decide to believe what God's Words and actions say about who we are? Jesus has freely provided and is providing all we need. But we do not have the fruit of the gift until we appropriate it into our life. Spiritual works of Christ are appropriated only one way. We must believe the resurrected Christ in our hearts and confess with our mouths.

41

*Rom 10:8-10: But what does it say? "The word is near you, in your mouth and in your heart" (that is, the word of **faith** which we preach): that if you **confess with your mouth** the Lord Jesus and **believe in your heart** that God has raised Him from the dead, you will be saved. For **with the heart one believes unto righteousness, and with the mouth confession is made unto salvation.***

The Greek word translated "saved" in this verse is "sozo", and is defined in Strong's as follows: G4982. sozo, sode'-zo; from a prim. sos (contr. for obsol. saos, "safe"); to save, i.e. **deliver** or protect (lit. or fig.):--**heal**, preserve, save (self), do well, **make whole, be whole.**

The Greek word translated "salvation" is "soteria", and is defined: G4991. soteria, so-tay-ree'-ah; fem. of a der. of G4990 as (prop. abstr.) noun; **rescue or safety** (physically or morally):--**deliver, health**, salvation, save, saving.

Obviously, these verses are not just talking about believing the resurrected Christ in the heart and confessing with the mouth to get into heaven when we die. They tell us how to appropriate the now salvation of deliverance from our bondages, and healing of what ever needs to be healed, including our broken heart. What is the process for appropriating the work Jesus has provided?

The process it to believe with the heart, and confess with the mouth.

If we are already believing what men have said instead of what Jesus has said, then there must be a renewing of our mind. Part of the process of believing in the heart is renewing our minds from what men and the enemy have said to what Jesus says. *(Rom 12:2)*

(Eph 4:23) A renewed mind is not automatically done for us. We must renew our own mind. Our free will gives us the responsibility of controlling what we think which affects what we will believe. Taking every thought captive begins with an act of our will. Choosing what we hear and what we allow to remain in our thoughts, is our decision. We must warfare against all the negative, limiting, degrading thoughts previously planted in our hearts.

2 Cor 10:4-5: For the weapons of our warfare are not carnal but mighty in God for pulling down strongholds, casting down arguments and every high thing that exalts itself against the knowledge of God, **bringing every thought into captivity to the obedience of Christ.**

We cannot stop thinking about something by trying to not think about it. For example, if I told you to, whatever you do, do not think about elephants, not small elephants, or large elephants, or pink elephants, you will think only of elephants. But if I said think about pie, chocolate pie with tall meringue, or apple pie hot from the oven with a slice of cheese on top, or a piece of hot home made cherry pie with a large scoop of vanilla ice cream on it, you are no longer thinking about elephants. When the old negative limiting thoughts come into our mind we must replace that thought by thinking about what Jesus the Christ says about us.

Thinking and speaking the Word of God excites the Spirit of Christ within and opens the way for spiritual power to be released to change us and the world around us. Nothing can stand against the released spiritual power of Christ within us. No thought, no stronghold, no argument, no words of man or the enemy, no high thing can stand against knowing Christ within and knowing who He really is.

43

If we are thinking and speaking the anointed Words of God, we cannot at the same time, be thinking the negative, critical, judgmental, limiting words of men or of the enemy. Thinking and speaking the words of the enemy opens the way for evil spiritual power to be released to restrain and oppress ourselves and others. If we hear or think a bad report and **believe it in our heart and speak it with our mouth,** the spiritual powers of darkness are released to bind according to our belief and words. *"**Whatever you bind** on earth will be bound in (or from) heaven, and **whatever you loose** on earth will be loosed in (or from) heaven."*

We should never critically judge a servant of God.

God is fully capable to judge and to correct His own servants. We never have all the information and understanding of the whole situation, and therefore will never make an accurate judgment. God on the other hand has all the information and will never make a bad judgment. *(Rom 14:4)* Our critical judgments cause oppression for others and ourselves. When we judge others and think and speak negative words about them we release the powers of darkness to bind the thing to the other person. And like a boomerang the powers of darkness will bring our judgment full circle and hit us with the same thing for which we have judged others. The power of evil will always flow through our judgmental, critical words. The power of God will always flow through the Words of Christ, the Anointed One within.

Mat 7:1-2: "Judge not, that you be not judged. "For with what judgment you judge, you will be judged; and with the measure you use, it will be measured back to you.

44

BASILEIA LETTER

Number 4

The kingdom is like a mustard seed, Not a stick of dynamite.

𝕴esus said, in *Mat 16:28: "Assuredly, I say to you, there are some standing here who shall not taste death till they **see the Son of Man coming in His kingdom."***

*Mark 9:1: And He said to them, "Assuredly, I say to you that there are **some** standing here who will not taste death till they see the kingdom of God present with power."*

*Luke 9:27 "But I tell you truly, there are **some** standing here who shall not taste death till they see the kingdom of God."*

If only some of those standing there were going to see Jesus coming in His kingdom, then some standing there were not going to see the kingdom of God. There were those at the time when Jesus preached the gospel of the kingdom, who did not see or understand the teaching of the kingdom. There were those who did not see the "Son of Man" come in His kingdom, and the kingdom present with power, when Christ Jesus returned in the Holy Spirit at Pentecost. Just as there are some today who do not yet see the kingdom of God, kingdom of heaven, coming forth now, on earth.

Luke 17:20-21: Now when He was asked by the Pharisees when the kingdom of God would come, He answered them and said, "The kingdom of God does not come with observation; "nor will they say, 'See here!' or 'See there!' For indeed, the kingdom of God is within you."

45

The transition into the new era of the kingdom is already happening. There may not be a definitive single event that marks the new era, but each individual will probably mark the day when they personally received the revelation of the kingdom. Yet, there are those who are experiencing the events of today, but have no idea that sin is being judged, and the kingdom is coming forth.

In the day that Jesus walked upon the earth teaching and preaching the gospel of the kingdom, many religious people totally missed it. The great events taking place around them were seen as something other than the Son of God proclaiming the kingdom of God. It was not just the heathen who missed it; it was the established Bible (Old Testament) preaching religious leaders who could not see. Many people who lived at the same time and in the same place where the mighty works of God were proclaiming the kingdom of God, were not aware of what was occurring. It is no different as the great events of the seventh millennium are unfolding and Christ again walks in his body (the purified bride church, the body of Christ) proclaiming the gospel of the kingdom. *(Mat 12:14) (Mat 23:13)*

*Mat 16:21: From that time Jesus began to show to His disciples that He must go to Jerusalem, and suffer many things from the **elders** and **chief priests** and **scribes**.*

The religious leaders of that day were so into the old way of the law, which was coming to an end, that it was difficult for them to adjust to the new era of the law of grace and the preaching of the kingdom. This led to their violently opposing Jesus and the kingdom He preached. They put themselves into the position of becoming enemies of the same God they sought to proclaim. The gospel of the kingdom can be very divisive. It leaves little room for straddling the fence. Either a person will see it, and align with it, or rise up and oppose it. As the preaching of the gospel of the kingdom

comes forth in the new era some very religious people will put themselves into the position of becoming at enmity with God by resisting
the gospel of the kingdom.

We must change with the times of God and not attempt to
adjust the times of God to us for our comfort. Change is sometimes
not comfortable especially for the very mature. Yet it is far easier to
change with the time than to oppose God. *(Acts 5:38-39)*

We must face the future,
forget the past,
and fulfill the present.

In recent times godly people are experiencing an increase of
spiritual light. At the same time, ungodly people are experiencing
an increase in the revelation of darkness. It is popular with ungodly
people to change with the times and to become increasingly evil in
their ways. It is necessary for godly people to change with the times
and become increasingly holy in their ways.

In chapter thirteen of the book *"Overcoming Life On A Small
Planet"*, we began a self image adjustment by looking at who we
are in Christ, and Christ in us. As we realize the power of God
within us to live righteously, and to promote the ways of God into
the world, we simply cannot excuse continuing an adulterated
lifestyle. Holiness is great fun, an exciting adventure. There is nothing more exhilarating than experiencing the powerful loving flow of
Christ through our "dustling" (made of dust) bodies. There is nothing more rewarding than seeing the power of God released to change
lives for good. There is no greater fulfillment for man than experiencing the kingdom of God in the seventh millennium. Why not
make the effort and endure the inconvenience of change? Even if it

means allowing God to adjust some of our previous interpretations of Scripture, it will be worth it.

Man is dependent upon God to reveal Himself. Though religion may make a valiant effort to know God, man can not know God by his effort. No amount of intellectual effort will ever lead to the knowledge and understanding of God. *(John 3:13) (1 Cor 2:14) (Col 1:27) (Rom 9:23) (Luke 10:22) (Mat 11:25) (1 Cor 2:10)*

God must choose to reveal Himself to man.

God sovereignly chooses to reveal certain aspects of Himself to whom He chooses, when He chooses. **The Word of God, the Holy Bible, is complete and contains the complete revelation of God, but it will not be revealed to a man until God causes revelation within the individual.**

We do not know all the reasons why God chooses to reveal or not to reveal more of Himself and His marvelous ways to man. The Bible makes it clear that the **condition of the heart** of man and God's sovereign timing are two factors involved. The more truth God reveals the more man has for which to be responsible. God in His great mercy allows periods of time for man to prepare himself for the next revelation by properly responding to the previous revelation. Receiving revelation of God and treating it irresponsibly by allowing the perversions that it exposes to remain, leads to destruction.

The powerful revelation of the kingdom of God is coming forth on the earth.

The revelation of God Himself dwelling within man to guide and rule the world, will bring blessing and peace to those who properly respond. But it will eventually bring destruction for those who will not align with it. God has allowed two millennia of grace since Jesus and His disciples annunciated the gospel of the kingdom. During this period of grace the gospel of the kingdom of God was not widely preached. God's messengers simply had little or no light from God on the gospel of the kingdom. Therefore, during this two thousand years of grace man has been free to receive Jesus the Christ by the Holy Spirit into himself; and yet was not fully held accountable for the gospel of the kingdom. This era is ending and a new era beginning. The twenty-first century is the beginning of the third millennium since Jesus proclaimed the gospel of the kingdom.

It has been firmly documented from the Bible that the history of man from Adam to Jesus spans four millennia. From Jesus to the year 2000 AD is another two millennia. Therefore, the history of man according to the Bible will complete six millennia in the year 2000, (give or take a few years to allow for man's errors of his calendar). The seventh millennium of man is beginning as the sixth is completed. Seven is God's number of completion.

The first two millennia were characterized by God's natural law, the second two were characterized by the revealed law of God. The third set of two millennia has been characterized by the law of the grace of God. The seventh millennium is characterized by the law of the kingdom of God.

The seventh millennium will see the revelation of the kingdom of God from heaven on earth.

The Gospel of the kingdom will be preached to all the world.

All the world must then, become responsible for the revelation of the kingdom. An improper response to the gospel of the king-

49

dom of Christ will cause the judgment of God to come upon vast numbers of people and great areas of the world's systems.

John 12:31: *"**Now is the judgment** of this world; now the ruler of this world will be cast out."*

1 Cor 11:32: *But when we are **judged**, we are **chastened** by the Lord, that we may not be condemned with the world.*

1 Pet 4:17-18: *For the time has come for **judgment to begin at the house of God;** and if it begins with us first, what will be the end of those who do not obey the gospel of God? Now "If the righteous one is scarcely saved, Where will the ungodly and the sinner appear?"*

Catastrophic events will become common place during a portion of the seventh millennium as many of the scriptures of the Book of Revelation are carried out in the earth. This is indeed the end of an era. The era of God's tolerance for rebellious, unresponsive man ends with the wrath of God becoming evident. All natural and supernatural systems of existence will bear the mark of the new era.

Even with all the catastrophic events occurring there will be those who will still not see the kingdom of God and repent of their evil ways. *(Rev 9:20-21)* But eventually every knee shall bow and acknowledge God as King of all His kingdom. Every person will meet God in His Grace or face Him in judgment. Even as some cry out for the mountains and the rocks to fall on them and cover them from the face of God, they will acknowledge Him as God. *(Rev 6:15-16) (Rom 14:11)*

Phil 2:10-11: That at the name of Jesus every knee should bow, of those in heaven, and of those on earth, and of those under the earth, and that every tongue should confess that Jesus Christ is Lord, to the glory of God the Father.

There are those who are still looking for these things to happen someday. Yet, they have already begun and are continuing to increase in intensity. Just as the grace and glory of God are already happening and are increasing in intensity. Because the kingdom of God begins like a seed and grows slowly but certainly, many people do not realize the changes and miss what is happening.

Jesus said the kingdom of God is like a mustard seed. A very small seed that continues to grow steadily into a large plant. He also said the kingdom is like leaven. A small bit of leaven added to a large lump of dough will grow to fill the entire lump. Can you imagine trying to stop the spread of leaven in a lump of dough? Nothing will stop the gradual but powerful growth of the kingdom of heaven on earth.

Mat 13:31-33: Another parable He put forth to them, saying: "The kingdom of heaven is like a mustard seed, which a man took and sowed in his field, "which indeed is the least of all the seeds; but when it is grown it is greater than the herbs and becomes a tree, so that the birds of the air come and nest in its branches." Another parable He spoke to them: "The kingdom of heaven is like leaven, which a woman took and hid in three measures of meal till it was all leavened."

As the kingdom of heaven, kingdom of God continues to grow in the hearts and lives of individuals, families, groups, and communities across the land, righteousness, peace, and joy, in the Holy Spirit, spreads across the earth like leaven. At the same time catastrophic judgmental events are occurring in the lives of individuals, families, groups, communities, and across the earth. *(Isa 60:1-3) (Mat 13:41-43)*

God knows how to, and will protect those walking in His kingdom from any harm from all the catastrophes. *(2 Pet 2:7-9)* With God it is possible to go through the fire and not be burned. *(Dan 3:26-27)* The peace and joy of God's kingdom disciples does not depend on circumstances. *(Phil 4:6-7)* Even if the body were killed a child of God would be present with the Lord and still experiencing peace, and joy. *(2 Cor 5:1-8)*

Psa 91:7-10: A thousand may fall at your side, And ten thousand at your right hand; But it shall not come near you. Only with your eyes shall you look, And see the reward of the wicked. Because you have made the LORD, who is my refuge, Even the Most High, your dwelling place, No evil shall befall you, Nor shall any plague come near your dwelling.

Walking in the kingdom of God lifestyle is the only really safe and joyful life on earth.

But it is only for those who enter the kingdom lifestyle. Walking in the kingdom means more than being born again. It involves growing up into obediently living God's way. We are not speaking of going to heaven when we die. We are speaking of entering into the victorious, overcoming kingdom of God life now. Many Christians have not entered and are not walking in the practical kingdom of heaven life experience now.

Mat 7:21-23: "Not everyone who says to Me, 'Lord, Lord,' shall enter the kingdom of heaven, but he who does the will of My Father in heaven. "Many will say to Me in that day, 'Lord, Lord, have we not prophesied in Your name, cast out demons in Your name, and done many wonders in Your name?' "And then I will declare to them, 'I never knew you; depart from Me, you who practice lawlessness!'

52

What is practicing lawlessness?

Many church members have a somewhat generic view of what constitutes lawlessness. People seem to have a concept that, anything worse than what they themselves are doing is lawlessness. Some feel better about themselves when they focus on, what they see as, worse lawlessness in others. Many respectable church members see themselves as not being in lawlessness because they have not murdered, raped, or even robbed. Therefore, some of the less respectable people, who recognize their disobedience and repent, will enter the kingdom of God lifestyle before them. *(Mat 21:31)*

Lawlessness means walking in anything other than obedience to God.

The grace of God flowing through Christ within the believer is the source of obedience. Our self-life desires can hinder or limit the flow of the Spirit of Christ within, and cause us to become disobedient to God. *(Walk in the Spirit and you will not fulfill the lust of the flesh.)*

Many Christians who would never murder, are deceived into the equally severe disobedience of manipulation or lying. Manipulation is working or making a lie. It may even be done without technically telling a lie. By whatever means, making things to seem as they are not, by what we do or say, is lying. Getting someone to do or feel what we want them to, or what we think is best for them, by manipulation is lying. Many people including Christians seem to think that, not telling the truth is lying only if the intent is to hurt someone; but, if the intent is not to hurt or harm, then it is not a lie. Therefore, many reason that telling or working a lie, for what they consider to be a good purpose, is not a serious matter with God.

Wrong! God's direction is to leave deceitful practices and speak the truth in love. *(Eph 4:14-15)*

Manipulation or "making a lie" will prevent one from entering the kingdom of God lifestyle. All of the wonderful peace and joy, the secure protection of the refuge of God, the powerful flow of the Grace and power of God in and through one's life, the entrance into the kingdom of God lifestyle will not happen to the one who lies. It does not matter if one has been a Christian for thirty years and is the pastor of the largest church in town, or if one is doing a life sentence in the state prison, manipulators, those who make a lie, and all liars will not enter the kingdom of God.

*Rev 21:27a: And there shall in no wise enter into it any thing that defileth, neither whatsoever worketh abomination, or **maketh a lie**.*

*Rev 21:8a: But the fearful, and unbelieving, and the abominable, and murderers, and whoremongers, and sorcerers, and idolaters, and **all liars**, shall have their part in the lake which burneth with fire and brimstone.*

*1 Tim 1:9-10: Knowing this: that the law is not made for a righteous person, but for the lawless and insubordinate, for the ungodly and for sinners, for the unholy and profane, for murderers of fathers and murderers of mothers, for manslayers, for fornicators, for sodomites, for kidnappers, **for liars,** for perjurers, and if there is any other thing that is contrary to sound doctrine.*

Liars are part of the same unholy and profane list with murderers of fathers, murderers of mothers, manslayers, fornicators, sodomites, kidnappers, whoremungers, and others that work abominations and defilements.

Many people including church members and preachers, may need to rethink their priorities relative to speaking the truth. It may seem expedient to tell someone something that sounds good rather than risk offending their ego or creating a confrontation. It may seem better to tell the preacher how good his message was even though one doesn't believe a word of it, and thinks the preacher is deceived. It may seem better to build the church rather than to preach or teach what one really believes. It may seem better to cover what one did wrong by not telling the truth when asked. It may seem better to stretch the truth into a lie to get that business deal, then one will be able to give a generous offering to the church. It may seem better to misrepresent things to that boy friend or girl friend, rather than risk damaging the relationship. It may seem better to tell Aunt Jasmine how beautiful her hat is, even though it looks demonic, rather than risk offending her.

But the thing that must be considered is:
Are these things worth failing to enter the kingdom of God lifestyle?

Lying is stealing. It is robbing the other person of the truth and the opportunity to respond to the truth, which might lead to change for the better on someone's part. Yes, telling the truth is risky but it can lead to improvement of the situation, while lying or manipulating will never clear the table and will always further complicate matters. Christ Jesus within will not lead one to lie but can help one in speaking and working the truth in gentle, kind, caring, real love.

Manipulation, lying, misrepresentation, and exaggeration are so ingrained into most cultures today that it is not only acceptable to lie, it is expected, and telling the truth is not socially acceptable in many cases. The judicial system in the USA is based on the expectation that everyone will stretch the truth into lies to improve their position.

Communications are carried out by trying to figure out what the other person really meant by what he or she said. Church members and wives rarely say what they really mean. They usually say something that is supposed to give you a clue and you are supposed to figure out what they mean. Or they complain bitterly about something that has nothing to do with what is really bothering them. Most people have a reason that sounds good for what they do or don't do. But they often have another reason that is real. The game is to try to figure out what is real by what is not said.

This would all be very comical if it were not the destruction of the potential kingdom of God way in our personal lives, homes, churches and governments. Trust is destroyed, communications break down, and intimate relationships between individuals and groups are impossible. There can never be oneness of spirit without openness and transparency.

If manipulation and lying are employed, trust is destroyed and can never be replaced without real **repentance** and commitment to openness and honesty. One must repent to God and change, but one must also repent to the parties involved and make recompense wherever possible. In the long run facing the risk of telling and working the truth in love, may be far less costly than making a lie.

Manipulation is not rooted in love, it is rooted in unlove.

Unlove is the lack of the presence of the manifestation of the love of God within, through Christ by the Holy Spirit. The emptiness of unlove causes one's inner needs to be so intense that it seems worth making a lie to try to get or hold on to something or someone, that one needs to feel better. **Fear** of not getting or losing something or someone we need, and **unbelief** that God will meet all our needs, may lead one to become like God and try to meet his or her own needs. To be self centered and self seeking is to be one's own god; which is **idolatry**, and leads to **sorcery** as the powers of darkness begin to assist the works of manipulation. This can all be subversively accomplished under the guise of **self** betterment.

Rev 21:8a: But the fearful, and unbelieving, and the abominable, and murderers, and whoremongers, and sorcerers, and idolaters, and all liars, shall have their part in the lake which burneth with fire and brimstone.

Begin now to seek the kingdom of God with your whole heart. Don't miss entering the wonderful kingdom life.

Mat 6:33 But seek first the kingdom of God and His righteousness, and all these things shall be added to you.

BASILEIA LETTER

Number 5

Sexual Freedom and The Kingdom of God

Jesus said, *"For **out of the heart** proceed evil thoughts, murders, **adulteries**, **fornications**, thefts, false witness, blasphemies. "These are the things which defile a man, but to eat with unwashed hands does not defile a man," Mat 15:19-20.*

Some local churches have in a general sense, through out history, adjusted to seek to meet the needs of the people in a cultural framework that will allow the people to feel some degree of comfort in attending. The rationale is that the people can only be ministered to if they attend, and they will not attend if the church is not tolerant of their chosen lifestyle. Others have been very intolerant and verbally attacked the lifestyle and the person. Or at least made the person feel that they were attacked.

In the USA, and much of the world today, one of the major issues is "free sex." Many people today including church members are confused. Especially many young people who have adopted the philosophy that it is their right and privilege to enter into sexual intimacy with whom they choose, when they choose. Many have come to accept unmarried couples living together intimately as an acceptable lifestyle. Others who might publicly loudly oppose the "free sex" lifestyles of today, have themselves entered into **secret** sexual affairs and encounters of their own.

Many people have come to believe their sexual lust is just the normal way they are, the way God made them. God does cause man to have a wonderful desire for sexual intimacy with a mate. But the same God gave definite instruction into how and when the desire for sex is to be fulfilled, and how and when it is not to be fulfilled.

God's instructions were not given to mankind to keep him from having fun.

Quite the contrary, the instructions given by God are designed for the greatest fulfillment and the most joyful life for men and women. The warnings given by God are to help keep people from devastating painful experiences in life and to cause them to experience abundant peace and joy in the exciting passionate realm of sex. The most beautiful, satisfying, loving, sexual experiences are for those walking in the kingdom of God; those who are seeking the kingdom of God above all else, and are walking in His righteousness, His right way of doing and being.

True sexual freedom in the kingdom of God is freedom to enjoy God's design of sexual intimacy with a mate to the fullest. No fornicator nor adulterer will experience the beauty of intimate union, in an atmosphere of spiritual love, openness, and transparency, free from any guilt or shame. There is no romance as good as the one God brings to pass, in His way, and in His timing. There is no fear, no stress, no selfishness, no jealousy, and no regrets in the union of a kingdom of God romance. The devil did not invent sex, God did. The devil and mankind only perverted it. Much of the world's people have chosen to ignore God's plan, given in the Bible, and come up with their own plan. People of God need to understand and come into order with God's plan for sex.

"Free sex" is not free at all, it is very expensive.

It will cost one entrance into the kingdom of God lifestyle. No person engaged in premarital sex, extra marital sex, nor any other

59

sexual perversions, nor unmarried persons living together in sexual intimacy can enter the kingdom of God lifestyle now. We are not talking about being born again. We are talking about the wonderful peaceful, joyous, safe and secure lifestyle of the kingdom of God. We are talking about the unrestrained flow of the grace and power of the love of Jesus the Christ, flowing from within the believer to overcome every obstacle and accomplish every work of God. We are also talking about being free from fiery judgments now.

*1 Tim 1:9-10: Knowing this: that the law is not made for a righteous person, but for the lawless and insubordinate, for the ungodly and for sinners, for the unholy and profane, for murderers of fathers and murderers of mothers, for manslayers, for **fornicators**, for **sodomites**, for kidnappers, for liars, for perjurers, and if there is any other thing that is contrary to sound doctrine.*

*Rev 21:27: But there shall by no means enter it anything that defiles, or causes an **abomination** or a lie.*

(Read, *Prov 6:24-35).*

*Prov 7:21-23: With her enticing speech she caused him to yield, With her flattering lips she seduced him. Immediately he went after her, as an ox goes to the slaughter, Or as a fool to the correction of the stocks, Till an arrow struck his liver. As a bird hastens to the snare, **He did not know it would cost his life.***

*Gal 5:19: Now the works of the flesh are evident, which are: **adultery, fornication, uncleanness, lewdness.** Eph 5:3: But **fornication** and all **uncleanness** or covetousness, let it not even be named among you, as is fitting for saints.*

Col 3:5: Therefore put to death your members which are on the earth: **fornication, uncleanness, passion, evil desire,** *and covetousness, which is idolatry. 2 Tim 2:22:* **Flee also youthful lusts;** *but pursue righteousness, faith, love, peace with those who call on the Lord out of a pure heart. 2 Cor 12:21: Lest, when I come again, my God will humble me among you, and I shall mourn for many who have* **sinned before** *and have not* **repented** *of the* **uncleanness, fornication,** *and* **lewdness** *which they have practiced.*

The key is repentance, a turning away from perverted sexual practice and a turning toward the grace of God, in Christ Jesus the Anointed One. One can never overcome sexual perversions by trying hard. Jesus is the answer. He has provided all one needs to be set free of every perverted habit. It is not a matter of trying to keep the law, it is a matter of the heart. The law makes clear to a person what is right and what is not, and leads one to repentance, but it has no power to make correction within the heart. Jesus paid for everyone's perverted practices at the cross. The resurrected Christ Jesus now lives within the believer to empower him or her to live righteously, and to walk in the kingdom of God lifestyle, with all its freedom and benefits. The choices are to repent and be changed or to attempt to justify one's unclean, lewd practices.

Practice of sexual perversions come from within the heart. Remember Jesus said in, *Mat 15:19: "For* **out of the heart** *proceed evil thoughts, murders,* **adulteries, fornications,** *".* Jesus also said in *Mat 5:27-28: "You have heard that it was said to those of old, 'You shall not commit adultery.' "But I say to you that whoever looks at a woman to* **lust** *for her has already committed adultery with her in his* **heart."**

Being filled with the presence of the Anointed One, Jesus Christ in one's heart, by the Holy Spirit can give power when the Word of

God is applied within, to completely destroy the old perversions of the past. There is no stronghold too difficult for the anointing of Christ which destroys the yoke of bondage. *(Isa 10:27 KJV)* The kingdom of God is righteousness, peace, and joy in the Holy Spirit, and the kingdom of God is within you, if Christ is in your heart. *(Rom 4:17), (Luke 17:21)*

> Every person who knows Jesus as saviour has the opportunity to enter the glorious kingdom of heaven lifestyle.

Those who have murdered, raped, committed adultery, had immoral affairs, practiced sexual perversions, had lewd involvements, been sexual addicts, kidnapped, gossiped, manipulated, stolen, divorced, lied and any other defiling abominable thing, have the potential to enter the kingdom of God and walk in the powerful glorious kingdom lifestyle, **IF** they will **repent** and by the grace and power of Christ through the Holy Spirit, **STOP** their sin.

These sins and perversions are not greater than the cross of Jesus. Any time one acknowledges his or her sin and repents, the blood of Jesus can again make him or her a new creation, fresh, pure, and clean, fit to enter into obedience to God by the power of Christ and enter into the kingdom of heaven lifestyle.

But if one attempts to justify his or her sin and continues in it he or she will not enter the kingdom of heaven lifestyle now, and is in line for a lifestyle of fiery judgments and lack of peace and joy. Even though one may have received Jesus as saviour and is believing He will get him or her to heaven after death, he or she will not enter the kingdom of heaven now. Jesus preached, *"Repent for the kingdom of heaven is at hand."*

This is not a new issue, it is an old problem in a new era. In the era of the revealed law those found in some of these activities were stoned to death. Some people, especially church members appear to think that verbal stoning, in the form of judgmental accusations, is the best answer available today. Jesus living in believers today will handle these problems just as He did when He walked on the earth and the New Testament was being lived out.

When Jesus met the Samaritan woman at the well He was aware of her perverted sexual lifestyle. Her life was strongly affected, and I believe forever changed, by the encounter of meeting Jesus. Jesus did not reprimand her with stern judgmental accusations. Instead of telling her how bad she was, He focused on telling her about the true God, and the great blessing of living water that she could have; the everlasting life she could begin experiencing now instead of the life she had been living. Jesus demonstrated the power of God to her as he told her of her personal life. Not only did she hear of the true God but she saw the power of God demonstrated in her presence.

*John 4:10-18: Jesus answered and said to her, "**If you knew the gift of God**, and who it is who says to you, 'Give Me a drink,' you would have asked Him, and **He would have given you living water**." The woman said to Him, "Sir, You have nothing to draw with, and the well is deep. Where then do You get that living water? **Are You greater** than our father Jacob, who gave us the well, and drank from it himself, as well as his sons and his livestock?" Jesus answered and said to her, "Whoever drinks of this water will thirst again, **but whoever drinks of the water that I shall give him will never thirst. But the water that I shall give him will become in him a fountain of water springing up into everlasting life**." The woman said to Him, "Sir, give me this water, that I may not thirst, nor come here to draw." Jesus said to her, "Go, call your husband, and come here."*

*The woman answered and said, "I have no husband." Jesus said to her, "You have well said, 'I have no husband,' "for you have had **five husbands, and the one whom you now have is not your husband**; in that you spoke truly."*

The woman believed in Jesus as the Christ and became an evangelist as she ran back into her city and told everyone that she had met the Christ and invited them to come and see for themselves. They did come and see and many were saved. Would this harvest have occurred if Jesus had rebuked the woman for her immoral lifestyle, and verbally stoned her with accusations? Would it have occurred if Jesus had just ignored her as if she were not present? Would it have occurred if Jesus had not told her of the better life of everlasting spiritual living water? What if He had not demonstrated the power of the kingdom of God to her by supernaturally telling her of her personal life?

Jesus never condoned her perverted sexual lifestyle.

He never said it was acceptable. He simply focused on the kingdom of God lifestyle and told her she could have it now. Repent, why? Because the kingdom of God is at hand, and its too good to miss.

On another occasion a group of religious leaders, scribes and Pharisees, brought a woman caught in adultery before Jesus. The religious men proffered that according to Moses she should be stoned. And then they asked Jesus, "But what do You say?" Jesus knelt down and wrote on the ground as though He was not hearing them.

*John 8:7-12: So when they continued asking Him, He raised Himself up and said to them, "**He who is without sin among you,*** *let him throw a stone at her first." And again He stooped down and wrote on the ground. Then those who heard it, being convicted by their conscience, went out one by one, beginning with the oldest even to the last. And Jesus was left alone, and the woman standing in the midst. When Jesus had raised Himself up and saw no one but the woman, He said to her, "Woman, where are those accusers of yours? Has no one condemned you?" She said, "No one, **Lord**." And Jesus said to her, "**Neither do I condemn you; GO AND SIN NO MORE**." Then Jesus spoke to them again, saying, "I am the light of the world. He who follows Me shall **not walk in darkness**, but have the **light of life**."*

If accusation and condemnation could have helped, the matter would have been well taken care of by the religious men. Again, Jesus did not ever condone or tolerate her perverted behavior. He brought it to a quick end by bringing her to a point that she could **go and sin no more**. Jesus is the light of life, the understanding, the energy, the source of all that is needed to follow Him and walk in His light. The Jesus in us will no longer condone or tolerate sexually perverted behavior in our lives, or in the lives of others. Nor will the Jesus in us condemn and accuse ourselves or others.

Jesus does not condemn, He fixes the problem.

*John 3:17: For God did not send His Son into the world to **condemn** the world, but that the world through Him might be **saved**.*

Condemning ourselves or others never fixes the problem. Coming to Jesus and receiving the grace and power of the living God within, will fix the problem. Then one can **go and sin no more**.

The cost for sexual disobedience is far more than we can imagine. Perverted sexual practices threaten destruction on a world wide scale. The pain of devastating experiences to the individuals involved is only the beginning of loss and destruction caused by "free sex". In the USA we are only beginning to see the result of not respecting and adhering to God's kingdom pattern for family. Families are stressed to the breaking point by sexual immorality. The bond of intimate closeness developed in a pure sexual relationship in marriage is broken by sexual indiscretions. When extra marital sexual activity is discovered lives are devastated, families torn apart, children's lives damaged and altered forever. Even when extra marital sexual acts are not discovered by the mate, there is a loss to the intimacy in the relationship. The passionate sexual desires are dulled and the keen edge of exciting intense ecstacy is lost, and may lead to disappointment, frustration, lack of interest and eventually contribute to a break up.

God's kingdom family pattern is the one that works.

(See, Chapter 17, "God's Kingdom Family Pattern," in the book, "Overcoming Life On A Small Planet".) Not only is it the one that works it is less costly and more fun. The breakdown of the family causes perversions in the children that lead to less productive lives with more disorders. Communities and eventually nations will buckle under the burden of cost of unwed mothers trying to raise children without a husband, expenses of hospital and doctors care for sexually transmitted diseases, the waste and expense of divorces, pornography with the sexual perversions and crimes spawned by it, and many other costly results of "free sex".

The emotional stress and damage from the results of sexual perversions ("free sex") fills counselors' offices, and may lead many to turn to drugs or alcohol as a source of temporary relief from the stress of their lives. Some turn to suicide. The price is very high, the cost goes on and on for "free sex".

But, perhaps the greatest cost is the broken hearts and dreams. The broken heart of the father who discovers his thirteen year old daughter is sexually involved with an older boy. The lost dream of the pregnant fifteen year old who wanted to become a scientist. The lost dreams of the young man dying with aids, and the broken heart of his mother. ----- Is "free sex", really free?

The people of the world are not eagerly moving toward religion that promises heaven when they die, but **does little or nothing about the hell they live in now**. As the gospel of the kingdom is preached and demonstrated by the supernatural power of God, *(1 Th 1:5)* as the people are seeing the abundance of peace, joy, and prosperity of life in the kingdom from heaven on earth, many are eagerly coming toward the kingdom of God. As they see the health, happiness, and healing of Gods people, as people are seeing spiritual power overcome and destroy the works of darkness on every front, many are ardently seeking the kingdom of God.

Isa 60:1-4: Arise, shine; For your light has come! And the glory of the LORD is risen upon you. For behold, the darkness shall cover the earth, And deep darkness the people; But the LORD will arise over you, And His glory will be seen upon you. The Gentiles shall come to your light, And kings to the brightness of your rising. Lift up your eyes all around, and see: They all gather together, they come to you; Your sons shall come from afar, And your daughters shall be nursed at your side.

God made the earth, its systems, and everything that is on the earth through Jesus the Christ. *(John 1:3) (Col 1:16-20)* Surely the one who made all that exist, has sufficient power and knowledge to fix it. Surely He knows the best way to operate and to govern it.

Another word for kingdom is government.

A kingdom is a government ruled by a sovereign. The individual governed by God will prosper. The family governed by God will prosper. The nation governed by God will prosper. The world governed by God will prosper in all its ways and systems.

Psa 144:15: Happy are the people who are in such a state; Happy are the people whose God is the LORD!

The sovereign power and wisdom of almighty, all wise, Father God is in the son of God, Christ Jesus. The potential of all the power and all the wisdom of Father God is available within the believer in whom Christ Jesus dwells, by the Holy Spirit. *(John 17:20-23)*

Fully releasing the governing of our lives from our rule to the rule of God through the Holy Spirit, allows God to rule as King of our lives; and causes the portion of the world over which we have authority to be ruled according to the government of God. God has chosen to give the dominion of the world to man. Every person has the God given power to decide to seek to rule one's own life from his or her own intellect, or to decide to seek the governing of God Himself. If man decides to rule by his own intellect, he is in disobedience to God and will be assisted by powers of darkness.

Whichever rules in the heart of man rules in the world. The world must respond to the beliefs and words of man. Whatever man believes in his heart and speaks with his mouth will have an effect on the world.

*Mark 11:23: "For assuredly, I say to you, whoever **says** to this mountain, 'Be removed and be cast into the sea,' and **does not doubt in his heart, but believes** that those things he **says** will be done, he will have whatever he **says**. (Rom 10:8-10)*

68

God made the decision to give man dominion in the world. He will not override the will of man. *(Gen 1:26-28)*

If one chooses to rule one's own life and participate in disobedient acts, such as "free sex", or any other disobedient act, the power and wisdom of God are restrained, and the powers of darkness are released with all their deception and cunning. If, however, one decides to completely release the rule of one's life to God, the power and wisdom of God are released, and the deception and cunning of the powers of darkness are restrained. The devil cannot do anything that man does not allow him to do.

And God can do anything man can believe.

When the will of man becomes aligned with the will of God the kingdom of God is come and the will of God is done on earth as it is in heaven. *(Mat 6:10)* First the kingdom comes within man and then into the world as man rules all that is given into his authority by the power and wisdom of God.

There are no earthly problems that are greater than the power and wisdom of God. Every need of man and the world can be met by the power and wisdom of God released in man. There are creative ideas and problem solving strategies that man as yet has not seen or even imagined. Solutions are waiting for man to bring his will into alignment with God's will. *(John 15:7-8) (Mat 19:26) (Mark 9:23) (1 Cor 2:9-10)*

Seeking to rule one's own life is seeking the kingdom of man. Seeking God's rule in one's life is seeking the kingdom of God. *(Luke 9:24)* Seeking the kingdom of man aligns one with the will of the enemy and causes deception and darkness that prevents one from seeing the solutions of God.*(2 Cor 4:4)* Seeking the kingdom of God opens the way for the wisdom and power of God to flow through one's life, and makes it possible to see the solutions of God.

Inordinate sexual activity is perhaps the enemy's most effective enticement for alluring people to seek to rule their own lives, and thereby fail to seek the kingdom of God. The enticement of "free sex" does not reveal up front that the wisdom and power of God will be stolen from the participant. The entire world suffers as multitudes are robbed of the power and wisdom of God to bring forth solutions and meet needs. Men make bad decisions without the wisdom of God and continue to bring greater disorder and destruction to the world.

The entire world can only be saved one person at the time. The decision that you make to either seek the kingdom of God, or to enter into "free sex" or other disobedience, will have an effect on the world. The world is groaning and waiting. *(Rom 8:19,21-22) (Mat 6:33)*

BASILEIA LETTER

Number 6

Competition and
The Kingdom of God

Competition first originated in heaven as Lucifer, a most powerful angel, decided to strive against God to become number one. *(Isa 14:12-14) (Rev 12:7-9) (Ezek 28:12-18)* The same powerful spirit works in the world today seeking to cause each person or group to compete with one another to try to become **number one, over all the others**.

There are only two most fundamental orders of life. One is following God in obedience to Him and His ways. The other is self will in competition against God's will and way. Life is ordered by God and His will, or it is ordered by another will in competition against God.

Competition between individuals and groups is a major factor in the world today. Competition is deeply ingrained in the life patterns of Americans. It has been revered for so long that most people think it is a very worthy ingredient of successful life. Children are taught to compete at home and in school. They are praised when they are better than others and when they win over others. Sometimes the entire town will show up at the game and cheer like crazy when they win over the neighboring town's children. But it is very quiet when they lose even by one score to a cheering rival group of children. Children's games become adult games, and everything revolves around their beating the other people. Competition is self seeking and involves covetousness, which leads to envy, which leads to strife and wars.

The first major competitive incident occurred between Cain and Abel. Cain wanted to do offerings his way, not God's way.

71

When Abel's offering, brought God's way, was accepted by God and Cain's was not; Cain become angry and killed his brother. *(Gen 4:3-8)* Cain's competition with Abel began with Cain's competition with God concerning who was to be number one in his life. Competition in our lives today begins with our competing with God for number one status.

Competition first became a major player in the scheme of human living in Nimrod. Nimrod was the great grandson of Noah. He departed from the faith of his fathers and tapped into the occult powers of darkness. Nimrod built the original great city of Babylon. He was the first to put competition to work within his army to train and toughen troops. He enticed and controlled men through immorality, competition, and sorcery. He conquered his neighbors and ruled over them.

Competition is not a kingdom of heaven principle. Cooperation and collaboration are kingdom ways.

Competition does serve a valuable purpose in Babylonian style cultures. It is valuable for balancing greed and motivating quality service in cultures where businesses must compete with one another to survive. In a similar way it can motivate individuals to greater performance. Competition is also generally believed by many to increase production, and in the short range it can stimulate production between individuals and groups. However, in the long range and in the bigger picture, competition decreases production and efficiency. Cooperating and collaborating will always prove to be more productive in the end. *(See pages 136-137, "Overcoming Life On A Small Planet")*

Competition in Babylonian culture is beneficial much like the law of the jungle is beneficial by eliminating the weak and preserving the quality of the species. Within many species males must battle to the death, or near death, for breeding rights. The survivor will be the most fit and will produce the best offspring. The individual or business that can become the most efficient and productive has the best chance for survival and should produce the best value in products or services. In a greed based economy these are noble principles. But the kingdom of God is not a competition oriented economy based on greed.

The kingdom of God is a service oriented economy based on love.

The new era of the kingdom is changing the way things are done. In the old Babylonian style system competing with others to have more than they, to be better than they, and to be esteemed by others more highly than they, was considered normal good behavior. It was normal for one business group to try to get all the business for themselves and force others out of business if possible. It is expected that a defensive lineman on a professional football team will try to injure the star quarterback on the other team, so his team can win and be number one.

As the kingdom of God is coming forth into our world, more and more people are seeing the value of living according to God's kingdom patterns. More and more are seeking the kingdom of God, who is the true number one, rather than seeking to be number one.

I wonder if in generations yet to come, kingdom of God people will look back upon this time with wonder at how Christians could have been so greedy and self seeking. As the transition continues, some, who live long, may even look back on their own life time and wonder at the change. Much the same as I look back over sixty years now and wonder how Christians of my generation could have been so prejudiced against other races.

I also marvel at how much more wicked the ungodly people have become in my lifetime. The rampant and open immorality and perversions, along with the level of violence, evil, and irresponsibility in America today were unthinkable just fifty to sixty years ago.

For those who are not old enough to know, America was a very different culture. Patriotism was big; the president was greatly respected; the dollar was sound; no one knew what inflation was; policemen were your friends; dope was only in New York slums; families had a mother and a father and children; the mother made a home and cared for the children during the day while the father worked and provided for the family; and they both were there with the children at night; anyone who engaged in immorality or sexual perversion was a social outcast; movies were clean and fun. It wasn't perfect, but it was very different from the general American culture today.

Multitudes of people who are seeking the kingdom of God today form a sort of subculture in which families still look and operate much the same as they did in the past. They are, however, in general more focused on God and more pure in their lifestyles than past generations. Since many participate only very sparingly and guardedly in main stream American culture, the perverted practices of modern Babylonian style culture are less likely to be implanted in their children. Kingdom of God subculture children can grow up untrained in the competition of a greed based economy. They have the opportunity to become the leaders of the new era of service oriented, love based economy.

Love is the primary
motivational force of the kingdom of God,
New Jerusalem lifestyle.

Unlove and its intense inner needs that cause greed are the rudimental motivational forces of Babylonian culture.

Jesus said, "love your neighbor as yourself". *(Mat 22:39)* He told the disciples to love one another as He had loved them, and that men would know they were His disciples by their love. *(John 13:34-35)*.

The Bible in *1 Corinthians, Chapter 13*, gives a picture of what love is like. In part it says that, *"love does not seek its own"* and that, *"love suffers long and is kind; love does not envy; love does not parade itself, and is not puffed up"*. Love is a giving thing that leads one to become a servant of others, not a competitor against others. One of the underlying desires of seeking to be better than others is seeking to rule over others, to be the boss. *(Mat 20:25-28)*

Competition leads to unnecessary strife between individuals, families, tribes, and nations. Competition roots in inner need, and fear of not having enough. Whether it is not enough land, food, jobs, business, or some other tangible thing, or whether it is not enough praise, acceptance, affection, love, or some other need, the fear is that I will not have enough unless I strive against you to get more. A belief that there is not enough for everyone, leads to wars and strife of every kind. I must strive to get mine before you get it, or from you if you already have it.

James 4:1-2: Where do wars and fights come from among you? Do they not come from your desires for pleasure that war in your members? You lust and do not have. You murder and covet and cannot obtain. You fight and war. Yet you do not have because ***you do not ask***.

There is a big difference between asking
for something and taking it.

A hungry but **independent** and **proud** person would rather steal something to eat than to knock on a door and ask for a meal. Asking is humbling and causes the person to feel he or she is not number one, not greater than others. Taking it by stealing or robbing at gun point allows the proud person to continue to feel that he is greater and more powerful than others. He is still number one, and in control of his own life.

Competition between peers is the result of individuals seeking to meet their own needs rather than asking God. The first question should be, "God, what do I really need?" instead of asking for what I determine that I need. If one can determine what he needs on his own, and ask God for it and get it, God has become subordinate and the person is still number one.

Competition is striving against God and against others to be in control. Whether it is a sister and brother arguing, or two boys fighting on the school yard, or a husband and wife yelling at each other, or battling it out in a divorce court, or Christians manipulating for the favored position in their church, or business men suing one another, or nations at total war with each other, the basis is still the same. It is a matter of being in control so things will be done my way and I will have whatever I determine that I need.

The greater the inner need, the greater the striving will be. The world's most competitive people are often those with the greatest inner need. The very richest men are often those who grew up in painful poverty, and from that severe experience of need have become very competitive. Unfortunately their inner need will never be satisfied by the money and power that they acquire. The real need is for the love of God within and nothing else will fix things for them, and allow them to stop striving and competing. Sometimes the greatest athletes are those who did not receive unconditional love as a child, and now, never feel they are good enough to be acceptable.

Subsequently they have a great need to perform extraordinarily, and are driven to intense competition.

Strife among peers is a very pervasive and costly problem. The inner needs of Christians and unbelievers alike often cause them to strive against one another with their words and actions.

Some people who grew up in an unstable environment in which bad things happened that they were unable to control, sometimes have a great subconscious inner fear of not being in control. Without realizing what they are doing, they will challenge and strive against anyone or anything which affects their lives and is not under their control. The strife may start in the form of contentious debate about seemingly unimportant matters. Powerful arguments, fighting, accusations, debasing comments, and rejection of any potential authority may explode from the person as the panic of the fear of not being in control possesses them. The intense competition of such persons will not allow them to appreciate their peer's views and accomplishments. It will not allow them to receive direction and correction from, or through others. They must be number one, in control at all times. Strife often seems to eventually erupt in every situation of life in which they are involved.

This and many other reasons may cause people, including Christians, to compete and strive with one another for control and dominance. In the kingdom of heaven lifestyle there is no strife.

*2 Tim 2:24-26: And **the servant of the Lord must not strive;** but be gentle unto **all men**, apt to teach, patient, In meekness instructing those that oppose themselves; if God peradventure will give them repentance to the acknowledging of the truth; And that they may recover themselves out of the snare of the devil, who are taken captive by him at his will.*

Americans are obsessed with competition.

It permeates the American culture and affects most every aspect of life. In recent years the obsession with competitive sports has grown by enormous proportions. The amount of attention, money, and other resources vested in competitive sports probably already exceeds any other facet of American culture. Competitive games including gambling, video games, and every other form of competitive play that can be imagined is growing rapidly in America. Sports and most other competition in America is thought of as "friendly competition". Much of it may have begun as a friendly game, but it has grown into very serious multi billion dollar industries with great consequences for winning or losing.

Is friendly competition really friendly?

The old meaning of the word "sport" is to make mockery or ridicule. The object of any sporting event may be to win, but the result is that someone is beaten and becomes a loser. Being the loser can cause a great deal of pain, frustration, and serious negative feelings which can significantly impact one's life.

Prov 18:14 KJV: The spirit of a man will sustain his infirmity; **but a wounded spirit who can bear?**

The winner may become filled with pride and haughtiness; and lose respect and concern for others, which may lead to problems in other life situations. Friendly competition may not be as friendly as one might think.

Prov 16:18: **Pride** *goes before destruction, And a* **haughty** *spirit before a fall.*

78

As a young man I loved to play poker. Friends and relatives would gather for a "friendly" game of penny poker. Though the stakes were very low, (a whole night's winnings might be three dollars) I felt very good when I won; but I remember feeling very bad when I lost. I began to notice that I just did not like the person who beat me as much as before. No big deal, I just did not care to be around them very much. I became a better player and won a lot of times. I began to notice that it was hard for me to get along with the ones that I had beaten. Especially when I would win a big pot by bluffing them out when they really had the better hand. After I became a Christian I realized that I lost when I lost because I felt bad. And I lost when I won because they felt bad. Either way there was a loss of friendship. Is friendly competition really friendly?

Most games are not for fun they are for winning by beating others. If a game is for fun, there is no difference in the fun no matter who has the largest or smallest score. Actually, it would not even be necessary to keep score if it were truly for fun.

In Babylonian style culture the "friendly competition" of sports is beneficial in several ways. It provides an outlet for aggression in people by providing a format for release within rules and controls. This is much better than releasing aggression on the streets. It provides a focus and motivation for some who are without direction or motivation in their lives. It often provides training in teamwork, discipline, and Babylonian style social skills. Since sports have become big business it can provide for money in the form of scholarships for young people, and for those who become really good, it can provide wealth. But one must keep in mind that in competitive sports, for every winner there is a loser.

In the kingdom of God New Jerusalem lifestyle, there are no losers.

79

Play is for fun, and work is for serving by meeting the needs of others. No one must be made a mockery or ridiculed for someone else to win. Jobs and businesses meet the needs of people by providing needed products and services. If a need is being adequately met by one business there is no need to start another business for the same purpose in the same market area. Instead the businessman will look for another need to meet, or assist the existing business in meeting the need at hand.

Love motivates the businessman and the worker to provide the best possible product or service for the best possible value for all concerned. *(Gal 5:13) (Col 3:23)* The intent of every business transaction is that all parties win, that no one be defrauded for the benefit of someone else.

There is no competition between individuals or groups in the kingdom of heaven.

There is no strife between individuals or groups in the New Jerusalem lifestyle. Every person seeks to take care of himself and others equally.

Mark 12:31: "And the second, like it, is this: 'You shall love your neighbor as yourself.' There is no other commandment greater than these."

Rom 13:9-10: For the commandments, "You shall not commit adultery," "You shall not murder," "You shall not steal," "You shall not bear false witness," "You shall not covet," and if there is any other commandment, are all summed up in this saying, namely, "You shall love your neighbor as yourself." Love does no harm to a neighbor; therefore love is the fulfillment of the law.

80

Luke 6:31: "And just as you want men to do to you, you also do to them likewise.

The only competition in the kingdom of God is with the devil, not with flesh and blood.

*Eph 6:11-12: Put on the whole armor of God, that you may be able to **stand against the wiles of the devil. For we do not wrestle against flesh and blood, but against principalities, against powers, against the rulers of the darkness of this age, against spiritual hosts of wickedness in the heavenly places.***

*2 Cor 10:3-4: For though we walk in the flesh, we do not **war** according to the flesh. For the weapons of our **warfare** are not carnal but mighty in God for pulling down strongholds.*

Every person on earth is involved, whether they want to be or not, in the great conflict between the kingdom of God, kingdom of light, with its New Jerusalem lifestyle, and the kingdom of darkness, with its Babylonian lifestyle. *(See pages 24-25, "Overcoming Life On A Small Planet")*

All strife in the kingdom of God is directly or indirectly against Satan and his kingdom of darkness. Striving is to live godly in Christ Jesus, and against sin. One is to strive to enter through the narrow gate. *(Luke 13:24)* One should also strive to have a conscience without offense toward God and men. *(Acts 24:16)* And the servant of God should strive in prayer. *(Rom 15:30)*

There is never strife against any person. There is never competition with any person for any reason. God is no respecter of persons and everybody has the opportunity to acknowledge God and seek the kingdom of God.

Acts 10:34-35 KJV: Then Peter opened his mouth, and said, Of a truth I perceive that **God is no respecter of persons***: But in every nation he that feareth him, and worketh righteousness, is accepted with him. Rom 10:13: For "whoever calls on the name of the LORD shall be saved."*

There is no sin too great for the blood of Jesus. The penalty for all sin of all people has been paid for at the cross of Jesus. *(Rom 5:17-18)*

2 Cor 5:15 and **He died for all***, that those who live should live no longer for themselves, but for Him who died for them and rose again.*

The way is open for everyone to come to Christ, and God is not willing that any should perish. *(2 Pet 3:9)* Any person seeking the kingdom of God must turn away from the darkness, and let go of it. Those who will repent of their sin and turn from darkness toward the light can be born again into the kingdom of God and grow into the New Jerusalem lifestyle. Those who will not let go of the kingdom of darkness and its Babylonian lifestyle, and continue to hold on to it will share in its destruction.

Rev 18:2-4: And he cried mightily with a loud voice, saying, "Babylon the great is fallen, is fallen, and has become a dwelling place of demons, a prison for every foul spirit, and a cage for every unclean and hated bird! "For all the nations have drunk of the wine of the wrath of her fornication, the kings of the earth have committed fornication with her, and the merchants of the earth have become rich through the abundance of her luxury." And I heard another voice from heaven saying, **"Come out of her, my people, lest you share in her sins, and lest you receive of her plagues.**

There are two spiritual pattern cities by which individuals can order their lives and by which the world is ordered. Just as there was an old natural Babylon which was destroyed, there is now a "Mystery Babylon" which is being destroyed.

Rev 17:5,18: And on her forehead a name was written: MYS-TERY, BABYLON THE GREAT, THE MOTHER OF HARLOTS AND OF THE ABOMINATIONS OF THE EARTH. And the woman whom you saw ***is*** ***that great city*** *which reigns over the kings of the earth.*

The other spiritual pattern city by which life can be ordered is New Jerusalem. Just as there is old natural Jerusalem, there is now a spiritual New Jerusalem coming forth from heaven.

Gal 4:26: but the Jerusalem above is free, which is the mother of us all.

Rev 21:2-3: Then I, John, saw the holy city, New Jerusalem, coming down out of heaven from God, prepared as a bride adorned for her husband. And I heard a loud voice from heaven saying, "Behold, the tabernacle of ***God is with men, and He will dwell with them,*** *and they shall be His people.* ***God Himself will be with them*** *and be their God.*

MAY GOD BE WITH YOU.

BASILEIA LETTER

Number 7

Business in the Kingdom of God

Jesus taught supreme matchless wisdom from heaven. The transcendental wisdom from the very core of heavenly understanding was spoken to the disciples and written for our instruction in how to live in the world. Successful and prosperous life are encased within the teachings of Jesus the Christ. Kingdom of God wisdom and understanding are revealed by the Holy Spirit for the believers instruction in doing business, and every aspect of life. Yet most of the world is ignoring these greatest of all teachings for doing business. Others simply do not understand that Jesus taught more than religious or church matters.

Many Christians have received their business training from the Babylonian system. They may have received their spiritual or religious training from Bible based teachings of the church. But, many have not realized that the Bible teaches how to do business in the most successful way. Most of the teachings of Jesus are explaining the practical kingdom of God on earth, from heaven. He taught what the kingdom is like, how to enter it, how to live and work in the kingdom, including how to do business, not just how to get to heaven when one dies. Many people do not realize that life came with an instruction book.

The Bible is God's instruction book for life.

Jesus and His disciples were on the way to Jerusalem when Jesus told them that He would be crucified there and rise again the third day. The disciples could not understand that this was only the next step in the kingdom of God coming forth. They expected the kingdom to fully appear when they reached Jerusalem. As they neared Jerusalem, He taught them with a kingdom parable to help them understand more about the kingdom of heaven on earth, and their part in it.

*Luke 19:11-13: Now as they heard these things, He spoke another parable, because He was near Jerusalem and because they thought the kingdom of God would appear immediately. Therefore He said: "A certain nobleman went into a far country to receive for himself a kingdom and to return. So he called ten of his servants, delivered to them ten minas, and said to them, **'Do business till I come.'***

He went on in the parable to teach them things about doing business and the kingdom of God. The Bible teaches more about business than just "business ethics", **Jesus taught foundational business principles and formulas that will shape the entire foundation of doing business.**

American Christians in general have developed a mental system for departmentalizing life. Different principles may be employed to achieve differing goals in each department. People tend to separate their "Christian or religious life" from their "business life," or their family life from ministry life, etc. In God's kingdom, New Jerusalem, lifestyle, these are all one life; and there is only one set of life principles. The purpose for one's life is the same at home, in church, in ministry, or in business.

The purpose for our lives is to glorify God, and to serve God by serving others and the world around us. The motivation and goal is for each of us to love God with our whole heart, and love our neighbor as ourself. The method is serving and caring for one another and God's creation. Serving one another begins with meeting the needs of others, but goes further to blessing others beyond their needs.

Caring and providing for ourselves, other people, and the world around us, is doing business in the kingdom of God.

Whether it is praying for someone and teaching the Word to meet a spiritual need, or teaching math to provide for a mental need, or growing and processing food to meet a physical need, or comforting someone with a kind word and a hug to meet an emotional need, or controlling emissions from a power plant to meet an environmental need, it is all doing business in the kingdom of God.

God has given, and continues to give gifts and abilities to each person to be used to do the business of providing for the world, including all its inhabitants. These gifts include talents, strengths, and material possessions. The gifts always remain the property of God. They are given into man's hands to be managed by man for God. The nobleman in the parable of the minas gave the minas to his servants to do business with until he returned to call for the results of doing business.

Luke 19:12: A certain nobleman went into a far country to receive for himself a kingdom and to return. ***"So he called ten of his servants, delivered to them ten minas,*** *and said to them, 'Do business till I come.'*

When the nobleman returned and called for an accounting from his servants, he praised those who had increased what he had given them, and rewarded them accordingly.

Luke 19:16-17: "Then came the first, saying, 'Master, your mina has earned ten minas.' "And he said to him, ***'Well done, good servant;*** *because you were faithful in a very little,* ***have authority over ten cities.'***

Under the wise management of the trustworthy servant, that which had been given into his hand had prospered. The nobleman then gave much more into the hand of the servant to manage for him. The nobleman knew that the servant had employed the correct principles to cause prosperity and the increase of his gift.

Which principles will provide for prosperity and increase, the Babylonian, or New Jerusalem type principles? Many people believe that the Babylonian style principles based on competition and greed will prosper more than the New Jerusalem type principles based on love and serving. It does seem logical that striving to get more would cause more prosperity than seeking to give more. It also seems logical that doing or giving the very least possible amount to get the very most possible amount, even to the extent of taking advantage of others, would cause more gain. It would seem that an armed bank robber with a bag full of cash, would gain more than a faithful trustworthy servant. A bank robber and a person who takes advantage of others in business, differ only in the social acceptability of their actions. And neither will prosper in the long range. Though Babylonian style principles may seem right to a man, they will lead to loss, destruction, and eventually premature death. The New Jerusalem style principles will lead to prosperity in every realm of life. They are the most profitable way to do business.

Prov 14:12-13: **There is a way that seems right to a man, But its end is the way of death.** *Even in laughter the heart may sorrow, And the end of mirth may be grief.*

Psa 37:1-5,9-11,29,35-36: Do not fret because of evildoers, Nor be envious of the workers of iniquity. **For they shall soon be cut down like the grass, And wither as the green herb.** *Trust in the LORD, and do good; Dwell in the land, and feed on His faithfulness. Delight yourself also in the LORD, And He shall give you the* *desires of your heart. Commit your way to the LORD, Trust also in Him, And He shall bring it to pass.* **For evildoers shall be cut off;** *But those who wait on the LORD, They shall inherit the earth. For yet a little while and the wicked shall be no more; Indeed, you will look carefully for his place, But it shall be no more.*

But **the meek shall inherit the earth,** *And shall delight themselves in the abundance of peace.* **The righteous shall inherit the land,** *And dwell in it forever. I have seen the wicked in great power, And spreading himself like a native green tree. Yet he passed away, and behold, he was no more; Indeed I sought him, but he could not be found.*

New Jerusalem prosperity
will always out last Babylonian riches.

Possessions gained by the Babylonian style of doing business will consume their owner and will not last. Prosperity must be measured not only in amount but also in duration. The bank robber with the bag full of cash who may be caught a few miles down the road has a lot of riches, but they will not last long in his possession. A Babylonian business person may have riches for a short time, but they will not bring true prosperity and the person will surely crash.

(Luke 12:20) And then whose will those things be which you have provided?

The meek and righteous will inherit the wealth. Inheriting the earth and land means receiving tangible assets of the earth such as food, clean water, gold, buildings, businesses, jobs, and everything of value on the land. The kingdom of God way is a very prosperous way of doing business.

My natural father passed along to me, only a few gems of wisdom. I have found some of those gems to be of more value than they seemed at the time. For example, he once said, "Its not how much money that you make that is important. The important thing is how you spend what you have." How we use what we have determines what we will have in the future. Our attitudes and actions of today become seeds that will grow into our future. The fruit of poverty, or the fruit of prosperity, will be produced in our future depending on which seeds we sow. Sowing and reaping is a universal law of God. It is the same for everyone and cannot be overruled except by God. It will come to pass; what we plant will be what we reap. *(Gal 6:7-10)(2 Cor 9:6)*

Using what God has given to us to meet the needs of others and the world around us, is seed sown to our prosperity. Consuming what we have for our own desires, and thereby robbing others of God's intended provision for their need, is seed sown to our poverty. God would not be a very good manager of His kingdom, if He continued to give more to the servant who was not producing. God is a good manager and will take from the ineffective manager and give it to the servant who manages well. Managing well, means using what we have according to God's instruction. Kingdom of God prosperity will come to the servant of God who learns to use all he has, including his spirit, soul, and body according to God's instruction. All of one's skills, abilities, intelligence, money, material possessions, and any other gifts must be used for God's intended purposes.

Luke 19:20,23-26: Then another came, saying, 'Master, here is your mina, which I have kept put away in a handkerchief.
'Why then did you not put my money in the bank, that at my coming I might have collected it with interest?' And he said to those

who stood by, 'Take the mina from him, and give it to him who has ten minas.'

But they said to him, 'Master, he has ten minas.'

For I say to you, that to everyone who has will be given; and from him who does not have, even what he has will be taken away from him.

If the money had been put into the bank, it would have been available for others to use to do business in the community meeting human needs. Fear caused the servant to hold on to the money, rather than put it to work meeting needs and thereby increasing it. Riches that are put to work meeting needs do not consume the owner. Clothing that is in use is not moth eaten, and gold and silver that are being used do not corrode.

James 5:1-3: Come now, you rich, weep and howl for your miseries that are coming upon you! Your riches are corrupted, and your **garments are moth-eaten. Your gold and silver are corroded,** and their corrosion will be a witness against you and will eat your flesh like fire. You have heaped up treasure in the last days.

The kingdom principle is to use what you have to do business by meeting needs.

This includes giving to the poor and needy; but it means much more than that. It means production that is profitable for all. One cannot give, what one does not have. Industrious production is involved in acquiring clothes, food, and other items to meet the needs of people. Someone must grow or produce the food, fiber, and other products; and someone must process them, transport them, store them, and distribute them. Jobs are created and many people have an opportunity to share in the process, and become involved in serving Jesus in others. Investment opportunities are created by the capital needs for facilities and equipment to produce and distribute the goods to meet people's needs. This provides the opportunity for others to share in the process by supplying funds, and become a part of serving Jesus in others.

Entering into the blessings and joy of kingdom of God living is tied to production that meets needs. We are to do good to all men but especially to those of the household of faith. *(Gal 6:10)* In the parable of the sheep and the goats, Jesus taught the principle of serving Him by serving others and entering into the kingdom of God lifestyle by doing so.

*Mat 25:37-40: Then the righteous will answer Him, saying, 'Lord, when did we see You **hungry** and feed You, or **thirsty** and give You drink? When did we see You **a stranger** and take You in, or **naked** and clothe You? 'Or when did we see You sick, or **in prison,** and come to You?'*

*And the King will answer and say to them, 'Assuredly, I say to you, **inasmuch as you did it to one of the least of these My brethren, you did it to Me.'***

We serve Jesus the Christ as we serve those in whom Christ dwells.

Our prosperity begins with our seeing Jesus in the hungry, in the thirsty, in a stranger, in the naked, in the sick, and in those in prison, (both naturally and spiritually). When Jesus in us enables us to feel the need of Jesus in our brethren, we are ready to go to work at our job doing business to serve Jesus, not just to get things for ourselves. The better we do on the job, in the business, or wherever we serve, the more will be given to us to manage for him. Bigger and better jobs, businesses, and ministries await the faithful productive servant. Poverty is the reward of the greedy, the fearful, or the unfaithful, unproductive servant.

If you are lacking in prosperity, get excited about serving Jesus in others.

There is a lot of difference in doing our job to serve Jesus in others, and working for a paycheck. If one is just working for the pay, the work will not be done from the heart. It will not be of vital interest to the worker, and he or she will tend to grudgingly do only the minimum amount required. But, if one is doing one's job or business to serve Jesus in others, it will be done form the heart with vitality and enthusiasm. Much more will be accomplished and the job or business will be much more fun. The heartiness of service will lead to prosperity and increase. Everyone around becomes excited by our hearty enthusiasm and we will become inspiring leaders. Good people are drawn to our enthusiasm and our sincere care for others. They will desire to help with the job or business and may become a part of our team.

When we are excited about what we are doing it is easy to arise early and eagerly approach the day with enthusiasm. One can more easily overcome the temptation to roll over and sleep a little longer because of the exciting potential of the day. Slothfulness will always lead to deeper poverty. *(Prov 6:9-11) (Prov 18:9)* Lack of enthusiasm and excitement indicates that one is not really seeking and serving the Lord. Seeking to commune with God and becoming connected to His will and plan for the day is the first step toward an exciting and profitable life. Boredom is a sure sign that one is not serving the Lord. Anyone who is bored is not connected into God's plan to serve Jesus by serving others.

*Col 3:23-24: And whatever you do, **do it heartily,** as to the Lord and not to men, knowing that **from the Lord you will receive the reward** of the inheritance; for you serve the Lord Christ.*

Our reward for serving heartily does not depend on man; it depends on God. The law of sowing and reaping is much bigger and more powerful than man. Even though man may attempt to withhold our wages, our reward will eventually come. It may not come from the place where we served but it will come, if we do not lose our heartiness.

*Gal 6:9: And let us not grow weary while doing good, for in due season **we shall reap if we do not lose heart.***

Although we are to do good to all men, our best is to be reserved for Jesus in others. We are not to give our most precious assets to swine, (those who are greedy, self-seekers, with an appetite for base things). Neither are we to give our most holy to dogs, (heathen, who have no appreciation for beautiful and delicate things). We will be harmed and will not prosper giving our best to such people or organizations. This balance principle must be considered in determining who and where to serve.

Mat 7:6: Do not give what is holy to the dogs; nor cast your pearls before swine, lest they trample them under their feet, and turn and tear you in pieces.

Because we seek to serve Jesus in others and do not serve just to gain, we will not defraud anyone. Cheating on the job or in business will short circuit the law of sowing and reaping and stop our prosperity. God hates business and job fraud and it will never lead to prosperity, whether it is cheating on the time card, stealing products or supplies, slipping a few dollars from the register, or defrauding customers with deceptive statements and advertising, or deceptive packaging, or short weights and measures. *(Micah 6:10-15) (Deu 25:13-15)*

Prov 20:10: Diverse weights and diverse measures, They are both alike, an abomination to the LORD.

*Luke 6:38: Give, and it will be given to you: good measure, pressed down, shaken together, and running over will be put into your bosom. **For with the same measure that you use, it will be measured back to you.***

Always give a good measure plus a little more. If you give only what is required or expected, you have sown nothing for the future. But if you do all that is required or expected, and then give a little more, you are sowing toward future prosperity. Many may notice if a job is not done well. Usually no one notices much if a job is done well, as expected. But everyone notices when a job is done well and then something extra is done. No one notices a well made bed in a motel room, but everyone notices a mint on the pillow. A little beyond the required or expected can buy a lot of goodwill.

*Mat 5:40-41: If anyone wants to sue you and take away your tunic, let him have your cloak also. **And whoever compels you to go one mile, go with him two.***

Settle disputes quickly. They will cost much more in lost time and production to debate and battle than to make quick agreement.

Even though you may suffer some loss in the agreement it may be much less than the total cost of lost production as all your abilities and creativity normally applied toward business are imprisoned in striving with an adversary.

Mat 5:25-26: **Agree with your adversary quickly**, *while you are on the way with him, lest your adversary deliver you to the judge, the judge hand you over to the officer, and you be thrown into prison. Assuredly, I say to you, you will by no means get out of there till you have paid the last penny.*

We have seen that working and doing business to get money is not the New Jerusalem way, but, that the kingdom of God principle is to work to serve Jesus in others. Neither is it God's kingdom way to invest money to get money. Putting our money to work just to get more money is not the kingdom of heaven principle.

Investing money to serve Jesus in others, by meeting needs for capital, is the kingdom way.

The first consideration in investing is not how much money will this make, and how fast will it make it. The first question must always be; what will this investment do to serve Jesus in others? Will it do good to all men but especially those of the household faith? What will this investment do, and how will this help to supply needs? This consideration will help an investor to become aligned with God's purposes in a venture that He can bless. Costly future losses may be avoided by applying this principle first. If a venture does little or nothing to serve Jesus in others, but is designed to get money, one need look no further at other factors regarding the investment. Get rich quick schemes are never tempting to one who does not even look at them.

The two most prevalent factors affecting Babylonian style investing are greed and fear. Greed causes one to try to get the most money in the shortest time. Fear of losing money restrains the Babylonian investor and heavily affects his investment decisions. When he sees others making money from some item, he may hesitate to purchase it in the early stages of growth because of fear. But when he sees others continue to make a lot of money then he will purchase it, usually at or near the top of the growth cycle, and just before it declines. When it decreases substantially fear of loss again motivates him to cut his losses and sell, losing from the investment.

The kingdom principle of investing to serve will cause one to seek to buy what no one wants now, but that will be needed later, and store it in readiness until it is needed. Or one may purchase items that are not usable in their present state and repair, alter, or upgrade them to make them useful. Or one may buy goods that are not needed in one geographic area and transport them to an area where there are needed. Or one may invest in buildings, machinery, tools, or equipment to provide for others to use in production for meeting needs. The key is to look for human needs and determine how you or your money can be used to help meet needs. Always buy and sell at the fair market price for the item, in the condition it is in, at the time. Always sell what people need when they want it.

Prov 11:26: The people will curse him who withholds grain, But blessing will be on the head of him who sells it.

Be content with what you have now.

Heb 13:5a. Let your conduct be without covetousness; be content with such things as you have.

Do not serve money. Serve God with money.

BASILEIA LETTER

Number 8

Love the world,
Not the evil world order!

For God so loved the **world**

that He gave His only begotten Son, that whoever believes in Him should not perish but have everlasting life. John 3;16

Do not love the **world**

or the things in the world. If anyone loves the world, the love of the Father is not in him. 1 John 2:15

These two verses of Scripture, at first glance, seem to contradict one another. One makes it very clear that God loves the world. While the other indicates that we are not to love the evil world system, and even goes so far as to say that if we do, the love of God is not in us

Doctrines developed in the past, and held by much of the church today, offer little or no hope for man or the world, in this present life. The essence of these doctrines are that the world and its systems are hopelessly tainted with sin and subsequently evil. In this view there is no hope for the present world to be cleansed and restored. Some of the fruits from the essence of these teachings are:

(1) A release of the responsibility of man to preserve and care for the natural systems of the planet. There is little or no incentive for man to cooperate with natural laws of God's order. The shorter range more immediately profitable actions are often chosen over those that align with God's natural order; which are designed for the continued existence of the planet's systems.

97

(2) A lack of appreciation for the wonderful creation of the beautiful life supporting planet. The glorious essence of God can be seen in the beauty of His creation. The beautiful intense blues of mountain lakes reflect more than the breath taking awesomeness of the magnificent mountain scenes; they also reflect something about our loving God.

The unfathomable complexity of all the physical, biological, zoological, meteorological, ecological, and other systems of the planet all speak of our God who created them. *(Rom 1:20)* They are all designed to intricately work together to support life on the planet, and to continue the life of the planet.

(3) The third fruit from these teachings is a lack of respect for the life man has been given, with its awesome and exciting potential. Man is the only part of God's creation designed to intimately relate to God, to actually experience knowing Him now in this life. And to represent God in the earth, to rule and reign with Him now in this present age. *(Rom 5:17) (Rev 5:10) (2 Tim 2:12)* A lack of appreciation for God's natural creation, all the plants, the animals, the forest, and everything else, leads to a lack of respect for the life of man himself. Man is linked to, and a part of, the world's systems.

These fruits do not line up with the words of Jesus the Christ and the character and nature of God. Jesus came *"that they may have life, and that they may have it more abundantly."* It is God's nature to give life, to heal, and to deliver. It is someone else who desires to destroy. *"The thief does not come except to steal, and to kill, and to destroy." John 10:10.* Is it God's plan and desire to destroy the earth, or to purify it? Jesus spoke of the wicked being removed and the righteous shining forth on earth. *Matt. 13:24-30, 37-43.* The Scripture also speaks clearly of God destroying those who destroy the earth.

*Rev. 11:18b "And that You should reward Your servants the prophets and the saints, And those who fear Your name, small and great, **And should destroy those who destroy the earth**."*

Since the essence of the teachings that the world is bad, and fit only to be despised, does not line up with the words of Jesus and the character and nature of God, we must reexamine the Scriptures that seem to affirm these teachings. Does God love the world's systems or despise them? Are we to love the world or to despise the world?

John 3:16, is one of the most well known Scripture verses. Most evangelical Christians have taught this verse to their small children. We use this verse to instill in children that God loves them so much that Jesus came to save them, and all who will believe.

We may read the verse,
*"For God so loved the **world**"*,
but we hear in our mind,
"For God so loved **me,** or **mankind**".

Certainly the individual and mankind are the focus of what is being spoken of here. But we are not the whole thing being referred to as the world.

The word translated "world" here is the Greek word "kosmos" which is generally interpreted as the world's systems. Strongs Concordance Greek Dictionary defines the word as follows: "G2889. kosmos, kos'-mos; prob. from the base of G2865; **orderly arrangement**, i.e. **decoration**; by impl. the **world** (in a wide or narrow sense, includ. its **inhabitants**."

Is it possible that Jesus came to save more than mankind, that He came to save the world? Could God desire to restore all other "kind" as well, including all the adorning and decorative systems, the "kosmos"? Since God has given mankind authority and responsibility to rule the earth, man must first be redeemed and brought into order with God and His ways in order to save or restore the world.

God chose to limit himself to rule through man on earth and has never rescinded that position. Man has a free will to make decisions.

God had to become a man to save the world.
God became a man in Jesus.

God's original created order is for man to have dominion and rule the world. *(Gen. 1 26-28)*. The man Jesus, seated at the right hand of the Father in heaven, now rules in the world as he lives within believers on the earth by the Holy Spirit, the Spirit of Christ. As men receive Jesus into their lives, and then yield control of their lives to the Spirit of Christ within, the will of God is done from heaven on earth. The kingdom of God from heaven rules the world and the ways of God redeem and restore the kosmos.

The key to the redemption of the world is the salvation of man. Thus man's redemption is the world's only hope.

In every instance the word translated "world" in *John 3:16-17*, is "kosmos".

*John 3:16-17: "For God so loved the **world** that He gave His only begotten Son, that whoever believes in Him should not perish but have everlasting life. For God did not send His Son into the **world** to condemn the **world**, but that the **world** through Him might be saved."*

In these verses God speaks of man being saved in relation to the world being saved.

In these verses God speaks of man being saved in relation to the world being saved.

There is no distinction made between mankind and the rest of the world as the object of God's saving love.

We have seen from other Scripture that God has delegated rule of the earth to man. Man is to carry out the order of God's design. The kingdom of God, the will of God, is to be done through man. **More specifically by Christ Jesus within man**.

To love the world, or not to love the world? Perhaps, God loves the world but does not love the evil of the world. Just as He loves man but does not love man's sin and evil nature. Scripture seems to indicate that we are not to love the world. A distinction must be made between the physical systems of God's creation and the evil world order set up by the devil. It is expedient that we take a closer look at some of these verses.

1 John 2:15-17: ***Do not love the world*** *or the things in the world.* ***If anyone loves the world, the love of the Father is not in him.*** *For all that is in the world; the lust of the flesh, the lust of the eyes, and the pride of life; is not of the Father but is of the world. And the world is passing away, and the lust of it; but he who does the will of God abides forever.*

The word "world" in the above verses is also translated from the Greek word "kosmos". Why is it that we are told to not love the kosmos when God said He so loved the kosmos that He sent His son to save it?

God loves the kosmos (world), and we are to love the kosmos (world) with His love. A closer look at the original Greek in *1 John 2:15-17* reveals that the translation is confusing at this point. Man is not being told to not have loving concern for the world, but is being told to not have the love of (**from**) the world. The world has it's own kind of selfish, lustful, greedy affection, the desires of the (sarx) flesh. We are not to have that love of the world. Nor are we to lust for the things of the world.

But we are to be filled with the love of God for the world. God loves the kosmos (world), and we are to love the kosmos (world) with His love.

The love of (from) God is a fully satisfying inner abundance. The individual filled with the love from God feels no frustrating need for anything else. Nothing further is required for the spirit and soul to be at perfect peace. From this inner abundance flows a great desire and potential to love the kosmos (the world and it's inhabitants). This desire leads to serving mankind and the world around us by seeking to make things better for everyone; **to bring the peaceful, prosperous, order of God to the kosmos**. The love from God is a giving kind of love.

On the other hand the love of (from) the world isn't really love, but it is **lust for the kosmos**. It is seeking to fill an inner need that exists because the love of (from) God is not filling the individual. In reality the world's kind of love (lust) is not love, but unlove (the lack of the presence of God's love within). The inner need created by unlove leads to the lust of the flesh, the lust of the eyes, and the pride of life. The inner need becomes like a great vacuum trying to fill the void with the kosmos (the world and the things in it, including other people). The kosmos is consumed, used, and destroyed as the inner need drives the individual to get more, have more, be more, control more, and experience more. The love of (from) the world is a taking kind of unlove.

The love of God is in Christ Jesus. The potential for the very love of God in your life and mine is in Jesus. If the Spirit of Christ rules our hearts, the love of God is manifest in our lives.

*John 17:26: "And I have declared to them Your name, and will declare it, that the **love (agape)** with which You **loved (agapao)** Me may be in them, and **I in them**."*

The usage in this verse seems to indicate that agape is the inner affection from which flows the social outworking agapao, practice of loving. Christ Jesus is the provision for mankind to have the agape love of the Father. Christ in man is the practical method by which the love from God fills the life until no room exist for the love (lust) from the world, for the things that are in the world.
There is a vast difference in having loving concern for the kosmos (as God also does), and seeking to devour or consume the kosmos from our inner lust of the flesh, lust of the eyes, and pride of this life.

Gal 5:16-17: I say then: Walk in the Spirit, and you shall not fulfill the lust of the flesh. For the flesh lusts against the Spirit, and the Spirit against the flesh; and these are contrary to one another, so that you do not do the things that you wish.

The Spirit of Christ Jesus living and ruling within, guides and empowers the individual to walk in freedom from the lust of the flesh and to be filled with the love of (from) God. It is impossible for one in whom Christ Jesus does not dwell to be filled with the love of God and to be free of the love of (from) the world.
Man is inseparably linked to the rest of the kosmos. To harm or destroy the world is to harm one's self. To bless or build the world is to bless and build one's self. As man takes care of the

103

world, the world takes care of man. I'm reminded of an old saying that farmers once used. They said, "If you will take care of the land, the land will take care of you." This same wisdom applies to all the kosmos.

Many Christians may need to rethink their world view. A belief that God does not love the "kosmos" may have led us to devalue much of what God loves, and sent His Son to save.

The world is not inherently evil. The world is a marvelous and wonderful creation of God.

The systems and order of the world are awesomely grand beyond all we can think. The complex intricacy of biological systems, ecological systems, and the physical make up of all things is more than all the minds of man together could ever understand. Yet it all fits and works together to perpetually sustain life. The beauty of the colors, shapes, and patterns of the mountains, lakes, forest, plains, and mighty oceans are marvelous beyond compare. The delicate, delightful fragrance of the rose, the flowers of the field, the spruce and fir tree, the pine tree on a still spring evening, all speak of God's love and provision for the world.

It is humbling to realize that God has put man in charge of caring for His marvelous creation. To not be concerned about caring for the people, animals, and the ecology of the world is to be apart from the plan of God. As man, by the power of the indwelling Christ, walks in accordance with God's ways the kosmos is healed. Mankind seeking the kingdom of God and His righteous way of being and doing moves man and the world systems toward healing and restoration. Mankind seeking his own way apart from God moves man and the world systems toward disorder and destruction.

The power of Christ in man is sufficient
to heal and restore the kosmos.

John 3:16a,17b: "For **God so loved the world, that he gave** *his only begotten Son,-- that the world through him might be* **saved.**"

John 1:29b: "Behold! **The Lamb of God who takes away the** *sin of the world!"*

The wonderful healing, delivering, restoring, kingdom of God (the rule of God) is now being spoken into the world. The past religious views are beginning to give way to the glorious, practical, reality of the way of God in all realms of life in our world. The great secrets of life and how to live it are being revealed in the purified hearts of God's children.

The evidence of the fruit of man seeking his own way, apart from God, is becoming increasingly visible as the world systems are wounded and fight back against the oppression of man's evil ways. Breakdown, and failure are common concepts in our afflicted world.

Our ailing world will not be healed by religion or politics. Laws passed by the governments of the nations of the world may help alleviate some immediate symptoms temporarily. But, they will never deal with the root of the problem and make real and permanent changes. The harsh administration of religious laws, rules, ceremonies, and traditions of man, may confuse or worsen the overall condition. The false peace and security created by some religious teachings, may bring a temporary sense of peace, but will not deal with the real problems of the world.

Only the Word of the kingdom from heaven, the kingdom of God, planted in the fertile heart soil of man, can begin the powerful changes required to really change the world. To the same degree that the enemy can prevent or pervert the Word of the kingdom, he can continue to deceive and oppress the world. If the Word of the kingdom is not planted and grown to fruition in the hearts of man, the world will continue to move toward disorder and destruction. The Word of the kingdom of God, planted and grown to fruition in the heart soil of man will overcome the enemy's work and move the world toward healing and restoration. Yet there are many religious people and unbelievers alike, who will not hear or grow to fruition the powerful, world changing, Word of the kingdom.

There are three major reasons why, not everyone will hear the powerful Word of the kingdom.

Jesus taught the three reasons in the parable of the sower and soils. He later explained the parable clearly to his disciples.

Mat 13:3-9: Then He spoke many things to them in parables, saying: "Behold, a sower went out to sow. (#1) "And as he sowed, some seed fell by the wayside; and the birds came and devoured them. (#2) "Some fell on stony places, where they did not have much earth; and they immediately sprang up because they had no depth of earth. "But when the sun was up they were scorched, and because they had no root they withered away. (#3) "And some fell among thorns, and the thorns sprang up and choked them. "But others fell on good ground and yielded a crop: some a hundredfold, some sixty, some thirty. "He who has ears to hear, let him hear!"

*Mat 13:18-22: "Therefore hear the parable of the sower: (#1) "When anyone hears the **word of the kingdom**, and does not understand it, then the wicked one comes and snatches away what*

*was sown in his heart. This is he who received seed by the wayside.
(#2) "But he who received the seed on stony places, this is he who
hears the word and immediately receives it with joy; yet he has no
root in himself, but endures only for a while. For when tribulation
or persecution arises because of the word, immediately he stumbles.
(#3) "Now he who received seed among the thorns is he who hears
the word, and the cares of this world and the deceitfulness of riches
choke the word, and he becomes unfruitful.*

The first reason that some will not hear the Word of the kingdom is because of the hard pressed soil of their hearts. The wayside
soil represents the soil of a roadway, where the heavy footsteps of
men, and the wheels of their ox carts and chariots, have pressed the
soil so hard that the seed cannot enter the soil, and will be easily
picked up and carried away by the enemy. The hard heart is a
wounded heart that has been hurt by the oppression of people. The
many afflictions brought about by the enemy through other people
have so perverted the heart that one cannot receive the loving and
positive message of the kingdom of God.

Jesus specifically refers to the **"word of the kingdom"**, in
this passage. One may be able to hear the gospel of being born
again or some other word from God, but the heart in this condition,
cannot hear the word of the kingdom. The ministry of Jesus to heal
the broken hearted must be appropriated to heal the wounded heart
before the Word of the kingdom can enter.

The second reason is the stony heart soil. The rocks prevent
the seed from having enough good soil to take root. Even though it
may sprout it will wither and die at the first difficulty, and will not
grow to fruition.

The rocks in the heart represent hardened preexisting strong
convictions. Strong, preconceived religious views or beliefs can be

rocks in the heart soil, that will not allow the Word of the kingdom to grow and bear fruit. When Jesus first preached the word of the kingdom, very few of the Pharisees with their strong religious convictions could grow the seed of the kingdom. Yet, some fishermen and even tax collectors could receive and grow the seed of the kingdom.

Strong convictions other than religious ones can also cause the Word of the kingdom to not grow to fruition. Rocks in the heart can be strong convictions of negative beliefs about life, how bad people are, how bad circumstances are, how bad the enemy is, etc.

The rocks of hardened preconceived convictions must be dealt with by giving them to God. One must take all of his strong religious beliefs and traditions, along with all the other rocks in his heart and lay them on the altar of God; allowing God to renew, refine, and return those He desires; and allowing God to discard and replace those which He desires. God is faithful and will not take away any good thing from His children. We can trust God. He will do what is best for us. **If there is anything we cannot leave on the altar of God, then that thing is our god.** It is more important to us than God.

The third reason some will not hear the Word of the kingdom is that thorn bushes will grow up and choke out the seed of the kingdom. The thorn bushes are the cares of this life and the deceitfulness of riches. Caring for the things of this life means being concerned about possessions, positions, and pleasures of natural life. Possessions can include money, houses, lands, family, and anything else we value. Positions can include any place in society or church we may hold, or desire to hold. Pleasures can be anything in which we delight.

The seed of the kingdom will not grow to powerful fruition in a heart that lusts for the things of the world. One must get his or her delights in the Lord not in other things. The thorn bushes must be dealt with by taking all we delight in to the altar of God and laying it there, allowing God to do whatever He desires with it all. God will return to us what He wants us to have and it will no longer choke the seed of the kingdom. We can trust God. He does love us. What He will do is best for us.

When the hard soil, the rocks, and the thorns, are all dealt with, then the good heart soil will grow the seed of the kingdom into the kingdom of God.

Mat 13:23: "But he who received seed on the good ground is he who hears the word and understands it, who indeed bears fruit and produces: some a hundredfold, some sixty, some thirty."

BASILEIA LETTER

Number 9

The Disconcertment of
The Kingdom of God

Jesus said, that He had not come to bring peace but a sword. He spoke of troubling our personal world.

Mat 10:34-36: "Do not think that I came to bring peace on earth. I did not come to bring peace but a sword. "For I have come to 'set a man against his father, a daughter against her mother, and a daughter-in-law against her mother-in-law'; "and 'a man's enemies will be those of his own household.'

Luke 12:51-52: "Do you suppose that I came to give peace on earth? I tell you, not at all, but rather division. "For from now on five in one house will be divided: three against two, and two against three.

The kingdom that Jesus preached brings change to our lives. Change can be good or bad, but in either case it is often very disconcerting for a season. The change in our world that Jesus came to bring is a change for good. A change for the betterment of our personal lives and for the world. We all know that God's goal for the world is not disconcertment and division. Yet, Jesus fully recognized that the magnitude of the change from the old order to the new kingdom of God order would, for a season, create great disconcertment and division.

Even in much less significant matters, change within our lives can bring disconcertment. Sometimes we have very little choice and must walk through the disconcerting experience. At other times we may postpone or fail to make needed or desired changes simply because it is not pleasurable to endure the initial loss of peace that the change will bring.

I personally have a recent involvement in a situation where I believe God wants to bring some very great changes, changes that could bring the people involved to a new and greater fulfillment in their walk with God and their ministry in the kingdom. The problem is that these changes are radical and very different from the life long traditions and experiences of the people. The old ways have worked and served those involved very well. When the new is attempted, the first response is sometimes the loss of the peace that we have been accustomed to following, and can be very disconcerting.

If you are like me, at this point you may be wondering, exactly what does he mean by disconcerting. The dictionary definition for disconcert is:

"disconcert 1. **to disturb the self-possession of**; perturb; ruffle. 2. to throw into disorder or confusion; disarrange.

From other Scripture we know that Christ **did** come to bring peace on earth and goodwill toward men. He is the God of peace.

*John 14:27: **"Peace I leave with you, My peace I give to you**; not as the world gives do I give to you. Let not your heart be troubled, neither let it be afraid.*

*Rom 14:17: For the kingdom of God is not eating and drinking, but righteousness and **peace** and joy in the Holy Spirit.*

*Rom 15:33: Now the **God of peace** be with you all. Amen.*

*Phil 4:9: The things which you learned and received and heard and saw in me, these do, and the **God of peace** will be with you.*

111

WE CAN WALK IN PEACE EVEN IN DISCONCERTING TIMES OF CHANGE, **IF WE KNOW FOR SURE WE ARE FOLLOWING HIS WORD AND WILL FOR US AT THE TIME.** If however we do not have a sure Word from God it may be very difficult to maintain peace within ourselves during times of change. Our feelings, and seeking for peace, may become very unstable guides when God is bringing change. Resisting the change because it just does not feel right and is disconcerting may lead to wrong choices. However, making major changes without a sure Word from God can also become a hazardous activity. In many situations time is better spent seeking direction from God, rather than either prematurely receiving or rejecting a specific change.

In some cases of urgency one may move expediently and try to the best of their ability to do the will of God, without having a clear word at the moment. Most often there is a way to alter the action later without devastating effects. One must, at times trust God to fix up what one has messed up.

It is not God's best for His people to make decisions as to what is right and wrong to do next. To decide within our own mind, can be partaking of the "tree of the knowledge of good and evil". To hear what is right and wrong from God and obey Him, is to eat from the "tree of life."

IT IS NOT OUR PLACE TO DECIDE, but rather to find out what God has already decided and represent that into the world.

Jesus did not decide what to do or how to do it within His own mind. He said that He only did what he heard and saw the Father doing.

*John 8:26 "I have many things to say and to judge concerning you, but He who sent Me is true; and **I speak to the world those things which I heard from Him.**"*

*John 8:28-29: Then Jesus said to them, "When you lift up the Son of Man, then you will know that I am He, and that **I do nothing of Myself; but as My Father taught Me, I speak these things.** "And He who sent Me is with Me. The Father has not left Me alone, for I always do those things that please Him."*

*John 5:30: "**I can of Myself do nothing. As I hear, I judge;** and My judgment is righteous, because **I do not seek My own will but the will of the Father who sent Me.***

*John 5:19: Then Jesus answered and said to them, "Most assuredly, I say to you, **the Son can do nothing of Himself, but what He sees the Father do; for whatever He does, the Son also does in like manner.***

God is doing tremendous things in our world. It will prove much more profitable to find out what God is doing and get in on it, rather than to decide something on our own and try to get God to bless it. And if what God is doing is somewhat new to us, it may temporarily cause some disconcertment in and around our lives.

In this, the time of the beginning of the seventh millennium of the history of man, the gospel of the kingdom is again being preached across the world as it was in the first century. The gospel of the kingdom that Jesus preached caused great disconcertment when He preached it in the first century, just as it is causing today. Christ living and speaking through His body on earth is again preaching the gospel of the kingdom and many are disconcerted.

113

The church must be prepared for change, and must be willing to lay down the old in order to receive the new work of God.

God has not changed. The Gospel has not changed.

Our ability to see and hear the fullness of the gospel of the kingdom that was lost to the church during the dark ages, is changing. As the people of God become more purified in their hearts, the resurrected life of Christ is more fully alive within and more revelation is a partial result of that process. More revelation brings change. Change can bring temporary disconcertment and division.

Many Christians that have been born again for years are just now hearing for the first time the glorious gospel of the kingdom that Jesus preached, the same gospel that the first century disciples preached. The restoration of all things that began in the reformation period is still continuing. We thank God for the restoration of the revelation of the Word that we have enjoyed in the past. We must continue to embrace the truth from the past and allow the further revelation of the now to melt away error and plant truth in our hearts. We must not turn back because of the temporary disconcerting feelings that may come our way in time of change. If we turn back we may miss out on the wonderful further plan that God has for us.

The seventh millennium outpouring has already begun.

It is as if there were a great ball of the fire of God come near the earth, and fingers of that fire swirl down toward the earth and happen to touch the earth here and there. Where these fingers of the fire of God come forth, renewal and powerful manifestations of the Spirit are common. Men and women are overcome with the presence of God and cry out to God confessing there sins. These spots of outpouring will continue and increase in number as we continue into the seventh millennium.

Some of the things occurring within these areas of outpouring may be more than we have seen in the past and can be disconcerting to the believer who as yet has not personally experienced this powerful ministry of the Spirit within themselves. It is important to not look back nor to try to return to yesterday. If per chance you are one of those who are hanging on to the familiar and secure ways of the past, because the new brings disconcertment to you, please turn again and instead of watching, get in the middle of what God is doing and the peace of God may flood your heart.

Another part of the seventh millennium outpouring, which can cause further disconcertment is a great increase in the revelation of the word of God. This outpouring is marked by God's removing the cover from great spiritual truths of His word. The word translated revelation in the New Testament, means to take the cover off. God is truly revealing fresh truth regarding His kingdom in this season. When a mystery is revealed it is finished because it is no longer a mystery. A secret that is uncovered and told is no longer a secret.

*Rev 10:7: But in the days of the sounding of the **seventh** angel, when he is about to sound, the mystery of God would be finished, as He declared to His servants the prophets.*

*Rev 11:15: Then the **seventh** angel sounded: And there were loud voices in heaven, saying, "The kingdoms of this world have become the kingdoms of our Lord and of His Christ, and He shall reign forever and ever!"*

Is it time for us to feast at His table of freshly revealed light of His Word, that will further enable the saints of God to manifest His love and power to bring forth the New Jerusalem lifestyle? Is it time for the saints of God to come out of Babylon and set their minds upon the New Jerusalem of God? Is it time for believers to become real in their souls and to seek Him with their whole heart? Is it time for the Holy Spirit of Christ to shine deep into our hearts and reveal the duplicity of inner motives? Is it not time for repentance for our seeking our own thing while at the same time seeking to serve God? And is it not time for the fire of God to burn the self seeking motives and all they have built within and around us? Is it not time to worship Him and praise Him unreservedly, full out, with our whole heart, soul, spirit, and body?

If it is time for these things, then,
It is time for the people of God to pray without ceasing.

To lift up holy hands and cry out with supplication and thanksgiving for the will of God to be done, and the kingdom of God to come, now, in our world.

It is time for intercessors and every saint of God to cry out to God with tears and great faith for the sick and needy church. Cry out for the sleeping giant to awaken and do the works of God. Call unto God and He will send the mighty works of the Spirit of Christ and multitudes of powerful angels. After the church awakens, shakes herself and is cleansed, then the lost will come. The evil of the city will change after the sleeping giant, the church, awakens, shakes, and cleanses herself and becomes the purified holy Bride of Christ.

You and I are very privileged to be on the earth now, and surely have come to the kingdom for such a time as this. A time that the

116

patriarchs of old desired to see, but could not. A time that the Apostles of the Lamb saw begin but did not see the fulfillment of their beginnings.

It would have been great to have been a part of the first century and to have seen the Lord in His earthly body, to have witnessed His ministry, and to have been in the upper room at Pentecost. **BUT it is just as great a thing that we have upon us, if not greater.**

The seventh millennium outpouring has begun and will continue to grow in breadth and depth and height in the days ahead.

Seventh millennium Christianity will eventually exceed first century Christianity.

Though there will be great turmoil and great tribulation, there will eventually be the full manifestation of total victory. God will at some time in this next millennium rule the kingdoms of earth and every aspect of our planet through His seventh millennium servants   men, women, and children sold out completely to God and God only.

Businesses, governments, education, homes, and every institution on the planet will serve the living God, as the servants of God rule first their own lives, then their own families, communities, states, nations, and eventually the planet according to the will of the Lord as directed by the Holy Spirit, the Spirit of the Lord, Spirit of Christ, Spirit of the King.

Yes there is a long way to go, and much tribulation will occur, and many around the world will not make it. But, we are seeing the start of the greatest work and move of God on Planet Earth. It is beginning with "The Seventh Millennium Outpouring", the mighty sovereign work of God shaking, tearing down, and forever changing the religious and carnal ways of the church and world; sovereignly healing the works and wounds caused by religion; sovereignly bringing deliverance from all the weight of our foolish and religious ways; pouring His love sovereignly into our hearts and lives.

In that love flows His grace, empowering His sons and daughters to do mighty exploits, and walk in righteousness, peace, and joy. His mercy flows through that love and grace to receive our messed up religious and carnal hearts, forgive us, and wash us clean, that we may become purified vessels for His mighty love and power. It is well worth walking through the disconcertment of the changing times to enter into the kingdom of God, New Jerusalem, lifestyle that God is bringing forth in His mature sons and daughters.

Renewal and revival are a part of the outpouring but it is more than "re" anything, because God is beginning a work that is more than has ever before been seen on earth. It is the establishment of His kingdom from heaven, on earth, one heart, one life, one step at a time. Individually, our first step is repentance from dead works. Even those of us who have felt that our lives were sold out to God and have sought to flow in His Spirit, must come to a new level of holiness. To whom much is given, much is required.

Personally, I thought that my life was totally sold out to God, that I owned nothing, that everything in my hands was only His, that my heart's only desire was to please Him and do His will, **yet more love has poured into me**, bringing more grace and holiness, more of His presence. In comparison to His presence and love now, I hate my life of only a short time ago. We cannot know what we do not have until God pours it into us. What will it be tomorrow? Today seems to be all the love, grace, peace, joy, and power that one can know. Will we hate this wonderful life tomorrow as God continues His outpouring of love into our hearts?

Acts 2:32-33: "This Jesus God has raised up, of which we are all witnesses. "Therefore being exalted to the right hand of God, and having received from the Father the promise of the Holy Spirit, He poured out this which you now see and hear.

Rom 5:5 Now hope does not disappoint, because the love of God has been poured out in our hearts by the Holy Spirit who was given to us.

As God produced life from Sarah's dead womb, so shall he bring forth the life of Christ in the dead womb of the awakening church. As he caused the dry bones to come together, and put flesh upon them and caused them to live, so is He in these days bringing life from death. Resurrection comes after death. Resurrection life is pouring out upon the church and again the dead womb shall bear a child, **the manifestation of the Son of the living God**. And the dry bones shall live and march in order to the commands of the Spirit of the living God. With man it is impossible, but with God it is happening!

God is bringing forth to His church, A new administration and a new order!

It is not a new administration and order to God, but it is new to the church, in that the church has not fully walked in it before. The new administration is the unbridled flow of the Holy Spirit. The manifestation of the Spirit of Christ coming forth unguided, unrestrained, not in any way controlled by man or his systems of church order or government. Israel asked for a king and lost the direct leadership of God personally administering their affairs. The church has been under schoolmasters of external rules and laws until this season. Now in this time, the old administration is being replaced with **the administration of the Spirit of Christ the King.**

The new order is the intimate love of God in the hearts of men. Because of His intimate love, God's ways will be kept by each person. No person in love with Jesus and filled with His love can walk in an unruly manner. God by His love and Spirit will guide, and will break the heart of anyone who steps into disobedience. Repentance will be swift and complete by the one intimately in love with the Spirit of Christ Jesus.

The systems of control established by men ruling over others is finished. The perversions of son-ship between brothers is over. All are sons of God and do not call any man their father. The perversions of what was called "spiritual authority" but was really the control of men is finished. These things will not continue to work in the days ahead. The day of the big name men of God is closing. The long prayer lines, seeking a touch through the big name man of God is fading away. God is pouring out His spirit through multitudes of nobodies. Obscure men and women, and small children are bringing forth the powerful anointing of God, as His Spirit is poured out upon our sons and daughters.

The fire of the Lord is already here to destroy the evil and sinful world and will continue to greatly intensify. Now the dismantling of the things that were good has also come. Men are finding their lives and ministries falling apart for no apparent reason. Personally, I was very busy for a time trying to build back the things that God kept tearing down. We will help God's work in progress, if, when we recognize He is dismantling, we help Him tear it down and stop fighting against what God is doing. If the new is to be built the old must be dismantled. Then God can rebuild the new in accordance with His plan and design.

He will burn or tear down anything that our heart goes after. God will not be satisfied with half of our heart, seventy percent is not a passing grade, ninety nine and nine tenths percent is not good enough. We must seek Him NOW, with our whole heart, even if it means the laying down of many good things in our lives. He is able to restore to us the things that He desires for us to have. Again, all of this can be very disconcerting but the end is well worth the temporary discomfort and lack of peace that may occur.

Break up the fallow ground of your heart.

Before the new can grow the old must be plowed. I live on a ninety six acre farm. When a decision is made to change the use of a field from pasture to growing a row crop, such as corn, the field must first be deeply plowed, completely disrupting the existing growth on the field. When the hardened ground is thoroughly broken up and softened by rain, then it is ready to receive the new seed and grow the new crop. This is a very disconcerting experience for the field that is being plowed.

Hosea 10:12: Sow for yourselves righteousness; Reap in mercy; **Break up your fallow ground***, For it is time to seek the LORD, Till He comes and rains righteousness on you.*

Scripture refers to the hardened soil as fallow ground. Our hearts are like that fallow ground. God is plowing deep in preparation for the seeds of the kingdom of God to be planted and the New Jerusalem way of life to grow. We are to work with God in breaking up the fallow ground of our hearts. God will supply the power, but we are to be willing and open our hearts to the plowing. Many of us have a portion of already prepared good soil in the center of our heart and life. But the edges and the corners are overgrown with the cares of life, the hardened ground of wounding experiences, and the rocks of convictions. We may yet be holding on to our old religious convictions and other strong beliefs that will not allow the seed of the kingdom of God to grow to maturity.

God loves us to much to stop until the work is finished.

BASILEIA LETTER

Number 10

Love and the Kingdom of God.

Jesus said, the greatest commandment of all is to love God. And He said that the second greatest is to love your neighbor.

Mark 12:30-31: 'And you shall love the LORD your God with all your heart, with all your soul, with all your mind, and with all your strength.' This is the first commandment. "And the second, like it, is this: 'You shall love your neighbor as yourself.' There is no other commandment greater than these."

Mat 22:40 "On these two commandments hang all the Law and the Prophets."

He did not say the greatest commandment was to do any of the other noble commandments of God. He did not say the greatest commandment was to be a mighty faith warrior, nor a mighty prayer warrior. Nor did He say it was to be a mighty preacher, nor prophet, nor teacher nor any other gift or calling of God. As important as these things are, LOVE is the only MOST important thing of all.

Theologically much has been said about the love God has for His children and the love we are to have for Him. But in practical terms, what does the love OF GOD and the love FOR GOD mean to you and me? And why is it the most important commandment of God? What kind of love are we to have for God?

In the natural realm, mankind is familiar with several different aspects or types of love. There is the love parents have for their children and that children have for their parents. This is a very strong fundamental kind of love that provides security and causes needs to be met. This love will usually last forever though it may take different forms in mature life. It is more of an understood continuous love that does not vary much though it may be felt more strongly under certain circumstances.

There is another love that one may experience between siblings. This is a much more dormant kind of love that may only really surface when certain experiences or needs occur, such as one of the siblings being threatened. Also, in the natural realm, there is a certain kind of love that one may, or may not have for their neighbor. Usually this is a very casual kind of love, and often is not much more than a generic concern for the well being of the neighbor.

Another kind of natural love is the very intense love that one has for one's sweetheart or mate. This very intense love is the most consuming of all natural love known to man. A man or woman in love will go to extremes to be with the one they love. They may become very dissatisfied when apart for a season. They may feel a deep longing that can only be satisfied by embracing the one they love. They find great joy in each others company and intimately share everything about their lives. They greatly desire to please one another and would knowingly do nothing to harm or hinder one another. They will go to extremes to protect and defend one another. There is nothing that they are able to do, that they would not do for one another.

The love God has for us and the love we are to have for Him is most like this last kind of love. The Bible refers to believers as the "Bride of Christ", suggesting a very intimate relationship between the Lord and His people. There is no greater experience in all of life than being in love with God.

Many Christians do not even know it is possible to share an intimate, exciting, passionate, personal love with God Almighty; the very one who created all things that exist; the one who spoke the earth and the stars into existence; the one with all power and all knowledge, who causes all things to continue; the very one who will judge all the world. *(Col. 1:16-19) (Heb 1:2-3)* One of the great mysteries to man is, "how can such an awesome God love me?" How can such a great God even know that I exist, much less be concerned for me and love me.

*Job 7:17: What is man, that You should exalt him, **That You should set Your heart on him.***

*Psa 8:4 What is man that You are **mindful of him**, And the son of man that **You visit him**?*

Rom 5:8 But God demonstrates His own love toward us, in that while we were still sinners, Christ died for us.

Knowing that God loves us and spared not His only Son to save us certainly gives us a great, but still somewhat remote understanding and appreciation of the love God has for us. Considering why He made us and why He saved us begins to direct us toward the greatest fulfillment of mankind, which is to fulfill God's design for man. The reason the greatest of all commandments is to love God, is because that it is God's designed primary purpose for man. God made man in His own image to intimately relate to Himself. *(Gen 1:27)*

We are for the primary purpose of loving God.
We are His desire.

Just as there is an emptiness in man when separated from God, there is an emptiness in God when we are apart from Him. There is a lack in the purposes of God when man is apart from the Husband,

Jesus, who loves His Bride passionately and deeply. This longing of God for us, and the longing in man for intimacy with God is very similar to the longing one feels when separated from the person one loves in the natural realm.

The joy, that one who is in love with God feels, when coming into His presence and intimately relating to Him, is very similar to the joy one feels when one is reunited with, and embraces the person one loves.

Spiritual oneness with God is His plan for His Bride, and is the ultimate fulfillment in life.

Many people are frustrated their entire lives because they do not know God or never come into intimacy with Him. They are never able to fill the void and lack of completeness in their lives, though they may try everything under the sun to bring satisfaction and completeness.

Probably the closest thing in the natural realm to being in love with God is romantic love for another person. Yet often this natural love can fade or be abused, and can be very disappointing at some point, and may never be fully satisfying. God will never disappoint His Bride. His love is forever fresh and complete. We can fully trust our lives to the love of God. God, unlike man is always faithful and will always have an adequate supply of whatever one needs to become all that God desires, and to experience fullness in life.

Giving one's life to God and living in intimacy with Him assures the most productive and prosperous life possible for the individual. One will be prosperous in the total sense of all areas of life, not just the gaining of material things, seen as prosperity by the carnal mind. God will supply encouragement, comfort, discipline, strength, guidance, and anything else needed to fulfill His purpose for one's life.

There is nothing in life that is as valuable as intimately relating to God.

Yet, many Christians busy themselves with many things that are of much less value. In any modern city, people are rushing about and are often greatly stressed in an attempt to get somewhere and do something in a hurry. The pressure of busy fast paced life can take a heavy toll on the body, soul, and spirit of Christians. *(Luke 10:40-42)*

It is possible to remain so busy about so many things that we no longer notice the longing and emptiness of our hearts for the one we love, the one who loves us. Have you ever stopped to consider how God must feel as His heart longs for His Bride to come and be with Him, and yet she just continues day after day rushing about busy about many things but missing the most valuable thing of all?

Is it possible that we need to reevaluate our motives for the very busy lifestyle we live? Is it possible that we have set such costly high standards for our lives that we have lost our life in the process of trying to pay the price? Is it possible that the cost for creature comforts and status in life has driven us to invest our lives in trying to pay for that which will not give us what we really want or need? Have we been tricked out of the very thing that will fulfill our lives and supply everything we need? Have we left our first love, and sold ourselves to buy bread that will not satisfy? Is God trying to get our attention? Is he calling out for His people to STOP and consider what we are spending our lives for, and how much it is costing? Is it costing the very thing we are made for, to spend our lives intimately relating to our Husband, our Lover, the one who will provide all we need for abundance in life and eternity?

Isa 55:1-3: **"Ho!** *Everyone who thirsts, Come to the waters; And you who have no money, Come, buy and eat. Yes, come, buy wine and milk Without money and without price.* **Why do you spend money for what is not bread, And your wages for what does not satisfy?** *Listen carefully to Me, and eat what is good, And let your soul delight itself in abundance. Incline your ear, and* **come to Me.** *Hear, and your soul shall live; And I will make an everlasting covenant with you; The sure mercies of David.*

Is God speaking to your heart? Do you feel a longing to be with Him in personal intimacy, to spend time in His arms in personal prayer and communion, to enjoy the brightness of His presence and the excitement of His Word? If He is speaking to your heart, please do not turn away from that voice and return to busyness, but make whatever changes are necessary to spend time loving Him and being loved by Him. There are those who have failed to respond to that call for so long that they no longer hear His voice calling for His Bride to come to Him. They cannot even spare the time to read this letter and will not hear the plea of God to come and rest in His arms.

All of the different types of human love are mirrors of the spiritual love we have with God. The different types of human or natural love may break down and at some point disappoint us; but the love of God is perfect in all of its different aspects. Not only are we to be in love with God as bride and wife of our Lord Jesus. But, we also love God and are loved by Him as our Father.

Jesus represents the Father to His children. He said, "If you have seen me you have seen the Father." Jesus is the "Everlasting Father".

*Isa 9:6: For unto us a Child is born, Unto us a Son is given; And the government will be upon His shoulder. And His name will be called Wonderful, Counselor, Mighty God, **Everlasting Father,** Prince of Peace.*

A godly earthly father knows the depth and undying continual love for His sons and daughters. He would give his life in an instant to save the life of his child. He knows the deep desire to provide for and protect his children. He sincerely delights in being with his children. He loves to play and frolic with them, to roughhouse with the boys, and sip make believe tea with the girls. He loves to help guide the bike when the training wheels are first removed, all the while encouraging and affirming his children. Children in his home feel very safe and know their strong father is their to take care of them. They know the rules and boundaries that he lays down are for their protection and feel very safe within them. They have an awesome respect and love for their father. And though they may not fully realize it at the time, they will come to appreciate the strong discipline that results from their disobedience and brings correction.

But what the children do not know is the great feeling of loss their father feels when he is apart from his children. They do not know the great heartache in their father when they pull away from him or rebel against him. Many fathers have gone to an early grave with a broken heart caused by rebellious sons or daughters, who someway really never knew how deeply their father loved them, never knew how much he needed them. They had always thought about how much they needed their farther, and never even considered that he needed them, needed their love and presence in his life, needed to hold them and give them his love and affection and receive theirs unto himself.

As it is in the natural so it is in the spiritual. However, our Heavenly Father is perfect in His love for us and will always be consistent in caring for us. He will always provide the direction, correction, training, and strength for our lives if we will come to Him. But what He really desires is to hold his sons and daughters on His big lap and love them. He delights in the joy of being with His children, and if your religious mind can handle it, He loves to play with His children. As His children grow up He will stand beside them with His big arm around them, face the whole world and say, "This is by beloved son; in whom I am well pleased, listen to him."

It does not really matter if you had a great natural childhood or not. Jesus came to fix all that is lacking. His blood, His grace, His mercy, His love is sufficient to completely renew and put into place anything that is lacking in our lives. We are adopted sons and daughters through Jesus and are joint heirs. His heritage is our heritage, and we can now come boldly into the presence of our heavenly Father and experience all that was lacking and live a full and abundant life with Him.

Only after we really know the love of our Father and are in love with our Husband, can we carry out the second greatest commandment, which is to love our neighbor as we love ourselves. The love for our neighbor must be very different from the natural kind of generic concern for the well being of our neighbors or the dormant kind of love for our siblings .

The internal spiritual love from our spiritual Father and Husband is to be reflected out from us into the world toward our siblings (brothers and sisters in the Lord), and our neighbors (those near by). By love, we have God's heart for them. By His love, we see Jesus in our brothers and sisters, and love Jesus in them as we love them with deeds of kindness, acceptance, support, mercy, affirmation, thankfulness, and even correction when needed. By love, we share His heart for the lost who wonder about as sheep without a shepherd. By His love, we feel His concern for the lost sheep that have gone astray. By His love, we can see the end of the lost and seek to do all we can to bring them to Jesus. By love, we have compassion and sincerely care for those who persecute us and spitefully use us.

The outworking of the love of God in us is the fulfillment of all the laws and the words of the prophets. Obedience to the ways of God are a natural product of our love for Him. Power and strength to live righteously flows in and through us as the love of God brings the grace of God into our lives and gives us the power to do the things we could not do in our own strength. God works in us both to will and to do his good pleasure. *(Phil 2:13)* His desires are fulfilled in us by His power and we become profitable sons in His great kingdom family.*(Heb 2:10)* Then the ways of God become the ways on earth and His will is done on earth as it is in heaven. *(Mat 6:10)*

His ways are the most prosperous ways. We will be a better son or daughter, and do a better job of whatever we are given to do. Because we do it better we will reap more and will enjoy more of His abundant life. *(2 Cor 9:6) (Gal 6:7-10)* Love, His love in us, will cause us to be better parents, better teachers, better doctors, better businessmen, better government servants, better ministers, better workmen of every sort. Living His way will cause less loss and waste from foolish activities and mistakes.

The grace of God is not a blanket covering for our continued disobedience.

The grace of God flows to us through the love of God as we intimately relate to Him. The unmerited favor is the love of God, which we do not deserve, coming to us and bringing His desires, His strength, His holiness, His power, His ways, into our lives, to cause us to live powerful, holy, righteous lives. Our trying hard to keep religious rules, ordinances, and laws will never bring us to holiness and purity in our lives. *(Gal 3:21)* Only the grace of God flowing through the love of God as we become intimate with Him will bring us to maturity and holiness in our daily lives.

The Greek word translated grace in the New Testament is "charis", (khar'-ece) and means **the divine influence upon the heart, and its reflection in the life.**

One may be significantly influenced by a teacher or a notable respected person such as a star athlete, or important state official, or some very wise man who takes the time to become intimate and show love for a person. The impact of their influence could cause change and improvements in one's life that would last forever.

How much more will the influence of Almighty God have upon the heart and life of one intimately in love with Him!? And will there not be a glorious reflection of His influence in one's life, reaching out to the world!?

In our weakness His strength is made perfect. *(2 Cor 12:9)* Yes, our flesh and our soul is weak within itself, yes we would always be rotten stinking sinners unable to bring forth the glorious works of obedience to God, daily crying out for His mercy because of our continued disobedient sinful fleshly state. But the grace of God, (the influence of the Almighty God of all creation, the righteous holy One) upon our heart empowers us to live as holy, righteous, powerful saints. No longer subject to the flesh and the sin nature of Adam. Able to walk in freedom over every work of the enemy, able to fully conquer our flesh and live in glorious righteousness, peace, and joy by the Spirit of Christ which now lives within us to do all the bidding of the Father in and through us. No! We are not stinking sinners covered by a blanket of grace to keep our true character hidden from God. We are filled with the very presence of God Himself. And are more than conquerors in all things by grace, the empowerment of the gift of the love of God. *(Rom 8:37)*

Wake up! God's arm is not shortened that He cannot bring us to righteousness. His hand is not too weak to mold and shape us into the image of Christ.

All things are under His feet and He has been given to be the head of the church which is you and me. *(Eph 1:22-23)* We can do all things through Christ who strengthens us. *(Phil 4:13)* Yes, we are nobodies, but the one who lives in us is SOMEBODY. His grace, His influence within our lives makes all the difference. And the reflection of His life into our world will and is changing our world. There is nothing too hard for the Lord. There is no evil stronghold, no Babylonian bondage that is to big for the one who lives in us. There is no work under the sun that is impossible to the Almighty Father whom we love and who loves us. Because He loves us the world and all it contains is for us.The power to overthrow every false god and evil work of man is now within the sons and daughters of God who know they are loved and know the grace flowing through the love of the Father.

Now is the time to fall in love with your Husband and become filled with His love and carry out the works of God in the earth. It is now that the kings of earth must bow to the king of heaven and the kingdoms of earth are to become the kingdoms of our God. Only because of love, and only when sons and daughters give up their busy stuff and fall in love with God, only when our lives do not matter any more except as they are filled with His desire, His presence, and His love and power will we see the fullness of the salvation of our God. Be still in His presence and in His love and you will see the salvation of God over the earth. *(Psa 46:10) (Exo 14:13) (Luke 3:6)*

Only by the Spirit of God
will the world come into the order of God.

And only by the love of God and our response to it will the Spirit of Christ have free reign to rule in and through our lives. Nothing is impossible to the one who believes and only the one in love with God will be able to truly believe the awesome words and works of God. Truly, faith works by love. There will be great love before there is great faith. There will be great faith before there will be great works of God redeeming the kingdoms of our earth.

Fear not little flock for it is your Father's good pleasure to give you the kingdom. *(Luke 12:32)* Perfect love casts out fear. *(1 John 4:18)* Once we are in the place of mature love with God we will not fear the faces of men or the spirits of darkness, and will have no problem in exercising the full potential of the power of God to destroy the works of the enemy and retake the kingdoms of this world. There is no fear in love and faith can work where there is no fear. Nothing is impossible to him who believes (has faith), and there is no limit of faith to the one completely in love with God.

Love is the most important principle in all creation.

Love will purify the harlot into a pure bride. *(Eph 5:25-27)* Love will cause us to not defraud our neighbor and naturally keep all the law. *(Rom 13:9)* Love will cause us to seek to provide for others which will in turn activate the law of sowing and reaping and we shall be adequately supplied because of our love. Love will cause us to be better servants to God and to others, and as we become faithful servants we become rulers in his kingdom. *(Mat 25:21)* Love causes us to not exercise authority in an overlord manner which will allow the authority of God to rule and establish His authority. *(Mat 20:25-26)* Love will keep us from costly disputes and disorders which steal the provision of God in our lives. *(Mat 5:25-26)*

By love coming forth in man and ruling in the earth, there will not be painful church splits and strife, no marriages for all the wrong reasons, and no divorces as a result. Love will stop all costly conflicts and deadly wars. Love will cause all the assets of man and earth to be used for good and not evil. Love will stop crime and empty the prisons. His love will prosper the entire earth. Only by His love will righteousness, peace, and joy reign over the earth. Love is the primary substance of the kingdom of God.

Is there anything as important as the intimate love of God in your life?

BASILEIA LETTER

Number 11

Freedom in the Kingdom of God.

Jesus said, you shall know the truth and the truth shall make you free.

John 8:31b-32: **"If you abide in My word**, *you are My disciples indeed. "And you shall know the truth, and **the truth shall make you free.**"*

What is freedom and what is not? Am I really free? How can the truth make me free? How can abiding in His word make one free? Can one truly become politically free, economically free, socially free, by abiding in the word of Christ, becoming His disciple, and knowing the truth? Or, is the Holy Bible, the Word of God, not true? And, if one can become free through this process, cannot an entire nation possibly become free? And if a nation can become free, cannot the whole world potentially become free?

In the past age the emphasis was on church as opposed to the emerging emphasis of the kingdom of God. In the church emphasis age, the Bible was generally interpreted as having value primarily only to one's "Christian life", or religious training and experience. The Word of God was not sincerely valued as the source of wisdom and guidance for governing our entire lives and the governments of the world.

Many Christians who have been educated by both religious and/or secular higher educational systems have been trained to not value the Word and ways of God as realistic guidance for all governing aspects of life in the world. This has resulted in a multitude of various forms of bondage or slavery. Social, political, financial, physical, spiritual, and many other forms of bondage have taken control of the world's people and subsequently its governing systems.

An inversion of truth has occurred which tends to see the Word and ways of God as bondages that limit the freedom of individuals to participate in activities of carnal pleasure. The truth is that carnal pleasures only temporarily satisfy and always create a desire for more. In order to continue the individual's sense of satisfaction, one must have new and increasing activities of carnal pleasure. Therefore they become a lifestyle of addiction or bondage, stealing the individual's personal freedom to make real and free choices in life. The activities of the person's life become those which lead to the fulfillment or satisfaction of the addiction and not those which lead to prosperity and true freedom in all areas of life and government. The lack of productive and prosperous activity creates a dependent person, one who is dependent on someone or something else to provide the necessities of life and external direction or control for life.

Freedom means to be at liberty; at liberty to make decisions without the despotic control of another external force. Some antonyms of freedom are: **dependence**, restriction, **bondage**, servitude, **slavery**, imprisonment, and **captivity**. Any **thing** that brings one toward dependency is leading away from freedom and toward bondage or slavery to that **thing**.

People in the church emphasis age did not understand the difference between independence and freedom. Many have been deceived into believing that independence from any guidance in their lives except their own mind was freedom. **Independence from all authority, including God, is not freedom!** Ungodly or carnal living is not freedom and does not lead to life. On the contrary it leads toward bondage and death, not freedom and life. Individuals, families, governments and all institutions and systems of life will fail if the deception of carnal independence from God and His ways continues long enough. Death is the final result of independence from God and His ways. We are either slaves of sin unto death, or slaves of God's righteousness unto life.

Rom 6:16-19, 20-21: Do you not know that to whom you present yourselves slaves to obey, you are that one's slaves whom you obey, whether of sin leading to death, or of obedience leading to righteousness? But God be thanked that though you were slaves of sin, yet you obeyed from the heart that form of doctrine to which you were delivered. And having been set free from sin, you became slaves of righteousness.

For when you were slaves of sin, you were free in regard to righteousness. What fruit did you have then in the things of which you are now ashamed? For the end of those things is death.

People in the kingdom emphasis age are beginning to understand that freedom comes only from knowing the truth that God is the creator and designer of life, and that He knows best how to live life, and how to govern in such a way as to produce true freedom and prosperity in every aspect of life.

The church age people, at best, have tried to adapt principles from the Word of God to develope laws and rules for governing in the world. Often the attempt to use the moral principles of the Word of God to establish rule in the world was met with much resistance by those who feared the loss of carnal independence. The subsequent democratic attempts to compromise the ways of God to satisfy the carnal minds and personal addictions of the people have increasingly deteriorated life over the entire world.

People during the past church emphasis age retreated within the church walls and left the world to its own end. The great fallacy of the isolationist philosophy of the church is that no one in the world is truly isolated from the results of the actions of others. In the emerging age of the kingdom of God, people are returning to life; returning to rule and reign with Christ, and are beginning to have an impact upon the world. The great giant, the people of God who were asleep and in bondage in the church, is awakening and moving into life in the world. Kingdom age people are realizing that the **renewal of their mind** to the Word and ways of God, can bring the ways of God into their own lives, and then into their families, their communities, their nations and eventually into the entire world. No longer are we focused on the problems of the world but upon the possibility and potential of the power of God to change the world.

John 1, teaches us that Jesus was the Word and became flesh and dwelt among us. That same Jesus was crucified, resurrected from the dead, ascended to the right hand of the Father, and returned to the earth at Pentecost in the Holy Spirit, not just to dwell among us, but to actually dwell within believers. To abide in the Word we must abide in Christ, we must abide in the Spirit of the resurrected Christ. Only as we walk in the Spirit can we be delivered from walking in the carnal mind of the flesh. *(Gal 5:16)* Only as we abide in Him and He within us by His Spirit can we know the truth and bring forth into the world His ways of life and government of all aspects of life in the world.

We can rule and reign with Him now in this life as we yield to His Spirit and renew our minds from our carnal and church age ways to His righteous and kingdom age ways. *(2 Tim 2:12) (Rev 5:10)* His thoughts are higher than our thoughts. *(Isa 55:8-9)* He must live in us and produce His thoughts, His way of thinking and doing. We shall live by the faith of the Son of God, or we shall die by our carnal minds. *(Gal 2:20) (Rom 8:13)*

John 15:4-11 "Abide in Me, and I in you. As the branch cannot bear fruit of itself, unless it abides in the vine, neither can you, unless you abide in Me. "I am the vine, you are the branches. He who abides in Me, and I in him, bears much fruit; for without Me you can do nothing.

139

"If anyone does not abide in Me, he is cast out as a branch and is withered; and they gather them and throw them into the fire, and they are burned.

"If you abide in Me, and My words abide in you, you will ask what you desire, and it shall be done for you. "By this My Father is glorified, that you bear much fruit; so you will be My disciples.

*"As the Father loved Me, I also have loved you; abide in My love. "If you keep My commandments, you will abide in My love, just as I have kept My Father's commandments and abide in His love. "These things I have spoken to you, that **My joy may remain in you, and that your joy may be full.***

Joy is an inner excitement of peace that endures. Joy is peace excited. Peace is joy at rest.

Carnal pleasures never bring lasting joy.

Certainly carnal pleasure is fun for a season, but will soon disappear leaving emptiness, until the next participation in an activity of fleshly pleasure. This is true for the nations of the world, just as it is true for individuals. The world, without the joy of the Lord, must depend on strife and war to obtain the ingredients for carnal pleasures.

One of the greatest natural carnal pleasures is to be ruler over other men, to be number one, to be better than others. Men involve themselves in conflicts that range from simple parlor games, to great sports activities, business ventures, and full out wars in an attempt to be greater and to have more than others. Individuals strive against individuals, families against families, tribes against tribes, and nations against nations, all in an effort to be number one, and to take the things that others have for their own carnal pleasure. The more riches one can obtain and the more luxury one can purchase, the more carnal pleasure one can have. I once saw a slogan on a shirt that read, "He who dies with the most toys wins". I later saw another one that read, "He who dies with the most toys, still dies."

The second greatest carnal pleasure is probably sexual stimulation and activity. The world has moved gradually and steadily toward immorality and extreme sexual perversions in its search for satisfaction from carnal pleasure. Just as common, if not more so, is the practice of overeating for carnal pleasure. Recreational immorality and recreational eating are common forms of seeking carnal pleasure to replace the Joy of the Lord that is lost from not abiding in Jesus.

One of the most severe forms of seeking carnal pleasure is the abuse of drugs and alcohol. For a short season one can alter the body chemistry with drugs and alcohol in such a way as to deceive the brain into a peaceful and pleasurable kind of feeling. But just like all other carnal pleasures it does not last. More and more is required to get the same feeling as the addiction grows into a life controlling bondage.

In the kingdom age men and women are learning that abiding in Jesus, in His Word, and in His love causes His joy to remain in them and their joy to be full, and dissolves the lust for carnal pleasures. The joy of the Lord is our strength to overcome the bondages of addictions to carnal pleasures and to walk in true freedom. The intense drive for carnal pleasure is destroyed by Christ in us. *(Col 1:27)* Ruling over others, being number one, having more things, sexual immorality and perversion, recreational overeating and all other carnal pleasures pale in the light of the inner joy of the Lord when we truly abide in Him and He abides in us.

Personal freedom of the individual eventually leads to national freedom.

Spiritual freedom leads to moral freedom, and then to financial freedom. Political freedom will eventually result from the masses continuing in personal freedom. Only by abiding in the ways of God through Christ Jesus can freedom come forth in the world.

Someone has said that freedom is never granted by the oppressor. There will indeed be a great cost in obtaining freedom in our world. Throughout history many have died in an attempt to gain and maintain a pseudo freedom or independence. Even many of those fighting for a pseudo freedom were not free themselves, but were servants to one form of carnal pleasure or another, or some form of humanistic or religious philosophy of government. Subsequently many who have won the wars for freedom have then imposed their own brand of bondage upon others.

The cost of freedom began with the death of Christ Jesus on the cross and the martyrdom of the first century apostles. No man can number the multitudes of godly men and women who have been slain, and shall be slain as the great war for freedom on the earth roars toward a climax and end. The weapons of our warfare are not carnal but spiritual for the pulling down of strongholds.

2 Cor 10:3-6: For though we walk in the flesh, we do not war according to the flesh.

*For the weapons of our warfare are not carnal but mighty in God for **pulling down strongholds, casting down arguments** and every high thing that exalts itself against the knowledge of God, **bringing every thought into captivity to the obedience of Christ**, and being ready to punish all disobedience when your obedience is fulfilled.*

The war is won or lost in the mind and hearts of men.

The true oppressor is not white over black, or communism against democracy, or gentile against Jew, or protestant against catholic, nor any other human or natural thing. The true oppressor is the spiritual enemy of God and man. The enemy uses all of these differences to inflame prejudice, fear, and strife in an attempt to rob the world of freedom. He desires to control and to become number one, equal to God. (Isa *14:12-14)*

The good news is that Jesus has completely defeated the devil and now lives in believers to destroy all the work of the enemy. *(Col 2:15) (1 John 3:8b) (Luke 10:19a)*

The bad news is that people of the world have been deceived and entrapped into seeking carnal pleasure, instead of delighting in the Lord and experiencing the Joy of the Lord. The joy of the Lord will overcome the enemy's ability to corrupt the individuals life, and thereby take away all of his ability to steal freedom from the world. *Neh 8:10b: Do not sorrow, for the joy of the LORD is your strength. "*

The devil has only the power given to him by the people of the world. God has given dominion to man and has defeated the enemy. God has not rescinded His position of giving rule of the earth to man. *(Gen 1:26-28)* Man lives or dies by the decisions that he makes. God will not intervene without man's permission. The plan and work of God on earth will not come to pass without man's permission and participation. God had to become the man, Jesus, to carry out redemption and the plan of God on earth. Only man had the God given authority to rule in the earth and it was necessary that redemption come through a man. Jesus was that man and now can live in man by the Spirit of Christ and carry out the will of God on earth. Only with the permission and participation of men will it be done, and only by the indwelling presence and power of the resurrected Christ can it be done.

Man, by his collective majority decision to turn from the ways of God and from abiding in Christ, to seeking carnal pleasures, has given power to the devil. The beautiful but cunning serpent of Genesis Chapter Three, who tempted Eve in the garden of Eden, has become the ferocious fiery red dragon of Revelation Chapter Twelve, by the power given unto him by the people of the world.

Is it possible that man now has the potential of Christ within to completely bind the enemy's power and bring forth the plan and will of God on earth, that the destruction of evil is now within the potential of Christ in man? Is it possible that the Word of God is true and that good can overcome evil? Could it be that the Spirit of Christ bringing forth His love in the body of Christ throughout the world can bring forth righteousness, peace, and joy in the Holy Spirit, and overcome the evil of the world?

If we look at the problem, the multitudes of evil men who are bent on destruction, and the great deceptive philosophy of seeking carnal pleasure that rules men around the world, certainly it does not seem possible to the natural mind that evil can be defeated and the kingdom of God can and is coming forth into our world. Looking at the giants in the land is exactly what the enemy wants us to do. *(Num 13:32-14-1)*

The victory waits only for men to have faith and believe the Word of God. Faith comes where there is righteousness, peace, and the Joy of the Lord. Faith in God cannot be strong in carnal pleasure seekers. The prayers and faith of righteous men will unleash the power of God and the great apocalyptic cataclysmic events of the book of Revelation can greatly alter the entire scheme of things in the world. The great outpourings of the Spirit of God upon His mature sons can bring forth renewal and people can repent of seeking carnal pleasures and turn to God by the millions.

Yes, it may be a bloody fiery road to the freedom of the World, but God can protect and deliver His children. The kingdoms of the world will become the kingdoms of our God. *(Rev 11:15)* We will rule and reign in the earth with Him. *(2 Tim 2:12)* We will overcome the evil one by the blood of the Lamb and the word of our testimony. There is nothing too hard for the Lord. *(Gen 18:14)*

Rev 12:11: "And they overcame him by the blood of the Lamb and by the word of their testimony, and they did not love their lives to the death.

In the church age, for the most part, Christianity was something that people added to their lives. It was a part of their lives that helped them to be good citizens and do a better job of their vocation.

In the kingdom age, serving the Lord is our vocation. Christ Jesus is our lives, not a part of our lives.

Everything in the kingdom begins with the King, Christ Jesus. Our very lives must be given into His hand whether we live long, or whether we die young in battle, we are the Lords and will be present with Him. Whether we live or die, we shall ever be with the Lord.

Rom 14:8: For if we live, we live to the Lord; and if we die, we die to the Lord. Therefore, whether we live or die, we are the Lord's.

Adding God into our lives as part of our life will never bring freedom to our lives and to our world. Only as men give themselves wholly to the Lord, will they find real purpose in the job they are given to do. They will do every task as unto the Lord and will be better at every work the Lord gives them to do. They will serve others with their whole heart as they serve God by serving others. More will be done and more prosperity will result from seeking to serve, rather than seeking to gain for carnal pleasure.

Kingdom freedom is in the heart and mind of the individual.

Truly the kingdom of God is within you. *(Luke 17:21)* We cannot be free in the world until we are free in our heart. The masses cannot be changed except they are changed from within, one heart at the time. There may be millions being changed in an instant, but the release of freedom is still in each individual heart.

Everything else will follow the mind and heart. The mind and heart will not follow everything else. We must come to the realization that the rule of the world is within the hearts and minds of men. What we think and believe is far more important than most have realized. The world and all of its complicated systems must respond to the faith and words of men. What men believe and say will manifest into the world.

The war becomes one for the minds and hearts of men. The first battle of the war is the redemption of man. Men must come into contact with the living God and become connected to Him through Christ Jesus. Until the life is yielded to God and the Holy Spirit is indwelling and filling the life, the heart and mind will be in opposition to the will and kingdom of God. The battle is won or lost in what men believe in their hearts.

The just shall live by faith, and the unjust shall die by fear and unbelief.

What men believe in their hearts, they will speak with their mouths. *(Luke 6:45)* What they believe and speak releases the dominion forces given to man and begins to bring forth into the natural world the things man believed in his heart. *(Mark 11:23-24)* Spiritual powers are poised to bring forth the thoughts and words of men into the world. The lips and the tongues of men are the source from which the sword of the Spirit, the Word of God, can be launched into the world. *(Eph 6:17)* As the resurrected Spirit of Christ dwelling within men speaks forth the empowered Word and will of God, it is planted into the hearts of men and into the world, and the world is changed, set free from the control of the enemy.

In the same way, evil words of unbelief, fear, and hatred are spoken forth from the hearts of ungodly men. Their lips and tongues become the source for the power of the enemy to bring forth evil words or curses to change the world and hinder the kingdom of God coming forth upon the earth.

Words spoken precede works.

A word spoken and received becomes a thought.
A thought retained becomes a belief.
A belief meditated and spoken becomes a work.

The strongholds of the enemy are in the minds of men. The minds of men are controlled by the thoughts within. The thoughts within man are generated by the inputs coming into the mind. What a mind sees and hears over time will become reality to that person. The person will act and react in accordance with his perception of reality, and his or her actions and reactions will effect change in the world. Therefore the key to bringing forth the kingdom of God,

God's freedom and ways of life into the world is the planting of the truth of God into the minds of men. By the preaching of the Word the world can be delivered and walk in freedom. *(1 Cor 1:21)*

There are two sources of input into the minds and hearts of men. One is the natural five senses, especially the eyes and ears, the other is the spiritual five senses, especially the spiritual eyes and ears. Everything seen, heard, or felt by man has an effect upon the mind of the person. Every word whether a picture or spoken word must contain and communicate a thought. The thought is planted in the mind of the one seeing, hearing, and feeling and can grow into a belief if heard or seen often enough, especially from what is considered to be a reliable source.

From the natural inputs one's mind is shaped into patterns of belief as a child and confirmed and modified as a mature person. Every communication, every word, thought, or feeling has its origin in either the truth of God, or the lies of the enemy. Though often subtle and hidden, every story, every word, or communication moves one toward the ways of God or toward the ways of the enemy, depending upon the origin of the communication. The culmination of the stored thoughts become the belief system of the life and will determine the destiny of the person, and will have an effect on the destiny of the world. Only by renewing the mind to the thoughts and ways of God can one be freed of the strongholds of thought patterns planted by the inputs of the enemy. And only by renewing the mind can one be filled with the powerful potential of God. *(Rom 12:2) (Eph 4:23) (Col 3:10)*

Spiritual inputs from the Spirit of God within the person can bring new pictures, words, and feelings directly from the Spirit of God into the mind of the believer. The visions, words, and feelings from the Spirit, if received and believed, can destroy old ways of thinking and bring new vision and power into the life and subsequently into the world. Spiritual gifts such as prophesy are vital for those who are not skilled at receiving from the Spirit within themselves. The prophetic word can give them a picture, word, or feeling from God that can be planted into their lives and help bring forth the will and plan of God for the person.

In the same way, evil pictures, words, and feelings can be received in the minds of men directly from the powers of darkness. The evil communications can alter the patterns of thought within the mind and bring forth the plan and will of the devil into the world.

The choices that lead to freedom of the world begin with the choice of what men will choose to see, hear, and feel. The things that are focused upon and allowed to remain in the mind and heart of men will bring forth the ways of God in the earth, or the ways of the devil. It is up to each of us individually to choose what we will hear and see, which will destine our thoughts, which will destine our actions, which will destine our lives, which will destine our world.

Freedom or bondage is a choice we make at the level of what we will look at and listen to, and what feelings and thoughts we will allow within our hearts and minds. The enemy desires that one believe that nothing can be done to change the world and everybody is doing it this way, or that way, so one might as well go ahead and do it the same way and enjoy carnal pleasures. He wants you to think something like, "I am only one person and can really do nothing to change the world, and no one is going to know what things I allow in my thoughts, so it really does not matter very much what I think and do".

As long as the enemy can, one at a time, keep the majority of the world, especially sons of God, thinking in this way he can continue his evil works of bondage in the world. The church will remain in retreat within its own walls and be of little or no effect in establishing the kingdom of God, the ways and will of God, into our world.

Praise God! Now in our time the sons of God are awakening and coming forth to proclaim the gospel of the kingdom from heaven on earth. Now in this day individuals are coming into intimacy with God that causes them to determine to seek and serve God with their whole heart. No matter, if the whole world does not go with them, these maturing sons of God will go anyway. It is not as important whether they live this way or that, as long as God lives within them and is present with them. Long life on the earth is not the first priority. The first and predominant priority is that the fullness of God come forth in their lives, and that His kingdom come, and His will be done, on earth as it is in heaven. Truly the model prayer given by our Lord has become the theme and purpose of our lives.

Mat 6:9-10: "In this manner, therefore, pray: Our Father in heaven, Hallowed be Your name. Your kingdom come. Your will be done On earth as it is in heaven.

When different men believe and speak different opposing words, the spiritual war is on. Those who have the greatest measure of rule and the greatest number of hearts believing, praying, and speaking will prevail. When multitudes come into agreement for the will of God, and pray and speak His will and Word, the will of God is done in our lives and in the world.

Do you see why it is such an important strategy of the enemy to divide and cause disagreement among believers? The great potential of millions of believers in agreement would bring a quick end to the enemy's work in the world. He could no longer hinder the kingdom of God.

The strategy of the enemy of keeping mens minds focused on carnal TV programing, movies, sports, video games, etc. is very important to him. They contain subliminal and subtle thoughts and ways, that will lead men away from the Word and ways of God. People, especially young people, will accept what they see and hear repeatedly, and it will mold and shape their minds, which will mold and shape their lifestyle. We cannot focus our thinking on the things of carnal pleasure and expect to live the kingdom of God lifestyle. Feeding our minds on sexual perversion, immorality, violence, and every other form of carnal pleasure, will produce those same qualities within one's character.

Feeding on the Word of God will produce the kingdom of God lifestyle.

BASILEIA LETTER
Number 12

Denominations and the Kingdom of God

Jesus said, *"And other sheep I have which are not of this fold; them also I must bring, and they will hear My voice; and there will be **one flock**. John 10:16.*

*John 17:11: Now I am no longer in the world, but these are in the world, and I come to You. Holy Father, keep through Your name those whom You have given Me, that they may **be one** as We are.*

The Scripture states in *James 5:16*, that the prayers of a righteous man avails much. We all believe that the prayers of the Lord Jesus will come to pass. The world and its people must come into order with the Words of Christ Jesus who is one with the Father. Jesus prayed earnestly and specifically for oneness in those who believe in Him. He also made it clear that he did not pray just for those standing before Him at the time, but also for those who "will believe".

*John 17:20-23: I do not pray for these alone, but also for those who will believe in Me through their word; that **they all may be one**, as You, Father, are in Me, and I in You; **that they also may be one in Us**, that the world may believe that You sent Me.*
***And the glory which You gave Me I have given them, that they may be one just as We are one**: I in them, and You in Me; **that they may be made perfect in one**, and that the world may know that You have sent Me, and have loved them as You have loved Me.*

*Father, I desire that they also whom You gave Me may be with Me where I am, that they may behold **My glory** which You have given Me; for You loved Me before the foundation of the world.*

Not only did Jesus pray for believers to be one, but he spoke of how and why believers are to become one. The glory which the Father gave to Jesus, and that Jesus in turn gives to believers is for the purpose of oneness. *(And the **glory** which You gave Me I have given them, **that they may be one.**)* How is it that glory given to believers by the Lord can cause us to be made perfect (mature) in one? Jesus said, "**I in them, and You in Me; that they may be perfect in one**." Christ Jesus in believers brings the glorious manifestation of the power and presence of God *(Christ in you the hope of glory. Col 1:27)*

How will believers become as one and walk as the unified body of Christ with all its many different parts and functions? **Only by the manifestation of the Glory of God in believers.**

Teaching doctrine will not create oneness. Never, can denominations teach each other enough doctrine to bring agreement and oneness. Doctrinal debate will never bring oneness. Neither will compromise of doctrinal teachings and positions bring maturity and oneness. Blending of religious traditions, ordinances, and practices can never make the body of Christ fit together as one.

Differences in believers and groups of believers are a part of the design of God. *(1 Cor 12) (Rom 12:4-8)* Individual believers have different functions in the Body and are therefore given different gifts and tools to do their different jobs.

Individuals tend to gather together in groups with those of like calling and gifting who are doing the same type job. Denominations are those different work groups with different jobs. Much like the labor groups and societies in the secular business world. The plumbers have their unions or societies, while the electricians have others; the doctors have their groups, and lawyers have others; welders and machinist have their groups while carpenters have others, and so on.

The important thing is for all the workers and the different groups to work together to accomplish the required tasks to meet the needs of mankind and the world. The understanding and principles emphasized in one group seem of less importance to another group. Each group sees their understandings as of greater value because they are more important to them in their particular job or function. Each individual or group may think of themselves more highly than they ought to think.

*Rom 12:3-4: For I say, through the grace given to me, to everyone who is among you, **not to think of himself more highly than he ought to think**, but to think soberly, as God has dealt to each one a measure of faith. For as **we have many members in one body, but all the members do not have the same function**.*

We would think it very ridiculous for a group of plumbers to have a serious contention with a group of electricians over a debate about whether pipe or wires were more important; or whether teachings regarding voltage, amperage, and resistance were more important than teachings regarding pressure, flow, and friction.

If these groups thought that their knowledge was complete and of ultimate importance, they would think the other group was wrong. And could consider them to be deceived and possibly dangerous to their group and others. If there were a third party involved who would benefit by the two groups waring against one another, the third party might help increase the contention between the groups by fanning the flames of differences.

Is this not exactly what has happened with the different jobs and different teaching emphasis that God designed to meet the various needs of His kingdom on earth? Has not the denominations, sects, and other religious groups contented against one another as the enemy has fanned the flames of differences? Is it not religious bigotry which says, "We have all the truth in our group, and if there is any we don't have it is not important anyway?" Does this same strong bias cause theologians aligned with different denominations to view the Scriptures with unequal prejudice of the value of one Scripture over another? Is it possible that one may so devalue certain aspects of knowledge and understanding that verses about those aspects may seem to not even exist as one reads the Scriptures? Is it possible that the enemy has blinded their spiritual eyes so that they cannot see truth beyond their select part? Is it also possible that because of this blindness one may contend bitterly with anyone who sees a part they do not see? *(John 12:40) (1 John 2:11)*

Within groups and denominations today the people usually have a group of leaders whom they respect. They receive their doctrinal teaching and guidance for religious practices from these leaders. For the most part these revered leaders can do no wrong and everything they say or do is right in the eyes of their followers.

The people may strongly emphasis a negative issue or character flaw regarding a prominent leader outside their group. The negative issue may be widely reported, severely judged, and continue to be discussed forever. But they will minimize and make excuses for the leaders of their own group and quickly forget the matter. **They will accuse one while excusing the other**. Perhaps subconsciously, or perhaps from design they will discredit the other teachers so that people will not listen to them and will look for something wrong in anything they should happen to hear from them. At the same time they tend to keep the people believing in their own leaders by disallowing harmful reports regarding the person or the teaching.

Rom 2:15b KJV: ---- and their thoughts the mean while accusing or else excusing one another.

155

Denominational and group teachers will often teach against teachings and practices of other groups. They will present an assortment of Scripture interpreted with a slant that presents a bias toward the particular view they propagate. They will then often tell of their own personal experiences or tell stories of other's experiences which seem to devalue or disprove the other position. Often the view of another group is misrepresented by over statement and improper emphasis. This causes a distorted view of the teaching and discredits the other group.

Manipulation, contention, strife, and debate may be ways of dealing with differences in the unregenerate world system, but they have no part in the kingdom of God. Debate is not the best way in the kingdom of God. **There is a higher authority for settling all of man's debates. Debate is only carried out among those of somewhat equal authority. When one of much greater power and authority enters the scene the debate is over.**

So it is that the glory of God is resolving denominational debate and strife. The current renewals and revivals coming forth in our world are releasing the power and glory of God and melting debates. As the glory of God manifest in awesome works, miracles, signs, and wonders, the debate and strife between individuals and groups is melting and denominational walls are coming down. The greater glory of the greater truth of the gospel of the kingdom is coming forth with power to renew our world. The gospel of the kingdom is never preached in words only but in the demonstration of the power of God.

*1 Th 1:5: For our gospel did not come to you in **word** only, but also in **power**, and in the Holy Spirit and in much assurance, as you know what kind of men we were among you for your sake.*

*Mat 4:23: And Jesus went about all Galilee, teaching in their synagogues, **preaching the gospel of the kingdom**, and **healing** all kinds of sickness and all kinds of disease among the people.*

*Acts 1:8: "But you shall receive **power** when the Holy Spirit has come upon you; and you shall be witnesses to Me in Jerusalem, and in all Judea and Samaria, and to the end of the earth."*

*Mat 10:7:8: "And as you go, **preach**, saying, '**The kingdom of heaven is at hand.**' "**Heal** the sick, **cleanse** the lepers, **raise** the dead, **cast out** demons. Freely you have received, freely give.*

*Mat 12:28: "But if I cast out demons **by the Spirit of God**, surely **the kingdom of God has come upon you.***

Individual Christians suffer greatly because they are cut off from the life and gifts flowing through groups other than their own. The following is just one example of how the body of Christ suffers due to separation. There are many other strengths and weakness within different groups, and many needs that can only be supplied by receiving the provision and gifts of other individuals or groups.

As an example, some denominations are focused on getting to heaven after death and are not greatly concerned with this life. They tend to see the work of Jesus as primarily to get people born again so they can have assurance of going to heaven someday. This is a needed evangelistic view to bring people to the first step, the new birth. The tragedy is that among these people there is little hope for victory in this life and no realistic faith in healing and deliverance. This results in a lack of power to prevent many unnecessary disabilities and premature deaths. The deaths and sicknesses are seen as the providence of God rather than a work of the enemy.

Other groups see an emphasis on the experience of God in this life to change people and the world for better. They may also see the potential for victorious living and defeating the devil now in this life. They may have great faith for healing and deliverance to set people free in this life. This view and work is desperately needed as well. The problem is that they may be so focused on this emphasis that they are negligent in bringing people to the new birth.

God desires, and we need all the work and provision of God through Christ flowing into our lives by the Holy Spirit. The body must be joined and not severed for each part to supply what is needed to the next part.

Eph 4:16 from whom the whole body, **joined and knit together** *by what* **every joint supplies**, *according to the effective working by which* **every part does its share**, *causes growth of the body for the edifying of itself in* **love**.

The continuing restoration from God continues to further reveal our need and His answers. In the passing church emphasis age, there was not receptivity for the authority of God to work through God's chosen servants to bring spiritual order among believers. The mighty miracle working apostles of God were not prevalent upon the earth. The apostolic wisdom and authority to bring spiritual order and connected unity to the diverse parts of the body were not in place. *(1 Cor 12:28)*

Among many groups the work of the evangelist, pastor, and teacher were the only accepted works. There was no greater authority to come on the scene to end debates and bring connection and order to the Body of Christ. This left only leaders of near equal authority to debate among themselves and divide the Body of Christ into many separate sects and denominations.

The lack of shared light and power between the groups caused a lack in the maturity of the different groups which provided open ground for the enemy to implant false doctrines. Thus darkness has infiltrated the diverse groups and caused death and destruction as well as prevented unity. Jesus did not come to abundantly bring debate, disability, and death. He came to bring life more abundantly. *(John 10:10)*

In the recent past God has restored prophets to the earth. Many groups have received the gifted prophets of God. The ministry of the prophet is added to the ministry of the evangelist, pastor, and teacher. The prophets ministry is pointing the way toward the restoration of the body and is preparing the way for the ministry of the apostles of God coming forth on the earth at this time.

We are just beginning to see the great impact of the powerful revelation, wisdom, and awesome miracle working gifts of the apostles. The ministry of the apostles is calling the body to repentance and refocusing believers toward the awesome power of the preaching of the gospel of the kingdom, and away from the darkness of doctrines of demons that divide asunder.

Truly the power and the glory of God coming forth today will help wash away our ignorance and melt our denominations into becoming joined as they were designed to be. The connecting of the body will further release powerful works of God upon the earth.

*Eph 4:11-16: And He Himself gave some to be **apostles**, some **prophets**, some evangelists, and some pastors and teachers, for the equipping of the saints for the work of ministry, for the edifying of the body of Christ, till we all come to the **unity** of the faith and of the knowledge of the Son of God, to a perfect man, to the measure of the stature of the fullness of Christ; **that we should no longer be children, tossed to and fro and carried about with every wind of***

159

doctrine, by the trickery of men, in the cunning craftiness of deceitful plotting, but, speaking the truth in love, may grow up in all things into Him who is the head; Christ; from whom **the whole body, joined and knit together** *by what* **every joint supplies,** *according to the effective working by which* **every part does its share,** *causes growth of the body for the edifying of itself in* **love.**

The phrase, "tossed to and fro and carried about with every wind of doctrine" has the connotation of various doctrines implanted by trickery and cunning craftiness of deceitful plotting. Thank God for the ministry of the apostles coming forth to bring understanding, priority, and order to the various doctrines. Together with the other gifted servants of the church the apostles will bring and end to many false doctrines that divide asunder.

The kingdoms of this earth are now becoming the kingdoms of our God. Our God reigns! He reigns not just in heaven, and not just in the church building, and not just in this or that denomination, **Our God reigns over the entire earth, and the will of God is being done on earth as it is in heaven. Truly the kingdom of God has come upon us. (Luke** *1:33) (Rom 5:17) (1 Cor 15:24-25) (2 Tim 2:12) (Rev 11:15) (1 Chr 16:31) (Psa 93:1) (Isa 52:7)*

We live in a new era. Some of us may have difficulty adjusting to the order God is bringing forth in this day. Please don't be concerned when you cannot figure it all out. We do not need to figure it all out. We must however, follow the leading of the Holy Spirit and move with what God is doing.

God will speak to men and send them with great power of the Spirit. They will effortlessly flow the miracle working power of God to heal, deliver, and set free. They will bring forth revelation, wisdom, and understanding that far exceeds their intellectual capacity. The revelation will expose areas of darkness and bring peaceful order to our understanding of the Word of God.

160

None will seek to be an apostle and none will need announcement or verification of man. They will simply be who they are, and do what they are sent to do. They will not be involved in commercialism nor in the promotion of ministries etc. Many of these men will be largely unknown to the world. They will quietly do what they are sent to do without fanfare.

There seems to be two extreme reactions to the restoration of apostles. On one hand, many groups continue to totally deny the office of apostle as valid today. While on the other hand, some groups tend to call almost anyone who ministers with any anointing an apostle. It is understandable that the body does not know how to respond to apostles. It simply is a very new experience for believers.

Some have called themselves apostles and sought to rule over a group of existing churches. *(Rev 2:2)(2 Cor 11:13)* They may have used human means of leadership and promotion etc. to seek to obtain a place of authority. Being called apostle or not being called apostle is not important to the apostle. Neither are positions of authority and high ranking offices of importance to the sent one of God. The only greatly important thing is the presence of God and knowing and doing His bidding. To the apostle, man's titles, rank, man's approval or lack of it, money, and everything else in the world is of little or no importance. Only God's approval and the presence and personal direction of God are of ultimate importance. *(Phil 3:7-8)*

The presence and ministry of the apostles in the first century were for the purpose of establishing the new era of the grace of God. It was a highly transitional period as the rituals and laws of the past gave way to the coming of the Messiah and the powerful grace of God began planting the kingdom of God on earth. None of the other gifts and offices could handle the job of planting the new and tearing down the old. The Spirit of Christ came at Pentecost and worked with the apostles performing awesome works. The apostles endured tremendous persecution from the system of religion that was passing away.

Can you see that the situation is the same today? The great gospel of the kingdom is again being preached. The world is in transition from the religious and political systems of the past to the glorious kingdom of God.

The apostles are being restored to again bring the world through an awesome transitional period. This transition will be even more intense and much greater in scope than that of the first century. The fulfillment of things begun at that time will come forth in this great transitional period. Greater works of every sort will occur. Great destruction will also come about as the way of the past is purged from the earth. Only the kingdom that cannot be shaken will remain when this great transition period is over. *(Heb 12:24-29)*

When the first century apostles began to preach the new revelation of the kingdom of Jesus Christ, it was vastly different from the doctrines and practices of religion in that day. The message of the kingdom coming forth today is just as vastly different and just as offensive to religion today as it was then. The extreme level of commitment required from the apostles of that day is also required today. Apostles do not always live long lives. But the more important thing to the apostle is to finish the course set before him, to accomplish the work given him to do. *(Acts 20:24)*

The great outpouring of the glory of God and the awesome works of the kingdom apostles is the power to bring unity to the body. The great revelation of the kingdom of God and its heavenly ways of governing life will become the focus instead of the individual parts of the denominational doctrines of the past. Yes, all the truth and valid teachings of the church will continue on into the kingdom age. But vast areas of doctrinal error and incorrect emphasis will be washed away by the greater revelation of the kingdom of God coming forth through the apostles of God.

Eventually every nation, every government, every authority on earth will be affected by the coming of the kingdom of God from heaven to earth.

The leaven of the kingdom is already in the lump of the earth, and the spread of it will not be stopped! The mustard seed of the kingdom was planted. It has sprouted, broken through the soil, and is now growing, and its growth will not be stopped! *(Mat 13:31-33)* Thank God for redemption and restoration of mankind and the earth to His wonderful kingdom lifestyle.

BASILEIA LETTER

Number 13

Holiness in the Kingdom of God

Jesus was called the "holy" Servant of God. *(Acts 4:30)* Many other people, places, and things are referred to as holy in the Bible. Believers are instructed to be holy and live holy lives.

*1 Pet 1:15-16: But as **He who called you is holy, you also be holy in all your conduct,** because it is written, "**Be holy, for I am holy.**"*

What does being holy really mean?

In a practical sense, what is holiness? As believers entering the kingdom emphasis age, what exactly is holiness to us? Are we holy? If not, how can we achieve holiness?

In the passing church emphasis age, different views were taught by theologians regarding holiness and how it could or could not be obtained in the lives of Christians. All of us who have been believers for very long have been taught and trained by one or more of these views. We may be questioning and perhaps changing some of our previously held views. Nevertheless, we each may remain persuaded to some degree by our past training.

In the emerging kingdom emphasis age, fresh light from God continues to confirm the Word of God and wash away many of our past religious views, as it enlightens us to higher kingdom principles.

The reality of holiness now in this life
is the kingdom of heaven way.

Some of the past religious views regarding holiness involved externally applied force from religious structures to keep rules, ordinances, forms, and rituals. The religious structures prescribed punishments, (either formally or informally) for lack of adherence to the system of rules and rituals.

Through the centuries many forms and degrees of punishments have been employed. These ranged from death by burning alive at the stake, to mild rejections such as, lack of personal warmth, lack of recognition, lack of acceptance, or loss of privileges. In the minds of some Christians, excommunication from the church threatens their eternal salvation. To others being "kicked out of the church" (sometimes referred to as "the left foot of fellowship") just means going somewhere else to church.

The attempt is to produce holiness in the people by causing them to exert their effort to not do the evil things that they desire in their hearts to do. The fear of being discovered and being publicly or privately punished causes the people to try harder to adhere to the rules and not do the things they really want to do. This is a hard and frustrating life for the people who must always be striving with great effort to not do the evil they really want to do. They may also live in fear that the times they have slipped will be discovered.

In an attempt to achieve holiness, some churches established rules regarding dress, appearance, participation in social activities or entertainment, level of giving to the church, church attendance, and other areas of conduct. These may be presented to the new convert or applicant and a signed agreement required before they are allowed to become a member of the church. Or the church member may be trained in less formal ways to keep religious rules and rituals after joining the church.

The attempt to produce holiness by establishing rules and causing others to keep them is the same approach used by the Pharisees in the early centuries. The Pharisees were generally esteemed to be most holy people, especially among themselves.

Jesus made it clear that this attempt at holiness would not enter the kingdom. The righteousness of trying hard to keep laws, rules, and rituals is not good enough to enter the, now at hand, kingdom of heaven age. Kingdom holiness must exceed even the best attempts to keep religious rules.

Mat 5:20: ***For I say to you, that unless your righteousness exceeds the righteousness of the scribes and Pharisees, you will by no means enter the kingdom of heaven.***

Another church age view proffers that we can never live holy lives in the reality of the practical world now. And that we are all sinners and sin every day by continuously coming short of the mark. But that we are positionally holy and righteous before God by faith in the cross of Christ Jesus. Usually, the belief is included that Christians will be able to live in practical holiness after the bodily return of Christ Jesus to defeat the devil and establish His kingdom.

In this view, the Christian is relieved of the responsibility of participating in the defeat of the enemy and the establishing of the kingdom of God on earth now. Also, in this view, practical holiness must wait for the bodily return of Jesus.

Neither of these views from the passing church age are potent to overcome evil and produce practical holiness in this life now. Form, ritual, and religious conformity may feel comfortable and assuring to the participant, but true holiness will not result from forms, rituals, and attempting to conform to religious codes of conduct.

Similarly, the belief that practical holiness is not a viable potential for life today, does not lead to practical holiness now. Believing in only positional righteousness causes a release of responsibility for real and practical holiness now. This also may feel secure and peaceful. Yet, it is dangerous and will not produce true holiness in life now.

Holiness is a matter of the heart
and requires a power greater than human effort.

Only the Holy One can produce true kingdom of God holiness. There is only One who is holy and therefore only One who can produce holiness. Jesus said that there is only One who is good.

*Mark 10:18: So Jesus said to him, **"Why do you call Me good? No one is good but One, that is, God.***

Jesus lived a perfectly holy life. He and He alone lived a life of true and complete holiness. Jesus did the works that He did by the power of the Holy Spirit. Jesus was led by, and empowered by the Holy Spirit.

*Luke 4:1: **Jesus, being filled with the Holy Spirit**, returned from the Jordan and **was led by the Spirit** into the wilderness, .*
*Luke 4:14: Then Jesus returned **in the power of the Spirit** to Galilee, and news of Him went out through all the surrounding region.*

Believers will only walk in holiness by the power of the Holy One, Jesus, bringing forth the power of the One who raised Christ Jesus from the dead, the One who empowered Jesus and the first century apostles, and the One who now empowers believers to live holy powerful lives. The indwelling Spirit of Christ brings redemption which clears the channel for the Spirit of God to flow freely into the believers life, producing true holiness. Power is required to live righteously.
The same power that heals the sick, cast out demons, and preforms miracles is the power that produces holiness.

*Rom 15:18-19a: For I will not dare to speak of any of those things which **Christ** has not **accomplished through me**, in word and deed, to make the Gentiles obedient; **in mighty signs and wonders, by the power of the Spirit of God.***

*1 Cor 6:11: And such were some of you. But you were washed, but you were **sanctified**, but you were justified **in the name of the Lord Jesus** and **by the Spirit of our God.***

Christ Jesus was:
- born of the Holy Spirit,
- led by the Holy Spirit,
- empowered by the Holy Spirit,
- resurrected by the Holy Spirit,
- and now lives in you and me by the Holy Spirit to produce the power of holiness.

*Luke 1:35: And the angel answered and said to her, "The **Holy Spirit will come upon you, and the power of the Highest will overshadow you**; therefore, also, **that Holy One who is to be born will be called the Son of God.***

*Rom 8:9-11: But you are not in the flesh but in the Spirit, if indeed the **Spirit of God dwells in you**. Now if anyone does not have the **Spirit of Christ**, he is not His.*

*And if **Christ is in you**, the body is dead because of sin, but the **Spirit is life** because of righteousness.*

But if the Spirit of Him who raised Jesus from the dead dwells in you, He who raised Christ from the dead will also give life to your mortal bodies through His Spirit who dwells in you.

It is the Spirit of Father God who raised Christ Jesus from the dead and now lives in believers to produce His holiness within us.

*Gal 1:1: Paul, an apostle (not from men nor through man, but through **Jesus Christ and God the Father who raised Him from the dead**).*

Holiness and power is only by the grace of God. The Greek word translated "grace" means the work of God within the heart and the outworking of that into the life. Some perverted definitions of grace were prevalent in the church emphasis age which distorted the picture of God living in us to produce true and practical holiness in daily living. Grace was generally seen as a covering for sin rather than a cleansing from sin by the gift of the power of God within.

Grace is cleansing from sin, not just a covering for sin.

The "Strongs Concordance and Greek Dictionary" defines "charis", the Greek word translated "grace", as follows:
G5485. charis, khar'-ece; from G5463; graciousness (as gratifying), of manner or act (abstr. or concr.; lit., fig. or spiritual; espec. **the divine influence upon the heart, and its reflection in the life;** including gratitude):--acceptable, benefit, favour, gift, grace (-ious), joy liberality, pleasure, thank (-s, -worthy).

The powerful presence of God within does not just empower one to not do evil things that one desires in his heart to do.

The Holy Spirit of God washes away the evil desires of the heart.

The brightness of the presence of God melts the darkness of evil desire and causes the will of God to be planted and performed in the purified heart. No longer is there a great striving within to

169

overcome various lusts and evil desires. Evil desires are overcome by the presence of God. Holiness includes freedom from the internal conflict.

Paul spoke of the inner conflict, of which he was delivered by Christ Jesus.

Rom 7:15 KJV: For that which I do I allow not: for what I would, that do I not; but what I hate, that do I.

*Rom 7:19-25 KJV: For the good that I would I do not: but the evil which I would not, that I do. Now if I do that I would not, it is no more I that do it, but sin that dwelleth in me. I find then a law, that, when I would do good, evil is present with me. For I delight in the law of God after the inward man: But I see another law in my members, warring against the law of my mind, and bringing me into captivity to the law of sin which is in my members. **O wretched man that I am! Who shall deliver me from the body of this death? I thank God through Jesus Christ our Lord.***

Paul could not attain victory over the inner conflict of sins of the flesh by trying hard to keep rules or rituals. Yet, he did not remain in subjection to the sinful desires of the flesh. He was not doomed to spend his life on earth in inner strife and conflict, sometimes winning and sometimes loosing the battle with the sins of the flesh.

Deliverance is through Jesus Christ our Lord, by the Holy Spirit.

*Gal 5:16-18: I say then: **Walk in the Spirit, and you shall not fulfill the lust of the flesh.** For the flesh lusts against the Spirit, and the Spirit against the flesh; and these are contrary to one another, so that you do not do the things that you wish. But if you are **led by the Spirit**, you are not under the law.*

Holiness is produced by the presence of God.

The great outpourings of the presence and power of God, by the Holy Spirit, in the seventh millennium are bringing forth the reality of practical holiness among believers who come to and remain in the powerful presence of God.

Repentance is quick for the believer in the presence of God. **One's sins are never as dark as when seen in the brightness of the light of the presence of God.**

Willingness and agreement are the part of the believer. The presence of the Holy Spirit convicts of sins and is present to cleanse, but a lack of willingness and agreement can prevent the work of the Holy Spirit from bringing holiness.

If one is not willing to come to the place where the presence of God is being poured out by the Holy Spirit, or if one is not willing to agree with God about one's sin, there may be no holiness imparted into the life. If however, there is willingness and agreement there will be impartation of holiness in the powerful presence of God.

Holy living is not something we do.
It is imparted to us by God.

Abraham believed God and gave Him glory. After carrying out God's instruction, righteousness was imputed to Him. Now in the kingdom age it is possible to remain in the presence of God so that life can become an experience of practical holiness; as righteousness is imputed to the believer by the Holy Spirit through Christ in the presence of God.

*Rom 4:20-24: He did not waver at the promise of God through unbelief, but was **strengthened in faith, giving glory to God,** and being fully convinced that what He had promised He was also able to perform.*

And therefore "it was accounted to him for righteousness."
*Now it was not written for his sake alone that it was **imputed to***
him, but also for us. It shall be imputed to us who believe in Him
who raised up Jesus our Lord from the dead.

If Abraham had not believed God and taken the actions prescribed by God, he would not have had righteousness imputed to
him. If Christians today refuse to fully trust the one who dwells
within them, the One who raised Christ from the dead, and refuse
to come to the places where the outpouring of the Holy Spirit is
taking place they may fail to have holiness imparted to them. They
may not see their sin and repent if they will not come to the places
of manifest presence of God coming forth in the outpouring of the
Holy Spirit.

The good news (gospel) of the kingdom is brought forth only
by the power of the Holy Spirit. A different gospel may be taught
or preached by the understanding of man in the power of the soul
and intellect of man. (Gal 1:6-12) (2 Cor 11:3) The glorious gospel
of the kingdom can only be brought in demonstration of power and
words of Christ Jesus by the Holy Spirit.

Mat 4:23: And Jesus went about all Galilee, teaching in their
*synagogues, **preaching the gospel of the kingdom**, and **healing***
all kinds of sickness and all kinds of disease among the people.

*Mat 10:7-8: And as you go, **preach**, saying, **'The kingdom of***
heaven is at hand.' Heal the sick, cleanse the lepers, raise the
***dead, cast out demons**. Freely you have received, freely give.*

*Mat 12:28: But if I **cast out demons** by the Spirit of God,*
surely the kingdom of God has COME UPON you.

When the gospel of the kingdom "COMES UPON" believers
in power, demons are cast out, sickness is healed, and the dead are

raised. The power of the gospel of the kingdom is the source of holiness in believers who have been "come upon" by the kingdom of God.

If there is no demonstration of the power of God, it is not the gospel of the kingdom and there will not be holiness produced. The vast numbers of miracles, healings, people being set free from bondages, the dead being raised, the blind seeing, the deaf hearing, and many giving their lives to God, being reported around the world are the signs that the kingdom of God has come upon us.

The mighty outpouring of the Holy Spirit is bringing renewal and revival as the gospel is being fully preached and demonstrated again on our small planet. Paul and the other apostles brought forth mighty signs and wonders by the power of the Spirit of God, in the first century, as they "fully preached the gospel".

*Rom 15:18-19: For I will not dare to speak of any of those things which **Christ has** not **accomplished through me, in word and deed,** to make the Gentiles obedient; in **mighty signs and wonders,** by the power of the Spirit of God, so that from Jerusalem and round about to Illyricum **I have fully preached the gospel of Christ.***

Just as Christ Jesus preached, taught, and demonstrated the gospel of the kingdom two thousand years ago, while in His natural body, He is today preaching, teaching, and powerfully demonstrating the same gospel of the kingdom, while in His earthly spiritual body. The purified believers are the body of Christ on earth. *(1 Cor 12:27)* He again lives within us to bring forth the gospel of the kingdom by the Holy Spirit.

In the church emphasis age incomplete versions of the gospel were preached with different emphasis among different groups. The meaning of the Greek word "euaggelion", translated "gospel" in the new Testament, is simply "a good message".

173

Strongs Greek Dictionary:

G2098. euaggelion, yoo-ang-ghel'-ee-on; from the same as G2097; **a good message**, i.e. the gospel:--gospel.

A number of "good messages" (gospels) are mentioned in the Scripture. The gospels of the New Testament are different aspects or parts of the great gospel of the kingdom. Jesus preached the gospel of the kingdom, which included the different "good messages" or gospels referred to by the writers of the New Testament. There is only one complete gospel and it is the gospel of the kingdom which includes all of the gospels of Scripture.

There are many references in Scripture to the gospel of Jesus Christ, or the gospel of Christ, or Christ's gospel. There is also mention of the gospel of God, and the gospel of the grace of God. Paul speaks of "my gospel" referring to what he preached. He also spoke of the gospel of salvation and the gospel of peace.

The gospel of being born again is one of the parts of the gospel of the kingdom, which was preached by many in the church age. The first step in coming to God is to be born of the Spirit. That is to give one's life to God and receive the Spirit of Christ. There can be no walk in the kingdom of God lifestyle now, and no hope of heaven after death, for the one who has not been born again.

This is obviously a primary part of the gospel. Yet, it is only a part of the greater gospel of the kingdom, and by itself, does not produce practical holiness in daily living. It is the beginning and the seed for growth into holy living.

The fullness of the gospel of the kingdom must be powerfully preached and demonstrated to produce holy people, living holy lives. As the Holy One lives within and empowers the person to live a holy life, true holiness is manifest into our world. The gospel of the kingdom is changing lives and our world as the great outpouring of the Holy Spirit "comes upon" believers, in renewals and revivals in places around the world.

Holiness is the presence of God.

Holy is defined as "having a **spiritually pure quality, referring to the divine, that which has its sanctity directly from God or is connected with Him**." To seek to be holy means to seek to become soaked or saturated in the presence of God. The baptism of the Holy Spirit means to be soaked, to be completely immersed into the Spirit of God.

Mark 1:7-8: And he preached, saying, "There comes One after me who is mightier than I, whose sandal strap I am not worthy to stoop down and loose. "I indeed baptized you with water, but **He will baptize you with the Holy Spirit.**"

Mark 16:15-18: And He said to them, "Go into all the world and preach the gospel (the gospel of the kingdom) *to every creature. He who believes and is* **baptized** (baptism of the Holy Spirit, by Jesus) *will be* **saved** (delivered, protected, healed, preserved, made whole); *but he who does not believe will be condemned."*

"And these **signs** *will follow those who believe: In My name they will* **cast out demons***; they will* **speak with new tongues***; they will* **take up serpents***; and if they drink anything deadly,* **it will by no means hurt them***; they will* **lay hands on the sick,** *and they will recover."*

Water baptism is a symbol. Spirit baptism is the powerful reality of being immersed into the Spirit of God. There is no power for holy living, no power for effective ministry to change lives and change the world apart from the baptism into the Spirit of God.

Show me your holiness without the Spirit of God and I will show you your deception, powerlessness, and ineffective religious works.

Show me the awesome manifestations of the power of God, and I will show you the mighty gospel of the kingdom of God, from heaven, being preached and brought forth by the Holy Spirit, to cause the kingdoms of this world to become the kingdoms of our God!

If our ministry is difficult and too hard for us, we are not preaching the gospel of the kingdom in the power of the Holy Spirit. Yes, serious adversity will attempt to overcome us at times. Yet, the awesome power of God will come forth as we continue to believe and faithfully preach the kingdom of God by the power of the Holy Spirit. We must be faithful and obedient to hear and obey the Spirit of God, as He leads us to places of His presence and holiness.

BASILEIA LETTER
Number 14

The Changing Church
In The Kingdom of God

Jesus said to the sick man at the pool of Bethesda, **"Do you want to be made well?"** The Greek word translated "well" is "hugies, hoog-ee-ace" and means to be healthy, sound, or whole.

John 5:5-6: Now a certain man was there who had an infirmity thirty-eight years. When Jesus saw him lying there, and knew that he already had been in that condition a long time, He said to him, "Do you want to be made well?"

As I was reading John 5:1-15, God spoke in my spirit and said, "This is a picture of my church without anointing." He caused me to see the church without anointing as a still pool in contrast to the mighty river of the anointed church flowing the power of God by the Holy Spirit.

In the emerging kingdom emphasis age, many churches of the past are being found to be not well, unsound, and in need of wholeness.

As the powerful anointing of Christ brings forth the power of God to save, heal, deliver, and demonstrate the gospel of the kingdom in mighty miracle working power, some impotent churches are being asked the same question that the sick man at the pool of Bethesda was asked, "Do you want to be made well"?

John 5:1-3: After this there was a feast of the Jews, and Jesus went up to Jerusalem. Now there is in Jerusalem by the Sheep Gate a pool, which is called in Hebrew, Bethesda, having five porches. In these lay a great multitude of sick people, blind, lame, paralyzed, waiting for the moving of the water.

Has it not been in the past and does it not continue, that in much of the powerless church, the religious leaders keep the feast of religious ceremonies while a great multitude of sick people lay waiting for the moving of the water?

A multitude of spiritually and physically blind, lame, and paralyzed people fill some churches. Many Christians are in desperate need of the reality of the power of God to heal them and make them sound, well, and whole, to form them into powerful men and women of God, free of the infirmities caused by sin and religion.

The still pool is referred to as "by the sheep gate" in the NKJV and "by the sheep market" in the KJV. These phrases are translated from the Greek word "probatikos, prob-at-ik-os", and means "relating to sheep". Apparently this pool relates to the merchandising of sheep.

Throughout the ages, some religious leaders have made merchandise of God's sheep. Shepherds that should have been feeding and healing the sheep have often fed themselves and failed to bring the river of healing and strengthening to the needy sheep.

Men with power and position of religious structure have often used and abused the sheep. Those who should be strengthened with spiritual food and healed with the power of faith in God, have often been left by the pool while the leaders and religious people feasted at religious ceremonies.

Ezek 34:2-4: Son of man, prophesy against the shepherds of Israel, prophesy and say to them, "Thus says the Lord GOD to the shepherds: Woe to the shepherds of Israel who feed themselves! Should not the shepherds feed the flocks?"

"You eat the fat and clothe yourselves with the wool; you slaughter the fatlings, but you do not feed the flock."

"The weak you have not strengthened, nor have you healed those who were sick, nor bound up the broken, nor brought back what was driven away, nor sought what was lost; but with force and cruelty you have ruled them."

Five porches had been built around the pool of still water, in which only occasionally there was a little movement of the water and someone was healed. Probably, only one porch was initially built and as the multitude of needy people increased, others were built. Have we not built great buildings around a pool of very little power and only an occasional stirring of the water, in the past church age?

I don't know what the porches at Bethesda looked like, but according to the definitions of the Greek wording, they may have had columns of stone supporting a roof. This was a substantial structure that provided for the sick to come each day and lay to wait for the moving of the water or wait to die. Probably, many died and were carried away from the porches to be buried. Is it not true that many have suffered needlessly and died prematurely on our grand porches around our powerless pools?

Whether we like to admit it or not this is a part of the heritage of the church that goes back to the medieval church of the dark ages. Is it possible that some of these ways and patterns have found a hidden place in us? Is it possible that we may have a wrong focus through a heritage of religion and erroneous training? Are we perhaps more concerned with our personal well being and church position than we think we are?

Is it possible that we might not be quick to do anything that might harm our reputation in the arena of church politics?

Is it possible that some of us may have become locked into the doctrines of powerlessness from the still pool of religion and are not aware of it?

The question is to us as it was to the man who had an infirmity for a long time, **"Do you want to be made well"?**

Are we willing to cast off the systems of man made doctrines and religion from the past to take a chance on moving into rivers of flowing, rushing, living water? Are we willing to take a chance on displeasing the ones over us in our religious structure by departing from the traditional still pool of religious theology?

John 5:7: The sick man answered Him, "Sir, I have no man to put me into the pool when the water is stirred up; but while I am coming, another steps down before me."

"I HAVE NO MAN", was the answer to the question. Are not the multitudes of sick sheep around the world crying out today for a man --- a man that will come upon their pitiful scene of sick people on grand porches around powerless pools and do something about it?

God is looking for a man to rise upon the earth -- a man who will make a difference. Jesus Christ is that man. When Jesus showed up at the pool of Bethesda everything began to change.

Today when Jesus shows up and the mighty presence of God is brought forth by the Holy Spirit everything changes. The spiritually and physically sick and afflicted meet the mighty river of God and are healed, set free, and empowered to live holy lives.

God has His Man and He is brought forth from a woman -- the wife of God. It is the purified holy Bride of Christ who is collectively becoming the Body of Christ, the manifestation of Christ Jesus into the world to change the church and the world -- to bring forth the rule and dominion of God -- the kingdom of God on earth.

180

Jesus Christ in His universal body on earth will stand and speak with power just as He did to the sick man at the pool, "Arise, and pick up your bed off the porch by the powerless pool and walk"--- walk in spiritual power and health in the anointing of God.

Have we made our bed on the grand porches by the powerless pool of religion without the movement and flow of the Spirit of God? It is now time for us to meet the power of God and be made whole, and then pick up our bed and walk---walk to the river of God.

John 5:8-9: Jesus said to him, "Rise, take up your bed and walk." And immediately the man was made well, took up his bed, and walked. And that day was the Sabbath.

"Do you want to be made well"? At first glance it seems the answer to this question would be obvious. Who would not want to be made well? Yet, as we read further we realize there may be a price to be paid after being made well. The religious structure is not always pleased when Jesus shows up and miracles take place. Certainly it is difficult for them to find fault with the sick being healed. It is easier to find fault and make a big issue of how or when it was done.

Great revivals of the past have been squelched by religious leaders arguing over doctrines, forms, and practices. Today mighty outpourings of God are producing multitudes of people giving their lives to God, miraculous healings, and deliverance from every form of bondage.

Yet, these outpourings and those working in them are highly criticized by some in the religious community. Like the Jews who criticized the man who was cured, they can only accuse those involved of not doing it the right way.

John 5:10-12: The Jews therefore said to him who was cured, "It is the Sabbath; it is not lawful for you to carry your bed." He answered them, "He who made me well said to me, 'Take up your bed and walk.'" Then they asked him, "Who is the Man who said to you, 'Take up your bed and walk'?"

One possible reason for not wanting to be made well is that it may cost loss of favor with those who remain at the still pool. Another reason might be that some do not know how sick they are. The enemy wants us to believe that what we have is all there is for us. He does not want us to know of the river of God flowing from the throne of God.

Rivers of living water of the Spirit of God are flowing into our world from the hearts of purified believers. The anointing of the anointed one (Christ Jesus) within believers is flowing the life, love, and power of God by His Spirit into the changing church. A corporate anointing of Christ is present as unified believers come together in praise, prayer, and worship.

*John 7:38 -39a: "He who believes in Me, as the Scripture has said, **out of his heart will flow rivers of living water**." But this He spoke concerning the Spirit, whom those believing in Him would receive.*

*Psa 36:7-9: How precious is Your lovingkindness, O God! Therefore the children of men put their trust under the shadow of Your wings. They are abundantly satisfied with the fullness of Your house, **And You give them drink from the river of Your pleasures. For with You is the fountain of life;** In Your light we see light.*

Rev 22:1: And he showed me a pure river of water of life, clear as crystal, proceeding from the throne of God and of the Lamb.

Jesus spoke of the living water in the conversation with the woman at the well. He spoke these words to her, "If you knew the gift of God". If religious men today knew the gift of God, the powerful water of life of the Spirit, and who Jesus is by the Spirit in His body today, they would surely want to be made well.

*John 4:10-14: Jesus answered and said to her, "**If you knew the gift of God**, and who it is who says to you, 'Give Me a drink,' you would have asked Him, and He would have given you living water."*

*"Whoever drinks of this water will thirst again, but whoever drinks of the water that I shall give him will never thirst. **But the water that I shall give him will become in him a fountain of water springing up into everlasting life.**"*

The flow of the river of life of the Spirit of God flowing from individuals together in unity combines to produce the mighty river of spiritual power and anointing that is changing individuals, churches, and our world.

In the passing church age a few "mighty men of God" were expected to flow the river of life for the multitudes. In the emerging kingdom age it is the power of the Spirit of God flowing through all of His people.

Not only were the sheep merchandised in past centuries but in more recent times the gifts of the Spirit have also been merchandised. Gifted men used their gifts to establish profitable ministries and positions.

When Jesus shows up things are different. Notice that after he cured the sick man He simply withdrew into the multitude. He did not attempt to gain anything from the working of the miracles. It was important that he give the healed man a final message so he looked him up later and gave him this important instruction for his life: *"Sin no more, lest a worse thing come upon you."*

John 5:13-14: But the one who was healed did not know who it was, for Jesus had withdrawn, a multitude being in that place. Afterward Jesus found him in the temple, and said to him, "See, you have been made well. Sin no more, lest a worse thing come upon you."

In another passage Jesus said the temple was to be a house of prayer but merchandisers had made it a den of thieves. Probably all of us have either preached or heard good sermons on the cleansing of the temple. And probably inwardly shouted a cheer for Jesus as we imagined Him disrupting the work of the merchandisers and expelling them from the temple.

Is it possible that while we cheered the work of Jesus, we ourselves have been subversively exposed to a system of practices that may have infected us to some degree with the perverted practices of the merchandisers without realizing it?

Is it possible that the increased presence of God coming forth in the temple of our lives and our churches is exposing deeply ingrained practices that may be tainted with the merchandising practices of the past?

Is it time for us to allow the increased light of the presence of God coming forth today, to brightly illumine and search our motives and methods? Or should we continue to reproduce the practices and patterns of the passing age into the emerging kingdom age?

It is time for change, just as it was time for change when Jesus arrived at the temple in Jerusalem. Obviously, Jesus had been there before. Surely, he had seen the tables of the merchandisers before. Yet, He had done nothing about them.

Why was this day the time for Him to take action against a long existing perversion in the house of God? What set the stage for the Son of God to come forth in power and bring powerful correction to the house of God on this day?

The worship and praise of the people released the power of the Lord.

Never before had palm branches and clothing been laid before him. Never before had He been received by the multitudes as "He who comes in the name of the Lord." Never before had acts of worship and shouts of praise for Jesus moved the entire city. Never before had Jesus been given the authority of the people to make these changes in the house of God. **Isn't this a lot like today? It Is Time!**

Today multitudes are worshiping and shouting out praises to God as the presence of God comes forth in the very midst of congregations around the world. The powerful presence of the Holy Spirit is bringing forth the awesome presence of the Lord in power to change us, to change our church, our city, and eventually our world.

Mat 21:8-13: And a very great multitude spread their clothes on the road; others cut down branches from the trees and spread them on the road. Then the multitudes who went before and those who followed cried out, saying: "Hosanna to the Son of David! Blessed is He who comes in the name of the LORD! Hosanna in the highest!" And when He had come into Jerusalem, all the city was moved, saying, "Who is this?" So the multitudes said, "This is Jesus, the prophet from Nazareth of Galilee."

Then Jesus went into the temple of God and drove out all those who bought and sold in the temple, and overturned the tables of the money changers and the seats of those who sold doves. And He said to them, "It is written, 'My house shall be called a house of prayer,' but you have made it a 'den of thieves.'"

The charismatic movement of the recent past came forth in the latter years of the church age emphasis of great mercy. Centuries of "still pool" religion began closing and a new season of stirring of the water began with a great move of spiritual gifts released upon ministers and congregations.

During the charismatic movement, the gifts of God without repentance were poured out upon flesh. The Holy Spirit was sometimes poured out upon spiritual children (those without maturity). Great miracles of healing, prophesy, words of knowledge, and even words of wisdom came forth from spiritually immature men and women.

Many of the gifted yet immature Christians became leaders who set the patterns of practice for the church. These patterns sometimes included merchandising the gifts and many became wealthy through selling the gifts of God.

Please do not miss understand what I am saying. God is not against our prosperity and purity in every area of life. Always having enough to complete God's plans for us is the kingdom way. Things will be added as we seek the kingdom of God and His righteousness first. Yet, did not Jesus say, "Freely you have received, freely give"?

Mat 10:8: Heal the sick, cleanse the lepers, raise the dead, cast out demons. **Freely you have received, freely give.**

New patterns--- kingdom of God patterns of maturity and purity are coming forth today. The stirring of the water of the charismatic error was great, but the mighty river of God that will change our world must flow through clean vessels. As people of God reach spiritual maturity and die to their self ways, the Spirit of Christ the King is manifesting through the Spirit of Him who raised Christ Jesus from the dead. (Rom 8:11)

The Spirit of the resurrected Christ is overtaking our religion and bringing forth the river of God to wash away our defilement and bring life giving nourishment and healing to God's people. The church is now becoming less "churchy", and much more alive.

It is time for the glorious Christ to be formed in His glorified Body on earth. **We are only beginning to experience what it really means to be the Body of Christ on earth.**

We may need to consider our ways. Is it possible that to some degree we have merchandised God's goods--- sold ourselves first, then the gifts He has given us, and the people he has given to us?

Is this possibly the reason our "still pool" is not moving? Is the church spiritually languishing while we take care of our own houses? Have we perhaps worked hard but with a mixed motive and reaped very little spiritual movement as a result?

Hag 1:4-8: "Is it time for you yourselves to dwell in your paneled houses, and this temple to lie in ruins?" Now therefore, thus says the LORD of hosts: "Consider your ways!"

"You have sown much, and bring in little; You eat, but do not have enough; You drink, but you are not filled with drink; You clothe yourselves, but no one is warm; And he who earns wages, Earns wages to put into a bag with holes." Thus says the LORD of hosts: "Consider your ways!"

"Go up to the mountains and bring wood and build the temple, that I may take pleasure in it and be glorified," says the LORD.

After answering the question "Do you want to be made well?" with an absolute, and unqualified YES, we must go up to the mountains--- to the high places with God. We must look up--- look higher to the mountains from which our help comes. Only on the spiritual mountain of God will we find the material to build the temple of God in which He will take pleasure and be glorified. *(Isa 2:3, Micah 4:2, Heb12:22-25)*

Psa 121:1: I will lift up my eyes to the hills; From whence comes my help?

Only clean hands and a pure heart can come to the high places of God and stand in His holy place of ministering the river of the Spirit of God's miracle working power to cleanse, heal, deliver, and make whole.

Psa 24:3-4a: Who may ascend into the hill of the LORD? Or who may stand in His holy place? He who has clean hands and a pure heart...

In a very practical sense we must draw nearer to God and He will draw near to us. Our focus must change from religious systems and trying to meet needs, to intimate worship and communion with Christ.

We can never cause the river to flow from us by trying to make it flow. The flow of the Spirit of God cannot be pumped, it must spring up from God Himself. We must come to Him without the religious framework of the past and seek Him with our whole heart at any and all cost.

James 4:8: Draw near to God and He will draw near to you. Cleanse your hands, you sinners; and purify your hearts, you double-minded.

It is once again time to press in--- time to press into God--- taking our eyes off everything else until we are with Him in the fullness of His presence. It is time to come together and praise Him full out--- worship Him with all we have--- and pray fervently. It is time to call upon Him for the outpouring of living water to flow upon us and from us--- time to cry out for the river of God to flood our families, churches, and cities with His glory.

The river of God flows from the combined water springing up from many hearts. All those gathered together must be in unity of the Spirit. All the disciples gathered in the upper room at Pentecost were in one accord when the mighty rushing wind of the Spirit of God came from heaven upon them. *(Acts 2:1-2)*

All the people marched around Jericho together in complete silence until the appointed time and then they all shouted together at one time *(Josh 6)*. The whole world was not in unity but all who were present were in one accord.

We will not enter into the river of God as a group until all present are in one accord. There will in no wise enter in anything that defiles. (Rev 21:27) The New Jerusalem -- the purified Bride of Christ will not be entered by those in discord with the Spirit and flow of God.

Only as all present put their focus on the Lord and seek Him with their whole heart can we come into unity. We cannot focus on religion, doctrine, or worldly things and move into unity. We must focus on Christ and in the power of the Spirit, seek His presence.

We are changed in His presence.

BASILEIA LETTER
Number 15

The Secret Place
In The Kingdom of God

Psa 91:1: He who dwells in the secret place of the Most High Shall abide under the shadow of the Almighty.

The word translated *"secret place"* is the Hebrew word "cether" (say'-ther) and has the meaning of a covering, covert, disguise, private, secret, protection, hiding place. It is almost always translated "hide" or "hid".

Where is the *secret place*? What does the *secret place* mean to me?

Today in some parts of our world, Christians are persecuted and martyred for their faith. In addition to persecution Christians are attacked by sickness and disease. It is very obvious to anyone with open eyes that there are severe problems encountered by many servants of the Lord. Is there really a *secret place* of protection under the shadow of the Almighty--- a refuge from the disorders of our world?

The first century apostles endured severe persecution. Were they unable to find the *secret place*, and therefore persecuted and martyred? Did they in some way miss Psalm 91 and its promises of protection under the shadow of the Almighty? I don't think so!

Obviously the *secret place* is not in a certain geographic location. Indeed, there are places where Christians can find refuge from persecution, but the *secret place* will not be found in a specific geographic location. **The *secret place* is in the Lord.** We can be sheltered and protected in the Lord.

*Psa 91:1-9: He who dwells in the **secret place** of the Most High Shall abide under the shadow of the Almighty.*

I will say of the LORD, "He is my refuge and my fortress; My God, in Him I will trust."

Surely He shall deliver you from the snare of the fowler And from the perilous pestilence.

He shall cover you with His feathers, And under His wings you shall take refuge; His truth shall be your shield and buckler.

***You shall not be afraid** of the terror by night, Nor of the arrow that flies by day, Nor of the pestilence that walks in darkness, Nor of the destruction that lays waste at noonday.*

*A thousand may fall at your side, And ten thousand at your right hand; But it shall not come near you. Only with your eyes shall you look, And see the **reward of the wicked**.*

***Because you have made the LORD**, who is my refuge, Even the Most High, **your dwelling place**.*

Obviously there are many questions and many facets to the answers to these questions. Yet the Word of God is true and Jesus (the Word from God) is truth. (John *1)* He is the way, the truth, and the life. (*John 14:6)* The Word was made flesh and is yet being made flesh as the indwelling Spirit of Christ lives in believers by the Holy Spirit.

Yet, there continues to be great warfare in the world for the souls of mankind. There is yet a generous abundance of sinful and prideful people in our world, including some who claim to be Christians. Where there is sin and pride there is a lack of faith, understanding, and victory in life.

Mankind is still very much in a process of finding out who we are in Christ Jesus. Therefore, much sin, sickness, disease, and premature death is prevalent in our world. Even many who try to do all they know, live in lack of victory. Christians who do not

191

know who they really are in Christ--- who do not know what He has done, and is doing, to bring the overcoming kingdom of God lifestyle into their lives will experience a lack of victory. They do not know how to appropriate the work of Christ into their own lives, nor how to warfare for others.

Knowledge of who we are in Christ will be revealed in the *secret place* of intimacy with our Lord. Victory over every circumstance in life is only possible as we come into intimacy with Christ. Only in His close presence with our ear pressed to His chest can we hear His heart beat and receive ultimate knowledge from Him. However, if there is impurity in our hearts and lives, our iniquity will prevent us from coming into the *secret place* of intimacy, and rob us of victory.

*Rom 10:2: For I bear them witness that they have a zeal for God, but not according to **knowledge**.*

*Job 36:8-12: And if they are bound in fetters, **Held in the cords of affliction**, Then He tells them **their work and their transgressions**; That they have **acted defiantly**. He also opens their ear to instruction, And commands that they **turn from iniquity**.*

*If they obey and serve Him, They shall spend their days in prosperity, And their years in pleasures. But if they do not obey, They shall perish by the sword, **And they shall die without knowledge**.*

Sin is at the core of all sickness, disease, and premature death in our world. **This is not to say that every individual person who is afflicted or persecuted is to blame for their own situation. It is a much bigger and more complex picture than that** . Sin entered through Adam and passed to all mankind. Had there been no sin there would have been no sickness, no disease, and no death. Jesus came to redeem mankind and our world from sin and the curse of sin. *(Rom 5:12-19)*

The knowledge of Christ and who we really are in Him can only be imparted by the Spirit. Only in the presence of God can we come to the realization of the awesome work and power of God available to redeem our world. We must come into the *secret place* of **intimate communion** with God to find the hiding place of protection and the power for victory to overcome evil in our world. We must **KNOW** Him in a deeper greater more intimate way than our past religion has taught us.

To bear the fruit of overcoming and living victoriously in the world we must intimately, closely, and continuously abide in Him. Our dwelling place must be with Him. Psalm 91:1, did not say whoever **visits** the secret place of the most high shall abide in the shadow (protection) of the Almighty. Jesus did not say whoever **visits** me occasionally, or even often, will bear the fruit of a victorious life.

Jesus said, *John 15:4: "**Abide** in Me, and I in you. As the branch cannot bear fruit of itself, unless it abides in the vine, neither can you, unless you **abide in Me**.*

*John 15:5: "I am the vine, you are the branches. **He who abides in Me, and I in him**, bears much fruit; for without Me you can do nothing.*

*John 15:11: "These things I have spoken to you, that **My joy may remain in you, and that your joy may be full.***

It is God's plan for His children to walk in full joy. It is His desire that the joy of the Lord remain in us through our abiding in Christ Jesus and He in us. The joy of the Lord in us does not depend on our circumstances.

Our joy depends on the presence of Christ
within us by the Holy Spirit.

193

Psa 31:19 Oh, how great is Your goodness, Which You have laid up for those who fear You, Which You have prepared for those who trust in You In the presence of the sons of men!

*Psa 31:20 **You shall hide them in the secret place of Your presence** From the plots of man; You shall keep them secretly in a pavilion From the strife of tongues.*

This may not make sense to our understanding of our circumstances. The presence and peace of God goes beyond the things of circumstances and understanding.

*Phil 4:6-9: Be anxious for nothing, but in everything by prayer and supplication, **with thanksgiving**, let your requests be made known to God; **and the peace of God, which surpasses all understanding, will guard your hearts and minds through Christ Jesus**.*

*Finally, brethren, whatever things are true, whatever things are noble, whatever things are just, whatever things are pure, whatever things are lovely, whatever things are of good report, if there is any virtue and if there is anything praiseworthy; **meditate on these things**.*

*The things which you **learned** and **received** and heard and saw in me, these do, and the **God of peace will be with you**.*

Paul knew how to abide in the *secret place* of peace in God whether circumstances seemed uplifting or whether things seemed downcast. He had learned to remain in that *secret place* when he was stoned and run out of town by the religious crowd, or when many were coming to the Lord and miracles were flowing through his ministry. Whether he was in warm fellowship with close friends, or was in a cold prison, he could know the presence and peace of God.

*Phil 4:11-13: Not that I speak in regard to need, **for I have learned in whatever state I am, to be content:** I know how to be abased, and I know how to abound. **Everywhere and in all things I have learned both to be full and to be hungry, both to abound and to suffer need. I can do all things through Christ who strengthens me.***

Personal well being is not the first priority of servants of God. Paul and every mature disciple of Christ, every sent one of God, knows that they are here to make a difference. We are sent to bring change in our world through Christ. First in the hearts of people and then our world.

As individuals multiply into multitudes walking in the Spirit and meditating the things of God, conditions and circumstances are changed in our world. The time in which we live is a time of major transition from the ways of fallen man ruling our world to the ways of God.

The transition began two thousand years ago as Christ Jesus proclaimed the kingdom of God way of life. Jesus paid the price for redemption of mankind and our world. And afterward, ascended to the right hand of the Father. The early apostles of the Lamb were then kept by the Comforter, the Helper, the Holy Spirit.

They were able to find the peace and protection of the *secret place* in the presence of God by the Holy Spirit. They brought forth and planted the seeds of the kingdom of God which have sprouted and grown through the years. We are partakers of the maturing growth of the kingdom of God.

Obviously, there has been many ups and downs. It has not been and will not be a smooth transition. Resistance from ungodly people, both heathen and religious, inflamed by the evil one who desires his kingdom to rule the earth, has brought many adverse and detrimental circumstances upon the people of God. While the transition is taking place there is a *secret place* of protection for the soul of those who continue to be used of God to bring forth His kingdom.

As kingdom warriors, we will be persecuted, and as many before us we may suffer and pay the supreme price --- the loss of our lives. Yet, we will never be touched by the devastating fear and destructive plagues of the enemy. We may pass from this life. We may be a casualty in the war. Yet, **we will never die.** We will only pass from LIFE unto LIFE. Whether we live or die we shall forever be in the presence of the Lord. (Rom 14:8) (2 Cor 5:8) In the *secret place*, we will live in victory over all fear of pestilence and destruction now. And when we pass from this life, we shall forever remain with Him in the *secret place* of His presence.

Psa 91:5-9 **You shall not be afraid** *of the* **terror** *by night, Nor of the* **arrow** *that flies by day, Nor of the* **pestilence** *that walks in darkness, Nor of the* **destruction** *that lays waste at noonday. A thousand may fall at your side, And ten thousand at your right hand;* **But it shall not come near you.** *Only with your eyes shall you look, And see the* **reward of the wicked.** **Because you have made the LORD,** *who is my refuge, Even the Most High,* **your dwelling place.**

There is more in the *secret place* **than peace and protection. In the secret place we receive impartation and instruction from God.**

Psa 32:7 You are my hiding place; You shall preserve me from trouble; You shall surround me with songs of deliverance. Selah

Psa 32:8 **I will instruct you and teach you in the way you should go;** *I will guide you with My eye.*

Yes, there is comfort and peace apart from our circumstances now. But there is more.--- Direction and power are released by the Holy Spirit to carry out our part in bringing forth the kingdom of God in our world.--- **His power and knowledge are changing our circumstances**.

The circumstances of our world are changing. The great men of faith of the past have not given their lives in vain. We have not given our lives in vain. We have become a part of the chain of people of God bringing forth the kingdom of God in the world. The awesome **love** of God shall rule the world as it rules our lives from within. The kingdoms of this world are becoming the kingdoms of our God as love empowers people of God to give their lives that others may come to the kingdom of God lifestyle in this life.

John 15:12-13: "This is My commandment, that you love one another as I have loved you. "Greater love has no one than this, than to lay down one's life for his friends.

Jesus clearly warned His disciples of the things they would face as He went to the Father. He also told them it was best that He leave them because the great "parakletos"(par-ak'-lay-tos) "intercessor, consoler:--advocate, comforter" would not come until He went to the Father.

John 15:26-27: "But when the Helper comes, whom I shall send to you from the Father, the Spirit of truth who proceeds from the Father, He will testify of Me. And you also will bear witness, because you have been with Me from the beginning."

John 16:1-7: "These things I have spoken to you, that you should not be made to stumble. "They will put you out of the synagogues; yes, the time is coming that whoever kills you will think that he offers God service. *"And these things they will do to you because they have not known the Father nor Me."*

"But these things I have told you, that when the time comes, you may remember that I told you of them. And these things I did not say to you at the beginning, because I was with you. "But now I go away to Him who sent Me, and none of you asks Me, 'Where are You going?' "But because I have said these things to you, sorrow has filled your heart."

*"Nevertheless I tell you the truth. It is to **your advantage** that I go away; for if I do not go away, the Helper will not come to you; but if I depart, I will send Him to you."*

It was a wonderful thing for the disciples to be with Jesus when He was here on earth in His natural body. It was not easy for the disciples to see Him go back to the Father. Yet, Jesus said it would be better for them than before. It was to their advantage for Him to go.

Today many long for His presence and think of how wonderful it will be when He bodily returns. Christians sometimes feel that something is missing, that there are things that cannot be fulfilled, victories that cannot be won until He bodily returns. Many wish they could have been there and walked with Him when He was here in His natural body.

We must come to the realization that what we have now is **better** than what the disciples had when they walked with Jesus in His natural body. There is nothing missing on God's part. Everything is in place to bring about the will of the Father, the kingdom of God now. There is nothing lacking on God's part to overcome the enemy and destroy His reign upon the earth.

Christ returned to the first century disciples in the Holy Spirit. They were **endued with power from on High** as the Helper mightily descended upon those who were waiting in the place instructed by the Lord. (Luke 24:49) (Acts 2) The power of God that flowed through Jesus before His ascension then came upon the disciples of Christ. They were changed from observers to **doers of the mighty works of God** to bring change.

Supernaturally God took up residence in the hearts of His people. (1 Cor 3:16) Holy Spirit is God just as much as Jesus or the Father are God. We have only one God manifest in three persons. (Mark 12:29) All of the attributes of the Father and the Son flow through the Holy Spirit. Our Helper is the most powerful, most loving, most wise, most knowledgable of all that exist. There is nothing beyond Him. He is the creator and the One who sustains all that exist. He is above all. All creation is subject to Him.

Jesus said, I and my Father are one. (John 10:30) And He said, **We** will make our home with those who love Me. (Rom 8:9-11) (Col 1:27)

*John 14:17-20: ...the Spirit of truth, whom the world cannot receive, because it neither sees Him nor knows Him; but you know Him, for **He dwells with you and will be in you.***

*I will not leave you orphans; **I will come to you.***

*A little while longer and the world will see Me no more, but you will see Me. **Because I live, you will live** also.*

*At that day you will know that **I am in My Father, and you in Me, and I in you.***

*John 14:23 Jesus answered and said to him, "If anyone loves Me, he will keep My word; and My Father will love him, and **We will come to him and make Our home with him**."*

We can meet with God and walk with Him in the *secret place* as we dwell together with God, NOW.

Christians today often rush about working and ministering seeking to do good. Putting out fires of difficulties of every nature in the lives of others. Seeking to bring the work or word to help suffering people and to bring correction to the rebellious.

Much activity is generated seeking to meet the needs of others. Additional jobs are taken on and extra hours of work put in to try to get things needed for the family. For many it seems difficult to search for the *secret place* amidst all there is to be done.

Yet, the answers we need, the power and guidance that will unlock the resources of heaven to overcome every situation of life, will only be found in the *secret place*. We must meet the Almighty and have His direction and empowerment before seeking to deal with the needs of our world. We must spend time close to Him, if we are going to be anointed (rubbed on) by Him.

Jesus went from one isolated place of prayer and communion with God to another, and released awesome miracles to meet the needs of people in between. Jesus today in us will do the same as He did in His natural body.

The world will not be changed--- the kingdom of God will not be established--- by our running around trying to put our fires. **The fires of hell will be quenched in the lives of believers as we find the *secret place* of power and guidance of God.**

We must find our *secret place* with Him. The first priority of disciples of Christ must be to love God with our whole heart. Only a hypocrite could say they love someone with all they have and yet not spend time in intimacy with the one they profess to love.

The *secret place* is that space in which all the world grows dim and leaves our awareness as we intimately bask in His embrace of love and glory. The comfort of the Holy Spirit in His embrace is awesome and complete. We are totally comforted no matter what our circumstances.

Our whole reason for being becomes to express our love for Him--- to worship Him with deep all consuming love. Our mouths and lives are filled with praise for Him as we exceedingly and amorously admire His glory. Our hearts are melted as He pours the liquid fire of His love upon us.

This out pouring of His love brings a great desire to obey Him--- to serve Him at all cost. The greatest desire of our heart is to please Him--- our only fear is that of disappointing Him. We are motivated to whole heartedly serve Him and carefully obey Him.

The empowerment and wisdom imparted to us in the *secret place* of intimacy with Him will enable us to change the world. Great creative ideas and solutions to unsolvable problems can be imparted into our hearts and understanding. Supernatural powers begin to work to change natural circumstances to cause them to come into alignment with the will of God and the job He has given us to do. Miracles are just God working in ways we cannot explain. Nothing is impossible to the one who believes. (Mark 9:23) And the one in intimate love with God will believe in Him without reservation and limitation.

There remains a season of great beauty as the powerful presence of God changes the people of God and our world. Eventually the perilous persecution will give way to a time when God's people will live in a world filled with the peace of God. All who have escaped with their lives through the time of transition and judgment will be holy--- cleansed of the Lord. The kingdom of God coming forth in our world is worth all the cost.

Isa 4:2-6: In that day the Branch of the LORD shall be beautiful and glorious; And the fruit of the earth shall be excellent and appealing For those of Israel who have escaped.

201

And it shall come to pass that he who is left in Zion and remains in Jerusalem will be called holy; everyone who is recorded among the living in Jerusalem. When the Lord has washed away the filth of the daughters of Zion, and purged the blood of Jerusalem from her midst, by the spirit of judgment and by the spirit of burning,

Then the LORD will create above every dwelling place of Mount Zion, and above her assemblies, a cloud and smoke by day and the shining of a flaming fire by night. For over all the glory there will be a covering. And there will be a tabernacle for shade in the daytime from the heat, for a place of refuge, and for a shelter from storm and rain.

BASILEIA LETTER

Number 16

The Loftiness of Man
And The Kingdom of God

Have you ever experienced the serenity of walking in a beautiful forest of majestic tall trees on a warm sunny day? There is a feeling of security and comfort in the cool shade of the huge trees. One feels at ease and protected by the canopy of giant branches meshing together far overhead. You tend to feel small in the presence of the giant trees, and may have a worshipful respect for the magnificent, stately, ancient trees.

This is how I felt as God recently spoke to me in a powerful prophetic dream. I walked about in the most beautiful oak forest I have ever seen. The trees were huge and over one hundred feet tall. They had magnificent limbs growing this way and that, forming unique patterns high in the trees. The tree trunks were very large and covered with distinctive rough oak bark. The trees were some distance apart but they were so large that they all entwined together forming a beautiful green canopy high overhead.

Beneath the trees, the floor of the forest was open and free of brush. There were no pesky briars or thorny berry vines, no small growth to make walking difficult. I strolled about with ease admiring the awesomeness of the giant magnificent trees. I felt they must be hundreds of years old. There was a sense of strength and personal protection realizing they had stood against the elements with no apparent damage for centuries. Though I could catch small glimpses of bright sun light through the canopy it was wonderfully shady and comfortably cool. There was no concern for heat or sunburn in such a protected environment. It seemed it would be a good place to remain forever and enjoy its comfort and protection.

I was well into the forest when I stopped short. The sound of a rushing strong wind came to my ears. Instantly I looked up toward the north from which the sound came. High above the earth one of the trees was being thrashed about by a strong wind from the north. Suddenly I heard great snapping sounds as the high limbs of the great tree began to break and started falling. Then the giant trunk snapped and the whole tree was crashing toward the earth. I turned quickly to the east and started to run when I saw that the entwined trees were being broken by the first falling tree. The trees were crashing in the east and I could not run in that direction. Instantly I turned to the south and started to run. But again the trees in that direction began to be broken by the others and were falling. By now the sound was horrendous as a great roar of snapping and crashing was everywhere. I turned to the west and it was crumbling as well. As a cloud of thick dust began to rise and fill the air around me, I instinctively ran a few steps and dove to the trunk of one of the great trees. I wrapped myself up against it and nestled up against the huge trunk as the roar of crashing continued and the dust boiled covering the entire scene.

I was unharmed and crawled out after the dust settled through the mass of tangled broken limbs to view a totally new scene. Not one tree, not even a very high trunk, or a very large piece of a tree was left. The entire magnificent forest was only a huge area of broken smashed pieces fit only for fire wood. It was still a bright sunny day with only a few wispy white clouds in the sky but all the sense of protection and comfort no longer existed.

As I awoke from this dream I was very moved and somewhat afraid. I knew beyond any doubt that the dream was a prophetic word from God and could instantly think of many negative fearful possible interpretations. But I am not usually used as a prophet of doom and was afraid to ask God the meaning. I really was not ready to know the full meaning of this dream and waited a day before asking God to reveal the interpretation of the dream to me.

I cautiously approached God with questions like, does this involve religion? I heard "yes", but with a sense that there was more. I asked, "does this involve the economy and political governments"? Again the answer, "yes". Knowing I was now ready God spoke on and said, **"It is the pride and loftiness of man"**.

For many days since this dream I have been consumed with it. Many questions have arisen as I went to the word and continued to seek God's guidance in more fully understanding the meaning of this word. What exactly is the pride and loftiness of man that has stood majestically for centuries and is now coming down? Why were trees used to represent the loftiness of man as opposed to great cities or tall buildings etc.? How does this relate to the glorious revival and the establishment of God's kingdom on earth now? When is this great crashing fall, which takes away the sense of security and comfort of many people?

*Isa 2:17-18: The **loftiness of man** shall be bowed down, And the haughtiness of men shall be brought low; The LORD alone will be exalted in that day, But the idols He shall utterly abolish.*

The loftiness of man makes a great covering for evil works of spiritual harlotry and adultery. Under the canopy of the lofty pride of men and their mighty works is a comfortable place for sin and evil works to prevail.

*Hosea 4:13: They offer sacrifices on the mountaintops, And burn incense on the hills, Under **oaks**, poplars, and terebinths, **Because their shade is good**. Therefore your daughters commit harlotry, And your brides commit adultery.*

Now is the time of great transition from the ways of fallen man to the ways of the kingdom of our God. The lofty pride of mankind is being exposed and soon will be brought down to nothing. The greatest crash ever is eminent as the prideful works of man come crashing down that the works of God's kingdom may flow through humble men and be established upon the earth. The lofty works of man in which we have trusted will crumble before our eyes.

*Zec 11:1-2: Open your doors, O Lebanon, That fire may devour your cedars. Wail, O cypress, for the cedar has fallen, **Because the mighty trees are ruined. Wail, O oaks of Bashan, For the thick forest has come down.***

In the figurative language of the Holy Spirit in Scripture, trees often represent the life structure of a man. Different types of trees have different characteristics and represent different qualities in man. The oak represents strength and long lasting stability. The oak grows slowly but makes a very strong hard wood and is therefore a picture of strong stable men.

*Amos 2:9: "Yet it was I who destroyed the Amorite before them, Whose height was like the height of the cedars, **And he was as strong as the oaks**; Yet I destroyed his fruit above And his roots beneath.*

It is vitally important for us to know the difference between the works of the pride and loftiness of man and the wonderful works and blessings of God. It is possible to come to some very frightening and unreal conclusions if we do not discern the blessings of God and the prideful works of man. We must consider carefully what is crashing down and what is being established on earth.

206

*Isa 2:12-21: For the day of the LORD of hosts shall come upon everything **proud and lofty**, Upon everything **lifted up**; And it **shall be brought low**; Upon all the cedars of Lebanon that are high and lifted up, And upon **all the oaks of Bashan**; Upon all the **high mountains**, And upon all the **hills that are lifted up**; Upon every **high tower**, And upon every **fortified wall**; Upon all the **ships** of Tarshish, And upon all the **beautiful sloops**.*

*The loftiness of man shall be bowed down, And the haughtiness of men shall be brought low; **The LORD alone will be exalted in that day, But the idols He shall utterly abolish**.*

*They shall go into the holes of the rocks, And into the caves of the earth, From the **terror** of the LORD And the **glory** of His majesty, When He arises to shake the earth mightily.*

*In that day **a man will cast away his idols of silver And his idols of gold**, Which they made, each for himself to worship, To the moles and bats, To go into the clefts of the rocks, And into the crags of the rugged rocks, **From the terror of the LORD And the glory of His majesty**, When He arises to shake the earth mightily.*

This is not doom and gloom! This is a marvelous outpouring of the glory of God!

Yes, it is an awesome shaking! But only those things that lift themselves against God are coming down. God is being exalted above all else in the minds and hearts of man and in the entire earth. It is the manifest glory of God that is coming forth in the earth. It is the terror and the **glory of God** from which man is fleeing into the caves, and that causes him to cast away his idols.

The LORD alone will be exalted in that day, But the idols He shall utterly abolish. (Isa 2:17b)

207

Have we not been praying and ministering to exalt the LORD and abolish idols? Man has made idols of the blessings of God. What does man have that he has not received? God is the source of every great idea of technology or science that has come forth. The many wonderful works of man today are entirely impossible without God. God is the source of all life and understanding. Trees were used in the dream because they show that the great works of man are from God. He grows the trees of mighty men and their works.

You could not be using your computer, nor driving your car, nor flying from place to place, nor watching TV, nor using any of the other marvelous scientific and technical works, if God had not given man a brain and enlightenment to do these works. Some of us would not even be alive if it were not for the wonderful works in the medical field. These and every great work of man, every building, bridge, city, all wealth, and every notable and noble work of man is an intended blessing from God. None of them could have been done without the gifts of God to and in man. Man did not get or do these things on His own. It is not by our own hand we have gotten this wealth.

The gifts of God become lofty works of pride when man believes that he has gained them on his own.

Deu 8:17-19: *"then you say in your heart, 'My power and the might of my hand have gained me this wealth.'*

*"And you shall **remember the LORD your God, for it is He who gives you power to get wealth, that He may establish His covenant** which He swore to your fathers, as it is this day.*

"Then it shall be, if you by any means forget the LORD your God, and follow other gods, and serve them and worship them, I testify against you this day that you shall surely perish.

The things which men do and do not recognize as coming from God and do not give God thanks for become "loftiness and pride" of man and will not stand in the glory of God. The great spiritual harlotry of Mystery Babylon is man's pride and loftiness. It is man worshiping himself and "his works" and all "his riches" above God. (Rev Ch.17&18) It is esteeming the glory of man and what he does above the glory of God.

In science, technology, finance, business, war, defense, religion, government, education, and in every area of man's works today there is much pride and loftiness of man. It will not stand. Only that which honors God shall be exalted in the earth everything else will be brought low.

The gifts of God become idols when men trust in them above the God that gave them.

We must trust in God for all of our needs and not in the wealth and things He has given. It is God who will protect us and provide for our victory in life. However, we also must not reject His great gifts and think of them as evil just because others may trust in them instead of trusting in the God who gave them.

Isa 31:1 Woe to those who go down to Egypt for help, And rely on horses, Who trust in chariots because they are many, And in horsemen because they are very strong, But who do not look to the Holy One of Israel, Nor seek the LORD!

Psa 49:6-7: Those who trust in their wealth And boast in the multitude of their riches, None of them can by any means redeem his brother, Nor give to God a ransom for him.

For I will not trust in my bow, Nor shall my sword save me. But You have saved us from our enemies, And have put to shame those who hated us.

It is God who gives power to get wealth. Wealth and all the blessings of God are for the purpose of establishing His covenant. Wealth and all the grand achievements of man are from God and are to be used for His purposes with great thanksgiving and praise to God for all He has done.

It is the pride of man that perverts the gifts of God and uses them to build his own lofty works and honors himself and not God. Sinful practices permeate the lofty structure and the prideful works become corrupt. The great Babylonian structure of mans lofty works apart from God is corrupted and is coming down.

*Rev 18:1-4: After these things I saw another angel coming down from heaven, having great authority, and **the earth was illuminated with his glory.***

*And he cried mightily with a loud voice, saying, **"Babylon the great is fallen, is fallen, and has become a dwelling place of demons, a prison for every foul spirit, and a cage for every unclean and hated bird!***

*"For all the nations have drunk of the wine of the wrath of her fornication, the kings of the earth have committed fornication with her, **and the merchants of the earth have become rich through the abundance of her luxury."***

*And I heard another voice from heaven saying, **"Come out of her, my people, lest you share in her sins, and lest you receive of her plagues.***

Revival is an urgent life and death matter for much of our world today.

The mixed ways of the past will no longer suffice. The mixture of godliness and the pride and loftiness of man is dangerous in God's people. We must become real with ourselves and God about what we really trust in. We can no longer trust in governments that do not honor God. We cannot trust in education that does not honor God. We cannot trust in religion and theology that honors man along with God. We cannot trust in financial structures that do not honor God. We cannot trust in the strength of man for it will all be bowed down.

*Psa 20:7-8: Some trust in chariots, and some in horses; But we will remember the name of the LORD our God. **They have bowed down and fallen; But we have risen and stand upright.***

Those who trust only in God will stand to bring forth the ways and will of God (the kingdom of God) into the earth. Powerful revival among believers by the manifest glory of God is bringing change from trusting in the lofty works of man to trusting only in God.

The values of the past are not the values of today.

The reformation of the church is coming about as pure hearted believers will no longer be led by the mixture of the ways of man with the ways of God. Purity and holiness are coming to new levels as true revival brings total abandonment of the pride and loftiness of man in religion and every area of life.

Men have valued the godless systems of the world which are filled with the pride and loftiness of man. Now pure hearted children of God are growing to value the glory of Almighty God above all else and at all cost.

The anointing of God empowers man for ministry and destroys the yoke of bondage, but the glory of God destroys all pride and loftiness of man. God's glory and man's glory cannot coexist.

In the passing church emphasis age there were two opposite views held regarding the works of man and the gifts of God by many doctrinal groups. Basically everything has been separated into two groups, **sacred** and **secular**. The sacred consisting of those things involving the church and religion and the secular consisting of everything else. In the emerging focus on the kingdom age believers are realizing that this is an improper division. The proper division should be **sacred** and **profane**. Secular is not the opposite of Sacred.

We are learning that God is involved in all life and is quite concerned with, and involved in secular matters as well as church matters. God is involved in working in all of His kingdom. Both a godly farmer growing food to meet needs of mankind and a preacher giving out spiritual food are ministers of God meeting the needs of people.

God uses man and works through man to meet needs of mankind. Man has three basic areas of need. Those which relate to the spirit, those which relate to the soul (mind, will, and emotions), and those which relate to the body. God is concerned with the whole man.

One of the opposing views has been that everything considered secular is dirty and should be avoided as much as possible. Although consorting with secular things to get money for living expenses must be tolerated and is acceptable practice. In this view people often did not recognize the hand and work of God in scientific, technological, and medical developments that meet needs of man.

Though it is true that the pride of man has often contaminated and perverted the use of God's provision through man, the intention of God in giving these good things is to meet the needs of man. In the emerging kingdom emphasis age believers are beginning to work to serve God by serving His people instead of working to gain for themselves. Whether their job is in the church or the marketplace, and whether it meets a spiritual need, or a mental need, or a physical need, it is a work of service to God and the person can be empowered by God to do the work.

Those who consider everything secular to be sinful and refuse to participate in the works of God coming through men may pay a great price. For example, to ignore and refuse the works of medicine because they come though man may cost unnecessary suffering and possibly premature death. To demand that God heal our eyes and refuse to wear the eye glasses He has provided may be rejecting the provision of God. To demand that God heal our cancer without taking advantage of medical provisions God has provided is about like demanding the ability to walk on the water instead of using the bridge man has been given the ability to build.

In the kingdom emphasis age people are learning that every good gift comes from above including those we may have considered as coming from man in the past. To not accept the provisions of God coming through man and to demand that God feed us, heal us, and meet all of our needs miraculously is a religious form of pride and loftiness of man.

The other opposing view is at the other end of the spectrum. This view ignores God as the source and trust in the works of man to meet man's needs apart from God. In this view people give credit to men for the works God has wrought. They may believe in doctors as their only healers and give God no credit for meeting their needs. They trust the doctors to cure cancer without God. This is a secular form of pride and loftiness of man.

One must seek God and His plan in every situation and never accept the word of man over the instruction of God.

In the kingdom age we are learning to use the gifts God has given us to meet the needs of others, and to give God thanks for all He does through us. The miracles of stunning technology today are no more or no less than other miracles God is doing in the world today. God is to be praised for all of His works and they are to be used according to His will and direction. Everything which is not is being made low. It is much better to trust in God than to trust in even the best of men and his works.

Psa 118:8-9: It is better to trust in the LORD Than to put confidence in man. It is better to trust in the LORD Than to put confidence in princes.

Probably most believers today are not aware of how much they trust in and are involved with the pride and loftiness of man. As the manifest glory of God comes forth in revival and believers experience His presence their values are exposed and changed. Experiencing the presence and glory of God causes everything else to become of less importance. Many are amazed as they come into the glorious presence of God in revival and see for the first time how much pride and loftiness they had.

Revival is God's chosen way to bring down the pride and loftiness of man. Now in this time there is opportunity to come into the presence of God and have our lofty pride purged from us. For those who will not, other severe methods will be employed. Both the **terror** and the **glory** of God can destroy the pride and loftiness of man.

It is urgent that we diligently enter the spiritual war now by finding our place in the mighty revival taking place in our world. Our enemies, the pride and loftiness of man can be pushed down. God is on the move in our world. Get in on revival and help destroy the loftiness of man in the glory of God.

The crashing fall of the pride and loftiness of man is eminent. One way or the other by glory or by terror the presence of God will bring down the pride and loftiness of man soon.

Psa 44:5-7: Through You we will push down our enemies; Through Your name we will trample those who rise up against us. For I will not trust in my bow, Nor shall my sword save me. But You have saved us from our enemies, And have put to shame those who hated us.

BASILEIA LETTER
Number 17

Renewal And The Kingdom of God

Barbara and I have been privileged to visit several areas of our country where major revivals and something called renewals are occurring by the outpouring of the Holy Spirit. There is no doubt in our minds that this is the most significant move of God we have seen in our lifetime. One of the most talked about things we have witnessed is a myriad of physical and emotional manifestations. Renewal, as it is happening today, is seen in a setting of people falling under the power and at the presence of God, along with shaking, crying out, laughing, and often lengthy times laid out on the carpet in a somewhat euphoric state. Many have asked either out loud or within themselves; What is the reason for this? --- Why is God doing these things?

I have been strongly affected by the presence and power of God in these meetings, and have seen many others powerfully changed. Often manifestations and miracles occur during the lively praise and worship time or in the ministry time when people are prayed for by a prayer team or prayer ministers.

Barbara's first encounter with renewal type prayer ministry was so different from what she was accustomed to that it was a bit frightening to her at first. Yet, after experiencing the powerful praise and worship ministry the awareness of God's presence was so powerful to her that she was more than willing to seek prayer ministry. When she was prayed for, she was aware of great internal changes taking place within herself including a sense of some things being pulled out and removed from her and then being replaced with more of the love of God than she had ever before known. These types of changes can make major differences in how a person thinks, acts, and reacts. The changes in Barbara's life are obvious and seem to be permanent. She and others testify of continuing to be changed each time they are ministered to by the Spirit of God in renewal services.

All of the things God does are not without purpose. Great numbers of people are being changed to be more like Jesus in renewal and revival services. The reformation of the church is continuing to take place as people of God are being changed by God through the many experiences of powerful manifestations and miracles in renewal.

God is creating a clean heart and renewing a right spirit within His people.

Psa 51:10-13 KJV: **Create in me a clean heart, O God; and renew a right spirit within me.**

Cast me not away from **thy presence***; and take not thy* **holy spirit** *from me.*

Restore unto me the **joy** *of thy salvation; and uphold me with* **thy free spirit.**

Then will I teach transgressors thy ways; *and sinners shall be converted unto thee.*

God's purpose for renewal and revival is the establishment of the kingdom of God --- first in His people and then into the world. The kingdom of God is God's government from heaven on earth.

Governments of men on earth come from the spirit and mind of men. What is within the spirit of men, what they think and believe will determine how they govern. Belief systems develop from the people's perspective of reality and become the basis for governing life. First the individual's life is governed by their belief system;

217

next, families, tribes, communities, cities, states, nations, and eventually the world is governed by the collective belief systems of men. Wars are fought and great pressures are brought to bear as different belief systems seek to rule in the world.

God's plan is now, and has always been since He formed man on the earth, for man to rule the earth --- to carry out the Father's plans and purposes on the earth --- for the will of God to be done on earth as it is in heaven. The government of God (kingdom of God) on earth is brought forth through man by the Holy Spirit from heaven.

The enemy (Satan and his spirits of darkness) seek to rule the earth by infiltrating and affecting the spirits and minds of men. The enemy is referred to as the prince of the power of the air. He seeks to be king and knows he must rule in the hearts of men to rule the world. His goal is destruction of all life and the planet.

The enemy has been effective in perverting the hearts of men and establishing his lying beliefs in the minds of men. Therefore, the earth is now being governed to a large extent by the ways and will of the enemy. The Scripture is clear that the goal of the enemy's rule is destruction, **not** peace on earth and good will toward men. *(John 10:10)*

Prosperity comes to the nation who's God is the Lord. He who seeks first the kingdom of God and His righteous way of doing and being will prosper and cause the earth to prosper. (Psa *33:12*) *(Matt 6:33)*

Many of the ways of thinking and governing on earth, which are now employed and respected by many people including Christians are not God's kingdom way, but are ways subversively implanted by the enemy over the past centuries. Though many of these ways are seen as acceptable and normal by many believers, they lead to disorder, discord, disunity, and eventually death and destruction.

Some of the enemy's ways are obvious and most believers seek to avoid them. But many of the ways implanted by the enemy are more subtle and have over time become accepted as normal good behavior by believers and non believers alike. **The kingdom of God will not be brought forth in the world through men with perverted hearts** --- men who are knowingly or unknowingly following another spirit and ways other than God's.

Therefore it is imperative that the hearts of men be changed to bring forth the new order of the kingdom of God on earth. In a very real and practical sense men must be renewed by the Spirit of God and implanted with the ways of the kingdom of God in place of the ways now functioning in the hearts of men.

RENEWAL and REVIVAL are methods God is employing to create new hearts and a right spirit within men. This is a marvelous work of God not of man. Notice that in Psalm 51, David is **asking God** to create a clean heart within him and to renew a right spirit within him. *(CREATE in me a clean heart, O God; and RENEW a right spirit within me.)*

In the passing church emphasis age, many people fought long and hard seeking to overcome their wrong ways and to obtain a clean heart and a right spirit. In the emerging kingdom age the presence and power of God has come to earth in a greater measure. In many places and among many peoples, the outpouring of the Holy Spirit is bringing a great awakening. As the awesome presence of God manifest many are overcome by the power of God and fall before Him. They are changed by God Himself **creating a clean heart** within them as they lay before Him soaking in His presence. Healings of past wounds and deliverances from wrong spirits are easy in the power and presence of God.

Just as David asked in *Psa 51:10-13,* many are receiving a **clean heart and a renewed right spirit in His PRESENCE** by the Holy Spirit; the JOY of His salvation is being restored, and they are upheld by His free Spirit.

(Create in me a clean heart, O God; and renew a right spirit within me. Cast me not away from thy presence; and take not thy holy spirit from me. Restore unto me the joy of thy salvation; and uphold me with thy free spirit.)

Many in the past have sought to obtain a clean heart and right spirit by the Word of God but have not had the experience of the Word dwelling among and within them by the presence of God manifest through the Holy Spirit. The study of the Word must lead us to the experience of God to receive the renewal of God. The joy of His salvation comes as we experience His presence.

Just to know something from the Word is not the same as experiencing it.

As we experience God first hand, we will become powerful in teaching transgressors the ways of God and sinners will be converted unto God. Evangelism becomes bringing forth the presence and power of God by the Holy Spirit to touch and impact sinners. Once they experience a touch from the presence of God they can and will accept the Word of God and receive the salvation of God. *(Then will I teach transgressors thy ways; and sinners shall be converted unto thee.)*

A great hunger is developing among God's people for purity and holiness in the presence of God.

Especially young people are sensing a great hunger for the clean wonderful experience of the glory of God. Across the world people are crying out for more of God, more of His presence, more of His cleansing, more purity, holiness --- more of the reality of the presence of God and His glory in and around their lives.

The contamination of polluted views and life are very odious to the one who has experienced the glory of God, but seem normal to those who over time have grown accustom to them. This may be likened to a person who first enters an area where the air is greatly polluted with chemicals and waste from uncontrolled industrial emissions. Their eyes burn and their nose throat and lungs hurt and they may gag as they attempt to breathe the contaminated air. Yet the people who have lived in this environment for a time go about their daily business and don't even notice the horrible stench and the caustic chemicals in the air. Much of the world's population, including many Christians, have lived for so long with the pollutions of immorality, greed, selfishness, anger, rage, violence, sexual perversion, drug and alcohol abuse, and filth of every kind, that they have adjusted to it and no longer notice how caustic and vile life has become.

Once they are exposed to the purity of the presence God, and compare life cleansed by the presence of God to life as it has been, they become painfully aware of how impure and polluted their lives and those around them have become. When they taste the purity and glory of God in the reality of experiencing His presence they hunger for more and more of His presence and purifying love. They develope a great distaste for the polluted life of the past and a great desire for the purity and holiness of God.

We now live in a world of people hungering for more of God to continually purify and cleanse their hearts from the pollutants of sin and the bondages of religion. God is calling forth a generation to be cleansed and then to be a part of cleansing the world. Great power and anointing is again being poured out as the apostolic work and government of God is coming forth into the world.

The old structures of church government are giving way as hundreds of thousands and even millions are finding new life and a new way in Christ Jesus. Truly, Jesus is beginning to be recognized as Lord of life and not just Saviour of the soul. First the individual's life is cleansed by the presence of God bringing the work of Christ through the Holy Spirit. Then the church is being cleansed and changed from all the control and traditions of man. All of the perversions of religion are melting as the presence and glory of God is manifesting. God's servants are becoming those without any ambition or desires apart from knowing and pleasing God. Simply to be with Him in His awesome presence --- to bask in His glory --- and to make Him know by bringing others to His awesome presence.

There has never been a time exactly like this and will probably never again be a time in which the presence of God is so mercifully pouring out His grace gifts to change the world. Those who hold to the past and cling tightly to the old church governments and practices filled with the perversions of religion and traditions of men with all their controlling mechanisms, will be greatly upset as were the money changers in the temple when Jesus turned their tables and drove them out. The hierarchy of religious rulers will confront the mighty work of Jesus coming forth with no better results than the leaders had when they questioned Jesus as to by what authority He did these things. In short Jesus told them that it is by the authority of the people who believed. *(Mat 21:23-27)*

The enemy has overplayed his hand. He has brought forth so much filth into our world and churches that he is becoming clearly exposed. The glorious presence of the light of God is shining forth into our dark world and creating a great contrast and providing a beautiful option for the multitudes of people who are trapped in darkness of sin and polluted religion.

Mat 4:16: The people who sat in darkness have seen a great light, And upon those who sat in the region and shadow of death Light has dawned..

Now is the time for every Christian to turn from the wicked ways that have slipped up on us and overtaken us as we have gradually adjusted to the pollution of the enemy in our world. *(2 Chr 7:14)* The wonderful love of God that awaits us in His glorious presence is so much greater than all of our past life that it becomes easy and reasonable to cast off our past with all the works of darkness and embrace the purity and holiness of our loving glorious Father in the great outpourings of His Spirit bringing renewal, revival, and reformation.

Much of the church in the passing church emphasis age has looked forward to the bodily return of Christ or the hope of escaping by death into the wonderful presence of our Lord. God is here to become one with us now. We no longer must wait for a future time or event to be in the glorious presence of God Himself. Now, at this time, in our world, the mighty presence of God is present to love us, heal us, deliver us, to save us to the utmost --- to create within us a clean heart and a right spirit. We can now embrace Him and share our deepest love with Him as His own Bride and become His very own Body in the world.

Freedom develops in the presence of God --- freedom from bondages of sin and its evil addictions that steal the joy and victory of our lives --- freedom from religious bondages that enslave us to forms, rituals, and the manipulation of religious men driven by religious spirits --- freedom to walk in the Spirit and flow the love and power of God to cleanse and heal --- freedom to be renewed and to renew our world by the power and presence of the Spirit and the Word of God. *(John 8:31-32) (Gal 5:16)*

In the passing church age many preached against sin and pronounced the judgment to come for sin with generally very poor results in stopping the invasion of the pollution of our world. There remains today those who see the pollution in our pulpits as well as our people and cry out against it, again with poor results.

In the emerging kingdom age the power and presence of God is made manifest in corporate gatherings. The people and preachers may not even need to be told of sin in their lives or to hear preaching against sin. Their sin is made clear to them in the awesome purity and presence of the glory of God. The great alternative of life in God becomes real to them and sin is clearly seen as sin and easily renounced in favor of the wonderful life of peace and love in the presence of God.

The reason some can only preach negatively against religious manipulation and sin is that they themselves are not yet experiencing the powerful presence of God changing their own lives and flowing through them to change others. Therefore, they have no real positive alternative to offer -- no real standard to hold up by the Spirit of the LORD, that will draw men away from religion and sin and toward purity and holiness in God.

*Isa 59:19: When the enemy comes in like a flood, The **Spirit** of the LORD will lift up a standard against him.*

BASILEIA LETTER
Number 18

Increasing Release of Glory
In The Kingdom of God

*Joel 2:28-29: "And it shall come to pass afterward That **I
will pour out My Spirit** on all flesh; Your sons and your daughters
shall prophesy, Your old men shall dream dreams, Your young men
shall see visions.*

*And also on My menservants and on My maidservants I will
pour out My Spirit in those days. "*

*Isa 9:7: **Of the <u>increase</u> of His government and peace There
will be no end**, Upon the throne of David and over His kingdom,
To order it and establish it with judgment and justice From that
time forward, even forever. The zeal of the LORD of hosts will perform this.*

Recently there has been a notable increase in the presence and
power of God. There is a continuing increase in intensity and acceleration of the outpouring of the Spirit of God. Burdens that were
difficult in the past are more easily moved with the anointing of the
Anointed One coming forth through pure hearted believers in this
season, as the outpouring of God is establishing His kingdom on
earth as it is in heaven.

Across the world many believers are uniting and coming together to pray for revival in our world. These prayer and worship
gatherings are often visited mightily by the presence of God demonstrating the power of the gospel of the kingdom with miracles
and changed lives. Life is being poured out and people, old and
young, are prophesying the message of God with power and accu-

racy. Faith seems greater and more easily obtainable than ever before. Now, in this emerging kingdom emphasis age, it seems easy to believe the things that Christians once struggled to believe in the passing church emphasis age. We have entered a new season on earth.

Things are changing rapidly as this era becomes more evident with each step of increasing intensity and acceleration. One of those steps was made very apparent to a small group, of which I was a part, gathered in the city of Greensboro, NC USA, for the purpose of seeking the face of God and praying for an outpouring of God's Spirit to bring revival in the mid-Atlantic region of the USA. As prayer was being made it was as if someone turned up the power of God switch to several times as much as it was before.

These prayer meetings were the first held by the group. They were ordered by the Lord as individually people were instructed to come together in Greensboro on this date to pray for revival. Not being of Jewish heritage, no one was aware at the time of receiving their instruction to come and pray, that it was Rosh Hashanah, the Jewish new year. The prayer began on Friday night September 10, 1999 and was continued the next morning of September 11, 1999.

In the Friday night session the presence of God became intense during a season of corporate prayer. The power of God moved in to heal and without laying on of hands or individual prayer, healings began to occur. The next morning a 79 year old man testified that when healing the heart was mentioned in the prayer he suddenly had the faith to reach out and receive healing of a bad heart valve. He had not been able to walk more than a few steps without stopping to breathe. The next morning he walked about the equivalent of two city blocks without even breathing hard.

This was just the warm up as the power of God was turned up in the Saturday morning prayer session. We were aware of the change as God spoke in our hearts that we had entered a new season, not just in this little group but world wide there was a shift, an increase that had to do with the Jewish new year and the new millennium.

Since that day, God has confirmed with the words of prophets in different places the intensification and acceleration taking place at this time and moving us toward the most awesome time on earth. Since that time, not only is much prophecy coming forth but also much revelation is coming forth to the apostles who have an ear to hear. Even the Book of Revelation which has been so difficult and so often interpreted erroneously in parts rather than as a whole, is being revealed as the covers are further being removed in these days. The mighty army of God spoken of in Joel 2 is clearly seen to be coming forth in this day as the Book of Revelation, which was written to be understood in this time is opening before us.

If you are reading this, you are alive in a day of major history of God being written in the earth. There has never before been a time like this time. It is indeed similar to the time of the first century but it is becoming even a greater time as the fruit of the seeds planted in the first century are now coming forth. The works that Jesus did, shall you who believe now do. The sum total of the works bought forth by Christ in believers will exceed those done in His earthly body and are the glory of God --- no longer just the hope of glory. *"Christ in you the hope of glory"* is becoming Christ in you the glory of God now.

A TIME OF WAR
By: Chuck D. Pierce (excerpt only)

This is such an exciting time for the Body of Christ. I believe with the beginning of Rosh Hashanah we shifted into a new, historical time frame in the Body of Christ. At this millennial shift, change and conflict are abounding throughout the earth at such an accelerated pace that we find ourselves groping for stability, footing, and positioning. The world is changing so quickly that many awaken with anxiety to each new day. Societal institutions are shifting at such a pace that from region to region the entire earth seems to be in a constant state of "earthquake". A word synonymous with conflict is "warfare". That war is the clash with an enemy, whether of a tangible nature or a discerned perception. God, the Omnipotent Creator of the universe and mankind, always has had a remnant leadership that arises in the midst of conflict, activating their faith and determining the course of events that molds the world for generations to come. God has a priesthood, a nation above all nations, that He draws near to Him and communicates His kingdom desires, so His Victory goes forth on the earth. He then says to this priesthood of believers, called the Church: "Rise Up and War until you see My purposes for this generation established!"

SPIRITUAL EARTHQUAKE IN BUENOS AIRES
By: Pastor J. Conrad Lampan

September 11th (Rosh Hashanah) something very unusual happened in Buenos Aires, Argentina: Over 450,000 evangelicals of ALL denominations gathered at a main street (The widest street of the world -- 120 meters wide). The crowd covered several blocks. **At 3:59 PM when they were praying the area was SHAKEN!**

All the evangelical churches were participating in unity such that pastors did not want to give their names, no list of personalities was read: it was only the Body of Christ praying in unity. At 3:59 the place was shaken.In many houses/apartments furniture was moved from its place. Interestingly enough the places that seemed to be more affected by the quake were those of the press: radios,

TV stations, and newspapers. They called the seismic office to inquire about a possible movement in San Andres fault and their system had not registered any earth movement. Some of them suggested that the sound from the audio system and the crowd shouting might have produced the quake but then one remembered that many political meetings have taken place there with much louder noise and nothing happened. Some newspaper reported: "curiously at that exact time the evangelicals were praying". The media can try many explanations but we know what happened: *"And when they had prayed the place where they were assembled together was shaken" Act 4:31*

Editors Note: The following prophetic word is very comprehensive regarding all facets of the current increase in the outpouring of God since Rosh Hashanah September 11, 1999.

WORD OF SEPTEMBER 26th, 1999
By Mark Wattenford

GOD' GLORY POSITIONED OVER GOD'S PEOPLE
Behold the promises of God are true and faithful. What He has spoken He shall perform. **The glory and the power has positioned itself over Gods people and the fullness of it is complete and lacking nothing,** though the hearts of Gods people wonder if it shall be sufficient to meet their expectations and the word of the Lord is, "Prepare thyself, for it shall not only meet your expectations but those things I shall bring shall over take your hearts and the abundance of the blessings that SHALL BE poured out shall be overflowing". I come with my reward with me, to call forth my chosen vessels, to bestow on them the authority that I send them forth with. Behold the authority and the power I shall open up upon my chosen vessels, how great it is and full of glory. They shall

indeed be the sons of glory who shall walk in this hour - in my spirit. And look at those who shall be stirred to jealousy because of those whom I have chosen. For those who are full of themselves have I not chosen and they shall wax cold in their hearts because of those whom I HAVE chosen.

ANOINTING WITHOUT MEASURE

In this hour my vessels shall walk as I walked in the earth, with an anointing that is without measure... not a portion, nor a double portion, but a portion that is without measure. Those things that were done in the past will be commonly done and many things that have never been done before will be done so that the world may come to have no excuse before God in that they shall see the works of God in full view and they shall be without excuse when they will openly reject God and they will therefore seal themselves for the judgment that shall soon after come.

COMMUNION OPENS MYSTERIES

Rise up in song my people for I shall walk among you as never before and the communion I shall have with my people shall be an open communion. The light of my glory shall rest upon the sons of God. **I shall sit among my people and speak to them the mysteries of the kingdom and I shall walk among them as they rise up and go forth. The books of the prophets NOW shall all be opened up, and the mysteries of them shall be fully brought forth into light.** The Pharisees have said that all mysteries have been revealed and that there are no new things to know... I shall bring forth such revelation of my word as never before seen and I shall shake every Pharisee with a quaking so that many shall fear what is coming forth in my word and in my revelation of my word.

THE NEW GENERATION ARMY

Behold I bring forth a shaking in the heavens and a shaking upon the earth. **I shall gather my people unto me and I shall take captive this new generation and shall draw them unto me and shall make of them the second wave of my armies.** Though they are young they shall wield the sword of my word and shall strike with accuracy that which the sword was meant to strike. I am raising up voices of thunder all over the world; voices that shall speak mightily like the world has never known. The fear of these thunders shall be wide spread and the dread of their coming forth shall pierce the hearts of men.

PROMOTION OF THE FAITHFUL

Behold, my reward is with me, to bestow upon the faithful what is due them. To promote my vessels that have remained in me - to greater places in me. The mantle of authority shall rise up in the earth as it has never been before. The sons of God and the Sons of Thunder are brought forth. They shall tear down strongholds with violence. They shall have no mercy upon the spirits that bind. They shall not give ear to demons or suffer the doctrines of men to take my people captive any longer. The day of deliverance is come to my people and I shall bring them fully out from captivity of the doctrines of men, the doctrines of demons and the traditions wherein they have been bound.

INCREASING GLORY

The cloud of my glory has formed and is positioned above my people and it is even now sending forth a light rain, but I say... this light rain is NOT for long as this cloud of my spirit and glory shall be rent and the pouring out of it shall catch all in surprise and it will be as a flood upon you where you stand.

231

The day shall rise with the light of its shining and all things hidden shall be revealed. The spirits that had power in darkness shall no longer have power as they shall be uncovered and brought into the light and judgment of my glory and my light. The dead shall rise, the blind shall see, the deaf shall hear, the lame shall walk, the sick shall rise up and they shall know again the Good shepherd that I am.

JUDGMENT OF SHEPHERDS

I shall not beat them as the hirelings have that have been over my people. And I come to judge them that have been over my sheep that have raised their hand up against my lambs and have beaten them and without mercy. Shall I not beat them who have beaten my sheep? Shall I give mercy unto those who have not shown mercy upon my lambs? I shall tear down with violence these kingdoms that these wicked shepherds have built for themselves. Repent you fallen shepherds who have built for yourselves kingdoms from the very blood I shed. Repent and turn lest I take the very stones of your own kingdom and cast them upon you, to destroy you and remove you from the earth. And why do you say I shall not remove you from the earth? I tell you I shall remove many from the earth in this hour who have offended me and have taken my name in vain and have beaten my sheep. I tell you the truth, it is YOU who have taken my name in vain, who have built up kingdoms for yourself and have bartered with the evil one that you might fill your bellies with the desires of your flesh and have paid for your lusts with the very cross of my death. My death was for the souls of men, but you have eaten it up to consume it and to use it for the desires of your lusts and the things of the flesh.

APOSTLES ESTABLISHED

The day of my rising is come. My prophets hear my voice.

I have now established the apostles of my choosing in the earth. They shall rise up and go forth and bring structure to my kingdom on earth. They have deep hearts of mercy, but they shall go forth and destroy what hinders my kingdom from coming forth. I tell you to search your hearts and ask of me whether it be filled with light or darkness, for there are too many who think they do not stand in my way, but who do stand in my way and are set for a breaking. Some I shall remove from their place and shall take them home because they have not heard my voice in this time and who stand in the way of my spirit. I am a God of Love and it is a long suffering love, but I will not suffer ruin to my kingdom in this time and I shall remove them that stand in the way. Those vessels I bring forth shall rise up with wings as eagles, they shall run and not grow weary, they shall walk and not grow faint. Some vessels I will raise up that men will not be able to kill. Were men to kill them, they shall rise up from death to continue. Time and time again they shall rise up. They shall not be taken off the earth unless I say. For all the sacrifices my people have offered up over many years, I bring now the reward for their giving. In this time those who have given up lands I shall increase and give them portions of the earth. Men shall deliver up riches into the storehouses of my people. I shall rebuke the devourer in this time and for a season he shall have no power to come against my chosen ones. I shall shut the mouth of the devourers as I shut the mouth of the Lions before Daniel.

CHILDREN MINISTER IN POWER

Your young children shall speak prophecy and have visions and I have appointed even them to witness and to preach the word of the kingdom in this time. They shall see my angels coming forth and with angels they shall speak and converse on many things. Think not slight of them or think them of little value for they are precious in my sight and I shall put words of wisdom in

233

these young vessels. They shall win souls into the kingdom through the purity of their hearts and the anointing I shall cover them with in wisdom. Speak to the darkness that has bound your families and I shall chase off the darkness that before has had place and rule in your houses. I shall rise up as a mighty and angry lion and shall run after darkness and shall chase it and drive it from my people.

HEAVENS OPENED

The earth has never seen before the heavens as it shall be opened up before my people. As Stephen saw the heavens opened so shall the people of God behold the heavens opened and the glory of my coming. The earth is mine and I now am risen up to take into possession all that is mine. The heavens are mine and I shall possess all that is in the heavens. I shall place my foot on the head of the serpent and for a season he shall not come against my chosen ones. I shall break the teeth of the lions who seek to come against mine anointed and the fear of my judgments shall come upon the hearts of men.

REMOVE ROBES OF RELIGION

To those who have the heart of Nichodemus who do hunger after me, I say... **remove the robes of your positions and the flatteries of men and follow after me and I shall give you instead the robe of righteousness and of holiness that you may enter into these things I bring into the earth.**

JUDGE WITH MERCY

To those who judge... seek my counsel while it is yet early that you may judge according to my counsel, lest I find that you are without mercy and I come to judge you. For those I find in this hour who have no mercy I shall strike with an iron rod in my anger. In this time the earth shall know the anger of God and the wrath of His displeasure for in the open I shall openly stand before them and offer mercy this last time and those who refuse I shall openly destroy before the eyes of many. The hearts of men shall fail them in this hour for the fear that shall come over them. Listen to my cry all yee nations, listen and know that I AM the lamb of God that was slain for your sake and none shall stand before my father who shall reject me. You shall NOT know God who refuse to know me and seek after my face.

HONOR FOR TRUE SERVANTS

My prophets I shall honor in this time and I shall make many jealous who think in themselves they have honored me and they have not. I shall pour upon my prophets blessings that shall anger those who think in themselves that they possess the kingdom of heaven and they do not. This is the day of the song of the prophets, but who can know what that means? This is the day of the power of the coming forth of my apostles. My arm shall strike the earth in judgment and the whole of it shall shake. Woe to them who say they possess my kingdom and do not, who say all things continue as with their fathers and everyday shall be as the other and God shall not move as these prophets say. You have not given heed to my chosen ones. You think in yourselves you are my counsel and I say, brace yourselves if you can for I shall shake all that can be shaken and if you hold on to anything that is not me you shall be carried off with the shaking.

DELIVER QUICKLY THOSE WHO ARE BOUND

Why do you not hear my voice, why do you not seek my face, why do you withstand the voice of my prophets, why do you not show mercy to them that are bound and even add further chains to them that are bound? For in this my anger is kindled greatly, that you have NOT brought liberty to the captive as I ordered you to do, but rather you have bound up further them that were in bonds. My wrath is kindled greatly because of this and I say... **run to them, run to them that you have bound and lose them quickly before I come and find that you have not done so.** I tell you the wrath of my anger for this is ALL consuming and I shall not have mercy on them who have done this when I am come and find they have not done as I said, and loosed them who are in captivity. You have but a short time to repent and right these things and you must RUN to lose them that you have bound for I come quickly and shall without mercy judge you if you have not done as I have said. Loose them who are bound!!

GOVERNMENT OF GOD

The kingdom shall be on earth as it is in Heaven. I bring the government of my Father among men. That which is in Heaven shall be seen on earth. My glory is come that it may enter into my people and that it may rest upon my chosen vessels. I shall raise up my temple of living stones. I go forth throughout the earth establishing my vessels and putting in place the stones of my temple. Who shall hear the words of my prophets and who are they who shall not be offended by the words of my apostles in this hour? There is a harvest and an ingathering that has never been before until now. A multitude shall rise up and enter into the kingdom as a field going forth from horizon to horizon. I shall remove striving from my people and I shall be in them with the power they have sought and yearned for. Before one shall finish praying I will have done it for them. Rise up and rejoice, for all things are come to be fulfilled and from this time forward you, my people, shall enter into all that is in me and you shall go forward in me unto the day that my kingdom is fully brought forth upon the earth.

BASILEIA LETTER

Number 19

Time of The Kingdom of God

Is it now time for the manifestation of the kingdom of God from heaven on earth -- time for the will of God to be done on earth as it is in heaven?

As we all know God is supreme over all creation including all the earth and all that is on the earth. So then why and how is it that the will of God -- the kingdom of God is not fully observed upon the earth? How is it that man can walk outside the will of Almighty God in disobedience to God and His ways? How can it be that the enemy kingdom or principality can exsert its self and its ways on earth? Is God with His omnipotent power and supreme wisdom unable to overrule the enemy and his ways? Is it not true that all of creation is under the rule of God who created it and His Son Jesus through whom all things were created and now consist?

Col 1:16b-17a: **All things were created through Him (Jesus) and for Him. And He is before all things, and in Him all things consist.**

Rev 4:11: "You are worthy, O Lord, To receive glory and honor and power; **For You created all things, And by Your will they exist and were created.**"

John 1:3: **All things were made through Him, and without Him nothing was made that was made.**

All creation heavenly and earthly was created and continues to exist and consist in order by the exerted energy of God. Everything created exist by the power and design of God through Christ Jesus. Christ Jesus has complete authority and therefore control over all creation--- He is before all things.

237

Col 1:15-19: He (Christ Jesus) is the image of the invisible God, the firstborn over all creation. For by Him all things were created that are in heaven and that are on earth, visible and invisible, whether thrones or dominions or principalities or powers. All things were created through Him and for Him. And He is before all things, and in Him all things consist.

And He is the head of the body, the church, who is the beginning, the firstborn from the dead, that in all things He may have the preeminence. For it pleased the Father that in Him all the fullness should dwell.

There is nothing impossible to Christ Jesus. The creator is fully able to recreate or change any part of creation, including things like bringing the truth of God's love and salvation to anyone --- healing deformed or diseased bodies--- or redistributing the wealth of the world in accordance with His will and purpose.

Man's part is to bring God's desires into the world by connecting with God and **hearing and obeying** the will of God. As God shows man things in the world which He desires to change, man has the ability to PRAY and take the desired change to God; and then to become an instrument in His hand to change the situation in connection with the power of God from heaven.

My friend and prayer partner, Billy, is used in intercession and is prone to be led away for hours or days of prayer and/or into divine encounters for ministry. One afternoon I was waiting for Billy to arrive at my log cabin in the East Texas rural area. He had called and said he would be there at a certain time. He arrived hours later than expected and told the following story.

God had directed him to take a sort of back trail way to get to my cabin instead of the usual way. He thought that it was just for a pleasant scenic diversion. But as he approached a travel trailer where a woman was sitting out front, God spoke to him to pull in and tell her about Jesus. It surprised Billy and wanting to be sure, he did not stop but drove by and stopped at the first opportunity to consider the situation. Being a man and alone in a rural area he was concerned that in might frighten the woman. Again it was made clear to him to go tell the woman about Jesus.

As soon as Billy started talking to the woman it was obvious that she was very distraught as she began sharing her situation with him. She had recently gotten out of prison for shooting and killing her abusive husband and was having a very hard time adjusting to life again. Nothing was working out for her and she did not know what to do.

Billy was able to tell her that God had sent him to help her. She was gloriously saved and her countenance instantly changed. Billy told her she needed to tell someone about her salvation. She thanked him and instantly took off to go tell her sister who was a believer.

In the weeks that followed the woman was very excited about her new found life and spent much time in the Word and prayer and had great fellowship with her sister and in church. It was later learned that her cousin had been crying out to God for the woman's salvation and asking God to send someone.

After several weeks of excited new life the woman suddenly dropped dead from a heart attack. She was only in her thirties and she nor anyone else knew of the illness. Billy shared how God had provided for her salvation and was a great witness to her family.

Because the cousin was connected to God within she could see the need of the woman and cry out to God to send someone. Because Billy was connected to God within and because he was willing to obey he was led at the precise time and to the precise place to deliver the love of Jesus and make an eternal difference.

These kinds of stories of men and women sent of God to make a difference in the lives of people and the world could be told many times over. Simple ordinary people who are connected and empowered by the Spirit of God.

Powerful ministries, churches, kingdom businesses, and nations can all be formed and reformed by the power of God. Nothing is impossible to the Christ within us as long as time remains.

Psa 104:30 You send forth Your Spirit, they are created; And You renew the face of the earth.

There was a man a number of years ago whom God directed to give money to send people with the good news to the lost world. This man worked for hourly wages and had a family of several children to support. He could give very little. He cried out to God to help him earn money to reach the lost. A series of miraculous events occurred as he continued to seek God. Job situations began to change and soon the man with only a high school education was earning as much in a day as he had earned in a week.

As he remained faithful to give and to continue to seek God, doors continued to open and soon he was the owner of a small business. As the man continued to pray, God would speak His desires for the little business and give instruction as to what to do next. In three years the little company had become a multi million dollar corporation, was free of debt, and was used in supplying funds for ministries to reach the lost.

In a recent report from a small village in India a visiting ministry team wrote the following in their report. "We saw many instantaneous, miraculous healings. One in particular struck me. A mother and father brought a little girl to me, probably about four years old. **They pulled up her shirt and showed that her stomach was distended in a terrible way. As I laid hands on her and prayed we saw her stomach go completely flat!** The God of mercy had shown Himself graceful to this little one. How great He is!"

The next day they wrote the following in their report. "The people drank in the teaching about the heart of the Father and were enthralled with the reality of a God who is interested in relationship, not religion. When the time for commitment came 35 Hindus, 25 women and 10 men, stood to their feet without hesitation to renounce all gods except Jesus. Two of these men were very advanced in years and had been strong in the Hindu religion. So in light of the fact that there were only 25 believers in the village before, there was some phenomenal church growth! Then we had the people line up for prayer and once again saw instantaneous, miraculous healings. **A child was brought to me with boils on his legs. Before my very eyes Jesus shrank them away to nothing.**"

There is nothing in all of creation that is above the Lord Jesus. He is the undisputed Lord of all and is the full expression of the Father. Jesus and the Father have the omnipotent ability to make any decision without any limitation. There is no force, no power strong enough to defy or challenge the decisions of God. Nothing can contradict or refute a decision made and spoken by God.

Phil 2:9-11: *Therefore God also has highly exalted Him and given Him the name which is above every name*, that at the name of Jesus every knee should bow, of those in heaven, and of those on earth, and of those under the earth, and that every tongue should confess that *Jesus Christ is Lord, to the glory of God the Father.*

Among the important decisions made by God regarding earth and mankind, two massively important decisions of immense magnitude have been made by Jesus and the Father. These two decisions have, and will continue to affect all existence on Planet Earth for all time.

The first awesome decision was made by Father God. **Father God decided to share the rule of earth with man. He gave man dominion on earth and limited Himself to the will of man regarding the life and fate of mankind and all creation on earth. God gave man a free will and the ability to choose. God, by His own decision limited Himself on earth by what man would decide.**

The second awesome decision was made by the man Christ Jesus. **Jesus decided to do only according to the Father's will and not according to His human will as a man. He decided to be obedient to the Father's will and do only what He heard and saw the Father doing.** *(John 5:19)*

Phil 2:5-8: Let this mind be in you which was also in Christ Jesus, who, being in the form of God, did not consider it robbery to be equal with God, but made Himself of no reputation, taking the form of a bondservant, and coming in the likeness of men. **And being found in appearance as a man, He humbled Himself and became obedient to the point of death, even the death of the cross.**

This is the decision that man should have made with his free will. But man instead decided to disobey the will of the Father in favor of his own will. Every decision of man that is not according to the will of God leads toward death (destruction, disorder, separation from the presence of God). Every decision made in accordance with the will of God leads toward life (prosperity, order, and the presence of God). Only in **time** of the existence of creation has God given dominion of earth to man. Man can decide which kingdom will rule earth -- the kingdom of God and light or the false kingdom of darkness of the evil one.

The potential for the kingdom of God ruling earth through man was redeemed by the man Christ Jesus, establishing again the will of God being performed by man on earth. Jesus became obedient even to the cross and provided that which was and is necessary for the redemption of mankind and the reestablishment of the kingdom of God on earth. Christ Jesus now lives in redeemed pure hearted believers to again bring man and all things over which man has dominion into alignment with the will of Father.

Time is a measurement of the continuation of created existence.

Along with height, width, depth, density, frequency or speed, time is a dimension of created life and existence. All creation emanates from God. Every created thing investigated to its deepest origin and simplest form will break down at some point and disappear into the spiritual realm as only energy from God.

If one investigates any item which consist of any materials, which are made of elements, which can be broken down into molecules, and then into atoms, and then into atomic structure of neutrons, protons, and electrons, which at some point in the investigation cease to be matter and are seen as energy, which can only emanate from God Himself the creator of all that exist.

Time and seasons are built into the natural creation of God. Physical and chemical activities act and react with one another in certain patterns and establish the existence of measurable time. Natural growth, degeneration, regeneration, movement and mass are all functions of change tied to time. Time and change are forever linked together. As long as creation remains, time remains. As long as time remains, change remains. There cannot be creation without time and there cannot be time without change.

There can be no matter without energy and there can be no energy without God. All energy and therefore all creation exist by the will of, and under the full authority of God. God and only God can alter the patterns of time and every other dimension or measure of created existence. God who is Spirit has complete and full authority and ability to alter all dimensions or measures of creation without limit. Therefore Spirit (God) rules over all creation (physical).

However, on the planet on which we live God has chosen to link His Spirit with man and to work or operate with the will of man. Spirit rules physical. Physical does not rule spiritual. The only way physical can effect the spiritual is through the Spirit in man.

Man is the only created being on earth which has a natural earthly body and a living Spirit within. The mind relates to the earth -- the earthly or physical realm and the Spirit relates to God in the spiritual realm. The connection or interface of the two in the heart of man is the Spirit /physical or God/man working together to rule on this planet.

Everything on this planet exist, consist in order, and is changed by the will and exerted energy (power) of God. Only man is given the opportunity to hear God from the spiritual realm and speak to God from the physical realm to the spiritual realm. Only man has the God given place of connecting with God and interfacing between Spirit God and physical creation. Only man working with God has the power to change the earth and things on earth to conform to the will of God from the spiritual realm. **God can do anything through man; and man can do anything through God, if both are willing.**

The kingdom of God is within redeemed man. As Christ Jesus abides in man and man abides in Christ Jesus the authority and power of God flows upon the earth to bring the will of God from heaven to earth. Christ in man will do as He did when He was on earth in his natural body. He will remain connected to the Father and do only what He hears and sees the Father doing.

All of creation must respond to the word of Christ Jesus flowing through redeemed purified man on earth now in this time. This is the **Time of The Kingdom of God.** Christ Jesus is now in this day being manifest in men, women, and children to change our world and bring forth the kingdom of God from heaven, to cause the will of God to be done on earth as it is in heaven.

The mighty river of the outpouring of the Spirit of God in our day is for the purpose of redeeming and purifying rebellious man so that the glory of God will be manifest into our world and the kingdom of God from heaven will rule the earth. The kingdoms of this world are becoming the kingdoms of our God as men are changed by the powerful presence of God and are empowered to hear and obey the Father.

Faith is being birthed in the earth as the hearts of man are bursting forth with the overflowing life of God in Christ Jesus flowing by the Holy Spirit out into the world as rivers of living water flooding the earth with the love and plan of God.

This is the **Time of The Kingdom of God** coming forth on earth. The time in which nothing is impossible as multitudes are swept up in the river of the love of God filling and changing millions of people. The youth of our world today will see the mighty hand of God flow in their lives and in our world in a way people of the past have dreamed and prophesied about but were not able to experience in their day. All the saints of the past will be fulfilled as the mighty return to the ways of our King, the kingdom of God lifestyle rules in the earth.

The powerful presence of God and the rivers of living water are coming forth from Christ in man to show forth the glory of God and establish His kingdom.

"Christ in you the hope of Glory"

BASILEIA LETTER

Number 20

Family And The Kingdom of God

Jesus is the head of the great family of God. The patterns of the universal family of God are the kingdom of God patterns for governing all institutions of life on earth including families, tribes, churches, businesses, states, and nations.

*Eph. 3:14-17: For this reason I bow my knees to the Father of our **Lord Jesus Christ, from whom the whole family in heaven and earth is named,** that He would grant you, according to the riches of His glory, to be strengthened with might through **His Spirit in the inner man, that Christ may dwell in your hearts through faith;** that you, being **rooted and grounded in love,** ---*

For centuries men have sought to successfully govern life with systems devised from the intellect of man. For the most part, in recent history, man has elected to ignore the kingdom of God patterns for governing. In the USA, an effort by some has been largely successful in eliminating God and His kingdom patterns from government and establishing substitute humanistic patterns. These perverted patterns devised by intellect and influenced by demons have spread to many nations around the world. In this kingdom emphasis age man must come to the patterns of God for governing life and begin to establish God's kingdom ways on earth.

God's basic pattern for all government is His kingdom family pattern. The family is the core of the kingdom of God governments on earth. The patterns established by God for family are the only ones that will really work in governments, businesses, churches, homes, and other governing institutions. All of life on earth must eventually come into the plan and patterns of God as His kingdom comes and His will is done on earth as it is in heaven.

Like many others, I grew up planted with the worldly patterns of family presented to me in the home of my parents. I did not realize that my family lifestyle was far from the kingdom of God way. Later in life it was shocking to me to find out that the stress and fear of my childhood was not the only way. A child tends to think that the ways of his or her home is normal and the same for all others --- that the lack of unconditional love and the disorder with its conflicts and power struggles is the normal pattern for family. As the child grows and experiences other situations he may become aware that all families are not the same.

I grew up quickly and was anxious to get out of the nagging, fighting, unhappy environment. At the age of seventeen I married and left five of my six younger siblings trapped in the family setting. My sister just younger than myself had already married at fifteen to seek a better life.

I did not know God nor did I have any idea that He had a kingdom plan for life and family. I only knew that surely something would be better than what I had. I vowed that my home would not be like the one I grew up in. Certain things that stressed me as a child would never be allowed in my family.

Though I had a desire for a better way, the patterns of life planted in me and the lack of God's ways in my life caused me to reproduce many of the same patterns. Coming to know God and His saving grace at twenty one years of age began to change everything. But it would be many years and much heart ache before God's kingdom family pattern would become known to me and begin to be established in my life.

The same type scenario was played out in my work life. Again, like others, I assumed that the principles trained into me by family, school, and job experience were the way to do things. Only later as

God began to reveal His kingdom family pattern for business, was I able to achieve much greater levels of prosperity and happiness than ever imagined.

The kingdom of God patterns for living on earth seem idealistic to most people today. Even for many Christians they seam too idealistic and difficult to implement into practical life. For the most part the people of the world have become so ingrained with substitute ways that the ways of God seem strange and sometimes frightening to them. However, the patterns and ways of the world which have been inspired by the enemy may seem natural and practical to them. In the kingdom emphasis age we will experience a change from the perverted ways of man to the establishment of the kingdom family pattern as the foundation for governing all institutions.

Righteousness, peace, and joy are characteristics of the government of God The people of the world seek peace and joy. Yet, for the most part they have ignored the source of peace and joy -- the kingdom of God lifestyle.

Now is the time of restoration to the righteousness, peace, and joy that only comes from the kingdom of God. The great facades and empty shells of seeking to govern life from the intellects of men are coming down. The kingdom of God reality and fullness of life are coming forth as the world endures the greatest change in modern history. It is the transition from the empty rule of man without God to the fullness of the kingdom of God ways ruling in and through man. It is the return to the patterns of God being reinstituted into the world. The people of earth by the thousands upon thousands must be reprogrammed with the patterns of God instead of the patterns of the enemy. The patterns of the enemy have been implanted through profane living and godless education into the foundations of all the world and have fostered many false beliefs and religions.

Only the power and glory of God can eliminate the influence of false beliefs and religions. **The acceptance of the practice of false religions will be dissolved by the mighty miracle working life changing presence and glory of almighty God.** As the power of God openly defeats diseases, destroys depression, and replaces the work of the enemy with righteousness, peace, and joy, the false beliefs and religions will be exposed as empty, powerless, shells.

Governments will no longer give equal status to false beliefs and religions when the glory and power of God is made manifest and undeniably demonstrated in the world. The governments of the world will no longer outlaw God and His kingdom ways from schools, and government institutions. Government officials will no longer use the excuse that all religions are equal and one must allow them all if one allows the true God to rule in the affairs of men and state. The mighty outpouring of God and the glorious undeniable manifestations of God Himself working through pure hearted men and women will change the world by changing individual lives. There may be very little success in trying to change the governments of the world until the people of God are changed and flowing in the river of the life changing glory and power of Almighty God.

The mighty outpouring of God's Spirit bringing renewal and eventually great revival to the world is preparing the hearts of man to receive and to begin to live the kingdom of God lifestyle. The kingdom family pattern must be learned and implemented into our lives and the lives of our children. The enemy's false patterns will be destroyed by the implementation of God's kingdom family pattern. The enemy's plan to destroy the kingdom of God governments of the world by perverting the family with his false patterns will be foiled.

The great spiritual family of God begins with the Father -- the giver of all life -- the creator of all existence -- the all powerful all loving God. The Son is the mediator between Father God and man -- the redeemer saviour -- head and Lord of all -- the husband of the Bride. The Bride is the purified church -- the New Jerusalem -- the ruling city of the Israel of God -- the mother of the children of God. The children are those born of the union of Jesus and His Bride and are in the process of growing up to maturity.

The patterns of the great family of God are the same for the natural family on earth. God has only one plan for governing-- only one kingdom family pattern. Everything else is either a perversion of God's plan or a counterfeit from the enemy.

God made man in His own image and gave man dominion over the earth. He made man and all the living things on earth from the soil of the earth, except for one thing. Woman was not made from the soil but was made from man. Man only, was created and he was created male and female. There is male man and female man. They are all of one creation. They each are given different equipment for different jobs and functions in the family of God. But each are the same to God spiritually.

The patterns for family are evident in *Genesis, Chapter 2 Amp.* God's pattern is that **before man has his mate** he is to: (1) have spiritual life breathed into him, (2) be walking in close communion with God daily, (3) have a good occupation and instruction for doing it, and (4) depend on revelation from God for direction for his life. **God's pattern is for man to be properly related to Him and established in His purpose before marriage.**

The wife is to be formed from the husband. Only woman was made "built up" from another living creature (man). The husband is the source of life to the wife. He must receive life from God and bring it to the wife. The instruction for the family's direction and spiritual life comes through the husband.

Therefore, a man must **leave** his father and mother and **cleave** to his wife, and become one flesh with her. She is to become his *"helper - meet, suitable, adapted, completing for him"*. He has the vision, the instruction, and the occupation or business direction from God. **She is to adapt to him, not him to her.** She is to become suited to him.

Many difficult problems arise from a husband or wife remaining tied to his or her mother's apron strings or staying overly dependent upon his or her father. The position of the parents of married children is one of advice, not control. It is not possible for a couple to cleave together and become one until they leave their parents.

God's pattern is that they leave dependency on parents and become their own institution and cleave to each other. She must look to her husband as head, not her father or pastor or anyone else. He must look to her for intimate help and completing, not to his mother or secretary or anyone else. **God's pattern is that only the husband meet the wife's need for headship, and only the wife meet the husband's intimate needs.**

The man and his wife are to be naked before each other, and yet not embarrassed or ashamed. **Intimacy is a part of God's pattern.** One major problem in marriages is a lack of intimacy. Intimate communication is vital to any marriage relationship. There is great fulfillment in loving intimacy between a husband and wife, much the same as there is in a loving, intimate relationship between man and God. Intimacy can exist only with transparency in an atmosphere of unconditional love when both are naked and open to each other emotionally, physically, and spiritually. There can be no great secrets, no deception, no hidden agendas, no defensive walls, no whitewashed coverings, and no manipulation.

True intimacy is a deep need for every married couple. **God's pattern is that nothing exist between the couple that hinders**

their being one flesh. One must speak the truth in love. However, a husband or wife must lovingly consider how and when to reveal information that might be hard for the mate to bear.

These patterns are the same for the relationship of God and man as they are for the natural family. The wife of Christ (the purified church) must be completely open and transparent with Jesus for real intimacy to exist. As Jesus is the head of the wife (church), the husband is the head of the wife in a natural family. As Jesus is to the church so the husband is to the wife. As the church is to Jesus so the wife is to the husband.

The natural family is to be a clear picture to the world of God's relationship to His wife, the church. The husband represents Jesus who must bring life and headship to the church (the wife). The children are the fruit or the production of the marriage. They are to become the image of their father, Jesus. The husband (Jesus) is to be closely related to Father God and do and say what He sees and hears the Father doing and saying. Wives, like the church, are to greatly respect and be subject to their husbands.

Eph. 5:22-24, Amp.: ***Wives, be subject - be submissive and adapt yourselves to your own husbands*** *as a service to the Lord.* ***For the husband is the head of the wife as Christ is the Head of the church,*** *Himself the Savior of (His) body.* *As the church is subject to Christ, so let wives also be subject in everything to their husbands.*

To understand God's family pattern we must distinguish the difference between person and office. **Man or woman is who we are. Husband and wife are offices in which we can serve.** The directives from God regarding His kingdom family pattern define the offices and the responsibilities of the different offices in relating to God and to one another. **These offices are what we do, not**

who we are. Some perversions occur when we lose that understanding and fail to make the proper distinction between the person and the office. For example, men may begin to think of themselves as primary and women as secondary.

The office of husband in the **universal church** is Jesus. The wife is the purified Bride part of the church. The children are the church in general.

In a **local church** type organization the office of husband relates to the chief elder or pastor or whatever the chief leader person might be called. The office of wife relates to the elders, associate pastors, or whatever the second level of ministry might be called. The children relate to the congregation.

The office of husband in **business** relates to the president, entrepreneur, or chief executive officer. The office of wife relates to the second level management or mid-management or whatever they might be called. The children relate to the worker type employees.

In a national **government** the office of husband relates to the king, president or whatever the chief leader person might be called. The office of wife relates to the heads of state, or generals, or advisors, or parliament, or whatever the second level of government might be called. The children relate to the citizens.

The pattern is the same for the universal family of God or for the natural family, or for the local church, or for a kingdom business, or for governments. The basic responsibilities of the offices are the same in each case.

The office of husband is primary. The husband must be closely related to God and commune with God in such a way as to know what God is doing and saying for the family. He must go to God and get what the wife and children need to meet their needs. **The primary responsibility of the office of husband is to love the wife unconditionally as Christ loved the church.** The love which the husband must have for the wife must be unconditional. It cannot be dependent upon her performance. God Himself is the only source of unconditional love. The husband must get it from God and bring it to the wife. This will bring life to the wife and have a great effect on bringing her to purity.

The husband must also get the direction for the family from God and bring it to the wife. The husband must hear and see what God is doing and bring it to the family. The husband must also hear the appeals, petitions, or suggestions of the wife and then make a decision by seeking to represent the will of God in the matter.

Eph. 5:25-32 Amp.: **Husbands, love your wives, as Christ loved the church and gave Himself up for her, so that He might sanctify her,** *having cleansed her by the washing of water with the Word, that He might present the church to Himself in glorious splendor, without spot or wrinkle or any such things - that she might be holy and faultless. Even so husbands should love their wives as (being in a sense) their own bodies. He who loves his own wife loves himself. For no man ever hated his own flesh, but nourishes and carefully protects and cherishes it, as Christ does the church, because we are members of His body. For this reason a man shall leave his father and his mother and shall be joined to his wife, and the two shall become one flesh. This mystery is very great, but I speak concerning (the relation of) Christ and the church.*

The office of wife is vital and distinct in function. As the husband is the head, the wife is the heart of the family. As the seed (word, vision, or idea) comes from God through the husband it must be planted in the wife, nurtured, and developed in her before it is given birth into the world as a child.

We have seen the wife's part of being subject to and of submitting to her own husband as head -- just as the church is subject to Jesus as head. Submitting to headship is very important in God's pattern. But it is not the most important function of the office of wife toward her husband. Her most important function is the same as the husband -- that is to love God with her whole heart and relate to Him in such a way that she can have what she needs to fulfill her responsibility toward her husband. The thing that she must have is just as important to her husband as love is to the wife. But it is not love; nor is it submission. As important as those things are, they are not her number-one responsibility to her husband.

The number-one responsibility of the wife is to RESPECT her husband. This is relatively easy to do if he is bringing love to her and is perfect in all of his character. However, this respect must also be unconditional.

As unconditional love flowing from the husband ministers life to the wife, **unconditional respect** flowing from the wife ministers life to the husband. Only God can provide this kind of respect. Respect is a reflection of love. **God's pattern is that unconditional love be reflected back by the wife to the husband as unconditional respect**. This respect will go a long way toward moving the husband to perform better as a husband. It becomes a strong motivational force for him to correct flaws and to do better. Nagging, debate, and disrespect have exactly the opposite effect.

Eph. 5:33 Amp.: However, let each man of you (without exception) love his wife as (being in a sense) his very own self; and let the wife see that she respects and reverences her husband - that she notices him, regards him, honors him, prefers him, venerates and esteems him; and that she defers to him, praises him, and loves and admires him exceedingly.

A Godly wife is a very valuable thing in God's creation. The wife is vital to bringing forth the will and plan of God on earth.

Without Godly wives, there will be no manifestation of the kingdom of God on earth. As it is with Jesus and the church, so it is with husband and wife.

The person in the office of wife has no more right to correct or overrule her husband than the church has to correct or overrule Jesus. But the wife has the right and the responsibility to petition or appeal to the office of husband and to make suggestions. Any attempt by the wife to usurp authority and rule over or apart from the husband will be seen as rebellion by the office of husband. Just as love from the husband ministers life to the wife and unlove from the husband ministers death to the wife, so also respect from the wife ministers life to the husband, disrespect from the wife ministers death to the husband.

The children are the fruit of the marriage -- the production of God. The office of child is a beginning office. Yet the children are being prepared to occupy the office of husband or wife as they mature. The need of the children is to be trained. God's kingdom pattern for family produces Godly children. Everything needed is provided for the children. The **primary responsibility of the children is to OBEY, honor, and esteem their parents.**

God's pattern is for the children to be **obedient** and **honor** their parents. It will be easy for children growing up in God's kingdom family pattern to know God. They see Him demonstrated in the husband/father and wife/mother. They see a clear picture of God's love in the love their father has for their mother. They are trained in how to reflect God's love as they see their mother respect and praise her husband, their father. It is easy for them to understand God's love and to know how to respond to it with loving respect and submission.

*Eph. 6: 1-3: Children, **obey** your parents in the Lord (as His representatives), for this is just and right. **Honor** (esteem and value*

*as precious) your father and your mother; this is the first com-
mandment with a promise: that all may be well with you, and that
you may live long on the earth.*

**In God's pattern, the father is responsible for training the
children.** Certainly the mother has a vital part in training the children. Her part is especially important to the very young. She is
especially equipped to nurture them with gentleness. The father is
the source of **training** and **discipline** for the children. The mother
will reflect the fathers love and help to train the children as directed by the father.

Eph. 6:4: **Fathers,** *do not irritate and provoke your children
to anger, do not exasperate them to resentment, but* **rear them tenderly in the training and discipline and the counsel and admoni-
tion of the Lord.**

The children feel extremely secure under the care and protection of a strong, loving father and a tender, loving mother. Fathers
have a strength that instills the feelings of safety in a child. That
same loving firmness gives them great assurance that firm boundaries exist for their protection. Only the special strength of a father
can provide the security of discipline and protection.

Remember these principles are the same for all kingdom of
God government. The basics of the kingdom of God family pattern
are: (1) The person God has placed in charge of an institution of
family, business, church, or state is to relate closely to God in the
"office of husband" and bring the unconditional love of God and
headship to the second level management (the office of wife). (2)
The second level management is to unconditionally respect the "office of husband". (3) The children, employees, congregation, or
citizens (the office of child) are to obey, honor, and be trained by
the father working with the mother.

BASILEIA LETTER

Number 21

Change And The Kingdom of God

Jesus said "repent (change) for the kingdom of God is at hand". The central message of Jesus was the kingdom of God and the need for man to change. The life changing message of Jesus is changing our world as individual lives are being changed.

Mat 4:17 From that time Jesus began to preach and to say, **"Repent, for the kingdom of heaven is at hand."**

Multitudes of people around the world are changing. The powerful presence of God is coming forth by the Holy Spirit b ringing the very life and power of Christ to live within believers who are willing to give up their past ways and be transformed (changed). Cities are being transformed as city officials and leaders of businesses, churches, and families are being changed by the powerful presence of God.

The transformation of a city begins with the renewing of individual minds to the kingdom of God ways. The glory of God is manifesting into our world on a personal level and then on a corporate level. Individuals must remove their mask or veil and become intimate with Christ. The presence of His glory at a personal level is life changing.

Rom 12:2: And do not be conformed to this world, but **be transformed by the renewing of your mind,** *that you may prove what is that good and acceptable and perfect will of God.*

2 Cor 3:18: **But we all, with unveiled face, beholding as in a mirror the glory of the Lord, are being transformed into the same image from glory to glory, just as by the Spirit of the Lord.**

Individuals who are being transformed are coming together in UNITY to praise, worship, and pray powerful prayers of intercession. Strongholds of evil spiritual forces that have held the people and their cities in bondage are weakening and are being destroyed as more and more people are coming into unity with the groups of worshiping intercessors.

The glory of God is released as the UNITY of praise, worship, and intimate communion with Him begins to bring forth miracles of healing and deliverance. More people are attracted to the miracles of God and many believe as they see the power of God demonstrated before them.

Deep commitment develops in the people as they are captivated by the reality of the presence and power of God. The release from darkness and the cleansing from evil brings freedom and joy. The city is transformed into righteousness, peace, and joy in the Holy Spirit. Crime goes down, domestic violence and stress at all levels are lessened, and prosperity increases in the city.

One of the many cities around the world where a documented transformation has occurred is Cali Columbia. Cali was once known as the cocaine capital of the world. Drug lords had bought up the finest mansions of the city. With their money and fear they ruled the city and much of the country. People in responsible positions of government and media who would not cooperate were murdered. The Cali cartel was said to be one of the richest, most powerful, and best organized crime organization of all time. Billions of dollars were at their disposal. Walls went up to protect the mansions of drug lords and murders were daily occurrences in the city. The drug lords not only ruled in political matters they had influence in the religious realm and participated in the occult practices that were strongly rooted in the city.

The churches were not very powerful. There was disunity among the pastors in the city -- churches were divided and each did there own thing.

259

Intercession made the difference. God sent a man who believed that if the church would come together in unity and pray God would change the city. They began by praying and asking God to show them how to pray. God led them to study the city and the strongholds and problems of each area and then to intercede for the specific needs of the areas. In 1995, this led to the first city wide all night prayer and worship meeting. Many opposed it but thousands came out and prayed powerfully for the city and against the strongholds of the enemy in the city. During the weekend of this first all night prayer meeting, for the first time since anyone could remember, there were no murders in the city. There was normally up to fifteen murders each day. Within ten days after the prayer meeting the drug cartel began to crumble. Soon over sixty thousand were attending worship and prayer meetings in the giant soccer stadium. In that same year the drug lords were taken down.

In the process the man of God who had been sent to bring forth the unity and prayer became a martyr. His murder led to much greater unity among what has become over two hundred pastors who united together in a covenant of unity. Today they are the backbone of the high profile prayer meetings and the miraculous transformation of the city.

Leaders in the city came to know the Lord and have given much favor to the work of God. The unsaved have found hope and are coming to the Lord in great numbers. Churches are exploding across the city and across denominational lines. One church has seven services on Sunday as thirty five thousand people attend.

The churches recognize that unity and prayer is what has allowed the mighty revival and transformation of the city. They know it is by the Spirit of God as He has come in great power among His people.

Nothing is impossible with God. This is the new thing God is doing in many communities across the world. This is the kingdom of God coming forth and changing our world.

Today the Spirit of God is moving from church to church and from community to community looking for a people who are **hungry, humble, and willing to change** to show forth His glory and establish His kingdom ways on earth. Yet again and again the mighty river and flow of the Spirit of God is turned away from churches and communities which are left to continue in their strife and division with one another. Unwilling to lay down their territorial rule and their traditions to join themselves with others in unity, prayer and worship. As the Spirit of God comes and knocks on the door bringing the gospel of the kingdom and is **not** received, the unwilling leaders are left to find fault with those whom God sends and strive against the change of God as they continue to defend their territory and the old religious ways.

2 Chr 16:9 : "For the eyes of the LORD run to and fro throughout the whole earth, to show Himself strong on behalf of those whose heart is loyal to Him. In this you have done foolishly; therefore from now on you shall have wars."

The words that Jesus spoke to the elders and chief priest in that many sinners would enter the kingdom of God before many religious leaders yet remain true. *"Assuredly, I say to you that tax collectors and harlots enter the kingdom of God before you". (Mat 21:23-32)*

Mat 7:21 "Not everyone who says to Me, 'Lord, Lord,' shall enter the kingdom of heaven, but he who does the will of My Father in heaven.
Mat 7:22 "Many will say to Me in that day, 'Lord, Lord, have we not prophesied in Your name, cast out demons in Your name, and done many wonders in Your name?'
Mat 7:23 "And then I will declare to them, 'I never knew you; depart from Me, you who practice lawlessness!'

261

It appears to be easier for sinners to change and enter the kingdom of God lifestyle than for some religious people to change and receive the gospel of the GLORY of Christ, the gospel of the kingdom. The traditions of the religious leaders of the first century were obviously too strong for them to be willing to change. The demons holding the immoral sinners may not be as effective in keeping people out of the kingdom as the religious demons ruling over religious systems. The powerful religious spirits of Pharisee, Jezbel, and Anti Christ and all that work with them seek to blind the minds of men to the gospel of the kingdom -- the gospel of the GLORY of Christ. They allow partial understanding of the gospel and seek to convince men that there is no more and cause them to fight against the gospel of the kingdom -- the gospel the GLORY of Christ now. They seek to prevent unity and true praise and worship of God and to replace it with an order or system with limitations and controls imposed through religious leaders. Anyone with more truth of the gospel is a threat to them

.

Mat 23:13 But woe unto you, scribes and Pharisees, hypo-crites! **for ye shut up the kingdom of heaven against men: for ye neither go in yourselves, neither suffer ye them that are entering to go in.**

Everyone wants to believe that it is someone else that is affected by the attack of religious spirits and -- it is someone else suffering from spiritual blindness and -- someone else who needs to change. We all tend to believe that what we have is right and is all we need. Our eyes must be opened. If we are not getting the desired results, if our own life, our church, and our city are not being transformed and the kingdom of God is not coming forth in them now, it is a clear evidence that we ourselves need to change. The enemy is not able to overpower the works of God. It is we ourselves that are not in order. We have power over the enemy and are here for the purpose of bringing forth the kingdom of God and to rule and reign with Him. God's power and plan are not lacking. The enemy is not able to over rule God. The lack is within men. We are the ones that must change. If what we are doing is not working, if unity is not coming forth and deep intercession, praise, and worship is not coming forth in our city destroying the works of the enemy and establishing the kingdom of God, we must admit it and change.

If we are not experiencing the powerful presence of God coming forth among us and deep intercession with praise and worship bringing forth unity among believers in our area, we are probably blinded spiritually in some areas. We may be resisting change thinking that we are defending the "gospel", or our denomination, or our place of rule in the church and city. Give it up! Let God change us until we also see, in our city, unity and prayer bringing forth the gospel of the GLORY of Christ -- the fullness of the gospel of the kingdom.

The gospel of the kingdom flowing through the mighty river of God will not continue to knock on the door of your house. You can be passed by and miss the wonderful works of God. We can be like the religious people of the first century and miss entering the kingdom of God lifestyle now. We can continue thinking that it is someone else who is causing us to be in strife and causing the disunity in our church and our community. Or we can face the reality that we ourselves or in need of change, we ourselves must be transformed into the image of Christ.

Some of us have fought the same battle in different places and at different times and have blamed the world and the devil for our continued lack of the reality of the kingdom of God lifestyle and the will of God being done in our lives, our church, and our city. We must admit that it is not God or the world or the devil -- it is us

that must change and become world changers. Are we the ones
with veiled faces unable to see the revelation of the kingdom of
God now? If we are to be transformed we must loose the veil of
religion and every other hinderance to seeing Him as He is now.

*2 Cor 3:18: But we all, **with unveiled face,** beholding as in a
mirror the **glory** of the Lord, are being **transformed** into the same
image from **glory to glory,** just as by the **Spirit** of the Lord.*

This verse is talking about us and the therefore in the next
verse tells us it is still talking about us, not lost sinners.

*2 Cor 4:1 Therefore, since we have this ministry, as we have
received mercy, we do not lose heart.*
*2 Cor 4:2 But we have renounced the **hidden things of shame**,
not **walking in craftiness** nor **handling the word of God deceitfully,** but by manifestation of the truth commending ourselves to
every man's conscience in the sight of God.*

This verse implies that it is possible for us to have *hidden
things of shame* and to *walk in craftiness -- handling the word of
God deceitfully.*
The subject has not changed in the next verse. The verse is
still speaking to us and is not just talking to sinners about the
gospel of being born again. It is talking to us about the gospel of
the GLORY of Christ.

*2 Cor 4:3 But even if our gospel is veiled, it is veiled to those
who are perishing,*
*2 Cor 4:4 whose minds the god of this age has blinded, who
do not believe, lest the light of the **gospel of the glory of Christ,**
who is the image of God, should shine on them.*

264

Is it possible that the phrase *those who are perishing* does not only refer to the eternal lost but to us who are living in debate, disunity, strife, and defeat and are not seeing the kingdom of God now in our lives, churches, and cities? Are we, like the religious people of the first century the ones who have veiled faces? If we are not seeing Him and experiencing the transformation of our home, church, business, and city into the kingdom of God we may be veiled.

No longer can I look to someone or something else to justify my lack of transformation into the fullness of Christ bringing forth His kingdom in my world. Lord it is me, standing in the need of change. In this time of the new millennium there is a shift in the things of God. **There is a hunger that exceeds anything of the past.** There is a consuming fire of God within that will not be satisfied with the ways and victories of the past. There is a universal call of God going out in these days. **Deep is again calling to deep**, but in a greater way than ever known in my lifetime. I simply must have more of Him or perhaps I must have Him to have more of me. The wonderful gifts and works of the past have been and are wonderful and my heart is grateful for them but they are not enough any more. There must be a greater intimacy a greater flow of His love and power a greater means of praise and worship -- His kingdom -- His righteousness-- His Glory must be seen and experienced in my life or I cannot be satisfied.

I was privileged to live a year in a some what remote log cabin alone with the presence of God. God was with me all day every day in a special closeness. It was the high point of my life. It was hard when the Lord ended that very special season and sent me out to be with people and to share what He had given me during that wonderful time of closeness. But even that no longer seems enough. It is wonderful for Him to be where I am but something within me desires to be where He is spiritually, not just Him where I am. I must have more. I must go to a higher place with Him. I must be changed again. I know there is much that must be changed in or about me but I have no understanding as to what it is. I just know that I must not continue at the same level of bringing forth His life and kingdom into the world. The results of ministry I have seen to this point are wonderful and I truly thank Him for them, but they are not enough. I must be more transformed. I must see homes, churches, and cities transformed into the glorious kingdom of God.

I know that I am not alone in this but that God is speaking to many of His people in the same way. I know there are others with this fire in their heart that will not be quenched. I know there is a great longing to see His people changed and the great harvest come in, but there is more. It is the longing to be where He is and to know and be known of Him in even a greater depth. **It is deep calling to deep.** I know there are others He is speaking to in this way who are also in tears often as the longing for Him and the fullness of His kingdom flood and overfill our hearts.

If you are still debating religious things and striving in this life, please consider the time and the call of God to seek Him with your whole heart now -- even to the point of giving up religious rule and systems. This is the time that all of God's people who have gone before us longed to see and did not see.

Let's not miss any of what God is doing in this time. Let's allow Him to change us and to make us into world changers.

BASILEIA LETTER
Number 22

Transformation To
The Kingdom of God

Jesus said that He came to fulfill the laws of God on earth -- to establish God's righteous ways of doing and being on earth as in heaven.

Mat 5:17: "Do not think that I came to destroy the Law or the Prophets. I did not come to destroy but to fulfill."

In Matthew chapters 5,6, &7 Jesus began to explain that his mission was to change the issues of the hearts of mankind to the ways of God and thereby bring forth the kingdom of God lifestyle on earth. He taught a new and living way which was greater than the old way and seemed backward to the minds of the hearers. He taught that adultery was a heart issue. He taught that murder is anger in the heart. He taught to turn the other cheek -- go the extra mile -- love your enemies -- bless those who curse you -- do good to those who hate you -- and pray for those who spitefully use you and persecute you. These and other issues of the heart fulfill the laws and plan of God on earth.

Jesus is the fulfillment of the law and plan of God. His perfect sinless life ended on earth with His crucifixion as the lamb of God to pay the full price for lawlessness (sin). Jesus rose from the dead, ascended to the Father, and then **returned in the Holy Spirit to indwell believers** and to complete the practical fulfillment of establishing God's kingdom lifestyle, first in the hearts of believers and then through them into the world, thus fulfilling the law.

Col 1:27: To them God willed to make known what are the riches of the glory of this mystery among the Gentiles: which is **Christ in you, the hope of glory.**

2 Cor 3:18: But we all, with unveiled face, beholding as in a mirror the glory of the Lord, are being **transformed** *into the same image from glory to glory, just as* **by the Spirit of the Lord.**

A great transformation is taking place in our world. God is moving upon people -- changing lives -- changing our ways of thinking and doing -- changing communities -- changing cultures -- changing our world. The metamorphic transformation now regenerating and reforming mankind is bringing forth God's kingdom of heaven ways on earth. The old worldly ways of doing things does not fit into the design of God now being made manifest in our world. God is now bringing into view what appears to mankind to be a new thing. It is, however, not a new thing but His old thing -- the way God has intended for life to be lived on Planet Earth from its conception.

Mankind has sought diligently to govern his life on the planet apart from the design of God. The alternate plans that mankind and the devil have devised and implemented have failed to bring true righteousness, peace, and joy to the people of the world. All of the problems facing mankind have been brought about by man's abandoning God's ways and seeking other methods of governing life. Consequently all of the problems facing mankind can be potentially overcome or neutralized by mankind ordering his life by the ways of God. Through many generations the souls of mankind have been trained in systems of beliefs and practices different from those designed by God.

In recent times God is magnifying and accelerating His presence and influence upon mankind. The outpouring of the Spirit of

God is bringing renewal and revival. Lifestyles are changing as people are being drawn by the Spirit of God and are turning to His ways.

Hunger for God is motivating many people to alter their lifestyles and provide time in their schedules to seek the intimate presence of God. The religious liturgy and ritualistic practices of the past have not fed the spirits and souls of the multitudes. Men, women, teens, and children are searching for more in life than occasional breaks from their busy lifestyles of pleasure seeking for halfhearted religious church services. Hours of viewing empty and often violent and sexually laden television programming are not satisfying the hunger of the hearts of the multitudes of spiritually starving people. This great hunger across the world is growing as the malnourished heart and soul of mankind is withering for lack of virtue. Secular education has for the most part focused on self improvement to gain power and wealth and has often proven to be lacking real virtue and satisfaction in life. Sexual promiscuity and extremes of dress and social practice provide no real nourishment to the soul starved for true virtue of God.

In this scene of only virtual reality and perplexing starvation for true supernatural reality, **a bright light of virtue is now shining into our world**. Starving people are becoming desperate as the reality they have longed for is beginning to come into view. Their spiritual senses are becoming intensified and their entire beings are quickened with excitement as the spiritual aroma of real spiritual food comes to their senses.

I can still remember as a boy walking down the street on a warm evening in the old fashioned neighborhood where I grew up. Doors and windows of the houses which were only a few yards from the sidewalk were open and the smell of supper cooking drifted out into the street. I was already hungry but when the smell of frying steak or chicken and other wonderful smells met me as I passed

269

the different houses I became desperate to get home for supper. My steps quickened into a run as excitement and anticipation tugged at my hungry body. I was filled with feelings of desperation to get home and be filled with Mom's good cooking.

The light of the presence and glory of God is now coming forth to dispel the darkness of the shadow of death from the church and the world. As people sense the supernatural presence of the Spirit of God coming forth in spots of revival here and there, their hunger is turning into deep desperation. As starved youth begin to taste the wonderful flavor of purity and holiness in the joyful presence of God they become desperate for more and desperate for others to come to the table of the Lord and be satisfied with the good food of spiritual reality. Life priorities change in view of the reality of God in their lives. Things that seemed very important become less important. Being in God's presence and serving Him becomes paramount in their lives.

Many mature or elderly people who have hungered for God and sought Him for many years are now experiencing their hunger turn into desperation as they sense the time has come of the outpouring of His Spirit. They have tasted of God's glory and must have more. The old ways of religion are crumbling and the new ways of the very presence and power of God are bringing reformation to the church. The church will never be the same again as the minds and hearts of men are being reformed by the presence of God.

Over the past four or five hundred years, **God has continued to move His church toward reformation through restoration.** Increasing parts and pieces of revelation and spiritual power have been restored to the Body of Christ through many moves of God over the past several centuries. In the past few decades, especially in the nineties, the moves of God seem to have increased in frequency and intensity. The fire of God yet continues to increase, restoring and reforming the church. Each of the previous recent moves have had, and continue to have, a distinctive part in the reformation. There is overlap in the moves and any personal need can be met by any of the current moves of God. Needs such as salvation, baptism of the Spirit, healing, deliverance, can all be met. Yet, each move can be identified as having an emphasis on one phase of ministry or reformation.

As an example some of the recent moves of God in the nineties can be easily traced to **Argentina. The great revival in Argentina emphasized supernatural power evangelism and deliverance.** The fire spread from Argentina to other spots in the world including a very significant outpouring in **Toronto**, Canada. **The emphasis in Toronto became the love of Father God bringing emotional and physical healing.** In Toronto prideful religious views were washed away along with past wounds as the pure love of God flooded souls and overcame diseases of soul and body. From Toronto many fires were spread around the world including a very significant one in **Pensacola**, Florida. **The emphasis in Pensacola became repentance and cleansing from sin as hundreds of thousands over a period of years rushed to the alters to repent and be purged.** And from Pensacola the fire spread to many other places including another very significant outpouring in the tiny town of **Smithton**, Missouri. **The emphasis in Smithton is the reformation of the church to the kingdom of God.** The move of God that began in Smithton, Missouri and has now moved to Kansas City, Missouri and is now becoming known as the "Smithton Outpouring of Kansas City" or "World Revival Church of Kansas City" is a significant next step in the ongoing revelation of God and reformation of the church. Thousands of pastors have been changed and many have taken the fire of revival back to their own churches. Over a quarter million people (250,000) from every state and over fifty nations have made the trip to Smithton seeking to be changed in the presence of God.

On March 24th of 1996 a bolt of spiritual fire like lightening suddenly hit **Pastor Steve Gray** and the Smithton Community Church in the tiny Missouri farm town of Smithton and a future world move of God was planted as a seed from God into the rich soil of the desperate hunger of Steve Gray. Over the next four years the seed sprouted and grew and World Revival Church of Kansas City was birthed after multitudes of people were touched and changed by the powerful presence of God at Smithton.

Steve and Kathy Gray along with the other servants of God who have been a part of helping birth this move of God are all just ordinary humble folks who have been touched by the fire of God and become extraordinary in their commitment to the work of revival. The level of commitment and loyalty of these people is extreme and is only exceeded by the vigorous life pouring forth from them. Those who stay don't seem to miss the natural worldly activities they no longer have time for in the outpouring of the Spirit of God. Everyone moves together as a team in attending the five services each week and serving the many guest who come to be changed. Everyone seems to some degree to recognize that this is an apostolic work brought forth by God to impact the church and the world with true reformation and they are more than willing to sacrifice personally to continue to be a part of the outpouring of God.

Some people have had difficulty understanding the intense commitment and loyalty of the Grays and those serving in this move of God. There are different callings and different places of service in the body of Christ. The apostolic type of work necessary to bring forth this awesome move that is touching the world is quite different from pastoring and teaching in a local church. The intensity and level of commitment required is different.

One can be a pastor who receives of the movement and then uses the reformed ways of God to serve his local body of believers.

Or in some other way one can continue to serve the Lord on a more local basis of meeting the needs of people and seeking to transform one's community to the ways of God. But, if a person decides to be a directly connected part of an apostolic movement like the World Revival Church of Kansas City, the level of commitment will be extreme. Can you imagine the amount of time and effort Paul and the other apostles spent during the transitional time of the first century outpouring of the Spirit of God. Even Jesus and the disciples with Him at times did not have time to eat and have normal rest.

Many other significant outpourings of God's Spirit have occurred and are yet occurring, not only in local churches but also in great itinerate ministries. These apostolic itinerate ministries also each bring forth different emphases, but by the same Spirit they are all bringing revival. For example, God has sent men like **Rodney Howard-Brown** with an emphasis of the joy of the Lord and the freedom it produces. Through Rodney God brought a demonstration of the power and joy of God and enlightenment exposing man made religion as an empty shell laced with doctrines of demons. Through another great evangelist, **Reinhard Bonnke**, God is bringing the salvation of cities as millions are coming together for gigantic open air meetings in Africa. In these unprecedented meetings hundreds of thousands are coming to Christ and multitudes of miracles and healings are taking place.

All of the men leading the powerful apostolic type ministries bringing forth reformation would probably have similar stories of becoming so hungry for God that they became desperate. **Steve Gray** says that he believes that for an instant in time he became the most desperate man in the world and God responded. He was so intensely desperate for the outpouring of God upon himself and his church that nothing else mattered and he could not go on. He refused to return to church and try to go on without revival. When he became intensely desperate God showed up in a lightening like

273

bolt of spiritual power and neither he nor his church has ever been the same again. Rodney Howard-Brown became so desperate that he told God, "God, you either come down here tonight and touch me, or I'm going to die and come up there and touch you." He frightened everyone around as he shouted for twenty minutes, "GOD I WANT YOUR FIRE!" He got what he cried out for in desperation. The world is yet being changed by ordinary men like these who reached a level beyond hunger for God and became desperate.

In the **Smithton Outpouring of Kansas City**, God has sent a move of real life purity, holiness, and power upon the earth bringing the seeds of the kingdom of God lifestyle to reform the church and change the world. The coming together of the fire of revival and the Word of the kingdom is being brought with clarity and power to believers and church leaders around the world. The Smithton outpouring is a balance of the miracle working, soul saving, delivering and healing power manifestations of God and a pure revelation and scholarly presentation of the living Word of God. Steve's preaching is well received and seems to be infused directly into the hearts of the people in the presence of God. Steve always has a fresh word from God and almost never repeats a message. The Smithton Outpouring is at this moment in time the next move of God and is truly planting the seeds of the kingdom of God lifestyle and bringing reformation to the church.

It seems that God has brought a balance of the previous emphases together in the Smithton Outpouring. There is the powerful manifestations of the Spirit but they are not the emphasis. There is the powerful Word preached and taught but that is not the emphasis. There is powerful prayer, salvation, filling of the Spirit, physical healing, miracles, emotional healing, deliverance, strengthening of families, restoration of pastors and leaders, prophesy and other gifts but none of these things are the emphasis of this powerful balanced move of the in-breaking kingdom of God in the

Smithton Outpouring. The church in general is not preached as right and all the rest of the world free game for bashing from the pulpit. Purity and holiness are practical and real goals and the preaching does not consist of bashing the lost and sinful people of the world. Rather the church is seen as the focus for revival, and when revived, the church will bring forth real change to the hearts and lives of the needy people of the world. The emphasis at the **World Revival Church in Kansas City and the World Revival Network is the revival and reformation of the worldwide church.** The world has only begun to taste the in-breaking kingdom of God flowing through this ministry. The impact of the kingdom lifestyle is destined to affect the world. **As powerful revival continues by the outpouring of God's Spirit through this and other ministries the church is being reformed and the whole world will never be the same again.**

Those seeking to live God's way must be reformed -- their souls must be retrained in the goals and ways of God's kingdom. Man must have new purposes in life and new ways of living. The principles of God's kingdom are redefining what life is about -- how to do business God's way -- how to have successful marriages -- how to rear godly children -- how to have a powerful church or ministry -- how to have peace and goodwill on earth.

Love is the greatest principle in the kingdom of God.

The pure love of God flowing from God through the Spirit of Christ within man, is first reflected back to God and then also flows out to our neighbor bringing the fulfillment of the law of God on earth. Because of this love, man is motivated and restrained to **obedience toward God and to goodwill toward mankind.**

*Matthew 22:36-40: "Teacher, which is the **great command-ment** in the law?" Jesus said to him, **"You shall love the Lord your God with all your heart, with all your soul, and with all your mind.** This is the first and great commandment. And the second is like it: **You shall love your neighbor as yourself. On these two commandments hang all the Law and the Prophets."***

True prosperity in every area of life is the natural result of walking in the love of God. God's love purifies mankind and changes his focus from himself to God and others. The person walking in this love no longer thinks first of himself and his need and how to get more of what he wants. The thoughts of his heart become, how can I serve God? -- how can I help meet the needs of others?

Seeking to serve leads to increased **production** as goods and services are needed to meet the practical and spiritual needs of others. One thinks, "how can I use what I have to establish systems and ways to meet the needs of others". **Business** is born and will be diligently brought forth as the principle of **heartiness** is evident in a heart felt work based on the love of God instead of greed and meeting one's own need. **Diligence** and **heartiness** in productive activity are normal results of God's love in us seeking to meet others needs.

The major kingdom principle of **LOVE** begins to bring forth many other lessor kingdom principles. We can identify the principles of **purification, prosperity, serving, heartiness, diligence,** and many others which flow from love.

The great universal kingdom law of **sowing and reaping** causes increased prosperity as we continue to increase service to others. Even the second greatest kingdom principle, **FAITH**, works through love. As God's purification, and plan flows through us, it becomes easy to believe God. It becomes easy to trust Him for greater things as we experience His blessing flowing through us in the production which He has put into our hearts to meet the needs of others.

Good balance of **management practices** (or **stewardship** to use a Biblical word) flows from love as we seek to not waste and to make best use of the provisions we have in meeting the needs of others. We are restrained from selfishly consuming the resources of time, energy, money, goods, and whatever else God has placed in our hands.

HOPE, the third greatest kingdom principle is birthed through the works of love and faith. We no longer live in a hopeless world filled with depression and no visible way to escape the doom and gloom of darkness. Hope is the positive, peaceful, joyful attitude of those who are trusting in God and serving Him by serving others.

These principles begin to produce **peace** and **joy** in the life which further lifts the spirits to higher levels of life and achievement (**promotion**) in the production of life. All these things working together begin to affect the **mental and physical health** of the one flowing in the love of God. Less time and money must be directed toward cures and recovery from disease, illnesses, and addictions of every sort. This results in less loss and more production of life.

A sense of **significance of life** develops from the God directed activities of meeting the needs of others. Life becomes exciting and we become enthusiastic through significant service. **Boredom is an impossibility for those actively serving God by serving others.** There is no need for time and money to be spent on costly entertainment and activities to fill an empty life, if the life is filled with the purposes of God. Again, this means more profit.

Loving our neighbor as ourselves fosters the principle of **agreement**. One becomes agreeable instead of disagreeable. Seeking to agree rather than seeking to dominate by proving ourselves always right, brings forth **submission** to one another and stops strife and disputes which lead to decreased production.

Christ is the very essence of kingdom principles. As His presence in-dwells us by the Holy Spirit, great increase of life is produced -- a true abundance of life. All of this leaves no room for lingering pain from past wounds nor resentment in any form. Thus our lives are healed and free of lingering pain. There is no need for emotional pain killers of alcohol and drug abuse or self administered pity to try to attract the attention of others to help us with our painful life experience. **FREEDOM** from all bondages is the natural result of the presence of God in one's life. And again, the great cost of these bondages is saved and profitable production is increased.

Kingdom of God principles lead to quality life decisions.

Walking in the Spirit and living in the kingdom of God lifestyle leads us to make decisions that will be most profitable for life. Relating to the Spirit of God within causes us to have His desires placed into our heart. We can then follow the desires of our heart into significant and productive life. Our hearts desire from God becomes the place of our greatest gifting and blessing.

BASILEIA LETTER

Number 23

Power In The Kingdom of God

Jesus said, *"you shall receive power when the Holy Spirit has come upon you." (Acts 1:8)*

--- Luke 24:49: *"Behold, I send the Promise of My Father upon you; but tarry in the city of Jerusalem until you are **endued with power from on high**."*

-- 1 Cor 4:20: *For the **kingdom of God is not in word but in power**.*

**How much and what kind of power were
the disciples to receive?**

What is the purpose of this power from heaven?

Does anyone have this power from heaven now?

**Can we have this power now?
If so, how do we get it?**

Do you want more power from on high in your life?

**If so, why do you want it?
How much do you want it?**

The Greek word translated power in the above verses is **"dunamis"**, and is defined in the Strongs Greek Dictionary as: "G1411. dunamis, doo'-nam-is; from G1410; **force** (lit. or fig.); spec. **miraculous power** (usually by impl. **a miracle itself**):--abil-

279

ity, abundance, meaning, might (-ily, -y, -y deed), (**worker of**) **miracle (-s)**, power, strength, violence, mighty (wonderful) work."

The power the disciples were to receive and the power of the kingdom of God is **a force of mighty miracle working strength -- a force from heaven that is beyond the natural -- a supernatural miraculous power.**

God Himself is the source of this power. The power that spoke all things into being and continues to cause all things to exist and consist -- the power that raised Christ Jesus from the dead is now potentially available in mankind. There are those who have tapped into the unlimited power of Almighty God. They have somehow entered into the realm of the supernatural miracle working power of God in this life now.

Barbara and I have chosen as God has directed us to invest our lives in being a part of the revival of power and presence of God in our world today. The more we spend time in the places where God is moving and with the men and women God is using to demonstrate His miracle working power, the more hungry we become for the powerful presence of God to bring forth great changes in our world -- to bring forth the kingdom of God destroying wickedness and establishing righteousness. The more we see wrecked lives renewed and changed -- people healed, delivered, set free and filled with joy, the more we desire Him.

One of God's chosen and anointed servants who is making a powerful difference, especially among the youth, is Bob Bradbury. Bob was a fisherman from Galilee, Rhode Island USA when at fifty plus years of age God and Randy Clark got hold of him in the early days of the great outpouring in Toronto, Canada. Soon Bob had sold his sea going fishing boat, airplane, boat building business and whatever else to pour out the power anointing God has graced him with.

Young people that range from street wise gang members to backslidden church kids are instantly changed as they encounter the power (dunamis) of God flowing through Bob. Preschool children, college students, and drop outs are all equally affected and changed by a power encounter as Bob simply tells them God loves them and wants to use them to change the world. He invites them to come and get a touch from God. The unsaved, backslidden, half hearted believers, and sincere believers all alike are powerfully touched as he prays for them or has some of the youth who have already received an impartation to pray for them.

In one of Bob's meetings, a weeping mother calls out to Bob from the congregation, "My fifteen year old daughter has strayed from God. I have prayed for eleven months and she only gets worse. What can I do." Bob replies, "Just get her here and the power of God will do the rest." In one evening the rebellious teen is transformed by the power of God as Bob gently lays hands on her and prays for her and invites other teens who have already been transformed to pray for her. The girls eyes fill with tears and she is obviously overwhelmed by the (dunamis) power of God. After a time on the floor being ministered to by the Holy Spirit her heart and life is transformed. Before the evening is over Bob instructs her in praying for others who have come for ministry and the power of God moves through her as even the adults fall under the power of God and receive from the Holy Spirit. Multiply this true story by thousands and you have some idea of what God is doing through one man. Then multiply it again by thousands and you will have an idea of what God is doing through thousands of people to change our world in this day. Cities are being transformed and nations are being affected by the power of God flowing through ordinary people who have received the authority of Christ to flow the power of God to other ordinary people who are hungry for more of God.

There is a season of God coming upon the earth in which many will come into the glorious reality of a relationship with God that will allow a release of the miracle working power (dunamis) of God into the world on an unprecedented scale. Never before has the world seen the awesome release of the mature sons of God walking in His supernatural power on such a large scale. Works of God that exceed the works of Jesus and the disciples in the first century will come forth on the earth as the conditions are met by the sons of God to receive the authority to flow the power of God. God greatly desires to release His power from heaven on earth through many sons. (Rom 8:19) (Heb 2:10)

God's purpose for releasing His power in mankind is the redemption of the world. The salvation of man for heaven after death is a part of that redemption, but God's purpose is larger and more comprehensive. **God's purpose in releasing power from heaven is to bring forth the kingdom of heaven on earth as it is in heaven.**

The unlimited power of God is potentially available to change the world with and through mankind. The entire planet can be changed from the ways of men and the devil to the holy ways of God. The sin of man can be wiped from the face of the earth and the glory of God established in every area of life on the planet. The power of the Creator is available to work with and through mankind to create the kingdom of heaven on earth. What will it take for this power to be flowing in your life?

Man must have specific authority from God to use the force or power of God in the world. Great **power** must always be accompanied by great **authority**. To be safe and effective, power must be restrained and focussed. Power must be released in the right place at the right time at the correct rate. It must be directed toward the target and restrained from other non target areas.

Another Greek word sometimes translated "power" in the New Testament is **"exousia"** and means primarily **"authority"**. It is defined as follows: G1849. exousia, ex-oo-see'-ah; from G1832 (in the sense of ability); **privilege**, i.e. (subj.) force, capacity, **competency**, freedom, or (obj.) **mastery** (concr. magistrate, superhuman, potentate, token of control), **delegated influence:--authority**, jurisdiction, liberty, power, right, strength.

Man must receive the authority (exousia) from God to use the miraculous power (dunamis) from God. There are conditions that must be met in the heart and life before these power gifts from God can be received by man. Many Christians seem to think that just because they are of the Christian faith they have power and authority over the devils and things of the world. Yet many continue to be plagued with demonic oppression and disorders in their lives and are unable to be a substantial factor in overcoming evil in the world. Many who seek to minister continue to find their efforts produce little or no real fruit and long for the power to make real change in peoples lives and subsequently the world.

All power and authority is given unto Jesus. (Mat 28:18) Only Jesus can give the miracle working power and authority of God to man.

*Luke 9:1 Then he called his twelve disciples together, and gave them **power** and **authority** over all devils, and to cure diseases.*

Later Jesus sent out seventy others and gave them power and authority over evil spirits and disease. Jesus often demonstrated power and authority over all the works of the enemy and over all nature. But only on a few occasions did He share that power with a few selected people. (Luke 10:1)

Before Jesus' crucifixion He promised that many would be given the power and authority to do the works that He did and even greater works.

John 14:12: *"Most assuredly, I say to you, he who believes in Me, **the works that I do he will do also; and greater works than these** he will do, because I go to My Father.*

At Jesus' resurrection and ascension the miracle working power of God, which was on the earth in Jesus, left the earth with Him. It was necessary for the disciples to wait in Jerusalem for the return of the power (dunamis) of God in Jesus by the Holy Spirit to in-dwell believers. At Pentecost the awesome power of God returned to earth and in-dwelled those believers who were chosen to be filled with miracle working power and given authority to change the world by overcoming the works of the enemy and establishing the ways and works of God.

These began immediately to speak by the Spirit with authority and began to manifest astonishing demonstrations of the Spirit . Their teaching and preaching became like Jesus with authority and demonstration of miracle working power. The people had been astonished when the power of God was evident in Jesus as he spoke with authority and power and cast out unclean spirits. Now they were seeing that same authority and power in these disciples.

Luke 4:31-36: *Then He went down to Capernaum, a city of Galilee, and was teaching them on the Sabbaths. And they were astonished at His teaching, for His word was with **authority**.*

Now in the synagogue there was a man who had a spirit of an unclean demon. And he cried out with a loud voice, saying, "Let us alone! What have we to do with You, Jesus of Nazareth? Did You come to destroy us? I know who You are; the Holy One of God!"

But Jesus rebuked him, saying, "Be quiet, and come out of him!" And when the demon had thrown him in their midst, it came out of him and did not hurt him.

*Then they were all amazed and spoke among themselves, saying, "What a word this is! For with **authority** and **power** He commands the unclean spirits, and they come out."*

Why did Jesus choose to give this power and authority to only a select few during His life on earth and why did He through the Holy Spirit come first only to those waiting in the upper room?

Why is it today that some are seeing these great miracles in their life and ministry and some are not? In these days of revival, more people are being chosen to receive authority to demonstrate the miracle working power of God. Yet there are others who call themselves believers who are not receiving it? What makes the difference in one who only wishes for the miracle working power of God to flow in and through their lives and those who actually see the miracle working power of God working through their lives?

Perhaps, the real question for you and me is: **How can I obtain the authority (exousia) to have the power (dunamis) of God flow through me?**

We don't need more theological discussions or religious formulas about this. We must have what the twelve and the seventy received from Jesus. We must have what Bob Bradbury and many others have in their lives today. What makes them different? How are they different from many others who wish they had the power of God and who seek it and may even try to act as though they have it, but do not have the reality of the power of God flowing through their lives?

How and why did these receive the impartation of the power of God? How can we receive the impartation of the power of God?

There may not be a simple one, two, three answer to these all important questions, but perhaps we can get some help from a brief look at some characteristics of those walking in (dunamis) power.

285

One thing that sticks out is that the twelve and the seventy had all been with Jesus. They had sold out and given up other things in life to just be with Jesus -- to walk with Him and be a part of what He was doing. Jesus is the anointed one and the anointing of power flows through Him. He is the one in authority and is the one who can impart that authority. The word in the Bible translated anointing means to be rubbed on with oil. Those who were close to Jesus were the ones who received. Those who were not close and were busy about other things in life did not receive the transference of authority and power.

The men and women of today who are demonstrating the power of God on a consistent basis and have authority to carry and impart the power of God all have sold out other things in life to focus on the one thing of being with Jesus. Often they have spent time with other men and women in whom the authority and power of God are present. The gifts and anointing are often transferred by the laying of hands by those who are anointed with Christ and filled with His power.

Only those who have been given the **authority** from Christ to receive the gifts and power will receive from the laying on of hands -- those with whom He has been intimate -- who have proven themselves trustworthy and have a pure heart and no other gods in their lives. God will not allow the authority to remain for an extended time on those whom He does not know and trust.

A touch from God is not the same as impartation. A touch can prepare one to give their life to God. But an impartation is for those who have figuratively sold all and can now be trusted with the awesome power of God. They will use what they are given only according to the desire of God. There are no other needs or priorities that drive them. Obedience to the Spirit of God is essential to walking in power. God will not release true spiritual authority to those who are not walking in obedience.

No amount of money or sacrifice can purchase the power of God for a believer with impurities yet existing in the heart. The wounded and yet unhealed heart containing any amount of resentment or bitterness in any form cannot obtain the authority of Christ to flow the power of God.

Acts 8:18-23: And when Simon saw that through the laying on of the apostles' hands the Holy Spirit was given, he offered them money, saying, "Give me this power also, that anyone on whom I lay hands may receive the Holy Spirit."

But Peter said to him, "Your money perish with you, because you thought that the gift of God could be purchased with money! **"You have neither part nor portion in this matter, for your heart is not right in the sight of God.**

"Repent therefore of this your wickedness, and pray God if perhaps the thought of your heart may be forgiven you. "For I see that you are **poisoned by bitterness and bound by iniquity."**

The authority and power of God is only in God. God desires to in-dwell believers and to demonstrate His power and authority through us. Yet, He is a holy God and cannot dwell with iniquity. True inner holiness in our hearts is the only place for God to dwell and to rest His authority and power. Sometimes the road of purification to holiness can take one through much **repentance and brokenness**. Only our love for God and our sincere desire for Him can bring us through deep purification. Seeking Him with our whole heart will bring us into a relationship with Him that allows His life and power to flow through us.

BASILEIA LETTER
Number 24

Waiting And Listening
For The Kingdom of God

Jesus did not say to the disciples, "Just show up at the next meeting." He said, **"Follow Me."**

He went to people who were busy doing other things and gave them promises and instructions like, **"Follow Me** and I will make you fishers of men -- go and sell what you have, give to the poor and **follow Me** -- let the dead bury the dead, come and **follow Me** -- deny yourself, take up your cross and **follow Me**". Jesus meant for the disciples then and the disciples of today to be with Him -- learn from watching Him and listening to Him -- do as He does and be as He is all day every day, not just show up at meetings. Jesus intends for all to be active in ministry (serving/waiting) in the kingdom of God. He desires for all to have an intimate relationship with Him -- to hear His voice and commune with Him.

One of the ploys of the enemy working through religious teachings of the passing church emphasis age has been to cause the people of the church to think they were supposed to sit in a pew and wait for the kingdom of God. Many have been seduced into believing that their responsibility toward the kingdom of God is to show up for meetings and watch the clergy do the "religious stuff". Jesus hates the doctrine of the Nicolaitans which divided the people into clergy and laity and separated the laity from spiritual life and responsibility except to pay tithes, and attend services.

Rev 2:6: "But this you have, that you hate the deeds of the Nicolaitans, which I also hate.

The people of the kingdom emphasis age today are understanding that waiting for the kingdom of God is much more than passively sitting in a church building. The writers of the New Testament who were passionately giving their lives for the kingdom of God never intended to imply that people should idly wait for the kingdom. The words they used which have been translated "wait" or "waiting" in the New Testament are not words of idle inactivity. The Greek words have meanings of serving, ministering, personal intimacy, and constant diligence.

*Mark 15:43: Joseph of Arimathea, a prominent council member, who was himself **waiting for the kingdom of God**, coming and taking courage, went in to Pilate and asked for the body of Jesus.*

Joseph of Arimathea was busy about the kingdom of God and even taking some risk in going to Pilate and asking for the body of Jesus. The Greek word in this verse translated "waiting" is "prosdechomai".

*Strongs Greek Dictionary: G4327. prosdechomai, pros-dekh'-om-ahee; from G4314 and G1209; to admit (**to intercourse, hospitality, credence** or [fig.] **endurance**); by impl. to await (with confidence or patience):--accept, allow, look (wait) for, take.*

Another word translated "wait" in the New Testament is "proskartereo" and means to be earnestly constantly diligently attending and adhering closely to a person place or thing in service -- to persevere and be instant in service.

*Strongs Greek Dictionary: G4342. proskartereo, pros-kar-ter-eh'-o; from G4314 and G2594; **to be earnest towards**, i.e. (to a thing) **to persevere, be constantly diligent**, or (in a place) **to attend assiduously all the exercises**, or (to a person) **to adhere closely to** (as a servitor):--attend (give self) continually (upon), continue (in, instant in, with), wait on (continually).*

289

Waiting for the kingdom of God means diligently serving much like a waiter waiting tables in a fine restaurant. It means serving the King by attentively listening for His request or instruction and quickly obeying His voice. A good waiter will not be distracted by other things but will have his ear tuned to hear the one whom he serves in readiness to respond. Serving in the kingdom means serving the Lord personally in praise and worship and indirectly by serving others in whom He dwells by the Spirit. *(Mat 25:40)*

The increased vigorous life coming forth in revival is causing increased activity of service to God and to His people. **Waiting and listening** for the kingdom of God is hearing and obeying God and is changing the church and eventually the world.

Spiritual revival leads to kingdom truth.

The awakening of the sleeping church is jolting many from their pews and into action worshiping, praising, praying, and serving God with dynamic energy. The great revivals of today are establishing the reality of life in God as His presence is again filling His temple — the hearts and lives of "ordinary " believers. Revived believers are actively pursuing God and His kingdom. Those seeking the kingdom of God lifestyle are no longer satisfied to give ten percent of their money and even a smaller percentage of their time and call it serving God.

Only serving Him with their whole heart — with their whole life can bring satisfaction to the revived children of God. The powerful presence of God has put a fire of desire within them that cannot be satisfied by idly watching and passively waiting. **The church watchers have become God chasers and cannot be stopped.** The reality of seeking first the kingdom of God has come into our world through revival.

The doctrine of the Nicolaitans is finally being destroyed. **Religion's invention of dividing the Body of Christ into clergy and laity is beginning to be dissolved.** The kingdom truth of the five fold ministry gifts of apostles, prophets, evangelist, pastors, and teachers in "ordinary" believers is coming forth by the Spirit in revival. Christ Jesus is beginning to be honored as head of the church in a practical real way. **The revolutionary reformation of church government has begun.**

The burden of headship that has been usurped by men and denominations is being returned to the shoulder of Christ. The body of Christ has greatly suffered for centuries as the people in the pew have been trained to reverence men as heads and depend on them for spiritual works and church government. Not only have the people failed to develop spiritual gifts and function but the "Reverends" have suffered under the undue burden of invalid headship.

The great overburden placed upon "men of the clergy" is being lifted in revival. No longer shall the weight of the congregation be on the back of the sacrificed life of the "Reverend — Minister — Pastor — Priest" or whatever title used for the paid minister — paid to do what God is now raising up a generation of willing volunteers to do in revival.

The overburden has destroyed many men who sought to fulfill a role as head of the church that God never intended. Not only has the burden been great but the temptation has also been great. Many have succumbed to the temptations and taken advantage of the undue worshipful reverence and respect of the people toward them as "heads of the church". The elevation of "clergymen" set them apart as virtual gods and not mere men. The intense affection for Christ that should have been focused on Jesus as true head of the church has been, in part, focused on "clergymen". It has been much too easy for men to become victims of the gifts and offerings of the people and begin to receive illicit affection and money to themselves. **Scandal, burnout, and failure became common terms relating to "clergymen" in the passing church emphasis age.**

Before the present day outpouring of the presence and power of God began to bring reformation, church leaders struggled with decisions. They often resorted to their own minds which were trained by seminarians in what they could intellectually glean from the Word. For centuries church "heads" and boards of deacons, elders, and denominational bosses have struggled, debated, and voted to make decisions for the church. **The reformed men and women of God are learning to listen for and hear God to receive what Christ has already decided and then represent that into the church.** Thus the burden of headship is being restored to the shoulder of Christ.

Isa 9:6: For unto us a Child is born, Unto us a Son is given; ***And the government will be upon His shoulder.*** *And His name will be called Wonderful, Counselor, Mighty God, Everlasting Father, Prince of Peace.*

Isa 9:7: Of the increase of His government and peace There will be no end, Upon the throne of David and over His kingdom, To order it and establish it with judgment and justice From that time forward, even forever. ***The zeal of the LORD of hosts will perform this.***

In a practical and real way, revival is bringing reformation. The good news is that believers, church governments, and eventually the world will be reformed to kingdom of God ways. The bad news is that **much of the old must be uprooted, torn down, destroyed and overthrown before the new can be built and planted back.**

As in the days Jeremiah it is the zeal of the Lord that is performing the reformation from government by men to the government of God — the kingdom of God. In Jeremiah Chapter One, Israel had forsaken God for other gods and established ways that had to be torn down and destroyed before God's ways could be replanted. There is a parallel in the church. In practice if not in theology other gods have ruled in the church.

*Jer 1:10 NIV: See, today I appoint you over nations and kingdoms to **uproot and tear down, to destroy and overthrow,** to build and to plant."*

The tearing down of the old can be a difficult and painful experience. The past is filled with fond memories of church experiences. Many Christian's faith seems anchored in the relics of the beautiful church buildings and the security of the familiar traditions and fond memories of the past. The future can seem very unsure when the past monuments of beliefs and systems began to crumble and burn.

I remember weeping openly recently as I watched a news video from Virginia. The video was of a beautiful one hundred and sixty two year old church building burning. Fire fighters could do little as the fire destroyed the historical landmark. As I watched the flames swirl up the tall stately steeple that had stood over the city pointing toward the heavens for generations, I felt great sadness and a painful sense of loss. I was impressed in my spirit that this is how many will feel as the old ways of religion are uprooted, torn down, destroyed, and overthrown. These same painful feelings will bruise them as they experience the old ways of the organized church being destroyed to make room for the planting of the kingdom of God ways and the building of the glorious "Bride Church".

293

Jer 31:28 Just as I watched over them to uproot and tear down, and to overthrow, destroy and bring disaster, so I will watch over them to build and to plant," declares the LORD.

As the children of Israel in the wilderness were unwilling to cross over and take the promised land, there will be those who will not make the transition to the glorious church. They will live and die unchanged retaining their old ways. While their children — the next generation will enter into the glorious revival of the presence of God and the extreme worship in the glorious church.

Who are the people of God that are crossing over into the promised land of the kingdom of heaven on earth? What are they like and what is their church and lifestyle like? Who are these people who are actively waiting upon the kingdom of God and listening for the sound of His voice -- these who will not move without the direction of the voice of their God?

They are those who move in unison together as a mighty army -- an army that remains in rank and file and never oversteps or sidesteps the will of their God. **A mighty army of "ordinary" believers filled with an extraordinary obsession for God** -- those obsessed beyond all reason with the very love of their God. Those in whom there remains no place for the devil to lay his hand or attach his hooks. A people without the religious bondages and prideful self righteousness of the past church age. A people who do not care any more about things that were once important but cares with their whole heart and life about the things of their God. A people who are dangerous because of their simple and real love that flows into and through them to the world. A people who forever will cling to the promises of their God and gladly give their lives to be in His presence and to serve Him with all their heart and strength.

These are the people of God coming forth into our world. They are the rulers, the workers, the teachers, the moms and dads, the soldiers from five star generals to buck privates who are one and the same unto their God. They will not rule as lord over one another but will serve one another as Lord. They are the scientist, the plumbers, the builders, and the farmers, they are the worshipers of God doing the work of God on earth. Anointed by His Spirit and filled with undeniable power and strength to do all the will of God.

The sons of the kingdom are with us now and shall continue to grow in numbers as the mighty revival of God planted by the fathers of our past and bathed in the blood of martyrs to our Lord shall cover the earth. From ocean to ocean and from mountain to mountain there shall be none who do not know of the glory of our Lord. The beginning is past and the work lies ahead of us and anyone having put their hand to this plow shall not turn back. The plowing must continue but the planting has already begun. The mighty revival of the presence and power of God shall sweep the whole earth and the planet and all of its people shall never be the same again. The harvest is upon us and shall not be stopped. At the same time the plower is plowing and the sower is sowing and the harvester is harvesting. (Amos 9:13)

What are these people like? They are like Christ Jesus. They are in fact those in whom Christ dwells bringing forth different aspects of His very life in different individuals - the possessors of differing parts of Christ who all coming together to form the whole body of Christ covering the earth. They are the risen Christ dwelling on earth to rule and reign as priest and kings. They are the physical embodiment of the glory of God. The "Christ in you the hope of glory" has become Christ living in many by the Spirit of Christ the manifest presence of the glory of God.

No earthly government or institution shall rule over the glory of God. The kingdom people will be led by Spirit appointed elders in local groups. The elders will be the loving authority to govern the local people of God. No longer will the church be a building made with hands. The local church will meet from day to day in houses or business places or great outdoor stadiums or wherever. Some elders will be gifted pastors tending the sheep. Others will be gifted teachers teaching the children young and old. And others will be evangelist reaching out to the local community harvesting their part of the world.

The apostolic government of God will be fluid and mobile. The powerfully gifted apostles and prophets will move from place to place bringing the wisdom and specific word of God for every need and in every situation. There will no longer be a "headquarters". The "quarters of the head" are in heaven and not on earth. God's chosen servant leaders will look toward the true headquarters in heaven and receive their direction for governing from the Spirit of Christ.

The apostles will receive direction for the overall body and the governing of the overall church will be in them. The prophet will receive the word for more specific an personal direction and correction.

The local elders will receive direction for the local group of believers and will know how to pastor, teach, and evangelize their areas. The elders will know which apostles to call for and when to call for them to come and bring light and government to their group. The apostles will have direction from God in agreement to go where the elders call them. If the elders should falter and need help, an apostle and/or prophet will be sent by God to bring authority and recovery to the situation.

BASILEIA LETTER

Number 25

Awakening of The Kingdom of God

Is there spiritual awakening in our world today?

Most of us tend to accept what we see around us in our local setting and what we see on the news as the way things are everywhere. And it may appear from what we see on TV, and in our local setting, that evil is abounding and God is not doing much about it.

Unfortunately, the TV news media does not do a very good job of reporting what God is doing in our world. You will hear and see about wars and evil works of men and nations from around the world. But mighty moves of God, such as thousands coming to Christ and awesome works of God that may affect entire cities and even nations will not be on your local news tonight.

Have we allowed the news media to be our primary source of spiritual awareness of the world?

Are we, like the Pharisees of the first century? Who in the day that Jesus Christ taught and preached the gospel of the kingdom, totally missed it. The great events and miracles taking place around them were seen as something other than the Son of God proclaiming the kingdom of God. Many people who lived at the same time and in the same place where the mighty works of God were taking place, were not aware of what was occurring. Religious leaders of that day were convinced that Jesus was not doing things the right way and that His doctrine was wrong.

Is it possible that Jesus is doing more in the world today than we know about? Is it possible that we are in danger of missing some great works Jesus is doing through the Holy Spirit in awakenings and outpourings in our world today?

There have been reports of many major outpourings and revivals in recent years and in past centuries in the USA and other parts of the world.

The outpouring of the Holy Spirit brought revival among the **American colonies** in 1734-5. Over 50,000 were converted. Jonathan Edwards described the characteristics of that move as, first, an extraordinary sense of the awful majesty, greatness, and holiness of God, and second, a great longing for humility before God and adoration of God.

In 1739 there were astonishing moves of God in **England.** The Wesleys and Whitefield along with about 60 others held a prayer meeting in London. The Spirit of God moved powerfully on them all. Many fell to the ground, resting in the Spirit. Whitefield started the next month to preach to the Kingswood coal miners in the open fields. By March, 20,000 were attending. Whitefield invited Wesley to take over, and so in April Wesley began his famous open air preaching which continued for 50 years.

David Brainerd, missionary to the **North American Indians** saw a powerful visitation of God in October 1745. Whole communities were changed by the power of the Spirit. Crime and drunkenness dropped, idolatry was abandoned and marriages repaired.

In 1800 a powerful outpouring and revival touched **America,** especially the frontier territory of **Kentucky**. Thousands were converted. Many strange reactions accompanied the move of the Spirit then, including strong shaking and loud cries.

A man named Jeremiah Lanphier started holding noon prayer meetings in **New York** in September 1857. By October, it grew into a daily prayer meeting attended by many businessmen. By March 1858, newspapers carried front page reports of over 6,000 attending daily prayer meetings in **New York** and **Pittsburgh**. In

Washington five daily prayer meetings were held at five different times to accommodate the crowds. In May 1859, there was only about 800,000 people in New York, of which 50,000 were new converts. Charles Finney was preaching in those days. New England was profoundly changed by the revival and in several towns no unconverted adults could be found!

The Ulster revival of 1859 brought 100,000 converts into the churches of **Ireland**. It began with four men starting a weekly prayer meeting in a village school near Kells, in the month of September of 1857— the same date that prayer began in New York.

The awesome moves of God continued and increased in the 1900s around the world.

A few of these outpourings were:

The Welsh revival, 100,000 were converted in **Wales** during 1904-5.

Azusa Street in **Los Angeles** 1906, drew people from around the nation and overseas. There were awesome miracles and manifestations of the Spirit.

In the **Belgian Congo** in 1914 it was reported that the whole place was charged as if with an electric current. Men were falling, jumping, laughing, crying, singing, confessing, and some shaking terribly. This particular one can best be described as a spiritual tornado. People were literally flung to the floor or over the benches, yet no one was hurt. In prayer, the Spirit came down in mighty power sweeping the congregation — bodies trembled with the power — people were filled and as drunk with the Spirit.

In **Rwanda** in June 1936, the famous East African revival began and rapidly spread to the neighboring countries of **Burundi**, **Uganda**, and the **Congo** (now Zaire), then further.

Argentina in 1954, the largest stadium seating 110,000 was filled for weeks as 300,000 made commitments to Christ and hundreds were healed each night for three months.

God's power visited Asbury College in **Wilmore, Kentucky**, on February 3, 1970.

The Jesus Movement exploded among hippie and counter culture **youth in America** in the early seventies.

Nagaland, a state in the North East of **India**, began to experience revival in the 1960s and continued in revival. By the early 1980s it was estimated that 85% of the population had become Christians.

Many other outpourings and major moves of God have been reported in recent decades —far too many to mention here. Hundreds of thousands of people have been and are being converted —countless miracles of healing and deliverance from every evil work and darkness have been and are occurring.

In the decade of the 90s there was an increase in the major moves of God in the USA and around the world.

But we do not see these things on our evening news nor in many of our denominational reports.

A major Christian broadcasting network reported 6 million conversions in their work **worldwide** in 1990, which was more than the previous 30 years of results combined.

Revival swept **Cuba** in 1988. One church had 100,000 visitors in 6 months! A miraculous healing in one church led to nine days of meetings in which 1,200 people were saved. The pastors were imprisoned, but the revival continued. In another church where over 15,000 accepted Christ in three months. In 1990 a pastor whose congregation never exceeded 100 meeting once a week suddenly found himself conducting 12 services a day for 7,000 people.

In **East Germany** small prayer groups of ten to twelve persons started to pray for peace. By October 1989, 50,000 people were involved in Monday night prayer meetings. In 1990, when these praying people moved quietly into the streets, their numbers swelled to 300,000 and the wall came down.

Reports indicate that more **Muslims** have come to Christ in the past decade than in the previous thousand years.

An estimated 3.5 million people a year become Christian in **Latin America** now.

Evangelists continue to have massive healing evangelistic crusades in **Africa**, often with hundreds of thousands attending in the open air. In February, 1995, in Ethiopia, up to 115,000 attended meetings daily. In five days more than 100,000 made commitments to Christ and as many were filled with the Spirit and thousands received healing. Around 10 million a year are becoming Christians in Africa.

In **Benin (West Africa)**, on January 26 to 31, 1999, in a six day evangelistic campaign 640,000 people came to hear the Gospel, and some 200,000 called upon the Lord for salvation. Chains of demonic darkness and voodoo were broken. The glorious delivering power of God burst upon the multitudes. Many were pitifully pain-racked, afflicted, possessed and even insane. But when prayer was made, miracles took place just as in Biblical times - the blind saw, the deaf heard, the cripples walked, cancer victims were cured and mad people became sane. Mister Adoni was totally blind for 12 years. He was instantly healed and can now see.

An estimated 12 million a year are becoming Christian in **China** now with unprecedented moves of God's Spirit, healings, miracles, and visions of Christ.

Over **two billion people** have seen the Jesus film, the full-length movie based on the life of Christ. Showings have occurred in 230 nations and territories. Eight hundred twenty-one organizations use the evangelistic film, in addition to Campus Crusade for Christ International, which coordinates its international translation and distribution. **Eighty seven million** (87,000,000) people have indicated decisions to accept Jesus Christ as personal saviour.

In **Argentina** it is estimated that evangelical Christians tripled in five years to three million, about one tenth of the population. There was not room enough in the churches, some removed the seats so more people can be packed in. Thousands of people attended open-air meetings every night of the week in large cities where miracle healings were commonplace in every service.

There have been major outpourings in this decade, in the USA, numbers of conversions and renewed souls are beyond counting as powerful outpourings of God have brought revivals. New life has surged into hundreds of thousands of people, including many young people and children. Lives are reportedly being changed, addictions broken, relationships healed, documented miracles of healing are occurring, and worship has entered into a new level of living praise to God.

In **Toronto**, in 1994, 120 people had gathered for regular services when the power of God swept in and began to powerfully move upon the congregation. Since that time the outpouring has continued to this date with multitudes coming from around the world to be changed and to receive from God. Millions around the world have been touched by this renewal and who can count the conversions and radically changed lives?

In **Pensacola** on Fathers Day in 1995, the power of God swept into a denominational church. Hundreds of thousands have been converted as multitudes of people from all over the world have come to this powerful revival that continues to this day. Day after day hundreds ran to the alter in tears to give their lives to God. Long lines formed early in the morning outside the church for the 7:00 PM service that evening.

In **Smithton**, a Missouri farm town of 532 people, on March 24, 1996 at 6:12 PM, the power of God hit like a bolt of spiritual lightning in a small community church. For over four years, hundreds of people packed into the church for each of the five powerful services held each week. Over 250,000 people from every state in the USA and over 50 foreign countries have attended. No attempt is even made to keep count of the many conversions and multitudes of changed lives.

In **Baltimore**, on January 19, 1997, The power of God suddenly was poured out during the Sunday morning service. Revival began with powerful works of God and intense worship and praise. Again no attempt is made to keep up with the numbers of changed lives.

Like the first century Pharisees we can criticize these works and renounce them as something other than the works of God. Or we can sincerely pray and personally investigate some of these hot spots of spiritual outpouring in our day, as I have done and continue to do. It may not be wise to reject or accept on the basis of what the news media or someone else says. Until you have been to some of these places and experienced the powerful presence of God for yourself, no one can explain it to you. And once you have experienced the presence of God as the first century believers did and as multitudes are experiencing today you will know the truth.

Why not start now to earnestly pray for true renewal and revival to come to your church and your city? Prayer and willingness to change or two consistent prerequisites for true revival and real revival leads to the kingdom of God ruling in our lives and then our world.

Spiritual awakening of the kingdom of God
through revival is the hope of the world.

The systems of the world cannot long continue to bear the burden of man's living apart from the ways of God. Nations have crumbled and will continue to do so under the weight of the cost of sinful pleasure and self indulgence. As the children of each generation without revival grow less able to make decisions that lead toward life and more unwilling to take responsibility for their own actions and lives, the cost increases. As the generations become more dependent, less productive, and unable to provide for themselves the cost becomes unbearable to governments and a strain on all the systems of the planet.

Thank God for spiritual awakening -- for with it comes awakening of reality thinking by God's people. Men's minds are being freed and the flow of godly wisdom is returning to cause mankind to find his way to real life and away from the seducing trickery of self indulgence and carnal pleasure seeking. People set free by the power of God in revival become God seekers who seek to know Him and to walk in obedience to His ways. Once freed from carnal pleasure seeking and self indulgence, the people begin to loose their bent toward violence. Without their appetites for violence and carnal pleasure, people become free to love and serve one another as they love and serve God with their whole hearts.

REVIVAL IS NOT OPTIONAL

And compared to the alternative it is not too costly. The alternative to not having revival in our world is unthinkable. The cost is beyond compare. To count the stars of heaven would be easier than counting the total cost of not having revival in our world. No amount of cost we pay for revival, either individually, or collectively world wide is too much. Any amount of cost of our lives and effort is worth paying for world revival.

God is pouring out His Spirit in this time and the potential for world wide revival is a reality in this day and the days just ahead. The time for religious debate and walls of separation between real life and God's people is past. Revival is destroying separations and will eventually destroy the separation of God and governments of many nations of the world.

National governments and ungodly ruling institutions are now feeling threatened by the reality of the kingdom of God coming forth in the World. They will be changed or brought down by the power and presence of God as revival and reformation sweeps the land. As God continues to pour out His Spirit and His people respond with unrestrained praise and worship and gather themselves unto Him in intimate prayer, revival is changing our world. No price is too great in response to the One who gave His life on the cross to become the resurrected Christ indwelling His people bringing revival to the world.

BASILEIA LETTER

Number 26

Innocence In The Kingdom of God

Jesus said, *I am sending you out like sheep among wolves. Therefore be as shrewd as snakes and as **innocent** as doves.* Mat 10:16 NIV

In this first century of the new millennium the Body of Christ is awakening to the reality of innocence. It seems we may have sought to be as wise as a serpent or shrewd as a snake and missed the Lord's instruction to be **innocent, harmless,** and **pure.**

Pastor Steve Gray of the Smithton Outpouring / World Revival Church said something that touched me deeply. He said, "Jesus is more real to me today than ever. As He has come nearer and nearer and I have had an even better glimpse of Him. **I have been shocked — not by His fire and power but by His innocence — a pure and innocent lamb that has never sinned — completely pure and innocent.**"

At the core of our Lord's matchless glory, His fire, and His power, is **His heart of innocence** -- completely and totally pure -- not even a hint of uncleanness nor a speck of disobedience to the Father. **He is the completely blameless and harmless innocent lamb of God.** In this time of outpouring, as His presence is more known to us and we become more intimate with Him, we are glimpsing more of His true character.

*Heb 7:26 NIV: Such a high priest meets our need--**one who is holy, blameless, pure, set apart from sinners, exalted above the heavens.***

We are beginning to grasp an understanding
of the relationship between utter innocence
and unlimited power.

The very center of His matchless glory, power, and authority
is His absolute perfect innocence and purity. As only a perfect gem
without inner impurity or flaw can perfectly flow the pure light
without distortion, only perfect absolute innocence can flow the
pure light and power of God. Any impurity or flaw would produce
distortion and become harmful when the light and power of God is
increased.

We desire to be like Him to be in the presence of His glory
and to flow His unlimited wisdom and power bringing healing,
restoration, renewal, reformation and revival to the world. But we
are not like Him and cannot do these things because we are not
innocent like him. Our man focused preaching and lukewarm
lifestyles mixed with cares of this life and desire for things of the
world are not innocent like him. Our zealousness to protect and
defend our narrow view of the very limited doctrines and religious
forms we cherish, causes us to become harmful and we are not
innocent. Doctrinal wars and debate over form do not flow from a
heart of utter innocence. Striving against brothers, back biting and
gossiping are not from a heart of innocence and are not harmless
and pure. Even our best is often not innocent like Him.

*Phil 2:14-15 NIV: **Do everything without complaining or
arguing, so that you may become blameless and pure, children
of God without fault in a crooked and depraved generation, in
which you shine like stars in the universe.***

While church members debate and actually get into fist fights
in the church over whether to use hymn books or an overhead pro-

jector, and while churches split over selecting the color of the new carpet and other such foolish strife, the world starves for the reality of God to show forth the pure and innocent heart of Christ.

While political church leadership attempts to cover its impurities and defend itself and friends and attacks others to protect a position of power over people, the prisoners of the pew starve and die for lack of real food from God. They are given only fake food. That plastic stuff that looks so real in the restaurant window but has no nutritional value and cannot really be eaten.

As we experience His innocence, our pride and self strength melts and our hearts are broken because of the impurity and defilement of our lives contaminated by self living and bad religious training. His glorious presence comes down as we give ourselves to Him in corporate praise, deep adoration of worship and focused prayer. Entering intimacy of His presence begins to reveal His innocence and our hearts are broken by the depth of his purity and innocence. Our lives are exposed to us and we feel as if we have walked into the perfect palace of purity in our dirty work clothes. We begin to understand the parable of the guest entering the wedding feast without a proper wedding garment.

Our hearts weep and tears flow as we see the innocence of our husband and recognize the uncleanness and unfitness of our lives to become the Bride and enter into further intimacy with the innocence of God Himself. Our bodies crumple to the floor and we cannot even open our eyes as our inner parts convulse with sorrow at our inability to enter into the fullness of intimacy with Him. In this deep repentance we feel great changes occurring as things are ripped out of our innermost being leaving gaping holes to be filled with His love and innocent purity.

Eventually we arise from the floor to lift our hands and hearts to Him in wonderful adoration from renewed hearts. Joy burst into our souls as we realize we are more like Him now than we were moments ago. The process continues as we are becoming the prepared Bride for the innocent Lamb the roaring Lion of God.

We have no pride or fear and will no longer remain in the pew as prisoners of religion. Revolution is inevitable as we enter into the glorious reality of the presence of God Himself and all tolerance for religions bondage of traditions and man centered doctrines leaves us. There is great love for God and His people, especially those remaining in the bondage of religious political systems. But there is no loyalty to the systems which may have retained a facsimile of the truth but have brought great perversion and distortion to the truth of the pure innocent Christ and His potential Bride.

Power and wisdom are directly and proportionately related to innocence.

We may have read many times *Mat 10:16 NIV, I am sending you out like sheep among wolves. Therefore be as shrewd as snakes and as **innocent** as doves.* Or in the KJV, *Behold, I send you forth as sheep in the midst of wolves: be ye therefore wise as serpents, and harmless as doves.* I have always noticed the contrast of being as wise or shrewd as a snake and as innocent or harmless as a dove and never before understood the relationship of these things.

Power and wisdom of God come to the innocent.

The harmless and innocent ones will hear and receive wisdom and revelation to function powerfully (shrewdly) in this perverse world. Only the innocent and harmless can be trusted with the great secrets of power and strategy from God. Only the innocent sheep can have the shrewd wisdom to deal with the wolves of this world and not become contaminated by the ways of the wicked.

The Body of Christ is now beginning to awaken to the potential power of purity. Our innocence will become the source of power to fuel the great revolution bringing an end to man centered and devil enhanced religious systems of the world.

Now is the time to seek Him with our whole heart and to lay down quickly those things He brings to our attention. We must enter collectively in the power of all in unity corporately to experience the glorious presence of God that changes us from glory to glory. We are becoming more like Him and He shall roar out of Zion in the unlimited power of innocence. The world is waiting and groaning for you and me and an army of young people to become innocent and harmless that we may be wise and shrewd -- the innocent army of God bringing a revolution of reformation establishing the kingdom of God on earth as it is in heaven.

From positional righteousness to real purity of innocence.

My heart was broken because of my sinful condition when as a young man of twenty one I encountered the saving grace of our Lord Jesus. My heart's desire was to be different, to be like Him and to be pleasing in His sight. Some things about me did change very quickly. I felt very bad every time a curse word leaked out of my mouth from my not yet renewed mind and soon I was mostly free of that profane habit. Yet many other things within and about me were not like Him.

My concerns about my debauchery were greatly eased by theological teachings of positional righteousness. Basically I was taught that my depravity was normal and that my disgraceful unholy inner life was covered by the blood of Jesus. Everyone was a sinner and now I was a saved sinner and would be in heaven because of what Jesus had done on the cross for me. My position was that of now being seated at the right hand of God with Christ, redeemed by the blood. When God looked at me He did not see my sinfulness but the righteousness of Christ. Certainly, I was to try to do my best but I could never expect to overcome sin in this life because of my sin nature. We all are sinners only some are saved sinners and some are lost sinners.

According to this teaching I was positionally innocent before God because Jesus had died for me and my sins past, present, and future were under the blood of Jesus. Because I believed in Jesus as the Son of God and had received Him as saviour I was secure and could not be plucked from His hand. Yet, my experience continued to be a roller coaster type of spiritual ups and sinful downs. Although I sought diligently to hide my lust and to overcome sinful habits and addictions my life was a battle of bitter frustration. Zealousness characterized my life. I fought hard against my own inner impurities and was severely harsh against sin in others.

I taught Sunday School, became an elder in the church, attended Bible College, began preaching, witnessed in the streets, and visited for the church. Yet, in all my zealousness, impurities remained within my own heart. I was not innocent and harmless as a dove and often wondered how and why most everyone close to me seemed to get hurt or offended by me. The intent of my heart was pure but it is from the abundance of the heart that the life speaks. (Luke 6:45)

Like many others around the world, My soul cried out, **"there must be more"**.

The "more" has now come. The outpouring of the Spirit has brought power from God to change our inner being to eradicate our sinful ways and fill us with His purity and power. No longer must we suffer in frustration as sin takes its toll upon the strength and glory of God within our souls. Freedom is upon us as the spiritual outpouring of God is bringing revival to our souls and reformation to the blessed Body of Christ who is becoming His purified Bride. No longer must we attempt to replace our lack of spiritual power with soulish zealousness. (Rom 10:2-3)

We can now be filled with the power of His presence cleansing our hearts and destroying our desire for the old ways. No longer are we focused upon our own lives and filled with needs. His love flowing in and through us is making us innocent and harmless. His presence has so filled us that we have no frustrating needs but are filled with abundant life to flow to others.

No longer must we devise doctrines to make room for our sinful hearts. Christ is not just a covering for our sin filled heart. Now, when God looks at us He can look directly into a pure heart filled with the innocence and glory of Christ Himself. The reality of God has come and the shadows are passing away.

The army of God is being formed. Pure hearts of ordinary believers have become the temple of God on earth and the attributes of God are becoming a reality in the innocent and harmless people of God's army. Truly nothing is impossible as pure hearts are filled with great faith and ability to know God and discern His will. Clearly receiving His instruction and having the faith to act upon it provides unlimited power to accomplish the will of God on earth as it is in heaven.

The outpouring of God coming forth in spots around the world in this time is not just for the purpose of our having a Holy Ghost party. The joy of the Lord is real and the excitement of miracles and manifestations along with the awesome praise and worship music are indeed producing many occasions of gloriously wonderful gatherings. The many testimonies of miracles and healing of bodies and lives is exciting. The stories told by those being saved and delivered as well as those returning to the Lord after straying away are uplifting. All of this is joyful and is indeed a part of the purpose for the great outpouring of God in the world today. But, if it does not lead to inner purity and innocence, God's purpose is not fulfilled. If we can experience God and His blessings and still leave the gathering to return to our old thought patterns and our old ways of doing and being, God's purpose is not yet fulfilled. If our lifestyle continues to be mixed with the spirit of the world, we are missing the purpose of God.

This is a new day for the church. The church that taught us self improvement, self love, prosperity for the sake of our blessing and tolerance for our sinful lifestyles is now over. The twelve o'clock whistle has blown, the final amen has been said and the entire church has gone to lunch. We must come to the realization that church as usual is over and is not coming back. Yes, many will hang on to the man centered gospel and the old ways of the church until they themselves pass away in the wilderness. Many will continue to carry forth the empty traditions of the past until they breathe their last natural breath. They have already breathed their last spiritual breath and are only waiting to die in their wilderness experience while seeking to prevent others from entering the promised land.

These are our spiritual mothers and fathers and there is a reality of honor for them. Yet, we must hate their ways and the ungodly part of the things they have taught us and demanded that we continue. Is this a part of what Jesus meant when He said in Luke 14:26 that we could not be His disciple if we did not hate our father and mother? We know that we are not to hate the church or our parents. But we must hate what they are saying to us that prevents us from going on with Jesus and being a part of what He is doing in this day. We must hate the encouragement to continue in our mixed ways of inner impurity and tolerance for sin. We must hate the thing that continues to tell us that we are doing well when inside we are filled with death and are not concerned about living a truly consecrated life unto the Lord.

Just as long as we are reasonably healthy and doing well financially we tend to be satisfied and don't really mind our immoral lifestyles and lack of the true presence of God in our midst. Much of the church today is yet saying, as long as we have really nice cars, the finest church buildings ever, time for the golf course, and plenty of entertainment why rock the boat. Why start a revolution bringing reformation and revival.

Only when the true presence of God shows up and begins to expose the bankrupt spiritual condition of the powerless church does it become obvious that something is terribly wrong. The lukewarm half hearted people who are mixed with the ways of the world will either be changed or deny the work of God and flee from His presence.

BASILEIA LETTER

Number 27
Pain & Suffering
In the Kingdom of God

Jesus said, *"O My Father, if it is possible, let this cup pass from Me; nevertheless, not as I will, but as You will.", Mat 26:39.*

*Heb 12:2a: Looking unto Jesus, the author and finisher of our faith, who for the joy that was set before Him **endured the cross, despising the shame.***

*1 Pet 2:20-21: For what credit is it if, when you are beaten for your faults, you take it patiently? **But when you do good and suffer,** if you take it patiently, this is commendable before God. For to this you were called, because **Christ also suffered for us, leaving us an example, that you should follow His steps.***

In my mind I can still hear the voice of President Franklin D. Roosevelt as he spoke the declaration of war in December of 1941. World War II was officially declared that night as my father, mother, my siblings, and I gathered in somber silence around the radio. In his deep, serious, and strong but mellow voice he spoke these words, **"I hate war. --- My wife Elenor hates war. --- We all hate war."** He went on to speak of the evil attacks against our nation and that because of evil, war was necessary. He then sought to encourage the nation to fight. He encouraged the men to fight for the lives and futures of their children and their families. He encouraged the families to sacrifice and give all they could to help their husbands, fathers, and sons that were going into mortal combat to stop the enemy.

315

This sleepy nation was suddenly awakened. The jolt of devastating attack had shaken us to the core and instantly the focus of the entire nation was on fighting and winning the war. We were so far behind in preparation and such a devastating blow had been dealt to our navy that we were not sure who would win the war. In the days, months, and years ahead the enemy advanced rapidly and we continued to retreat on all fronts with heavy casualties. Almost every person in the USA was affected personally by the pain and suffering of the war. Though we cried a lot, our focus was never on the fear or the pain but on winning the war and the hope of victory. Hundreds of thousands of young men laid down the tools of their trade and picked up a rifle with a bayonet fixed on it and became fighting men. They endured the pain and suffering of battle and died trying to stop the enemy's advance.

Pain is never a gift from God except as an indicator of disorder. It is not His desire for mankind. Yet, because of the evil of man, pain and suffering are very real. Those who will live as Christ in the world will be partakers of His pain and suffering.

2 Tim 3:12-13: **Yes, and all who desire to live godly in Christ Jesus will suffer persecution.**

Jesus came to earth and accepted the cup of suffering for the joy of the glory of the kingdom of God. Had there been no evil in the world, Jesus would not have endured pain and suffering. If there were no need in the church and no evil in our world today, we would not be compelled to endure pain and suffering today.

Col 1:24 I now rejoice in my sufferings for you, and fill up in my flesh what is lacking in the afflictions of Christ, for the sake of His body, which is the church.

316

In the days of this writing we are living in a time of great mercy of God. A time in which the outpouring of the Spirit of God is bringing renewal and revival to many spots in the world. Renewal is bringing great blessing and joyful presence of God and even something called by some a "Holy Ghost party", so called because of the great joy the presence of God brings. There is great praise and worship expressed in music, dance, shouts of rejoicing as well as times of quite intimate communion with God. Physical manifestations of the Spirit and miracles are not uncommon.

Many of these revived and rejoicing believers were once a part of other churches and religious systems. Some have given much of their lives and resources to their previous church fellowships and denominations only to find that they were unwelcome and unwanted when the powerful presence of God swept over them. Often evil reports and false accusations are brought to slander those who are revived by the Spirit of God. Family members sometimes reject them causing painful splits within families which sometimes brings financial losses and loss of social position. In some parts of the world believers are beaten, imprisoned, taken into slavery, and sometimes martyred because of their love for Jesus.

There have been those of the church in the past who have given their all and sought to serve God with their whole heart and to reach the world. They were the exceptions, the ones who were different, the revivalist, the missionaries, the saints who gave up secular life to serve to the best of their ability with their whole heart. Often spending their entire lives and seeing very little fruit in a spiritually sleeping world. Here and their a great awakening would occur only to be eventually smothered by the religious church of the past and drowned with tradition and debate over form and strife among denominations.

In the passing church age, religion has lulled its followers to sleep with lullabies of peace and doctrines of false security brought forth by religious demons.

*1 Tim 4:1 Now the Spirit expressly says that in latter times some will depart from the faith, **giving heed to deceiving spirits and doctrines of demons.***

*Jer 6:14 They have also healed the hurt of My people slightly, **Saying, 'Peace, peace!' When there is no peace.***

Most of the religious world did not even know that a spiritual war was going on and that the enemy was subversively infiltrating the religious and secular world with corrupt beliefs that robbed believers of the joyful and powerful presence of God which would have brought forth His kingdom in the earth.

For the most part, the church slept and did not even show up for the war and has lost by default.

The rule of the earth has been given over to the enemy without even a fight.

The lives and souls of multitudes of men women and children across the world have been lost. Our families are destroyed. Our children are spiritually raped and murdered and robbed of all potential power in the kingdom of God while we are comfortable with our favorite TV shows of filth and violence and our beliefs of liberal self gratification, and while the church fights over doctrines and debates manifestations.

318

Though there were many victories, **the church of the past has failed** to conquer the enemy and bring forth the kingdom of God. We cannot blame the devil whom Jesus has defeated. We cannot blame the lost and heathen world. They knew nothing and had no potential without the church becoming powerful to reach them. We must put the blame where it belongs, on ourselves. **Believers who have been deceived and have swallowed a camel of false doctrine and strained at gnats of truth.** Believers who considered ourselves, our lives, our comfort, and our religion above the kingdom of God. Believers who did not even know there was a kingdom of God here and now. A sick and deadly religious group of half hearted lukewarm powerless believers consumed with our own controversies and strife over useless wrangling over doctrines of baptisms and ordinances of which we knew nothing of the reality of the life these things proclaimed.

Today much of the sleeping church only wakes up to fight against the true move of God coming forth in powerful revivals around the world. They are harsh in defending their sacred doctrines and do not know that they are defending mixtures of truth and doctrines of demons and religious traditions of men. The church has been so trained in inner combat and to ignore the enemy who has taken them captive, that even those being set free tend to turn their guns upon each other and from habit and training they debate the different streams of revival and moves of God rather than joining together to destroy the enemy and bringing forth the kingdom of God.

The hearts and minds of men, women, and children are being changed by the powerful presence of God coming forth in our world today. The great transition from dead religion to the reality of the outpouring of the presence and power of God is bringing great change into our world. No longer are we the center of the gospel. No longer are we the center of our own world. Christ Jesus

319

is receiving His rightful place as king of our lives and eventually king over all the kingdoms of our world. There is no more place for lukewarm and half hearted Christianity. The presence of God is consuming His people like a consuming fire as revival sweeps our hearts.

Heb 12:28 -29: Therefore, since we are receiving a kingdom which cannot be shaken, let us have grace, by which we may serve God acceptably with reverence and godly fear.
For our God is a consuming fire.

The dying religious churches must give up their prideful position of believing they know everything and have all there is of God and bow their lives and beliefs before God. They must cry out for His mercy to cover them while there is yet mercy in this time of transition. This time of mercy will not last forever and the days of judgment will come upon the church. (1 Pet 4:17) She will be judged because of her lack of repentance from deception, spiritual darkness and blindness, which led her to oppose the move of God upon the earth today. While she thought she was the elite and chosen of God, rich in spiritual knowledge, she is a doomed and dying generation that must repent or die in the wilderness. Thinking herself to be rich she became naked and poor and now is in danger of being left behind as the mighty move of God upon the earth is bringing transition from the man centered church age to the God centered kingdom of God age. Now is the time for wise men to repent and pay the price to make the great changes necessary to get out of lukewarm religion and into the powerful presence and flow of God.

*Rev 3:16-19; "So then, **because you are lukewarm, and neither cold nor hot, I will vomit you out of My mouth. "Because you say, 'I am rich, have become wealthy, and have need of nothing'; and do not know that you are wretched, miserable, poor,***

320

blind, and naked; "I counsel you to buy from Me gold refined in the fire, that you may be rich; and white garments, that you may be clothed, that the shame of your nakedness may not be revealed; and anoint your eyes with eye salve, that you may see. "As many as I love, I rebuke and chasten. **Therefore be zealous and repent.**

The true people of God of today will never back down, never turn back and never quit. The revivals and the move of God today will not be smothered by religion or stopped by debate and strife. The people will not be stopped by suffering, pain, or death. This move of God will take the earth as young people across the world come to know the true love of God and become pure in their hearts to carry the cross of Christ into glorious blazing resurrection life.

The glory of God is now coming forth on the earth in His sons and daughters.

Christ Jesus is now being valued above riches, knowledge, worldly esteem, marriage and family and yes, even life itself. The most important thing to the pure hearted sons and daughters of God is not their own life, not even the lives of their children as deeply important as these things are, the most important thing is Jesus and his presence with us and His glory revealed.

A generation of people are coming forth upon the earth with a new value system. One that does not ignore the things of natural life but one that values God so far above all else that there is no close second. **To the rest of the world and to the devil and his demons this is a most frightening thing.** Nothing can be used to entice or divert the arising army of God. There is no place for the world or the devil to get their hooks into the self abandoned and empowered children of God.

321

We are entering the time for which the servants of God have waited throughout history. The time of redemption on a scale never before seen and that will never be seen again. A time when absolutely nothing is impossible to those who truly believe. A time that will see the destruction of the past religious world and the evil secular world which will not repent. The unrepentant will cry out for the mountains and the rocks to fall on them and hide them from the face of the completely innocent glorious all powerful God. The more the enemy and religion kills, the more children will be raised up by the mighty hand of God. The great harvest of the earth has begun in the pure hearted children of God who no longer count their lives as precious to themselves and value Christ Jesus above all else.

This is spiritual warfare in its total reality. This war will be won in the presence and power of almighty God himself coming in the outpouring of His Spirit bringing a pouring out of the Spirit of God through His people. It will be won in praise, worship, dancing, rejoicing before the Lord, and intimate oneness with Jesus. It is the reality of "Christ in you the hope of glory." In revival today Christ Jesus is returning to earth in His people to establish His kingdom and to rule and reign with His saints. The devil and the religions of the world cannot stop the very presence of God in His people walking upon the earth in the power of Christ doing all the works that Jesus did and more. (John 14:12)

This is not the time for human effort to attempt to do the works of the church. **Church growth is not the issue. The issue for the religious church is church destruction.** The old must come down to make place for the new. The only question is, will the people who have sought God in the religious man centered systems, turn and repent and seek Him with their whole hearts? Or will they wait to be torn down and destroyed by the work of the enemy who has seduced and deceived them? Will they seek deliverance and come out of the open prison door and receive sight for their spiritual blindness as many others already have?

Jesus is today proclaiming the opening of the prison for those who are bound (in religion), those who mourn in Zion (the church). The sons of God are anointed of the Lord to proclaim good tidings to those who may have thought they were rich but are really spiritually poor, blind, and in bondage to a mixture of truth and deception.

Isa 61:1-3: *"The Spirit of the Lord GOD is upon Me, Because the LORD has anointed Me To preach good tidings to the* ***poor;*** *He has sent Me to heal the brokenhearted, To proclaim liberty to the captives,* ***And the opening of the prison to those who are bound;*** *To proclaim the acceptable year of the LORD, And the day of vengeance of our God;* ***To comfort all who mourn, To console those who mourn in Zion,*** *To give them beauty for ashes, The oil of joy for mourning, The garment of praise for the spirit of heaviness; That they may be called trees of righteousness, The planting of the LORD, that He may be glorified."*

Wake up people of God! This is for you! The bondages of religious doctrines and false security brought forth in the darkness of past religious bondage can no longer hold you. The religious prison doors are open. There is comfort and beauty for you. There is power, joy and praise in the presence and glory of the Lord waiting for you now. Come out from among the unclean religious systems and God will be a Father to you. You will find life in His presence and experience His love in a greater way than ever before.

2 Cor 6:17 - 7:4: ***Therefore "Come out from among them And be separate, says the Lord. Do not touch what is unclean, And I will receive you." "I will be a Father to you, And you shall be My sons and daughters, Says the LORD Almighty."***

323

*Therefore, having these promises, beloved, let us cleanse ourselves from all filthiness of the flesh **and spirit,** perfecting holiness in the fear of God. Open your hearts to us. We have wronged no one, we have corrupted no one, we have cheated no one. I do not say this to condemn; for I have said before that you are in our hearts, to die together and to live together. Great is my boldness of speech toward you, great is my boasting on your behalf. **I am filled with comfort. I am exceedingly joyful in all our tribulation.***

BASILEIA LETTER

Number 28

Victory In the Kingdom of God

"Basileia Letter" is changing. As we enter the time of great harvest of the earth there are many changes to come forth. To be effective in turbulent times we must be quick to change and to flow with what God is doing. "Basileia Letters" and the books "Overcoming Life On A Small Planet" and "The Seventh Millennium" are written for the purpose of teaching some of the fundamentals of the kingdom of God and helping to bring people through the process of reformation from man centered church to God centered kingdom of God living on earth.

This work has just begun. There are relatively few people who have truly grasped the gospel of the kingdom and the potential that lies within the hearts of believers to rule and reign with Christ now in every area of life and government. Even the most powerful moves of revival and reformation in the world today have only a start of the revelation of the potential of the glory of Christ in man ruling and reigning in the world. Therefore the work of these books and letters shall go on for many years and perhaps centuries to come as one by one believers find the truth of the kingdom of God now.

These and other works by other men of God are the beginnings of kingdom understanding. It had to start with those who had nothing to loose. The established church and ministry leaders cannot be first in bringing forth the fresh revelation of kingdom. They have to much to loose by the rejection of those believers who are yet unable to change and flow in the new stream of restored revelation. God in his mercy temporarily withholds the enlightenment of leaders of revival and reformation movements to the fullness of the gospel of the kingdom now to prevent confusion of the troops who are required to bring about the harvest that is at hand. New and fresh wine can be too much of a taste change for the survival of unity in the ranks of the army of harvesters in our world.

Therefore, God has chosen to gradually re introduce the gospel of the kingdom through non threatening methods and non threatening men. He has chosen to use unknown and in many cases older men of God who have largely finished their season of gathering and therefore no longer need respect as significant or popular leaders. A base of believers who are receiving the gospel of the kingdom are coming forth and the kingdom is coming up like grass covering a field and not like great trees. Intermingled with the grass of the field are the tiny new trees that will eventually grow to become the great trees of future kingdom of God leaders.

Prophets Point The Way

Prophets are not designed to be great gatherers, but plowers that destroy the old, and planters of the new kingdom seed that covers the fields as grass and one day shall grow the trees of the future. God is raising up young prophets with strong words of the gospel of the kingdom. And of course the enemy is raising up false kingdom prophets who plant seeds of a kingdom that looks like the kingdom of God but is really tares.

"Basileia Letters" will, in the near future, all be bound in book form and along with Overcoming Life and Seventh Millennium will continue to be made available to the body of Christ. These works can be helpful in discerning the true and false prophets of kingdom as well as helping to plant and grow the seeds of the kingdom of God into the kingdom lifestyle in our world. These books can be requested and Basileia Letters downloaded from our web site: http://www.basileiapublishing.com/

In the kingdom of God, Victory is God ruling over all the kingdoms of earth through His people, not just ruling in the church or the individual.

Many believers are yet looking to the bodily return of Jesus to bring victory. Until the masses realize that Jesus has already done everything he will ever do to destroy the kingdoms of the enemy without our participation, the kingdoms of this earth cannot become the kingdoms of our God. Until believers understand that the ball is in our court, that we are empowered by God to destroy the work of the enemy and establish the rule of God in the earth, it cannot yet be done. The kingdom of God is not waiting for God to make another move. It is waiting on mankind to realize and move into what God has already provided through Christ Jesus. **The honor of God must be restored on earth by mankind.** Man dishonored God in the Garden of Eden and surrendered the kingdoms of this world to the enemy and until the kingdoms are returned to our God He is dishonored on earth.

Until this final victory is achieved the Basileia Letters and other books we have mentioned will not have finished their work. The fulfillment of my life and the lives of all the men of God who have come and gone before me and have seen the kingdom of God yet afar off cannot be complete until the day the kingdoms of this earth become the kingdoms of our God. Our mission must be completed in future generations if this generation will not come to the reality of giving our lives to restore honor to God in recapturing the kingdoms of this world. He has given us His great power within us and is now working with us from heaven. Jesus must remain bodily in heaven while He battles for earth in His Bride -- His Body on earth.

The fullness of victory remains incomplete -- not because of God or anything He needs to do -- but because of man and what he chooses to believe. Mankind does not want to accept the responsibility which he ultimately cannot escape. He wants victory to completely rest in God and have nothing to do with himself. The enlightenment of the truth that God will do nothing further to redeem the kingdoms of earth without man's willing participation is hard for man to accept. Men love darkness which covers their lack of willingness to die to self and honor God by redeeming the kingdoms of earth with the awesome power of God available through a willing participant.

To cover his lack man has invented doctrines of perversions of God's grace. God's grace gifts of power are to overcome the world and destroy the work of the enemy for the purpose of redeeming the kingdoms of this world for our God and restoring honor unto His name. God's grace is not a whitewash covering for man's sin of non participation and self centered living which only honor the devil and not God. God's grace is the unmerited favor of the power of God given to believers to redeem the kingdoms of the world. Christ Jesus has done everything to redeem the kingdom and is restoring honor to the Father by bringing righteous living and obedience forth in the world through His body on earth, the purified Bride church.

For now, our victory is the redemption
of His kingdom within the individual
rather than full corporate kingdom.

While the purified Bride church groups are growing and the grass of the fields is coming forth and the kingdom is waiting for believers to believe, we are blessed with personal victory and increasing victory in groups. In spots around the world the kingdom of God is coming forth in groups as revival fires continue to spread. Individually and in some groups we are restoring honor to God and recapturing portions of the kingdoms of this world as the work of the enemy is being destroyed and righteousness established in the earth.

The important thing is that we each finish our part. That we remain faithful to the end to carry out all God has put within our hands to do and to be. It is important that we complete the portion of destroying the kingdom of darkness and establishing the kingdom of our God that we are gifted to do during our time on earth. It is important that we leave a legacy for the future generations that have a fresh chance to take back the kingdoms of earth and restore honor to our God. Each generation has the opportunity to begin where the previous one finished. Our greatest hope is to hear those words, "well done good and faithful servant" and to know we have had a part in restoring His honor and bringing His kingdom forth on earth.

The great harvest has begun. Millions are gathering to hear the salvation message and experience the presence and power of God flowing through His servants. Praise, worship, strong corporate prayer and righteous living is restoring honor to our God. The great army is being assembled as multitudes are finding personal redemption in God and giving their lives to serve Him. These masses of mostly young believers must eventually hear and receive the gospel of the kingdom and become soldiers carrying the gospel of the kingdom to all the world. The political world, financial world, the world of education and every facet of our world will all be transformed as the mass of believers each do their part in conducting the business of the world.

The natural course of judgmental destruction set in motion by mankind living apart from God's ways for centuries will bring great adjustments in the world toward the kingdom of God in the future. For now in this time of mercy and visitation of the presence of God we must fan the fires of revival and seek to bring forth the glorious presence of God leading toward the great world harvest.

Our future periodical publications at Basileia Publishing will reflect that change. Our thought at this time is to publish a shorter communication called "Doxa Dispatch". Doxa is the New Testament Greek word for glory. This communication will remain true to the gospel of the kingdom and seek to spread the fire of His glory and fan the fires of revival moving toward the great harvest. This will be your last "Basileia Letter." May we suggest that you reread them in the books, "Basileia Letters Volume 1 & 2". Look for kingdom wisdom in the new shorter Basileia publication "Doxa Dispatch" coming soon.

~~~~~~

Author's Note

Wherefore I will not be negligent to put you always in remembrance of these things, though ye know them, and be established in the present truth.

Yea, I think it meet, as long as I am in this tabernacle, to stir you up by putting you in remembrance; Knowing that shortly I must put off this my tabernacle, even as our Lord Jesus Christ hath shown me.

Moreover I will endeavour that ye may be able after my decease to have these things always in remembrance.

For we have not followed cunningly devised fables, when we made known unto you the power and presence of our Lord Jesus Christ, but are eyewitnesses of his majesty, 2 Pet 1:12-16.

In His love,
Brother Ron

Made in the USA
Monee, IL
20 September 2020

43064602R00125

DYNAMO PRESS

JASMINE WALT

BOOK ONE OF THE BAINE CHRONICLES:
FENRIS'S STORY

FUGITIVE BY MAGIC

MW01505612

Cover illustration by Judah Dobin

Cover typography by Rebecca Frank

Edited by Mary Burnett

Electronic edition, 2017. If you want to be notified when Jasmine's next novel is released and get access to exclusive contests, giveaways, and freebies, sign up for her mailing list here. Your email address will never be shared and you can unsubscribe at any time.

❄ Created with Vellum

1

FENRIS

Home sweet home.

Those were the first words, rife with sarcasm, that echoed through my head as I stood outside the farmhouse, hands in my tunic pockets. The sight was nearly enough to make me turn on my heels and leave for good. As I stared at the crooked chimneys, the peeling paint, and the rusty rainwater pipe, I wondered how I'd fallen so far.

But then, what had I expected after buying this place sight unseen? At least the house was fairly big—family-sized, the advertisement had said—and though the proportions were not pleasing, I could live with them.

Taking a deep breath, I did my best to ignore the unpleasant exterior and approached the door. The owner had painted it a very unfortunate shade of green. When I gripped the tarnished handle, I had to remind myself of the reasons that brought me to this dilapidated farmhouse.

After nearly being arrested by Garrett Toring, who had come far too close to exposing my secret, I had used the cover of Solantha's disastrous quake to flee. It had pained me to leave Sunaya and Iannis behind, especially knowing they would be

spending many long, arduous months cleaning up the aftermath, but it had no longer been safe for me to remain in Solantha. I needed to be far from any mages intent on catching and executing me. And, as I'd just experienced, Abbsville was a tedious three-hour steambus ride away from the closest mages here in Watawis. I also needed to live away from other shifters, who would soon notice how unlike them I was and sniff out any magic I might use.

When I'd first left Solantha, I'd thought I could simply disappear into another city and live out my days using a magical disguise. But just a few weeks ago, I had nearly been caught through my love of old manuscripts and magical scholarship and had been forced to leave the city I'd been hiding in. Abbsville, a tiny human town with a population of around eight hundred, was the perfect place for me to settle. This hamlet had no shifters or mages to out me, and there was not so much as a single bookshop or public library to tempt me into old habits.

Besides, I thought as I went into the house, *the mountain ranges and endless forests are quite lovely.* This place was ideal in many ways for a shifter—I would be able to run free and hunt on full-moon nights. If I stayed away from the farms, there would be no issue.

I'd attempted to be discreet with my arrival, but I must have been noticed because less than three hours later, a visitor arrived. As I sat at my kitchen table, sipping coffee and gloomily considering all the improvements I would have to make to this place, I heard a steamtractor approach. Its high-pitched whine ripped through the pleasant spring morning, drowning out the songs of twittering birds.

Annoyed, I set my cup aside and pushed back the dusty curtain. The clumsy vehicle was still some five acres away from my doorstep.

As the steamtractor lumbered down the unpaved road, I

zeroed in on the young man driving it. He was big and muscular, dressed in a straw hat and suspenders—no more than twenty-three. There was an open expression of curiosity on his face, for which I couldn't blame him. A stranger from out of state had just taken up residence in an all-human farming community. I was an anomaly, and I'd known when I'd bought the place I would be dealing with nosy neighbors.

I only wished they'd given me at least one day to settle in before showing up.

The young man killed the tractor's engine with a last loud belch, and I relaxed as blessed silence filled the air once more. Well, not really silence. The sounds of nature rushed back in—the twittering birds, the rustling trees, the water trickling through the ancient plumbing. But these were easily tuned out —in the four years since I'd become a shifter, I'd learned to acclimate to my sharper senses, to "turn down the volume" so I would not be so easily distracted by every little noise.

I made it to the front door just as my visitor knocked, and pulled it open. The sweet smell of ripe strawberries wafted from the basket looped over the man's arm. Not what I had expected.

"Good morning," he said, looking quite taken aback—maybe he thought I hadn't heard him approach? But no, it was more likely that he hadn't expected a shifter to answer the door. With our distinctive eyes, we were immediately set apart from humans. The corner of my lips twitched, and I smoothed my expression into something polite but friendly.

"My name is Marris Dolan—my family runs the farm next to this one, and we've been leasing the farmland from Ackleberry Farm for the past three years. Are you the new owner?"

"I am. Jalen Fenris Shelton," I said, holding out my hand for him to shake. He took it, his grip firm but nonthreatening, and I added, "I go by my middle name."

"Fenris, eh?" Marris smiled. "I knew a shifter by that name

once. I must say, I didn't quite believe it when I heard the rumors that a wolf shifter had taken over Ackleberry Farm. But we're happy to have you—my ma sent me over with this as a house-warming gift. From our greenhouse." He hefted the basket slung over his forearm, holding it out to me.

"Thank you." I took the gift, then stepped back. "I suspect you're here to talk about the lease, so why don't you come in?"

Marris gave me a sheepish smile. "I'm sure you'd have preferred a day or two to settle in, but Ma insisted."

I waved him in. "It's no trouble at all," I said, closing the door behind him. I led him down the hall and into the living room, off to the left. It was spacious, mostly because almost all the furnishings had been taken by the previous owners. They had left a bed with a lumpy mattress in the guest room, an old set of pots and pans and cracked dishes in the kitchen, and a set of horrid floral couches and a scratched-up coffee table here in the living room. The holes in the walls suggested artwork had once hung here—holes I would eventually patch and perhaps cover with decorations of my own.

The "fully furnished" promise in the ad had been more than a little misleading. But judging by the pieces they had left behind, the previous owners had done me a favor by taking away any other horrors.

"I remember these couches," Marris said with a grin, patting the cushion on the loveseat he sat on. "There's a spring that would hit me in the rear every time I sat down here as a child."

I chuckled. "I became acquainted with that spring earlier today," I admitted. I was about to sit down on the couch when I remembered my manners. "Would you like some water or coffee? I'd offer you food, but aside from these lovely strawber-ries, I'm afraid my pantry is terribly empty."

"I'd love some coffee," he said, perking up. "I caught a whiff

of whatever you brewed, and it smells downright divine. You bring that from the city or something?"

"Yes, in another state." I'd picked it up during my travels, but I was running low already. I hoped they had decent grounds at the general store, though I did not have high hopes, given Marris's reaction. I retrieved my cup of coffee from the kitchen, refilled it, and poured a second one for him. After a moment's thought, I washed some of the strawberries and fished out a bowl from the cupboard to put them in. It had some hairline cracks, but there was nothing better available.

"Thank you," Marris said as I set everything down on the small coffee table. He took his mug and blew on it, and I plucked a ripe strawberry from the bowl.

"Mmm," I said as the sweet, tart flavors burst in my mouth. When did I last have a freshly picked strawberry? "These are delicious."

Marris beamed. "My ma will be very pleased to hear that. Those strawberries are her pride and joy."

"Why didn't your ma come with you?" I asked, frowning. "Or your pa, for that matter?"

Marris's expression sobered. "My pa died last winter, so I'm the man of the house now. Ma's been anxious ever since, which is why she asked me to come talk to you about extending the lease right away. With your land, we are running twice the cattle we could on our own. But the farm took a bit of a hit over the winter, and we've only just managed to get things back up to speed."

Reading between the lines, I gave him a reassuring smile. "I'm not planning to raise the rent," I told him. "What you've been paying is perfectly sufficient, and if you need an extension, we can discuss it."

"Oh, thank the Ur-God," Marris said, letting out a sigh of

relief. "Ma will be so happy to hear that. She'll probably send over a dozen fresh-baked strawberry pies to thank you."

We laughed, then spent the next few minutes discussing the terms of the new lease. I had no interest in farming the entire acreage. Unless I were to hire several hands, I would have to make constant use of the agricultural spells I'd mastered so long ago. Setting aside the fact I was rusty, that would draw too much attention. I did inform Marris I would be taking back a few of the meadows so I could run some horses, however.

"Do you know what horses might be locally available that would be suitable for a shifter?" I asked. "Most equines instinctively shy away from wolf shifters, so I will need to find some with steady temperaments."

"Mmm, that's a tough one," Marris said, cupping his triangular chin in his hand. He was clean-shaven, unlike me, and I reminded myself to trim back my beard—it had become quite overgrown during the last few months of travel. "We have a couple of foals that will be up for sale, but you need something trained and large enough for your weight." He measured me as though trying to estimate it mentally. "Shifters tend to be heavier than they look, I understand."

"Yes, we are." I wondered where he had picked up on that fact. It was due to the higher proportion of muscle to fat.

"Not many people breed horses anymore, what with steam machines taking on so much of the hard work," he observed. "Prices are down, so you probably can get a bargain when you find something suitable. I'll keep an ear out."

"Thanks."

"By the way," Marris said, "I didn't mean to give you the impression that you aren't welcome here when I was surprised to see you were a shifter. I had a shifter friend—actually, I made quite a few shifter friends while I was away. I only returned to the farm last summer, just in time to see my pa before he passed.

A few of the locals might take a bit to get accustomed to you, but I can guarantee you, Mr. Shelton, that my particular group of friends and I harbor no prejudice against shifters. In fact, I'd like to invite you to come down to the local pub this Tuesday for our weekly game of cards."

"That's very kind of you," I said, masking my surprise. My first instinct was to refuse, but doing so would only create the impression I was a mysterious recluse. Besides, this card game would be a good opportunity to spread my fictitious backstory around and cement my new persona throughout the community. "I would very much like that."

"Great! Looking forward to it." Marris grinned, then checked his watch. "I suppose I ought to get going," he said, setting down his empty cup. "I can tell you've still got a lot to do around here. Is Mrs. Shelton coming with the rest of your belongings?"

I shook my head. "I'm afraid there is no Mrs. Shelton, and all the belongings I have are already within the house." I gave him a wry smile. "I sold everything when I decided to move out here, so I will have to buy new furnishings and supplies."

"I see," Marris said slowly. He looked around with a frown, taking in the sparse, shabby furnishings and dingy walls. "Why don't you let me take you into town to pick up some provisions then?"

"Oh, there's no need to trouble yourself—" I began.

"You don't have a vehicle or horses yet, and it's a long walk, especially when you've got to carry supplies back," Marris said. "Luckily, they do deliveries. I understand not wanting to impose, Mr. Shelton, but it's no trouble at all, and you can't live off strawberries and coffee forever."

"Very well," I said, giving in. I had been planning to hunt for game in wolf form, but explaining that to Marris would only underscore how different I was from the rest of the community.

"If it really isn't too much trouble, I'd be happy to get a ride into town."

I regretted my decision as soon as I stepped onto the porch. *Of course we're taking the steamtractor,* I thought as I followed Marris down the stairs to where the rusty monstrosity was parked. *The man had used it to drive here, hadn't he?*

Hiding my reluctance, I climbed into the cab with Marris and did my best not to react when the engine let out a huge belch of black steam. "Sorry about that," Marris shouted over the shrill whistling as he turned the tractor up the road. "Bessie's going on eighteen years. We'd replace her, but we don't have the money just now."

"Bessie?" I asked, and Marris laughed.

"Yeah. My younger sister Dana named her when she was four years old, and the name just stuck. We're odd like that," he said, grinning.

I smiled. Marris's youthful, cheery nature was a refreshing change from the solitary months I'd spent drifting from place to place and keeping a low profile. Leaving my comfortable existence in Solantha behind had been as difficult as it had been to abandon Nebara and my position as that state's Chief Mage. No, even more so. It had been awful to let my parents think I was dead, and terrifying to start life over as a shifter, but a large part of me had been relieved to let go of my political career. Once awakened to the ugly truth, I could no longer go on with my nose buried in my ancient manuscripts as I strove to ignore the suffering and injustice around me.

Leaving Solantha, on the other hand, had been a true sacrifice. I had just found my footing, and had created a family of sorts with Sunaya, Iannis, and our friends. Sunaya had been part-daughter, part-sister to me, and I missed her snarky witticisms and no-holds-barred attitude toward life. She didn't know it, but our friendship had helped me settle into my skin as a

shifter. Without Sunaya and her cousin Rylan, both jaguar shifters, I would not have been nearly as confident about embracing my nature. I likely would have disguised myself as a human hermit instead.

That might have been a better choice than what you are doing now, I told myself as the tractor rumbled onto the main road leading into town. The scent of cow manure stung my nose as we passed grassy fields full of ruminating bovines and heavily fertilized farmland. The new identity I'd created for myself would not stop the townsfolk from speculating about me, and they would pick over every small detail. There was only so much to talk about in a town of less than a thousand people.

The tractor pulled up to the general store, a long, rectangular building with dark wooden slats for siding and sliding doors in the front. Several horses were tied up to posts on the far side of the building. Their tails swished in agitation as the steamtractor approached, belching steam with abandon. I expected the horses to stamp their hooves or snort nervously, but aside from the flicking tails and ears, they did not react. They must be used to the sound, since most farmers used steam-tractors nowadays.

"Good morning," a pretty redhead with corkscrew curls sang as we walked in. She was wearing a blue and white dress that clung to her buxom figure, and Marris's eyes roved over her. I heard his heart rate turn up a notch. Her nod to him was casually friendly, but when her gaze met mine, it lit up with entirely too much interest. "Who is your new friend, Marris?"

"This is Mr. Shelton," Marris said as we came up to the counter. "He's the new owner of Ackleberry Farm. Mr. Shelton, this is Barrla Kelling, the store owner's daughter. She's also the biggest gossip in town, so careful what you say around her." He grinned.

"Pay this lughead no mind at all," Barrla said sweetly,

holding out her hand for me to shake. I grasped her delicate fingers, and she held on just a little bit longer than necessary. "All that time he's spent away has addled his brain, I'm afraid. Your secrets are safe with me." She winked.

I highly doubted that, even though my shifter nose didn't detect a lie in her words. Barrla was likely the type who thought she could keep a secret but would blurt it out to her friends at the first opportunity.

"Is that Marris I hear?" a voice boomed from the back. A large man with a bald head and a thick mustache came out, his white shirtsleeves rolled up to expose brawny forearms. His bushy red eyebrows rose at the sight of me. "And who is this?"

"Jalen F. Shelton," I said, holding out my hand. "I'm the new owner of Ackleberry Farm."

"Is that so?" he boomed, and I had to suppress a wince. Was the man hard of hearing? "Sallia, come meet our new neighbor!"

A woman who was the spitting image of Barrla, but twenty years older, came rushing from the back as well. "My goodness," she exclaimed, her eyes widening as she took me in. "A shifter! My, I don't think we've ever had one of you around in Abbsville."

"Ma," Barrla scolded. "That's so rude!"

"Well, we haven't."

"It's all right," I said, holding up a hand. "I am aware my presence is unusual around these parts."

"I'll say," Mr. Kelling said, crossing his arms over his chest. "I heard rumors a shifter had bought the property, but I didn't pay them any mind. Did you really buy the farm with cash? I know the Ackleberrys were asking a pretty sum for it."

"I did," I said, the back of my neck prickling beneath their avid regard. Barrla wasn't the only one bursting with questions. "I came into an inheritance after my uncle died, and with no one left in the family to tie me to the city, I decided a change of envi-

ronment was in order." I pulled a gold coin from my pocket and placed it on the table. "Is this enough to start an account here?"

Barrla's eyes widened. "It sure is, Mr. Shelton," she said, sounding awed. "You can buy anything you like with this."

"And then some." Mr. Kelling laughed, clapping me on the back with enough force that a human would have stumbled. "I imagine you're tired of letting us talk your ear off, so let's get down to business. How can we help you?"

Despite Mr. Kelling's words, he and his family continued to pepper me with questions about my past as they retrieved the items I requested and rang up my order. Which city had I come from? Did I have any experience with farming? Was there a Mrs. Shelton? Barrla seemed particularly interested in the answer to that question, though her mother frowned at her. It did not surprise me in the least to know Mrs. Kelling did not want her daughter getting close to a shifter, but it seemed strange a small-town girl like Barrla would be interested at all. One of the reasons I'd chosen this town was because the human females here would not have any romantic interest in me—it was one thing to blend in, quite another to start a family among humans. It was a complication I certainly did not need in my precarious life.

I ordered enough food and supplies to last a good month, and Mr. Kelling promised to have everything delivered to my farmhouse by the end of the day. With a loaf of bread and a round of cheese tucked beneath my arm, I bid them all a good day and headed out of the store.

"Wow," Marris said, hot on my heels. His smile seemed a little forced as he regarded me. "Seems like you've got a potential sweetheart already."

I bit back a grimace. "Barrla is simply fascinated by the novelty of meeting a shifter," I said lightly. "I appreciate you

taking me to the general store, Marris, but I think I'll walk home from here. It'll help me familiarize myself with the place."

"Oh." Marris seemed a bit put out, but he quickly recovered. "Fair enough. Still coming to the card game this Tuesday?"

"Of course. I'm looking forward to it."

We parted ways. I walked up the road, the tension that had crept into my neck and shoulders melting away. I felt as though I'd just escaped an interrogation. Was everybody going to ferret out my life story as soon as they met me? I would have to make doubly sure I had my story straight, because I couldn't afford to slip up. Just one inconsistency would spread like wildfire throughout the place.

And it would be a damn shame if I had to leave just after I'd gotten here.

MINA

"There, there," I soothed, rubbing my patient's furry jaw. He whined, flicking his tail back and forth on the operating table, so I used my other hand to gently rub the top of his head to distract him. Magic seeped through the tips of my fingers, through his cheek, and into the abscessed molar that had pained him for the past week, according to his owner.

"Good boy," I crooned as the dog finally relaxed. His jaw slackened as the spell took over, deadening the affected area. Now that the numbing spell had taken effect, I focused on the cantrip spell, letting the magic seep into his brain. Soon, his eyelids drooped as doggy fantasies danced through his mind— not a hallucinogenic, but close enough.

A sleep spell would have been better, but my magical repertoire was extremely limited. Even so, I was grateful for the spells I did know—they saved me a fortune in sedatives.

"Mina," a voice called just as I was picking up my forceps. Startled, I dropped them back onto the metal tray with a loud *clang,* whirling around just in time to see Barrla burst through the doors into my surgery.

"Barrla," I scolded, and she stopped short. "You can't just burst in here like that while I'm in the middle of an operation. What if I'd accidentally cut this poor dog's face open?"

Of course, there had been no danger of that happening—I hadn't been holding a scalpel and wasn't anywhere near the dog's face. The real reason my heart was pounding was because Barrla had nearly walked in on me while I was doing magic. If she'd come in just a minute sooner...

"I'm so sorry, Mina." Her cheeks colored as she realized her mistake, and she seemed to notice the dog on the table for the first time. "I was just so excited that I *had* to come talk to you now. But I can come back another time..."

"No, no, it's fine." The crushed-puppy look on her face was making me feel guilty. Besides, I *was* curious. I waved her over to the stool near the counter. "This isn't a complicated operation. Just hang out for a few minutes."

"Great," she chirped, bouncing back onto the stool. I bit back a wince as she pulled one of her romance novels out of her skirt pocket to read, hoping fervently that she wouldn't ask me if I'd finished the one she'd lent me. Barrla had an entire shelf full— they were all from a series called Furry Nights, and each story centered around a shifter and human pairing. Naturally, the women at our bi-weekly book club made fun of Barrla for her taste in "low-brow smut" when she'd read a few passages from one of her favorite novels. Since she was my closest friend, I'd jumped to her defense.

No good deed goes unpunished, I thought as I gently pried open the dog's mouth. Barrla had taken my defending her right to read whatever she damn well pleased as a sign *I* would be interested in reading a shifter romance, and she had eagerly pressed the book into my hands. It was still sitting on my nightstand, collecting dust, nearly two weeks later.

Thankfully, Barrla was too absorbed with the book in her

hand to remember to ask about the one she'd lent me, or pay attention to what I was doing, so I was able to extract the rotten molar in short order. I was going to have to lock the doors to the surgery next time, I reminded myself sternly as I sewed up the dog's gums. Barrla was my closest friend, but even she could never learn my secret.

"All right," I said after I'd finished washing up. "Why don't we have a cup of coffee, and you can tell me all about the latest scandal?"

"Ooh, you're going to *love* this," Barrla gushed as she followed me through the back and into the living room. The modest house I'd been renting for the past couple of years doubled as my veterinary clinic and my home. The front half of the house was private, with a small living room and kitchen that shared an open floor plan and one bedroom. The rear half had been converted into a surgery with a small waiting room with its own entrance. It was cramped and far from ideal, but since I couldn't afford to have my own clinic, I made do.

I brewed a pot of coffee on the stove, then brought two steaming cups—Barrla's laden with cream and sugar, mine black—to the sitting area. Barrla was already sitting on the frayed but comfortable yellow couch, and I joined her, careful not to spill the hot brew in my hands.

"Okay, so do you remember the plot of *Falling for the Wolf*?" she asked eagerly.

"Huh?"

"Oh, come on, I must have told you about that one a thousand times!" Barrla flipped her hair over her shoulder with a huff. "It's the one where a strange shifter moves into town, buys a huge house with an inheritance from his great-grandfather, and falls in love with a local human girl."

"Right." Barrla had told me about so many of the Furry

Nights romances that I'd lost track. "So, what does this have to do with your big news?"

"Because fiction is finally becoming reality," Barrla squealed, her eyes sparkling. "A shifter has moved to Abbsville, and, just like in the book, he's got this great big inheritance and he used it to buy a farm out here. He was just at the general store, and I got to talk to him for a good ten minutes while he was ordering stuff."

"*What?*" I jolted in surprise, nearly spilling my coffee. "Are you talking about that Mr. Shelton who bought Ackleberry Farm?" It was hardly my notion of a rich man's mansion, but it had a lot of fertile acreage.

"The very same." Barrla leaned in, a conspiratorial look on her face. "Mina, he put a *solid gold coin* on the table and asked if that was enough to open an account. He's *rich!*"

I stared. Everybody in town had heard of the mysterious Mr. Shelton who had purchased Ackleberry Farm. We'd been on the lookout for him for the past two months, expecting some vehicle laden with furniture to roll into town. But there'd been neither carriage nor steamvan these past few weeks. How had he already moved in without anybody noticing? Abbsville was a tiny town, especially when one considered that most of its eight hundred residents lived on their ranches and not in the small cluster of homes located near the general store and post office.

Maybe he came in on foot, I thought. *He's a shifter—he could have run here, or even flown, if he's a bird shifter.*

That last bit was absurd...bird shifters were quite rare. But it did beg another question. "What kind of shifter is he?"

"A wolf, of course!" Barrla leaned back. "Weren't you listening? The book is called *Falling for the Wolf.*"

"Of course it is." Chuckling, I leaned back against the cushions. "And do you plan to be the leading female in this real-life romance?"

"Well, the leading female in the book was a redhead, so how could I not?" Barrla fluffed her curls, and I choked back another laugh. "I can already tell he's hot for me, Mina. He was so attentive, and *polite*, and so handsome..." She trailed off with a sigh, stars in her eyes. "Do you think our babies will come out furry, or will they look normal?"

That sobered me right up. "Barrla, just because he's similar to the shifter in that romance novel doesn't mean you ought to marry him. He's a shifter, and you're a human. He'll outlive you by at least two hundred years."

"A longer lifespan just means he'll be virile forever," Barrla declared. "There's no need to be such a wet blanket, Mina— romance will always find a way, regardless of age or class."

I shrugged. "Well, it'll be up to you to convince him that you're his mate." There was no point in arguing with Barrla— once she had her mind made up, it was nearly impossible to change it. I wondered how Barrla would react if I told her that, as a born mage, I might live even longer than her new shifter beau.

"Even if you're going to pooh-pooh my romance, you have to admit Mr. Shelton's arrival is fascinating," Barrla said, drawing me away from my thoughts. "Why do you think he's come out all this way? He must have known he would stick out like a sore thumb, moving to such a small town with only humans."

"Indeed," I mused, running my tongue over my teeth. "If he's running away from something, surely he'd want the anonymity of a big city, where he could blend in?"

"What, you mean like a criminal?" Barrla scoffed. "No, our dear Mr. Shelton is far too noble for that. He's an educated man —you can tell by the way he speaks."

"An educated man?" I blinked. "That's unusual for a shifter. They are not very interested in studying, as a general rule."

"Well, I would bet you a silver coin that this one is. Smart,

rich, *and* handsome." Barrla sighed again. "I suspect he's recently widowed and came out here to start anew. There was a touch of sadness about him, so he'll need time to grieve, of course. But I'll be there when he's ready," she said with a sly smile.

"I think you ought to find out if he really is a widower before you go jumping to conclusions," I said dryly. But I didn't give her too much of a hard time about it, because even if Barrla was wrong, this was still fascinating. What if he'd had a falling out with his clan and run out here to escape his troubled past?

You're projecting your own issues onto him, I thought. *Not everybody has crappy family skeletons in their closet.*

I let Barrla gush about Mr. Shelton for a bit longer, then kicked her out as tactfully as possible—I had a cat coming in ten minutes who needed to be spayed, and my complete concentration was required for that. As I closed the door behind her, I couldn't help but wonder if the newcomer would be able to fit in as well as I had. For me, blending in hadn't been much of a problem—I looked human and had done an excellent job hiding my meager magical skills. But with distinctive shifter eyes, Mr. Shelton would have no way to easily disguise himself. He was bound to run into some prejudice, especially from Abbsville's older residents. A few, like old Mrs. Roor, were bigoted and hated any non-humans, whether shifter or mage.

I'll be extra-welcoming when I meet him, I resolved as I headed into the back room to prep for surgery. He was another outsider, and outsiders had to stick together, right?

Even if I could never tell him my own secret...

FENRIS

Despite having the pantry fully stocked with ham, jerky, cheeses, and bread, I decided to go hunting. Mr. Kelling and his daughter had come by to drop off the provisions and had dawdled a good half hour longer than they needed to, the daughter doing her best to pry more information about my past from me. Dealing with her questions had been exhausting, and since I did not want to appear a surly curmudgeon by rebuffing her on my first day in town, I'd been forced to humor the young woman.

By the time they'd finally left, I'd felt confined, my wolf itching to be set free. I waited until the sun had set, then shifted into my beast form, trading human skin for thick, coarse brown fur, square teeth for sharp fangs, and blunt fingers for padded paws that moved soundlessly in the night.

When I'd first become a shifter, the wolf and I had been two distinct beings fighting for purchase in one body. The animal had been an unwilling victim of the experiment Iannis and I had plotted, and it had taken time to gain his trust. But over the years, the two of us had gradually merged into something like

one being—"I" but a distinctly different "I" than when I had been just a mage. While I was in human form, the wolf lurked in the background, coming forth only when something of interest piqued his senses. And in beast form, I was content to sit back and let him roam free, only reining him in when we encountered other humans.

Tonight, I let him loose, running silently through the fields as I hunted for prey. I was careful to steer clear of pastures—the last thing I needed was to be shot or stabbed by an angry farmer who feared for his chickens or sheep. That would certainly get me driven out of town. I stuck to empty fields and the thick forests beyond them, enjoying the rush of the wind through my fur, the crunch of dirt and leaves beneath my feet, and the scent of prey thick in the air. There were squirrels and rabbits, hedgehogs and pheasants, even the occasional deer, though they mostly roamed further north, avoiding the human town.

The scent of rabbit caught my nose long before I heard the rustle in the bushes. I bounded forward, my jaw already outstretched, and caught the hare between my teeth as she leapt from her hiding place. The crunch of neck bones between my teeth was more satisfying than I liked to admit, but the wolf side of me felt no shame. The hare was prey, nothing more.

As I ripped into the freshly killed animal, gorging first on the intestines, I reflected on how that element of savagery colored the way mages and humans looked at shifters. Of course, mages had created all shifters at one point, as cannon fodder and spies in their wars, culminating in the great and final Conflict. Though shifters were no longer slaves, mages tended to look down on us as primitive, only a step above real animals. When I'd been a mage myself, my own attitude had been one of tolerant condescension.

It did not help the shifters' cause that they had hardly any magic beyond the ability to shift, and most of them shunned

schoolrooms and higher learning. For all that, shifters were powerful and often cunning, and their—*our*—talents were more useful than that of the average human. If not for the fact that humans outnumbered shifters ten to one, shifters could easily overpower the race from which they'd been created.

Not that I particularly want that, I thought as I licked the blood from my fangs. No, I would prefer that we all peacefully coexisted. The Northia Federation was huge—there should be enough room for all of us to live and do as we pleased, so long as we did not harm others. What did it matter what god we worshipped or what level of skill and intelligence we possessed? Did I not have as much right to live my life as the farmers who peacefully toiled the land here or the Chief Mages who governed from their lofty chambers?

The wolf side of me huffed at my thoughts, and I smiled inwardly. He considered my ruminations a waste of mental energy. What point was there in wishing for had-beens or could-bes? There was only the *now*, and what one did with it. As far as my wolfish half was concerned, hunting down and consuming a fat hare was far more useful than wishing for things that one could not have.

I was headed back to the farm when the sound of hooves crunching on dirt made my ears twitch. A frisson of energy crackled down my spine as I froze, listening intently. There was a small creek running through the forest valley, and it almost masked the sound—but just below it, I heard the hooves again. At least two horses, maybe three.

Time to investigate.

I crept through the undergrowth, careful not to make a sound, until I reached the creek. Peering from between two bushes, I saw three sturdy horses laden with saddlebags trot by. I frowned at the riders astride them—they wore black and had covered their faces with bandannas. Were these burglars?

Highway robbers passing through? My hackles rose, and I debated whether I should attack. I could probably take them, unless they carried hidden arms, but killing or maiming seemed like overkill for simply riding through the forest with hidden faces. Better to simply spook the horses and send these men running off, away from the woods so close to my new property.

"This almost feels like old times," one of the men said, and I froze. That voice was unmistakable—it was Marris, my new neighbor! "Makes me wish we could go back."

"Those times are gone," another man said in a gruff baritone. "Don't think they're ever coming back, either."

"I'm just thankful we've found this opportunity," the third man said. "We ought to hurry up, though, before someone notices we're missing."

I stood still for a few moments, watching them trot off into the distance. When it became apparent they were headed toward Abbsville, I followed to make sure that they weren't getting into any trouble. I stayed downwind and back far enough that the horses wouldn't notice they had an extra member in their party.

As I trailed them, ears cocked, I hoped one of the trio would say something to give away what they were up to. But their journey home was silent. The saddlebags looked very heavy, but I was too far away to sniff out the contents. Had they just come back from looting someone's farm? But what could they have taken? They carried no livestock or fresh kills—I would have smelled that much—and none of the local farmers would have that many valuables.

Besides, Marris hadn't struck me as the sort of man who would rob his own neighbors. It would be stupid, considering how small the population was. Yet, clearly, he and these other two were up to something, in secret. The men with him must be

the "particular friends" he had referred to when he'd come to my house earlier, but what was so particular about them?

After a good ten minutes, the three men bid each other goodnight, then split off in different directions—likely homeward bound. After a moment's hesitation, I decided to follow their example and head to my own farm. I could attempt to retrace the horses' steps, but that could wait for daylight.

In the comfort and safety of my house, I sat back on the floral couch and mused over this latest discovery. From the way Marris was talking, it was quite possible he and his companions were former Resistance soldiers and had returned after the movement's collapse. That would certainly explain the "old times" he was referring to and why he was so familiar with shifters. If they were former Resistance, I doubted they knew anything about the leadership's plan to turn on their shifter compatriots—his liking for shifters had been genuine. Most of the foot soldiers had been kept in the dark and sent only to do very specific tasks. Even many officers had no idea of the corruption in their ranks—like Rylan, Sunaya's cousin, who had been a captain. Just because they were former members of the Resistance did not automatically make Marris and his friends bad people.

Even so, it was better to find out what they were up to sooner rather than later. If it was something harmless, I would hold my peace, but if anything illegal or revolutionary was going on in my immediate vicinity, it could draw the attention of the Watawis Mages Guild. The last thing I needed was for the local Chief Mage's officials to stumble upon my retreat, especially so soon after I'd bought the farm. The papers I'd gotten for my new identity would pass a federal inspection, but my presence here was extremely unusual, and it would no doubt invite poking around from the authorities.

I'll try to learn more at the poker game on Tuesday, I decided as I

turned out the lights and headed to bed. Hopefully the pub was a decent establishment—I was not looking forward to being stuck in a room full of rowdy drunks and clouds of foul-smelling tobacco. But that was a small price to pay for keeping my identity secret.

4

MINA

The sound of a creaky steamtruck pulling up outside my house alerted me to the arrival of my ride. Startled, I glanced up from my desk to the clock on my wall, seeing it was half past five.

Crap!

"Give me a minute," I shouted as Barrla banged on the front door. "I'm not ready yet!"

"Oh, for the Ur-God's sake, Mina!" The front door slammed open, and I winced—I must have forgotten to lock it again. "You're still back there working, aren't you?"

Grimacing, I put my ledger away, then poked my head out of the surgery door to see Barrla standing in my living room with her hands planted on her curvy hips. She wore a cherry-red dress with frilly white material hemming the bell sleeves and knee-length skirt. The neckline dipped impressively low for an otherwise modest dress, showcasing her ample bosom.

"Hoping to run into a certain shifter tonight?" I teased.

"Don't try to change the subject," Barrla warned, narrowing her pretty blues at me. "Come out so I can see what you're wearing."

Sheepishly, I stepped into the living room, revealing the plain top, jeans, and boots that were my normal work attire. Barrla shook her head. "I knew it. You completely forgot about the party, didn't you?"

I gestured helplessly at the surgery behind me. "I had paperwork to do."

"Paperwork, shmaperwork." Barrla grabbed me by the elbow and began hauling me toward my bedroom. "You're lucky you're a natural beauty, you know, and that it doesn't take much to get you ready."

I don't know about that, I thought as I stripped down to my underwear. I dutifully sat down in the chair in front of my small vanity and let Barrla attack my hair with a brush and the bobby pins I kept in my closet. I had wavy blonde hair that came down to mid-back, and it didn't require much maintenance beyond washing it occasionally and running a brush through it. My skin was decent, but my bone structure was too sharp—cheekbones too prominent, and there was a tiny dent in my chin I fervently wished I could cover up with magic. Trained mages could use spells to cover blemishes and even change their appearance entirely. I would have felt much more secure if I'd been able to do that when I ran away from home. But I was largely untrained, and the only spellbooks available in this state were locked up tight in the Mages Guild's library in Willowdale.

And that was one place in Watawis I could never go, not without risking exposure.

"There." Barrla stuck one last bobby pin in my hair, and I looked up. She'd fashioned my hair into some kind of updo, with loose curls piled at the top and two wavy strands hanging down by my face. I tried to tuck one behind my ear, but she smacked my hand away. "Uh-uh. Now let's see what you've got in the closet."

In the end, we settled on a pale blue dress with lavender

flowers stitched into the A-line skirt and matching blue flats. It was one of three good dresses I owned, and my favorite, as I felt the pale blue went well with my blonde hair. Barrla smudged some silvery-blue eyeshadow onto my lids to accentuate my silver-gray irises, swiped some pale pink gloss on my lips, and tossed my coat to me.

"Look at you. Dressed to kill in under fifteen minutes." She shook her head, but a grin was tugging at her lips. "You could look like this every day if you took the time."

"I'm sure the horses will really appreciate my eye shadow," I said as I followed her out.

Barrla laughed. "You always have an answer for everything, don't you?"

Terad, Barrla's brother, was sitting in the cab of the steamtruck outside. Realizing I'd kept him waiting, I apologized as we got in, but he waved it off.

"He's used to it," Barrla teased, and my cheeks colored. As Terad put the truck in gear, I couldn't help reflecting on how wrong Barrla was. I didn't have an answer for everything. I only had various coping mechanisms to keep anybody from getting too close and finding out the truth about me.

I knew quite well I could become one of the prettiest girls in town if I made an effort. The trouble was, I didn't want to attract male attention. As a mage who would likely live for hundreds of years, marrying a human would be folly. Marrying one in a small town would be worse, because even if I tried to keep the secret within the marriage, his family was bound to find out. We all lived far too close to one another. Only the fact that I knew so little magic in the first place, and never used it in the presence of others, saved me from too much scrutiny. If I started dressing like an eligible woman looking for a husband, my privacy would go right out the window.

It was for this very reason that I'd been on the fence about

going to Mrs. Boccol's sixtieth birthday party, where we were headed now. Everybody would be there, and dressing down was not an option. But Mrs. Boccol would take it as a personal insult if I did not come. I had saved her prized sow after the animal had accidentally swallowed rat poison last year, and the woman practically considered me a family friend.

"Besides," Barrla had said, "there will be food, music, and dancing. How can you say no to that?"

It had been impossible to refuse her.

"So, do you think Mr. Shelton will be there tonight?" Barrla asked eagerly, turning around to face me. "He's probably not acquainted with the Boccol family, but everybody knows he's a shifter now, and surely the Boccols will have invited him out of sheer curiosity?"

"No doubt they will have sent an invitation," I said, amused at Barrla's excitement. "The question is whether he'll have accepted. The man did just move here—he likely has his hands full setting everything up around the farm."

"I hear he's hiring people to help out with renovations," Terad piped up. "People to do roofing and other repair work. Was thinking about applying myself."

"Oh, you should," Barrla exclaimed, clapping her hands together. "Maybe you can use the opportunity to find out more about him."

Terad snorted. "If I go to his house, it'll be to work for him, not you, Barrla. I'm not your personal spy."

As the two of them bickered in the front, I leaned back against the patched upholstery and let my thoughts drift. I did like music and dancing. Most of the time, I managed to rebuff any unwanted advances from my dance partners. But there was one man I sincerely hoped would not attend—or, at the very least, would be too far into his cups to dance by the time he saw me.

"What are you grimacing about?" Barrla asked, noticing my expression through the rearview mirror.

"Just thinking about Ilain Roor."

"Ugh. That lout." Barrla's pretty face twisted into a similar expression of distaste. "If he gives you any trouble, just holler for me, Mina. I'll smack him upside the head with my shoe."

My lips twitched. "I'm not sure that will have any effect, considering how hard his head is."

"Seriously though, Mina," Terad said, his deep voice growing serious. "Let us know if he gives you any trouble. There's no need to deal with him by yourself, not with nearly the entire town gathered there. He can be a real ass when he's had too much booze."

That was true enough, I thought as we passed through the gates of Boccol Farm. The cab bounced as the wheels rolled over the cattle guard, making every single rusty joint creak and whine in protest. Terad's shoulders stiffened. I knew he was self-conscious about driving the rickety vehicle onto Boccol Farm—the Boccols were one of the richest families in Abbsville, and Terad had a sweet spot for their middle daughter Celara.

A large variety of vehicles, including horse-drawn carriages with the animals unhitched, were already parked outside the stables. One of the Boccols' hired men was guarding them. Terad parked in a free spot, and the guard gestured us toward the whitewashed ranch house. Colorful lampions marked the way and added to the festive atmosphere.

"If Mr. Shelton is here, he'll probably have come with Marris," Barrla said as we climbed out of the cab. She was practically vibrating with excitement as we turned toward the house. "Do you see the Dolans' tractor anywhere?"

"I do hope he shows," I said, remembering my resolution to be extra-welcoming to the only shifter in town. "I'm very curious to meet him."

"You'll probably get along famously, since he's half-animal," Terad said, laughing. "I've never seen you meet an animal that didn't fall into the palm of your hand."

"Hmm." Barrla's eyes narrowed at that, as if she wasn't certain she liked the idea of her shifter beau bonding with me. "Do you think that's really true?"

I rolled my eyes, deciding this had gone far enough. "Shifters are people first and foremost," I said, perhaps more sternly than I needed to. "They have vastly different temperaments and personalities, just like humans. I've had occasion to meet a few during my years at veterinary college, and none of them had any inclination to curl up in my lap or at my feet."

Barrla giggled. "Well, of course not," she said, grabbing my hand. "There's no need to get so defensive, Mina; it was just a question. Let's enjoy the party!"

Barrla practically skipped up the steps and through the wide double doors, which had been thrown open to let guests freely come and go. Every light within the house was ablaze, the warm glow spilling from the open doors and windows like welcoming beacons, drawing everybody inside. The sound of a fiddle and harmonica playing a gay tune, mixed with cheerful laughter and conversation, instantly lifted my mood.

After we greeted the hostess and wished her a happy birthday, I spent the first hour exchanging pleasantries with the other townsfolk, catching up on the latest gossip, and being regaled with endless stories of what their animals were up to. Everybody seemed to think that was what a veterinarian preferred to talk about, and while that wasn't strictly true, I didn't see the harm in indulging them. While we made our rounds through the house, Barrla was constantly craning her neck, no doubt on the lookout for her shifter beau. I had to admit I scanned the room once or twice as well, but had yet to catch sight of him.

"Don't look so anxious, Barrla," I murmured, squeezing her

arm. "Everybody's bound to notice, and if you keep winding yourself up like this, you'll scare the wits out of Mr. Shelton by the time he arrives."

Barrla deflated. "You're right," she grumbled, pushing a lock of coppery hair away from her face. "It's just that the dancing has already started, and I was so looking forward to doing my first set with him."

"Why not let him come to you?" I suggested, looping my arm through hers. "There's always a line of men waiting to dance with you, and the woman who's most in demand is the one men will gravitate toward. Show him that you're a prize, Barrla, and he'll be sure to pop out of the woodwork at some point."

Barrla's eyes sparkled. "That is an excellent idea," she said, straightening up to her full, if diminutive, height. "I knew we were friends for a reason, Mina."

I chuckled as I led her to the dance floor. Sure enough, the moment we approached, three men made a beeline for Barrla and asked her to dance. She was swept off within seconds, and as she whirled across the floor with one of them, I felt a pang of envy. Barrla could have any man she wanted in the town—she had no dangerous secrets to hide, no fear they would reject her if they knew the truth about her. The only reason she hadn't settled down yet was because those silly shifter romances had filled her head with fanciful notions about what true love should be, and as she'd complained more than once, the local young men seemed boring compared to those fictional heroes.

"Hey, Mina," a familiar voice said from behind me, and a shiver crawled down my spine. "I was hoping you'd be here."

"Mr. Roor." My tone was cool as I turned to face my unwanted suitor. He'd cleaned up for this shindig. The normal scruff had been shaved off his blocky jaw, and his dirty-blond hair was pulled back into a tail at the nape of his neck. He wore a plaid red-and-white shirt that strained across his broad shoul-

ders and jeans with a giant shiny buckle that had the Roor Farm's logo stamped across it. He was handsome, in a brutish sort of way, but the leer in his eyes as he gave me a once-over, coupled with the spots of color on his cheeks that came from too much alcohol, was enough to make me step away.

"You look amazing tonight," he said, grabbing my wrist before I could melt into the crowd. "Good enough to eat."

"Thanks." I forced a smile, trying to get rid of the mental image his words evoked. "Gotta dress up for a birthday party."

"Oh, I know," he said, his voice deepening as he moved a bit closer. "But we don't get many opportunities to spit and shine our shoes, so we may as well make the most of it, right? Come dance with me."

"Sorry." I jerked my wrist from his grasp. "I just got here and haven't eaten yet."

His brown eyes darkened. "You've been here over an hour already," he growled. "I saw you the moment you walked in. Now it's time for you and me."

"Excuse me?" A chill raced down my spine at the growl in his voice. "I don't remember giving you ownership over my time."

Roor rolled his eyes. "Come on, Mina," he said, grabbing my hand again. "Everybody knows we're meant to be together. My mother keeps asking me when we're going to get married. I get that you like to play coy, but it's time for this cat-and-mouse game to end. Just admit that you want me already." There was a slight slur to his words, I noticed now that we were closer, and his eyes were too bright.

"You're drunk," I snapped. "You don't know what you're saying."

"Excuse me," a deep, husky male voice said. "Are you Mina?"

Startled, I turned to see a man standing just a few feet away. He was just shy of six feet tall, with a solid build and a neatly trimmed beard covering a strong jaw. Yellow shifter eyes locked

with mine, and my heart momentarily stopped as I realized who I was facing.

"Y-yes," I stammered, thrown completely off guard. That had to be Mr. Shelton. How did he know my name?

The shifter smiled, revealing perfect teeth. "Sorry to intrude, but Mrs. Boccol asked me to fetch you. It's urgent. She needs to speak with you. Alone." He held out his arm to me.

"I'll come with you—" Roor started.

"I'm sorry, but she said alone." The man tucked my arm in his and pulled me into the crowd, leaving Roor sputtering behind us. A wave of relief swept through me, followed by a prickle of awareness across my skin as I felt the hard muscle of my savior's arm under my hand.

"Mrs. Boccol doesn't really need to see me, does she?" I murmured as he steered me into the drawing room, which was only slightly less busy than the dance area. Much of the older crowd was here, gathered in the sitting areas and playing cards and dice.

"No, she's quite happy playing cribbage over there in the corner," he said, a hint of amusement in his voice. "I intuited that you might welcome an excuse to get away from that brute."

"I did." Smiling, I extricated my arm from him. Unlike Roor, he let me go easily. "I suppose I'll have to thank you, Mr...." My cheeks colored. Why was I blanking out on his name?

"Shelton," he said, his lips curling into a smile. "But you can call me Fenris."

"Fenris." I tested the name out on my tongue. It suited him well, I thought, taking the time to look at him now that I didn't have Roor breathing down my neck. Fenris was dressed in a white linen shirt and royal blue slacks with a matching vest—a bit sophisticated for our small country town, but the outfit showed off his broad shoulders and trim waist. He was drawing considerable attention from the older ladies in the room, who

were stealing glances at him from behind their cards. The quasi-elegance of his clothing and the graceful way he carried himself should have been at odds with his rugged masculinity, yet somehow it all seamlessly fit together.

What stuck out like a lighthouse were those yellow eyes. They glowed with a preternatural light, and a wildness lurked in them that I recognized. It was present in all predators, even the most domesticated.

Even a shifter who walked and talked like a human.

"How did you know I needed rescuing?" I blurted out, partially because I needed to fill the silence. The two of us had been staring at each other for a full minute, and I didn't want anybody watching us to get the wrong idea. "Were you watching me?"

"Not on purpose," he said, tucking his hands into his pockets. "But I was close enough to scent your agitation, and I followed it to the source. You looked quite uncomfortable with that young man's advances, so I made up an excuse to get you away from him."

"You can scent emotions?" I asked, intrigued.

He nodded. "It's not an infallible ability, but it does come in handy during negotiations...or while rescuing damsels in distress." He winked.

A grin tugged at my lips despite myself. "I heard a rumor that you might be an educated man, and from the way you speak, it seems that might be true. Did you go to university somewhere?"

"Somewhere." A smile flitted briefly across his lips, no doubt meant to distract me from the guarded look that had entered his eyes. "You sound like you've had a bit more schooling than most of Abbsville's residents. What do you do for a living?"

I let him turn the conversation toward my veterinary practice and training for a bit, though I was curious to know why he

didn't seem to want to talk about his past. Could my hunch that he was running from something be on target?

He seemed quite interested in my profession and quizzed me about my experience. "I've been looking at buying some horses," he said, "but as I am new around here, I'm not sure who to approach. I was explaining to Marris the other day that I need horses that will not spook—many tend to shy away from me because of the wolf scent, but I know from past experience that it is possible to accustom them to me if they start out with a steady temperament."

"I know just the man you should see," I said, beaming at the opportunity to repay him for his assistance. "One of my clients breeds high-quality horses, and I am sure he would be happy to sell some to you. In fact, I am planning to go to his farm Wednesday morning to check on a breeding mare. I could take you along if you'd like?"

He gave me a slow smile. "I would like that very much."

We made plans to depart at eight o'clock in the morning, and then I asked him to escort me back to the dance floor. My hope was that Barrla would still be out there and I could hand him off to her for that dance she was so looking forward to. But as we approached, Roor stepped in front of us, blocking our way.

"You liar," he growled at Fenris, his slur far more pronounced than it had been earlier. "Mrs. Boccol didn't call for Mina at all. You just wanted to get your filthy shifter paws on her!"

The crowd quieted a bit, and I realized the people standing nearby had turned to watch. "Roor," I said, stepping forward and drawing his attention to me. "There's no need to make a scene."

"'Course there is," he said, grasping my arm. "You're my woman, aint'cha? What kind of man would I be, letting some filthy cur put his hands all over you?"

I half expected Fenris to retort, but he stood there silently,

looking remarkably impassive even though Roor had a good six inches and fifty pounds on him. "I am *not* your woman," I snarled, trying to yank my arm out of his iron grip.

"You damn well are, and tonight I'm going to show you," he growled, his grip on me tightening. He leaned in, and I reeled back at the rank stench of liquor on his breath. Terror gripped my throat hard, and an old memory suddenly hit me, one I hadn't thought about in months.

"What are you gonna do about it?" my cousin Vanley whispered in my ear, his big hand gripping my breast as he pressed me up against the wall. "You can't scream, can you?"

I struggled against his groping hands, tears sliding down my cheeks. The magical gag of air he'd shoved in my mouth prevented me from calling for help, and his parents weren't home. But he only laughed, letting his hand drift lower.

"One day," he breathed, his tone full of quiet, lethal venom. "One day, I'm finally going to get you alone, where nobody can find us. And then we're going to have some fun."

"Mina." A gentle hand curled around my shoulder, pulling me out of my stupor. "Are you all right?"

Shaken, I whirled around and looked into yellow shifter eyes filled with concern. The chills racing through my body and turning my skin clammy subsided as that gaze grounded me, reminding me of where I was.

"Get away from her," Roor snarled, shoving at Fenris. "This is none of your business."

Fenris somehow managed to look down his nose at Roor, despite being five inches shorter. "I suppose I won't hold that against you, since you're drunk," he said coolly. "But touch me again, or the lady, and we will have a serious problem."

Roor bared his teeth and let me go, taking a wobbly step forward. As he did, he stumbled, his eyes sliding closed. The spectators cried out as he sank to the floor and began to snore,

and two of his friends, who had been egging him on from the sidelines, rushed forward to grab him.

"What is the meaning of this?" Mrs. Boccol demanded, her shrill voice cutting through the commotion. The crowd parted as she came through, two of her sons at her side. "Is this a fight? I don't tolerate brawls of any kind underneath my roof."

"Not at all," Fenris said smoothly, stepping forward. "This young man has simply had too much to drink and said a few unkind things to Mina here. He fell over of his own accord, in a drunken stupor."

The other witnesses in the crowd began to voice their agreement—they'd all seen Roor practically faceplant into the ground before he could start the fight he'd been spoiling for. I turned around to see his friends drag him off, shooting murderous glares our way—they clearly did not support our version of events, but with so many witnesses, they could do little except take their friend away to sober him up. I lifted my chin and turned my back on them— good riddance. Hopefully, this embarrassing scene would make Roor think twice before pulling something like this again.

As Mrs. Boccol and her sons made their apologies to Fenris and me, Barrla and Terad burst through the crowd. "Oh my goodness, Mina, are you okay?" she gasped, her blue eyes sweeping me up and down, as if to check for injuries. "Someone said Roor tried to attack you!"

I waved that off. "I'm fine," I said, not wanting her to get all riled up. "Mr. Shelton was with me, but it turned out he didn't have to do anything at all. Roor lost his footing and fell to the ground."

"Serves the bastard right," Terad grumbled. "I think he drank half the wine tonight. He never could control himself around alcohol."

"Wait, did you say that Mr. Shelton was with you?" Barrla squealed. "Did you actually meet him? Why didn't you tell me?"

"He's right here—" I started, turning around, but the words died on my lips. Fenris had disappeared into the crowd. "Well, he *was* here, I guess." Flummoxed, I shrugged my shoulders at Barrla. "I was bringing him here to meet you, actually, before Roor got in the way."

"Just one more reason to hate that brute," Barrla spat, her face darkening like a thundercloud. "Getting in the way of my happily ever after. If I ever see him, I'll give him a talking-to for sure!"

Terad and I exchanged helpless smiles at Barrla's tirade, then watched her go off in search of the elusive Mr. Shelton. But as she walked away, I couldn't help but wonder what had *really* happened to Roor. If I hadn't known better, I would have said he'd been hit with a sleeping spell. But that was impossible, because I hadn't used my magic or even mastered that spell. And shifters like Fenris couldn't use magic except to change forms.

He's probably going to be blamed for this anyway, a voice in my head said, and my insides squirmed with guilt. Roor had already been angry with Fenris for intervening in the first place, and it was obvious that he would not take no for an answer as far as I was concerned.

So much for being extra-welcoming, I thought despondently. *You've only managed to make him new enemies, and during his very first week in town, too!*

You'll have to make it up to him on Wednesday, I told myself as I headed to the refreshment table. I just hoped that Mr. Handmar, the horse breeder, could deliver.

"There you go," I said, stepping back as the tabby dug into his meal. I was happy to see he had an appetite —he'd stayed overnight after I patched him up from a near-fatal altercation with a dog. Sometimes, animals lost their appetite for a bit after dealing with trauma. Thankfully, little Timber seemed to be just as hungry as any cat, and he eagerly lapped at the wet food I'd put in the bowl on the floor.

As I watched him eat, the doorbell rang. Glancing at the clock, I saw that it was nine a.m.—at least an hour before my next appointment. Who could be calling? Was it Fenris coming to discuss what had happened last night?

My heart jumped in my chest at the thought of the mysterious shifter standing outside my door, and I sternly told it to pipe down. There was no real reason for Fenris to be at my door, I told myself as I picked up the cat and put him back in his cage. He protested until I put the food in, too, then settled down contentedly to finish his meal. No, more likely the visitor was somebody with an injured animal.

"Good morning," I said, opening the front door, but then

faltered in surprise. Constable Foggart was standing outside—the local law enforcement officer. "What can I do for you, Constable?"

"Morning, Miss Hollin," he said, his lips stretching into a somewhat strained smile beneath his handlebar mustache. "Mind if I come in for a few minutes?"

"Of course not." Alarm bells started going off in my head, but I smoothed my expression into cool politeness and showed the constable in to my living room. "Would you like something to drink? I still have some coffee left over from the pot I brewed this morning."

"Coffee would be great, thank you."

I busied myself getting him a cup while he sat his great bulk down on my yellow couch. Sugar but no cream, I remembered belatedly from the last time he'd come—six months ago, when his Rottweiler had taken a nasty tumble and sprained his leg. The constable didn't have his pet with him, though, which meant this had to be official business. And I had a bad feeling I knew what this was about.

"So, how can I help you?" I asked after I'd handed him his coffee.

"I really hate to be doing this at all," the constable said as I took my seat across from him. He looked decidedly uncomfortable as he took his first sip of coffee. "But Mrs. Roor has filed a complaint against you for use of illegal magic."

Terror slammed into me, so fast and hard that, for a moment, I couldn't breathe. Had she somehow found out about me?

"What?" I managed to say.

"I know, it's a ridiculous claim," the constable said with a shrug, as if trying to distance himself from the whole matter. "But she heard all about her son passing out at the party last night and is convinced you used some kind of hex to make him fall into a stupor. She also insists that Mr. Roor's 'obsession' with

you, as she calls it, must be the result of a love potion that you've been slipping him."

The terror that had seized me subsided immediately, replaced by sizzling outrage. "That's insane," I snapped, fisting my hands into my lap. "I can't *stand* the man, and anybody who knows me can attest to that. It's all I can do to fend off his advances every time we run into each other. Why in Recca would I give him a love potion?" I laughed at the absurdity, shaking my head. "Besides, Constable, if I had any magical talent at all, it would have been discovered long ago, during the mandatory testing in school. As I understand it, wild magic bursts out uncontrollably when a child reaches his or her teens. At twenty-eight years old, I'm a bit past that point, wouldn't you say?"

"Yes, you are definitely an adult, there is no question of that," the constable said, his jowls vibrating as he shook his head. "And when you lay it out like this, it does make Mrs. Roor's story sound quite flimsy. It's not like we have a black market for hexes and potions here, like they have in the city. Likely she is just grasping at straws to try to cover up the embarrassment from last night. But I had to investigate the claim, and after questioning some witnesses last night, I have to say Mr. Roor's sudden collapse does seem a bit strange. From what I understand, he usually holds his liquor better."

I snorted at that. "Maybe he thought he needed some extra liquid courage to get me to dance with him," I suggested, even as an uneasy feeling grew in the pit of my stomach. I couldn't argue with the constable's observation—the collapse *had* been strange. But there was no other explanation, because I hadn't used magic to cause it.

"Possibly," the constable said, a curious look now on his face. "Are you truly twenty-eight? You don't look like you're more than twenty."

"I am." I rose from my chair and fetched my certificate from veterinary school. "Look at the date on here."

He took the framed certificate from me carefully. "That's five years ago," he murmured. "Indeed, you definitely would have to be older than twenty. I've never heard of a fifteen-year-old graduating from any kind of vocational school."

"Yes, and besides, I've been practicing here for over two years now," I reminded him, taking the certificate back. "All the women in my family tend to look young, Constable." Which was not a lie, since I came from a family of mages. "Sometimes I'm not certain if it's a blessing or a curse," I added with a wry smile.

The constable chuckled. "I think I know which one my wife would choose."

We talked for a few more minutes while he finished his coffee, and then he bid me a good day, apologizing once more for the intrusion. The moment I closed the door behind me, I let my cheery smile drop. My stomach was hollow, carved out by a sense of bleakness I hadn't felt in a long time. I'd thought that I could maintain this ruse longer than two years, and things had been going so well. I'd allowed myself to make friends, and this small house with its tiny veterinary clinic had begun to feel like home.

A place where you must hide your true nature can never be home, I told myself as I sank down into the couch cushions. A headache began to throb at my temples, and I pressed my fingers against the pain, trying to soothe it. This incident had been far too close for comfort—I was going to have to leave soon. My lack of aging was becoming too obvious, and now I was coming under suspicion for a crime that I hadn't even committed!

If only I could use my magic to change my appearance, I thought ruefully. Then I could go anywhere, be anyone. But I had tried in the past, and though I could make minor changes to my features

that made me look a bit older, I could only keep the illusion up for an hour or so. And if I was doing anything remotely taxing, like bookkeeping or surgery, the spell would lapse immediately.

Oh well, I thought as I headed back to check on the cat. Sure enough, he'd finished his food and was now contentedly curled up in his cage. I reached in and gave him a rub behind the ears, and he nuzzled my hand with a deep purr that made me smile, banishing the despair that had settled into my bones. Working with animals, even the most recalcitrant ones, always lifted my spirits. Regardless of where I went, there would always be animals to tend to, and as long as I had that, I was mostly fulfilled.

Besides, I only had another two years of hiding out. Once I reached thirty, I could return to my hometown and claim my inheritance. There was a large fortune waiting for me once I reached my majority. I could use it to arrange my life as I saw fit without interference from my so-called guardians.

A flash of anger lit inside me as I thought about the relatives who had so carelessly used and abused me. *They're not worth thinking of,* I told myself firmly, pushing those old memories aside. No, I had to focus on the plans for my future. Surely I could wait out the last two years here, so long as I kept my head down. It was not that long, considering how many years I had to look forward to, and now that I'd cleared things up with the constable, all I needed to do was stay away from Roor.

Even so, I resolved to pack a bag and deposit what little savings I had under a new name at a different bank. I would hate to have to start over without a copper to my name. It was too bad that I'd never learned to make gold, like all trained mages could. My practice was prospering, but many of my clients were hard up for money and paid me with eggs, meat, and other forms of barter. Nobody in Abbsville seemed to have much ready money,

aside from the Boccols and one or two other well-to-do farming families.

There is the shifter, I thought, thinking back to what Barrla had said about Fenris. I wondered where he had gotten all that money and what had brought him to Abbsville. Of all the places in the Federation that a wealthy, single shifter could have moved to, why did he choose a tiny town that was populated solely by humans? The guarded look that had entered his eyes when I'd asked him about his education told me he did indeed have a past that he did not wish to discuss.

We really are both outsiders, I mused as I prepped the surgery for my next appointment. And we had gotten along quite well during those few minutes of conversation. Perhaps we could become friends, though I didn't know if it was worth it to try and establish any kind of relationship. After all, once I left Abbsville behind, I would never see any of my friends here again.

FENRIS

As promised, I arrived at the Purple Pig at seven o'clock sharp on Tuesday evening, my first visit to Abbsville's sole pub and the town's general watering hole. The place reeked of stale tobacco smoke, but I'd come prepared—a special charm was pinned to the inside of my collar that helped mute the stench around me, making it bearable to my shifter nose without dulling it completely. The pub wasn't packed, but it was still plenty busy, with nearly every seat filled and the buzz of conversation filling the air.

"Hey, Mr. Shelton!" Marris was sitting at a table in the corner with two other young men. They had a pitcher of beer in the center of their table and tankards full of the frothy amber beverage. "Right on time."

I headed toward them, ignoring the stares of the other patrons. Everybody in town knew of me at this point because of that unfortunate incident at Mrs. Boccol's birthday party. Perhaps using that sleeping spell on Mina's assailant hadn't been the wisest choice, not with so many witnesses around, but most seemed to have accepted that the brute had been overcome by drink, and it had been a harmless enough solution. Far more

civilized than having to resort to fisticuffs, as would have been Roor's preference. The man had been itching for an excuse to punch me for daring to lay my "filthy paws" on "his woman."

I wonder how she's doing. The thought flitted briefly in my mind, along with the image of her, beautiful and vulnerable and headstrong all at once as she tried to fend off the brute pawing at her. I'd smelled the acrid tang of fear on Mina when he'd refused to let go—her mind had gone someplace else, and I strongly suspected this was not the first time she had been subjected to a man's unwanted attentions.

She'd been a delight to talk to, her eyes sparkling with a level of intelligence I'd yet to glimpse from any of the other women I'd met in this place. And when I'd woken the next morning, it had taken everything in me to stop myself from going to check on her. I'd already interfered enough, and she didn't need another man sniffing around her after she'd only just fended one off.

But that was neither here nor there at this moment. Right now, I was here to play poker, drink beer, and see what I could find out about Marris and his nighttime activities.

"Thank you for inviting me," I shouted over the noise, bumping Marris on the shoulder before I sat down in the empty chair and accepted the mug of beer that was pushed my way. "If we are going to drink and play together, you might as well call me Fenris."

"I've already bet that you're gonna clean us out," one of the other men said—a lanky fellow with rawboned features and stringy yellow hair. I recognized his scent and build—he was one of Marris's friends from the other night. "What with that keen nose and all."

I laughed. "I'll try to keep my nose out of this," I promised, and they all grinned at me.

"This is Cobil," Marris said, indicating the man who'd just

spoken to me. "And this other guy here is Rotharius, but we call him Roth for short. We've known each other since we were in diapers."

"Nice to meet you," Roth said, extending his hand. He was a big man, even taller than Roor, but I sensed a gentle, easygoing nature about him. "You're the talk of the town."

I bit back a sigh at that. "I wasn't aware that the resident veterinarian was supposed to be off-limits," I said. "I'm looking at purchasing some horses, so I consulted with her last night on who would be the best person to buy them from."

"Sure you did," Marris teased, grinning at me. "I saw you with her at the party last night—she was the only woman you talked to who didn't look like she was boring you out of your skull."

"She is very pretty and intelligent," I allowed. "But she is hardly my type."

Cobil gaped at me. "Hardly your type? What are you—gay?"

Marris elbowed him in the ribs, and Cobil yelped. "He means she's not a shifter," he said, rolling his eyes. "Which is understandable, though it makes me wonder why you chose to settle down here, where there are no eligible shifter females. You planning on ordering one in, like a mail-order bride?" He waggled his eyebrows.

I chuckled. "I hadn't thought much about it," I admitted, though that was a lie. The truth was that I would love to have a family, but I wasn't in a position to settle down with anyone. Apart from being a wanted man, my predicament was similar to my friend Sunaya's—I wasn't quite a shifter or a mage, and didn't fit in with either crowd. No shifter female would want to marry me if she knew I had magic, and I could hardly keep a secret like that from a spouse.

"It's a real shame," Roth said, "because Mina showed more interest in you than I've seen her show any man. It's high time

she settled down with someone—she's rejected every eligible fellow in the area. I hear she's never even allowed anyone to kiss her."

"Really?" I found it hard to believe that those rosebud lips had never touched any man's. She really was most appealing, the way her golden hair had been piled on top of her head, begging for a man to sink his fingers in and undo the knot, and those sparkling silver-gray eyes...

Realizing I was daydreaming about her, I yanked my thoughts back to the present. "Well, no matter. I'm sure someone will come along eventually for Miss Hollin. Now, are we going to get on with the game?"

Marris called for a refill on our pitcher, and Cobil pulled out a deck of cards and began dealing out the first hand. It took me several rounds before I started to catch on—it had been a while since I'd played poker—but I eventually settled into a rhythm, winning some here, losing some there. I didn't need to use my nose to read them—my shifter instincts had attuned me to the intricacies of body language. It was easy enough to tell when someone was bluffing or when someone else had a good hand and was trying to hide it. But I was here to ferret out information, not clean out my new friends' pockets. I had more than enough money, and I could always make more if needed.

"You say the three of you have been together since you were in diapers?" I asked after losing the fifth round. Cobil gleefully scraped the handful of coppers on the table toward him—his second win of the evening.

"Oh, yes," Roth said. "Me and Marris are next-door neighbors, and Cobil's mother makes and sells the best pies in town, so we saw him regular enough." He grinned. "We ought to get Mr. Shelton here a peach pie with some whipped cream. He'll think he's died and gone onto his reward."

"Please, call me Fenris," I reminded him. I wanted them to

feel at ease around me, and I knew that in addition to being a stranger, my obvious wealth wasn't doing me any favors. Hence my strategy to lose more than I won tonight. "Did the three of you go away together, too, since you are all so close? Marris mentioned to me the other day that he only recently came back."

"We did." Cobil's eyes narrowed. "What's it to ya?"

"Now, Cobil, I'm sure our new friend is just curious." But a wary glint had entered Marris's eyes too. "Where did you say you were from again, uh, Fenris?"

I held in a sigh. "Uton," I told them. It was one of the Federation's southwestern states, and hopefully none here would be familiar with it. "Barnas, specifically."

"That's home to one of the largest wolf shifter clans in the Federation," Roth said. "You're from that clan, then?"

"We had a falling out," I said evasively. "A misunderstanding regarding a lady, you could say."

The three men nodded sagely. "We know how that goes," Marris said. "Just last week, Ria Smorth, who was engaged to this one's brother"—he jerked a thumb toward Cobil—"eloped with another guy who she'd been secretly seeing for years. I'm guessing you were the 'other man' in the equation?"

"I don't really like to talk about it," I said, pretending the memory still pained me. "But I came out here because I wanted a fresh start. No meddling shifter clans, and no Mages Guild breathing down one's neck, either."

Marris's eyes sparked at that. "Yeah, it's one of the best perks to living in a small town like this. Those lofty mages consider us beneath them, aside from tax time, and, thankfully, that's only once a year." His expression darkened at the mention of taxes, and I imagined that nobody in Abbsville much liked it when the tax collector came. I knew from my time in Ncbara, which had plenty of farming communities, that

most farmers struggled to save up enough cash for the yearly tax day.

"As for where the three of us ran off to," Roth said, leaning in and lowering his voice, "we joined up with a Resistance recruiter who was passing through the area. The three of us were young, restless, and looking for adventure."

"Not to mention we all wanted to fight against the vile mage regime," Marris added. "Like you said, we don't much have to deal with them out here, but it is very unfair that they tax us so heavily while giving us so little in return."

I nodded, unable to argue with that. Sunaya had mentioned something similar to Iannis when she'd first come to Solantha Palace. The system certainly needed an overhaul, though not the kind of overhaul Thorgana Mills, the late shadowy head of the Resistance, had in mind for the Federation. I was glad she was no longer around to spin her web of intrigue, though I doubted her death spelled the end of the Resistance. There was always someone else ready and willing to take up such causes, and the only way to truly stop them was to fix the flaws in our government that were stirring up all this unrest in the first place.

"Anyway, the three of us served as infantry. We fought mostly in the south, about as far away from Abbsville as you can get," Marris continued, a wry smile on his lips. "We had some adventures out there, let me tell you. And as I mentioned before, we had some shifters in our unit that we got on pretty well with. But when we found out that the leadership was planning on betraying them, our shifter comrades cut their losses and went home."

Cobil shook his head in disgust. "Unbelievable," he muttered, lifting his tankard to his lips. He took a long drink, then slammed the mug down on the table. "Still gives me chills

to think about how many of our comrades they were planning to kill."

"We thought about leaving at the same time, but we hadn't been paid in a while, so we decided to stick it out at least until the next payday so we could bring something home to our families," Roth said. "Unfortunately for us, payday never came, and we were forced to come back home empty-handed."

"Some of our troop advocated robbing the locals," Marris said darkly, "but we weren't having that. Stupid fucks would have brought an entire mob down on us all. Besides, we were supposed to be fighting *for* those people. So yeah, we trekked back up northwest to this tiny town. Our mothers were pretty damn happy to see us, at least." He grinned briefly, but a shadow overtook his face. "Others, not so much."

"I can imagine." I sat back in my chair, studying them. "I can also imagine that it has been hard for the three of you to settle back into small-town life after all that fighting and adventuring."

The three men nodded. "We're waiting for a better opportunity to come along," Roth said, "but in the meantime, we make do with farming land and chasing skirts." He winked at me. "Marris, especially, is trying to get a certain redhead to look at him."

"Evening, boys," a balding, rotund man with a handlebar mustache greeted us. It took me a second to place him—Constable Foggart, Abbsville's local head of law enforcement. I bit back a smile as he came to a stop next to Cobil—I couldn't help but think of what Sunaya would say if she were forced to come work here as an enforcer. She would walk all over Foggart and likely have the run of the entire place within a week or two. A pang of homesickness hit me, and I forced myself to pay attention to what was going on.

"Don't think I've introduced myself properly," the constable said, holding out a meaty hand. "I'm Constable Davin Foggart."

I shook his hand. As I did, I noticed a similarity to Cobil in the lines around his mouth and the shape of his eyes. "Are you two related?" I asked.

"Cousins," Cobil said with a grin. "You'd never know it seeing as how respectable Davin is now, but according to grandma, he was a regular rabble-rouser in his youth."

"Yes, well." Constable Foggart coughed, the tips of his ears reddening. "No need to talk about me when we have such an interesting guest at this table. Tell me, Mr. Shelton, what brings you to Abbsville?"

I gave the constable the same story I'd told Marris and his friends. He did not seem convinced that a broken heart was what led me to Abbsville, but Cobil and the others quickly steered the conversation in a different direction, distracting him. Marris gave me another wink as they harassed Foggart about inviting them over to his house for another barbecue—the young men seemed to sense my need for discretion. After a few minutes, the constable finally left.

I held my breath, waiting for the men to press me for more details. But they simply dealt another hand, and, in low voices, began to regale me with tall tales of their time in the Resistance. From the occasional knowing looks and grins they gave me, I gathered they suspected I too was a former Resistance member, and I did nothing to correct the assumption.

"You don't have to worry about us ratting you out," Roth said as he swept up another small pile of winnings. "We may not have served together, but we were all part of the same cause. Resistance members always stick together."

I shrugged. "I am not worried," I said as Marris dealt another hand. "After all, you do not know anything to betray, now do you?"

The men snickered, and we played a few more rounds before I bid them good night. As I walked home, relying only on the half-full moon to light my way, I reflected on the night's conversation. Marris had said the three of them were waiting for the next opportunity to strike back at the mage regime... Did their sneaking about at night have anything to do with that?

All of these Resistance veterans and sympathizers...they were a complication I did not expect. What would these young men think if they knew I had a hand in the downfall of their cause? It didn't seem as though they were still particularly loyal, but from what I'd gleaned, they still considered any member of the Resistance, former or current, to be a friend rather than a foe.

What Marris and his friends would think about me is the least of my problems, I reminded myself. If the Watawis Mages Guild got any inkling that there was Resistance activity down here, they would come down hard on Abbsville. And even though I barely knew these men, I found I did not want them to be caught and punished. After all, they had only been fighting for what they believed, and they had abandoned the Resistance once they discovered the betrayal planned by the late Benefactor.

As I turned down the road leading to my lands, I decided to continue monitoring their nocturnal activities. Any pointed questions regarding that subject would only make them suspicious, and while I believed I'd gained a bit of their trust, they were not ready to confide whatever it was they were up to with those heavy saddlebags.

I only hoped that whatever I found was mostly harmless. If not, I might have to decide between delivering them to the mages' rough justice or leaving town myself before I was swept up in some illegal exploit.

This is silly, I thought as I smoothed my skirt with my left hand for the thousandth time. In my right, I gripped the reins of my single-horse cart, and I tugged left on them, urging my mare Fria onto the dirt road that led to Fenris's home. *There was no need for you to dress up. You are going to be looking at horses, not out on a date!*

"Dress up" might have been overstating it a bit. I'd pulled a faded red-and-white checkered dress from my closet and had taken care with my hair, brushing it out before twisting it into a bun atop my head. I'd debated putting on a bit of makeup but decided I'd already gone far enough. At least I'd put on sensible shoes—a pair of sturdy leather boots that would protect my feet while I was examining the mare. Luckily, she wasn't close to dropping her foal, or I would have had to take my ugly coveralls.

It would have been far more sensible to dress in my usual blouse and jeans, but showing up to my new neighbor's house so plain, when I'd looked almost fancy the last time I'd seen him, rankled me for some reason. I could tell from the look in his eyes that he'd found me attractive, and I wasn't quite willing to ruin that impression just yet.

Even if we were just going to be friends.

I pulled Fria to a stop outside Fenris's house and made to get out. But before I could so much as put down the reins, the front door opened and Fenris stepped onto the porch. I blinked at the sight of him in an understated black tunic—quite different from the outfit he'd worn at the party. No one around here wore tunics—they were old-fashioned, even in a small town like this.

"Good morning," he said, giving me a smile that sent tingles along my skin. He took a step toward the cart, and Fria snorted and stamped her foot in response.

"There now." I hopped down from the cart, very thankful for my boots when they instantly sank two inches into the mud. It had rained hard last night. "Calm down, Fria," I said, moving around to the front of the cart to stroke her velvety nose. "Fenris is a friend."

"Her hesitation is only to be expected," Fenris said, a sigh in his voice. He approached slowly, and Fria snorted again. "As I was explaining yesterday, most horses do not take kindly to a wolf shifter in their midst."

"Well, Fria doesn't yet know how perfect a gentleman you are," I said lightly, still stroking her soft nose. With each touch, I pressed a little bit more magic into her—a soothing spell I often used to quiet agitated animals when my presence alone wasn't enough. I didn't dare speak the Loranian spell aloud, but chanting it in my head seemed to be enough. The mare quieted, nuzzling my palm.

"There." I turned my head, and my heart jumped—Fenris was standing right beside me. His eyes were narrowed on the hand I still had pressed against Fria's nose. "Is everything all right?"

"Hmm?" He blinked. "I'm just surprised she quieted so easily."

"I have a deft touch with animals," I said mechanically—my

canned response whenever somebody brought this up. Which was true enough, but it sometimes took a little magic to get the beasts to do what I wanted. Breaking eye contact, I moved toward the cart. "Let's be on our way, shall we?"

Fenris nodded, and if he was still suspicious of my actions, he didn't say anything more about it. My palms were clammy as I gripped the reins. I had to force myself to take slow, calming breaths as I guided Fria back down the dirt road.

He doesn't know you used magic, I told myself firmly. *He can't. He's just a shifter, and he wouldn't know of such things anyway.*

But he wasn't just a shifter, was he? He was also an educated man with quite a bit of money at his disposal. A true puzzle, this Jalen Fenris Shelton, and one I was itching to figure out. It was hypocritical of me to want to pry at him for his secrets while guarding my own so closely. But I'd never met someone like him before, and try as I might, it was impossible to stop wondering about his past.

As we drove, we talked about horses, and I found myself relaxing—this was common ground, and a subject I had a fair bit of experience in. "I do hope you find a suitable animal to buy," I said as Fria and I navigated around a steep pothole in the road. "With the increased use of steamcars and trucks in the cities, and even here in the countryside, the market for horses is rapidly dwindling."

Fenris nodded. "Very few people used horses in Barnas," he said. "If not for the special magical charms installed on all the vehicles, the air would be constantly clogged with foul steam. And the noise...I grew used to it, of course, but the high-pitched whine of steam engines is hard on a shifter's ears."

"I can imagine." *So he's from Barnas.* I slanted a look at him out of the corner of my eye. I hadn't really thought too much about how his heightened senses would affect him—I'd always assumed they were an advantage for shifters, but perhaps that

wasn't always the case. "I'll tell you what. If you promise to pay fair value for any animal you purchase here in Abbsville, I will throw in six months of veterinary services for free."

Fenris's eyebrows rose. "A very generous offer, but I assure you it isn't necessary. I am happy to pay fair value both for horses and your services."

I smiled. I didn't know very many people who would have refused an offer like that—but then again, he was well-off. Perhaps he didn't feel it was fair to take advantage of me, especially since it must have been obvious I was barely making ends meet, like most Abbsville residents.

"I don't mind doing a favor occasionally," I said as the gates of Handmar Farm came into view. "You did help me out the other night when Roor was pestering me."

Fenris's expression darkened. "It seems like that wasn't the first time something like this has happened," he said. "How long has he been harassing you?"

I shrugged, uncomfortable with this turn of conversation. "He only really noticed me in the last year, when I treated his dog for food poisoning. And this was the first time he's been that aggressive...normally he presses me into a dance or two, tries for a kiss, and leaves me alone if I refuse him."

"It doesn't appear that he's gotten the hint," Fenris said, and I was surprised to hear the anger in his voice. "I would suggest you take precautions at home, in case he comes calling."

My skin went cold at that. I hadn't considered that Roor might come to harass me at my own home, but after the humiliation from the other night, he might very well try. I would have to do a better job of keeping my door locked, and perhaps find a weapon to defend myself with.

Is this really what my life has come to here in Abbsville? I thought miserably as we drove through the gate. Being forced to

fend off brutish men was the exact reason I'd run away from home in the first place.

"There you are, Miss Hollin," Mr. Handmar cried as he strode out from one of the paddocks. I parked the cart outside the corral, then unhitched Fria. I usually let her loose while I was here so she wouldn't have to suffer with that bit in her mouth while I was doing business. It was a half-spoon bit, not those horrible things that cut into horses' mouths, but I didn't like forcing horses to wear them any longer than necessary.

"Good morning, Mr. Handmar," I said as the breeder came up to greet us. Fenris rounded the carriage, and I introduced him. "This is Mr. Shelton, our newest resident here in Abbsville."

"Ah, yes, I'd heard that a shifter had moved into town." Mr. Handmar eyed Fenris curiously as he held out a hand for him to shake. "What brings you here to my farm?"

"I am looking to purchase a couple of horses, actually," Fenris said. "Miss Hollin here says that you might have some of even temperament that I can train to get used to me."

"Hmm." Mr. Handmar looked doubtful. "Why don't we get Miss Hollin's horse settled, and I'll see what we might have for you?"

Fenris and I exchanged glances as Mr. Handmar took Fria and led her to the corral. Once he'd relieved her of her tack, we headed toward the paddocks.

"On second thought, it might be better if I bring the horses out," Mr. Handmar said, hesitating. "Don't want to have you walk in there and spook them all at once."

"Mina," two youthful voices cried, and I smiled. We turned around to see Kelton and Hartley, Mr. Handmar's sons, sprinting from the house toward us. The twins had tanned skin, mops of curly brown hair, and identical smiles that melted the hearts of every woman around. No one could resist them, not even me.

"Hi, boys." I giggled as they pounced on me at once, wrapping me up tightly in hugs. "What have the two of you been up to?"

"Math." Kelton screwed his face up in distaste. "Ma says that just because we're farm boys doesn't mean that we can't get a 'good education.'"

"And she's quite right," Mr. Handmar said sternly. "Now have you noticed that we have a new guest?"

The boys instantly released me, spinning around on their heels. "This is Mr. Shelton," I said as Fenris gazed down at them, a bemused look on his face. "He just moved to Abbsville this week."

"Pleased to meet you." Fenris held out his hand, and both boys shook it, wide-eyed.

"Are...are you a shifter?" one of them asked, awe in his voice. "You've got those freaky eyes!"

"Kelton," Mr. Handmar scolded, but Fenris only laughed.

"They are a bit freaky," he said, "but they help me see better when it's night."

"Can you transform?" Kelton asked eagerly, bouncing up and down on the heels of his mud-spattered boots. "Oh please, say yes!"

"Shifters only transform during the full moon—" Mr. Handmar said, but there was a flash of light. Suddenly, a huge wolf with coarse brown fur was standing before us. The twins screamed, scrambling back, but Fenris rolled onto his back, letting his tongue loll out. Submissive behavior, I thought wonderingly, to let the children know they were safe to approach.

"He wants us to rub his belly," Hartley shrieked, beside himself with delight. The two boys rushed over to Fenris, who began wiggling around in the dirt as the boys petted him. I grinned at the oddly domestic sight—this was a side to Fenris I

had certainly not expected to see when I'd brought him here. I didn't know how much of this was an act for the children, and how much was animal instinct, but I was very happy to see that he was playing along.

"All right," Mr. Handmar finally said after a few minutes of this. "Time to let Mr. Shelton get back to business."

"But, Pa," the boys whined.

"No 'buts.' We've work to do."

Grumbling a bit, the boys got to their feet. Mr. Handmar told them to stand by—they were experienced riders and would help demonstrate any horses Fenris was interested in. Fenris got to his feet. After a quick shake, he changed back into human form in a flash of light.

We all stared—we expected him to be covered in mud, but he was immaculate. "What happens to your clothes when you... when you transform?" Mr. Handmar asked.

Fenris shrugged and pulled out a tiny stone from his pocket. It sparkled as he held it up in the sunlight, and my eye was drawn to the layer of shimmering iridescence. "There are charms one can buy in the big cities that help with that sort of thing," he said, then tucked it back into his pocket. "Now, you said you had a horse to show me?"

As Mr. Handmar went into the stables to fetch some horses, I chewed on my lip, deep in thought. Fenris was certainly nothing like I'd expected. He was well-mannered, educated, good with children, and it seemed he wasn't averse to using a little magic, when most shifters hated and feared it. What other surprises were wrapped up in the handsome, eclectic package that stood beside me?

"This is Makar," Mr. Handmar said, leading out a dappled gray gelding. "One of my more easygoing horses, so I'm hoping he takes to you."

"He's beautiful," Fenris murmured, taking a step forward.

The gelding tossed his gray mane as Fenris approached, but otherwise did not react when the shifter pressed a hand to his hide. Fenris did a careful inspection, checking the horse's teeth and hooves and running an experienced hand along their legs.

Finally, he stood back and nodded with satisfaction. "I am interested in this one," he said.

Mr. Handmar brought out three more horses for Fenris's inspection, and he selected a dark-colored stallion called Midnight for further inspection. We led his two selections to a paddock near the farmhouse that Mr. Handmar used for demonstrations, and the boys saddled up the two horses to put them through their paces.

"Impressive," Fenris said as Kelton guided Midnight through the obstacle course set up in the paddock while Hartley rode the gelding. In addition to the hurdles of various heights and forms, there was a sand pit and a small waterhole. "Your boys are excellent riders, Mr. Handmar."

The breeder beamed. "Been in the saddle from the moment their ma let me take them out of the house," he said proudly as the stallion made another jump. "Gotta start them young."

An irritated neigh had us all whipping our heads back to the paddock just in time to see a magpie dive close to the stallion's face. My heart leapt into my throat as the horse swerved and missed his footing as he came down from the jump. Mr. Handmar gasped in horror as the horse's leg went sideways with a loud crack, and the animal let out a shrill scream of pain that cut me to the bone.

"Kelton!" Mrs. Handmar screamed, rushing out of the house as her son tumbled from the horse's back. The boy managed to roll free before the horse crushed him beneath its weight, then lay on his back in the dirt, eyes glassy with shock.

"Damn," Mr. Handmar swore as he flung open the paddock gate. He and his wife gathered up their son and rushed him out

of the paddock toward the house while the horse still lay help-less on the ground. Hartley jumped down from Makar and held the gelding's reins in his small hands, his face pale. Now that Kelton was safely out of harm's way, I approached the stricken stallion, dread sitting heavy in my chest.

"His leg is broken," Fenris said softly as I knelt in the mud.

Yes, it is, I agreed silently as I inspected the leg. A clean break. But I couldn't say that aloud. "It is not broken," I lied firmly, waving him away. "The injury is treatable. Please," I said, dropping my voice. "Please go distract Mr. Handmar and his family while I tend to this. I don't want them to panic."

Fenris stared at me. The moment stretched out, and I was worried that he would balk. But he nodded, then went to Hart-ley, who was standing at the gate with Makar. Tears shimmered in the little boy's eyes, and I was struck by the urge to comfort him. But my duty was with the horse, who needed my comfort far more than the little boy. Fenris gently put his arm around the boy while taking the reins, and I knew Hartley was in good hands.

Sucking in a breath, I turned back to the stallion, who was trying, futilely, to stand back up, panicked snorts emitting from him. Struggling would only compound the damage, so I used my strongest calming spell to keep him prone. As Fenris directed Hartley to find compresses and liniment, I gently pressed my hands to the horse's leg. The animal quivered beneath my touch, his eyes rolling with pain and fear.

"Shhh," I said, then chanted a painkilling spell underneath my breath. If I'd had the time, I would completely numb the leg and induce the horse into a stupor, but I knew it was only a matter of minutes before the Handmars came back, and I couldn't let them see what I was doing. Gritting my teeth, I grasped both ends of the leg, then set it in one smooth motion. The horse whinnied, but it was not the pain-filled scream he

would have made without the spell. Praying to the Creator that Fenris would distract them long enough, I closed my eyes, then pressed my hand on the break and silently intoned the healing spell.

As the magic seeped into the broken bone, pain hit me, and I had to clench my jaw against a whimper. The cost of healing an injury, I had discovered long ago, involved drawing the pain into oneself so that the magic could do its work. My shin began to throb with agony, just as if I had been the one to break it, and I held back tears. The agony stretched on for several minutes before it began to subside, the magic finally done with the brunt of its work.

A rivulet of sweat ran down my spine, and I could feel perspiration gathering at my brow. Opening my eyes, I ran a hand across my forehead and met the horse's gaze. His large brown eyes were pain free, and I exhaled in relief. A wave of tiredness hit me—healing such a large injury so quickly had sapped quite a bit of my magic. But it was worth it, if I could save the horse's life.

"Come on, boy," I said, getting to my feet. "Let's see if you can stand."

As I gently coaxed the horse to his feet, the front door banged open. The Handmars rushed down the stairs. "My word," Mr. Handmar said, and I turned to see him and his wife heading toward the paddock, their arms full of the supplies Fenris had requested. Fenris and the children were right behind them, and my breath froze in my chest as I met the shifter's yellow eyes. Was that a knowing look in them? But no, I must have imagined it...

"I was certain Midnight's leg was broken," Mr. Handmar said, his eyes wide with astonishment and relief. "How in Recca is he standing again?"

"The injury wasn't as bad as it looked," I said casually,

patting the horse's side. "The leg is just bruised, not broken. A little massage and encouragement was all it took. Even so, I'd advise you to have him take it easy for the next couple of days," I said sternly. "It was a very near thing."

"I'll say," Mrs. Handmar said, beaming.

The boys broke free from Fenris's side and rushed into the paddock to hug me. "Thank you for saving him, Mina," Kelton said, his voice teary as he pressed his face into my belly. "I felt so awful when I thought I might have killed him."

"It wasn't your fault," I said gently, brushing my hand against his mop of curls. "Accidents happen to everyone. Even your pa."

"That's right," Mr. Handmar said gruffly, coming into the paddock with Fenris. Crouching low, he ran his hands up and down the stallion's legs. "Incredible. I guess his leg really wasn't broken."

"Excellent," Fenris said, patting the horse's shoulder. The stallion flicked his tail, but he seemed content to let Fenris touch him. "Because I would like to buy him."

Mr. Handmar and I exchanged surprised glances. "Really? You don't want to give him a few days first and make sure his leg is really all right? I would hate to sell him to you only to find out that he's permanently damaged."

Fenris smiled. "I have every confidence in Miss Hollin's abilities," he said, running a hand along the stallion's mane. "If she says the horse is fine, then I believe her."

After Mr. Handmar put the gelding through a demonstration as well—his wife wasn't about to let her sons near the paddock again today, not that I could blame her—Fenris arranged with the breeder to buy both horses. To my surprise, he pulled three gold coins from a small pouch tied to his belt and paid upfront.

"That's a bit too much for just two horses," Mr. Handmar said as he took the coins, sounding bemused. "I'll have to give you change."

He pulled out several silver coins from his purse, and Fenris winced. "I'll take those and add them to your account at the general store," I said quickly, palming the coins. "Shifters are allergic to silver," I explained.

"Oh!" Mr. Handmar started. "I apologize—I'd completely forgotten about that. I have to confess, I'm not certain how much I've heard about shifters is actually true and how much is just myth."

Fenris smiled. "It's quite all right. You now know two things —that we're allergic to silver and we can shift any time we want, regardless of the full moon. I'm happy to answer any other questions you might have, if you're ever curious to learn more about my kind."

"I may take you up on that," Mr. Handmar said, "but another time, perhaps. I think we've all had quite enough excitement for today!"

While Mr. Handmar and Fenris drew up the paperwork for the sale, I went to check on the pregnant mare—the reason I'd come here in the first place. She was doing fine, only a few weeks away from her due date, and after I was done, I met Fenris back at the cart so I could hitch my horse. We tied the gelding behind the cart so we could take him with us, and Mr. Handmar said he would deliver the stallion in about a week, after he was certain the horse was fully healed and ready to go.

We said farewell to the Handmars, then drove back to Fenris's farm to drop him and the gelding off before I returned home to tend to more patients. The first few minutes of the ride were silent, for which I was grateful. Fenris's gaze was far too keen for my liking, and I wasn't sure if I could successfully fend off his questions.

Unfortunately, the silence did not last nearly as long as I would have liked.

"I know a break when I see one," he said in that deep bari-

tone of his. "Under normal circumstances, that horse would have been put down, so I am glad you were able to save him with your magic. How often do you do that sort of thing?"

I nearly dropped the reins. "How..." Twenty questions exploded in my mind all at once, and it took me a few minutes to sort them.

"I don't suppose it would be any use to tell you that you are mistaken?" I asked, cringing inwardly. "A gentleman does not contradict a lady, after all."

"I'm afraid not," he said, sounding amused. "Magic has a very distinct scent—not unlike burnt sugar."

My cheeks flamed—clearly, denial was of no use. "You seem strangely at ease about this," I said, after a long pause. "Aren't shifters supposed to be afraid of magic?"

Fenris shrugged. "I spent most of my life in a big city filled with magic users," he said. "Getting used to magic was a necessity for me. And you haven't answered my question," he pointed out with raised eyebrows. "How often do you do this?"

My cheeks warmed. "I only know a very little bit of magic," I confessed, seeing no point in lying since shifters could scent lies from truth. "Mostly just what I need to help the animals I treat. I am a perfectly legitimate, human-trained vet," I added, lifting my chin.

Fenris grinned a little, as if amused by my standoffish behavior. "I never thought to suggest otherwise," he said. "You can be a well-trained vet and still use magic."

"I...you truly aren't bothered by my magic?" I asked, anxiety seeping into my tone despite my efforts to remain calm. I knew it was unlikely for Fenris, an outsider himself, to rat me out to the town, but I couldn't discount the possibility. He was a stranger, after all, and I could not let myself forget that, no matter how at ease I felt with him.

His expression sobered instantly. "Not in the least," he

assured me. "I am no stranger to secrets, Mina—we all have our skeletons in our closets. I will never tell a soul about what I saw today, and I doubt Mr. Handmar will say anything either, even if he should suspect. But I don't think he does—in my experience, humans are quick to accept the first explanation that makes sense to them, and he has no reason to think you have any powers with which to heal a broken leg."

I let out a long breath. "If this was the only incident, then perhaps I would not be so worried," I said. "But even if you and Mr. Handmar do not say anything, I am already under suspicion for practicing magic."

Fenris sat up straighter in his seat. "What do you mean?"

I bit my lip. "The constable came by to see me the other day about it," I told him. "Roor's mother has accused me of using a hex or some other form of magic to cause him to stumble and pass out the other night. Which, of course, I did not do—as I said, my magic is very limited."

"Is that so?" Fenris sounded startled. When I glanced at him, I thought I caught a flash of guilt in his eyes. But what would he have to feel guilty about? "That seems awfully petty of her. It's obvious to anybody who was there that Roor had far too much to drink that night."

"Yes, you would think so," I said bitterly. "The Roors are rich, but not popular. Mrs. Roor is a vile bigot and does not like anyone except her son. I'm not sure she even likes him. She hates shifters on principle, and mages as well. Most of all, she hates me for her son's persistent infatuation—she thinks I'm leading him on, though it's anyone's guess why she believes I'm encouraging him in any way. But she is quite capable of denouncing me to the Mages Guild as an illegal magic user, simply for the pleasure of causing me difficulties."

"That would be most unjust." Fenris's expression darkened, and I was surprised to see how troubled he looked by my revela-

tion. "I am sorry this has happened to you—you certainly do not deserve to be persecuted because one man cannot take no for an answer. If you need any help, please do not hesitate to call on me."

My heart warmed at his concern. "I will, thank you," I said, though I wasn't quite certain what he could do about it. I did not want to bring more trouble to Fenris's doorstep, not when he was still so new in town. Besides, I didn't need a defender. What I really needed was a tutor to help me get a better grip on my magic, but a shifter would not be able to help with that, even one comfortable with using magical charms.

At least he's not going to betray my secret. Which was a pleasant surprise. It felt...good, to be able to tell someone the truth about myself and know he was not going to judge or condemn me. Perhaps we might become friends after all—if I wasn't forced to flee Abbsville in the near future.

I'd better take more care about doing magic with witnesses nearby. Because if I had another slip-up, it would spell the end of my life here.

FENRIS

After Mina dropped me off, I took Makar to the stables, which I had already prepared with water from the well, fresh hay, and sacks filled with oats. I thought about feeding him first but then decided to brush him down—the grooming ritual would speed the bonding between horse and master as the gelding got used to my scent.

As I checked the horse's hooves, my mind drifted back to the surprising discovery I'd made today. I'd suspected there was something different about Mina from the moment I'd met her, but even so, the revelation that she could use magic had not been what I was expecting.

Well, this certainly explains why she looks so young for her age. Young, pretty, and a mage... The memory of her scent washed over me, a combination of lilacs and sunshine, and a tingling warmth spread through my body. Shaking my head, I forced myself to stop thinking about her, but it was difficult. I'd spent hours with her today, sitting in the cart so close to that sweet, fresh scent, feeling her body heat radiating from beneath that thin dress. She'd been close enough to touch, and I'd been

tempted more than once to reach out and see if her peach-colored skin was as soft as it looked.

This is ridiculous. I finished with the horse's hooves and grabbed the curry comb. Mina was far too young for me, and she did not need to be encumbered by a fugitive with dark secrets lurking in the shadows. I sometimes longed to settle down with a mate and raise a family, but those were mere daydreams. I could not bring danger on any other person when I could be discovered and arrested at any moment. There was still a death sentence hanging over me. Until I had established myself in my new identity and was certain I had permanently evaded capture, I could only dream about letting someone else into my life.

Not wanting to dwell on that problem, I returned my attention to Mina's predicament. Was she a human-mage hybrid, with a mage mother or father out there who had never taken responsibility for her training? Or had she been born with magic into a human family? Either case would have made for a very difficult upbringing. And how had she evaded the obligatory testing for magic during her school years? That was supposed to be impossible.

And yet, I thought, *this is the second case I've encountered recently of a full-grown adult possessing hidden magic.* Just how many more were out there, keeping their heads down, hiding behind mundane professions, and doing their best to keep their talents a secret? At least Mina could use her magic to some extent in her profession, which was impressive if she didn't have any training. Sunaya, who was quite powerful, had no control over her magic when she'd first been dragged to Solantha Palace in chains.

Of course, that was due to that blasted magic block that had been put on her when she was a baby, I thought crossly. The spell had protected Sunaya when she was a child and allowed her to pass

the testing without detection, but the mage who'd cast it had not factored in how powerful she would become, and it had begun failing in her adult years. She was very lucky Iannis and I had found her, rather than another Chief Mage, or she could very well have been executed.

But that was neither here nor there. Mina was obviously not in the same situation—she had no magical block on her powers, just a lack of training. She had surprisingly good control of her abilities for someone who wasn't tutored—she had done a marvelous job with that horse's broken leg in such a short amount of time. Judging by her expertise, she'd been using her magic for quite some time to treat her animal patients and had gotten away with it so far.

Yet now the danger of discovery loomed over her pretty blonde head. My mood soured at the thought of that lout, Roor. With his mother making such a fuss about Mina, it was only a matter of time until she landed in big trouble. And it was *my* fault, I acknowledged, guilt sitting heavy in my stomach. My fault for using my magic in front of all those guests to immobilize Roor.

Then again, Mina would have been suspected sooner or later even without my interference. I bet that she had a success rate far above the average veterinarian. It was amazing, considering how easily she had healed that leg, that she had gone undetected for this long.

Another example of how stupid and wasteful it is to stamp out non-approved magic, I concluded as I finished brushing the horse. I gave him a pat, then fetched a bag of oats and poured it into his bucket. I watched the horse for another moment, then once I was satisfied he would be all right, headed back into the house. As I washed my hands at the kitchen sink, I thought back to how anxious Mina had looked after I challenged her about having magic, and how relieved she'd been when I assured her that her

secret was still safe. She'd probably been dreading being found out for years, imagining what it would be like to be ostracized, driven out of town, or, in the worst case, imprisoned for illegal magic, as Sunaya had been. I could not stand by and watch her fears come to pass.

There was no reason I could not be of assistance, so long as I was discreet about it and did not act on the attraction I felt. Nothing more than friendship could come of this.

And why would anything more come of it? I scolded myself. *You have far too high an opinion of yourself to think that spending time with Mina could lead to a romantic relationship.* As I understood it, she could have any unmarried man in Abbsville. In fact, from all accounts, she had rejected most of them. And I was a shifter, to boot. Why would she see me in any different light?

But then, her standoffish attitude toward men was likely because she needed to hide her magic. Just as I was reluctant to let a woman into my life because of my dangerous secrets, she would also be hesitant about letting a normal human get that close to her. In a small town like this, she could not easily find anyone who would be willing to keep her magic a secret. It was admirable how well she'd managed to fit into this human community, but, underneath that, she might be just as lonely as I was.

That does not mean she would be receptive to advances from you, I told myself sternly. A shifter would be just as unsuitable a match as a human. Then again, was there *any* acceptable match for an illegal magic user?

Tired of my circular and unproductive thoughts, I made myself a sandwich, then went back out to the stables and saddled the gelding. It was high time I did something useful, and now was as good a time as any to find out what Marris and his friends had been up to the other night.

It did not take me very long to retrace my steps—my wolf

side had an excellent sense of direction, and there had been enough markers for me to find my way. The gelding objected when I'd first swung myself up in the saddle, but a touch of magic—perhaps even the same spell Mina had used to quiet her mare when I'd first approached—was enough to relax him. Soon, we settled into a steady rhythm.

It feels good to have a mount again, I thought as we passed beneath the forest canopy. The last time I'd ridden a horse for any length of time was when I'd fled Nebara, when I'd still been Polar ar'Tollis, the renegade Chief Mage. Riding as Fenris required a bit of readjustment, as my current body was vastly different—Polar had been tall and lean, whereas my shifter body was shorter and stockier, with more muscle, thicker thighs, and broader shoulders.

It was not long before I found the glade with the brook where I'd spotted Marris and his friends. The place looked much more cheerful in the afternoon light, and I pulled the gelding to a stop, taking a moment to inhale the earthy scents of the forest. Oak and maple were predominating, though beneath them I could smell scat from various forest animals mixed in with the dirt and a few pungent mushrooms. I dismounted the gelding, then tied him to a tree and crossed the brook so I could try to pick up any scent traces my new friends had left on the other side.

It took very little effort to track their scents. A few minutes later, I found a deer trail with recent hoofprints stamped into the dirt. *This must have been where they came from,* I thought, following the path. It led me to a side valley, completely hidden —I never would have known it was here if I had not used my shifter senses to retrace Marris's steps. The trees thinned out as the hills rose on either side, casting the place in shadow.

Further down the valley were some rocky cliffs tucked into the hillsides that rolled up into the mountains. To my surprise, I

discovered a sturdy wooden door in the rock face with a big shiny padlock. I examined it for any hint of rust or wear, but found none, telling me it was fairly new. Had Marris and his friends installed it? The scent confirmed my hypothesis.

Excitement began to course through my veins, although I was quick to temper it with caution. There was no telling what I might find behind this door, though my nose determined there was nothing living lurking here, nor any dead bodies. The scent of Marris and his friends was unmistakable, but it did not appear that anyone else had been here recently. A spell muttered beneath my breath easily undid the lock. I eased the door open and stepped inside.

Behind the door, a tunnel led further into the cliff, so dark beyond the first curve that even my shifter eyes could pick out very little. Not wanting to leave the door open in case anyone else came by, I shut it behind me, then conjured a ball of white fire to help light my way. The flames flickered above my palm as I silently crept down the tunnel.

It was a mine. I lifted a rusty pickaxe from a heap of stones. A quick sniff told me Marris and his friends had used it recently...and that they were mining gold. My eyebrows rose— this was a highly illegal activity. The mining of natural gold had been strictly banned by the highest authority, the Convention of Chief Mages. All currency, whether it be gold, silver, copper, or pandanum, was created by the various Mages Guilds and rationed out carefully via the accredited mages in yearly allotments.

Since a forger could easily create counterfeit coins out of mined gold, doing so carried an almost automatic death sentence. Still, some people thought it worth the risk. Without using a detection spell on individual coins, or having a shifter nose that could sniff out the lack of magical residue, the forged coins would look the same. Nobody would know the difference.

Was that what Marris was doing? I examined the evidence as I wandered further into the mine. Sure enough, there were more traces of gold ore in the walls—quite a lot, in fact, considering the piles of rubble meant a significant portion had already been mined. The Benefactor had used such illegal gold to fund her operations, but she had access to professional forgers and conveniently owned a chain of banks to launder the illicit coins. I doubted Marris and his friends had the skill to mint coins, and who else out here could?

I spent a few more minutes snooping around the place, then carefully closed everything up and hiked back to where I'd left my gelding. I was not certain how I felt about this discovery—if Marris, Roth, and Cobil were discreetly selling off the gold to a counterfeiter, that was one thing. But what if they were using it to fund the Resistance? That was high treason against the Federation, and if the authorities traced the gold back here, it would spell doom for these young men, and likely all their associates, including their new shifter neighbor. Hanging was the mandatory sentence for conspiracy and counterfeiting currency. They were playing with fire.

Of course, having fought with the Resistance was already a high crime, so they might think they had little to lose at this point. But the thought of those lively young men strung up on gibbets did not sit right with me, no matter how guilty they were.

No, I could not simply ignore this matter. For the short term, I would keep Marris's secret until I found out what the illegal gold was being used for. Then I would have to decide what to do about the clandestine operation conducted under the town's very noses before these young fools brought disaster down on the whole place.

MINA

The next evening, Barrla and I set out for the town's weekly book club meeting. It was held in a different place each week. This time around, we walked to the house of Mrs. Cattin, the pastor's wife. Barrla had baked fresh cinnamon tarts, and the most delicious smell was wafting from the basket she had slung on her arm. It blended wonderfully with the fresh springtime scents drifting on the air. Despite the worries that plagued me recently, I sighed contentedly.

"I'm glad to see you're in good spirits," Barrla said, looping her free arm with mine. "You've been out of sorts ever since the constable showed up at your door the other day."

I frowned. "Yes, and seeing as how I'd like to stay in good spirits, I'd prefer not to talk about it."

Barrla winced. "Sorry," she said, squeezing my arm. "I'll change the subject, then. Anything interesting happen since we last spoke?"

"I'm afraid not," I lied. I didn't want to tell her about my outing with Fenris, because that would lead to telling her about the horse's injury, and the fewer people who knew about that, the better. Besides, I was worried Barrla might think I was

spending too much time with her new "shifter beau," and I didn't want that to come between us. She was very good-natured —one of the qualities I loved about her—so I didn't think she would mind too much, but I didn't see any reason to destroy her hopes.

We arrived at Mrs. Cattin's house just in time. The other ladies were seated in the parlor, enjoying the refreshments that had already been laid out. The pastor's wife greeted us warmly and exclaimed over Barrla's tarts. I'd brought some cheese pastries, which she also accepted, and Barrla and I helped ourselves to treats before sitting down.

We were the youngest members of the club—the other ladies ranged from their late thirties all the way up to their nineties, though admittedly, Mrs. Harpton, a great-grandmother, was twice as old as the next eldest. Most of the younger girls in town were too busy to make time for a book club—or rather, too busy batting their eyelashes at the men. But Barrla and I loved to read, and the other women were happy to have us, so we went to nearly every meeting. Usually, it was the social highlight of the week—there wasn't very much to do out here in Abbsville aside from work and the occasional party or festival.

"All right." Mrs. Cattin clapped her hands. "Let's pull out our books. Who would like to go first?"

"I will," Mrs. Tamil offered eagerly, shooting her hand up in the air. She clutched a mystery paperback in her hand. Mrs. Cattin gave her the nod, and she opened the book and began to read a passage.

Because Abbsville was so small, and had no public library, it was impossible for us to borrow and read copies of the same book at the same time. Our solution was to each bring the book we were currently reading and read aloud a typical passage. Afterward, we would discuss it for a bit, then move on to the next lady and book. If someone decided they liked the story,

they could then borrow the book from the owner when she was done reading it. Most of the women couldn't afford to buy new books very often—Barrla, Mrs. Cattin, and I were the only ones who did so regularly—and in this manner, the other women were exposed to new reading material, and we were all able to exchange our small collections.

By the end of the hour, several of us had decided to borrow books from one another, and I was greatly looking forward to reading Mrs. Tamil's new mystery novel. I collected the book from her since she'd already finished it, then prepared to leave before the customary gossip session started. But Barrla was still in conversation with Mrs. Vamas, and I'd promised not to leave without her.

"And how are you doing, Mina dear, after your terrible ordeal with the constable?" Mrs. Staffer, a motherly widow in her late forties, asked me. I stiffened as the entire room turned toward us, but I could hardly rebuff her when she was looking at me with such concern. "I heard all about those nasty accusations from Mrs. Roor. That woman delights in mischief-making. And if she had brought her son up right, he would not drink so much and would have an easier time finding a woman to take him on."

"Thank goodness she doesn't come to our book clubs." Mrs. Cattin sniffed. "I'm not sure I could abide her nonsense. Really, accusing Mina of using magic. What else will she come up with —that hogs fly?"

"I appreciate the support, ladies," I said, doing my best to smile. "Really, though, I wouldn't worry about it. The constable hasn't come back to bother me about it since, and he assured me he didn't really believe the claims either."

"I wouldn't write off the situation too quickly, Mina," Mrs. Staffer warned. "Mrs. Roor told me the other day that she was

not satisfied with the constable's report. She has written to the Watawis Mages Guild asking for an investigation."

My blood iced over.

"Well, I hope the mages fine Mrs. Roor for wasting their time," Barrla said sharply, her blue eyes sparkling with anger. She came over to me and squeezed my hand, and I was startled to realize that my skin had gone cold. "Surely we would have all seen something out of the ordinary by now if Mina truly could use magic? She's lived here for years!"

"You know..." I said thoughtfully, acting as though this didn't faze me in the least. "When I was speaking with Mr. Shelton at the party, he told me that shifters can smell magic, and that it has an odd scent, similar to burnt sugar."

"Burnt sugar," one of the women exclaimed. "How strange."

"What else have you learned about him?" Barrla asked eagerly, her eyes now sparkling with excitement rather than anger. She clutched my arm tightly, like a small child begging for a piece of candy. "Has he told you anything about his past?"

The conversation quickly devolved into a question-and-answer session about Fenris. Where did Mr. Shelton get his fortune? Was he planning to marry? Why had he moved to Abbsville? That farmhouse really was much too big for a single man, one of the women declared.

"Oh, I simply must get him alone again," Barrla said, pressing a hand to her chest with a sigh. "He really is so very handsome, with that beard and strong jaw, just like the shifter from *Falling for the Wolf*." To my amusement, she pulled the very same book from one of her skirt pockets. "His yellow eyes flared with lust as he took her into his muscular arms," she began to read out loud, "and he crushed his lips to hers in a *scorching* kiss that seared every coherent thought from her mind. All she could think about was the feel of his iron arms banded around her and

the hardness of his bare chest pressed against her pebbling breasts…"

"Oh, stop it!" Mrs. Cattin exclaimed, her cheeks flaming. The other women were shaking their heads at Barrla, scandalized by the racy passage. "What would Mr. Shelton think if he knew you were picturing him while reading such naughty words?"

"I think he might find it rather sexy," Barrla said saucily. "What do you think, Mina?"

I choked back a laugh. "Mr. Shelton is a hard man to read," I said, not wanting to encourage her too much. Somehow, I got the sense that bubbly Barrla was not his type—she was very pretty, and she had a good head on her shoulders, but she was not an intellectual. I suspected Fenris would want a woman who shared more of his interests.

Still…he is a man, intellectual or not, I mused. Surely he found Barrla attractive, and if she spent enough time with him, she could very well entice him to her bed. What kind of lover would he be? Would he be rough and animalistic, like the shifter from Barrla's book? Or would he be attentive and thorough, using his heightened senses to find a woman's sweet spots and make her sing with pleasure?

Heat flooded my veins at the thought, and I had to quickly push away the sudden flurry of mental images before the other women noticed the blush rising to my cheeks. There was no point in trying to romanticize him. He was probably just like any other man when making love.

Not that I had very much experience with men. My one sexual encounter had been with a colleague in the town where I had first started practicing veterinary medicine, and it had not ended well. I had accidentally set the sheets on fire with my magic when I'd gotten close to my climax. My cheeks flamed as I recalled the embarrassing incident, and I turned back to the refreshment table before the other ladies noticed. I had

managed to convince my lover that it had been a freak electrical accident, but I had never attempted to have sex again. It was too dangerous for me to allow someone to get that close to me.

That incident was also what had led me to Abbsville. I'd felt compelled to move before any other "freak accidents" could give me away.

"Oh, before I forget, I have something absolutely juicy to tell you all," Barrla squealed, clapping her hands together. "But you must promise not to discuss a word of it outside the room."

This caused another flurry of excitement, and we agreed to take the secret to our graves.

"Someone has been leaving gold coins in the post boxes of several farms over the past few nights," Barrla said in a hushed voice, leaning in as if there might be someone listening at the windows. "Not a fortune, mind you—just enough to pay the yearly taxes coming up, or a little over."

"Oh, yes, I've heard something about this," Mrs. Canterbew exclaimed, her eyes widening. "This happened to my neighbor the other night. She was beside herself with joy. So it was not just her, then?"

"Do you know who is leaving these mystery gifts?" Mrs. Staffer asked eagerly. "I sure could use some gold to help pay the taxes this year."

"Us too," Mrs. Bartow said, sounding a little dejected. "We had a bad harvest this past year—we're not sure how to make ends meet."

As the others speculated about who the mysterious benefactor might be, I found myself wondering if Fenris could have been the culprit. He had plenty of gold...but no, a new arrival would not have any idea who was in need, or how much they fell short for the year. It had to be a local, someone who had intimate knowledge of the families that lived here and their

economic circumstances. Yet who in Abbsville could afford such largesse? Not even the Boccols were that rich.

Well, whoever it is, I'm very grateful, I thought as Barrla and I finally left. I just hoped that whoever was doing this wasn't bringing trouble upon themselves or stretching themselves too thin in the process.

10

FENRIS

The sound of hoofbeats pounding down the road caught my ears as I was pouring oats into Makar's feed bucket. The horse swiveled his ears in the direction of the sound but did not appear otherwise alarmed, so I patted him on the head and walked out of the stables to see who my new visitor was.

"Fenris!" Marris hailed me as I rounded the front of the house. He trotted up on a gelding of his own, then hopped off the horse to greet me. "I've come with this year's rent."

"Excellent." I smiled at him, even as alarm bells went off in my head. I'd given Marris and his family a few months to get the coin together—how did they have it so soon? "Why don't you come inside so I can get you a receipt?"

Marris eagerly accepted my offer to get out of the sun. After tying his horse to one of the posts outside my porch, he followed me inside. I sat him down at the breakfast table with a glass of water, then went into my bedroom to fetch a piece of paper and a pen.

"Here you are," he said, reaching into his pocket as I sat

down. "Five gold coins, as promised." He slid the money across the table.

"Thank you." I took the coins and put all but one in my pocket. As Marris took another drink of his water, I surreptitiously lifted the coin to my nose and took a whiff. As I expected, there was no trace of magic on the precious metal.

"Marris," I said slowly, placing the coin back onto the table. "Where did you get the money?"

"From the family coffers, of course," he said nonchalantly. If I were human, I might have believed him. But his scent changed subtly, soured by the faintest trace of fear, and I knew I had him.

"You should know better than to lie to a shifter," I said lightly, knowing if I grew stern with him, it would only push him away further. "We can scent whether a person is telling the truth...and we can also scent if coins are counterfeit." I picked up the coin again and tapped it against my nose. "Authentic coins are made by the Mages Guild and smell faintly of magic. This coin here has not even a tiny bit of magic in its scent, which tells me it was created from mined gold. So, I ask you again, Marris—where did you get this?"

Marris's jaw had dropped, but he clenched it at my question, his eyes narrowing. "I don't see why I would need to tell you that," he said tightly. "As long as we pay the rent, why does it matter where the gold comes from?"

"Because if I pay my taxes with these coins, and the Mages Guild discovers they are counterfeit, I will be investigated by the authorities. Something I very much do not want," I said calmly.

Marris's eyes widened in shock. "I...I suppose I never thought of that," he said. "But the Mages Guild would have no reason to suspect anything. They just want to get paid, don't they?"

"Why don't you start from the beginning," I prodded gently, "and tell me where this gold came from. I have no intention of

running to the Mages Guild if you are not doing anything dangerous, but I must know exactly what I am dealing with if I'm to avoid the worst kind of trouble."

Marris sighed. "As you probably know, the Resistance has been funding some of its operations through gold mined from a few caves across the Federation," he said, scooping a hand through his hair. "Aside from the last few months of my service, we were always paid well, and our gold was never turned away from any establishment, so we didn't care that it was technically counterfeit." Marris rolled his eyes at that. "The irony doesn't escape me, mind you, that naturally created gold is considered 'fake' while magically created gold is considered 'real.'"

I cracked a smile. "The thought has occurred to me as well," I said. "Are you telling me that this gold you have is from your time with the Resistance?" I did not want Marris to think I had already discovered his secret.

Marris shook his head. "When we came back from the fighting, half of the local farms were in danger of being auctioned off for tax arrears due to the terrible harvest last year. These were our neighbors, people we'd grown up with, and we couldn't bear to see their homes being taken away. We were up late one night thinking about it, when Roth pointed out that there was a gold vein hidden in the area that we had accidentally discovered back when we were kids."

I raised my eyebrows, as if surprised. "So this gold is local?" I asked, hefting the coin in my palm. "You mined it yourselves?"

"Yes." For a moment, Marris looked extraordinarily proud of himself. "It took us a bit to figure out how, but we managed to get the tools together. The hardest part wasn't the mining, to be honest—it was finding someone who could turn the gold into coins. We finally got in touch with a jeweler in another town, and he's been transforming the nuggets into coins for a cut of the profits. He had to produce the dies first, which took quite a

while, and it's only just these last few days that we finally have some actual coins to use."

"Right on time for tax season, I see." I smiled, even as my mind churned with the implications. "You are only using the gold on behalf of the local townsfolk?" I pressed.

"We're not sending it off to the Resistance, if that's what you mean," Marris scoffed. "I still believe in the basic concept, but after all the bigotry and hatred that's come to light, I wouldn't support them if you paid me. My loyalty is to Abbsville now," he added, "and I'll do whatever it takes to make sure my neighbors don't go hungry or lose their homes."

"That is very admirable of you," I said, masking my astonishment. My nose told me he was being frank, which indeed seemed to be his default mode. I had not been expecting that Marris would use the gold for such a selfless cause—in my experience, most people tended to hoard their riches rather than hand them out free of charge. Despite everything, I could not help liking the scamp.

"However," I continued, injecting a stern note in my voice, "this counterfeiting is not without risk. If the Mages Guild does take notice, they will send a team to investigate, and you probably know the penalty is hanging. Already, one Chief Mage I know about is aware of the Resistance's use of illegal gold, and he will have informed his fellow Chief Mages to be on the lookout for such coins." In fact, it had been Sunaya and I who first spotted the counterfeiting with our shifter noses. At the time, it had seemed natural to immediately inform the Mages Guild, but as I sat here, I realized there were unintended consequences.

Marris looked slightly troubled by my warning, but after a moment's consideration, he shrugged. "That may be so, but Abbsville is such a tiny town that the Federation won't be looking this way," he insisted. "But if you want, I can change out

these coins for real ones. It might take me a couple of days, though."

I shook my head. "No need," I said, finally placing the last coin into my tunic pocket. "I shall accept these, just this once." After all, I was perfectly capable of adding the magical scent to these coins, though I could not tell Marris that. "But be sure to pay me with genuine ones next year."

Marris eagerly agreed, then thanked me for accepting the coins and agreeing to keep his secret. As I watched him leave, I wondered just how long this secret would stay under wraps. From what I understood, this entire region had suffered from a bad harvest, and if Abbsville was the only town in the area where everyone could pay up, that anomaly could draw the interest of the state's tax inspectors.

"I guess I'd better go doctor these coins now," I muttered, heading back inside. I could only hope that the tax inspectors would be too happy about the money to look closely, but that didn't mean I could take any chances with my own payment.

MINA

Rain drummed on the rooftop of my house, matching the staccato of my fingers as I tapped them against the tabletop. In my right hand I held a pen, the end of which I chewed absently as I considered the tax report I was filling out.

A plaintive meow from across the room had me setting down my pen. There on my sofa sprawled a little black-and-white kitten—a tom I'd taken in the other night when he showed up on my doorstep, soaked and shivering from the sudden downpour that had assailed Abbsville. Feeling sorry for the small creature, I'd taken him in and fed him, with the intention of finding him a new home.

"I can't spend all day scratching your ears," I told him, picking up my pen again. "I have work to do, you know."

The kitten only meowed again, this time lifting his head imperiously. From the way he sprawled across my furniture, I could tell the little tom already thought he was home.

"Perhaps I should give you a name," I mused, still staring at him. The cat held my stare, unblinking, then hopped off the

couch and padded toward me. "What about Felix?" I asked as he wound his way around my legs, purring far too loudly for an animal of his size. He rubbed his chin against my ankle as if in response to the suggested name, and I giggled as the motion tickled my exposed skin.

"Oh, but I can't name you, can I?" I said with a sigh, scooping him up and putting him in my lap. If I named him, I would have to keep him, and since I was moving in two years, if not earlier, that didn't seem like a wise idea.

"You are very cute," I told him as I scratched beneath his tiny chin with the nail of my forefinger. "I should have very little trouble finding a home for you. Some little girl is bound to take one look at you and fall in love."

The cat purred louder, angling his chin against my finger. As I continued to scratch him, my mind drifted back to my current predicament—whether I should wait out my last two years in Abbsville or attempt to start over in another town. It would have been convenient if I'd learned transmogrification before running away, I reflected, looking out the window at the pouring rain. If I had that skill, I could create gold like any full-fledged mage, though I would have to do it secretly and in small amounts. Then I could afford nicer furniture instead of the creaky chair I sat upon and the scarred wooden table upon which my tax papers lay. I might very well have been the one to leave presents of gold for friends in need rather than the mysterious donor who had popped up all of a sudden. It still seemed too much of a coincidence to me that this happened just as Fenris moved into town, but I couldn't see how he would know who to leave gifts for.

Then again, I thought, *if I had not run away, and had managed to complete my apprenticeship, I'd be allotted a certain amount of gold every year simply for being a mage.* That didn't seem very fair, not

when the residents of Abbsville worked so hard and received so little, but it would have made my life much easier. I worked myself to the bone just to make ends meet—I'd stayed up until four in the morning with a colicky horse last night, and had woken at eight to patch up a dog that had gotten into a nasty fight with a stray cat. As the only veterinarian in town, I could hardly turn away pet owners in need.

But even with all the hours I worked tending the pets and farm animals of Abbsville, I made so little in ready cash that I did not have to pay taxes, for which I was grateful. I was still required to hand the form in to the tax mage when he came to town, but at least I did not have to hand over any of my hard-earned coin.

Using my left hand to pet the kitten, I finished filling out the form with my right, then signed it and put it in an envelope. I attempted to stand, but the kitten purred louder, snuggling deeper into my lap. Smiling, I settled back down and instead reached for my cup of tea. As I sipped, petting the cat and staring out at the empty, flooded streets, a sense of peace over-came me. I loved evenings like this, where I could sit inside and curl up with a cup of tea and a good book—or, in this case, a cuddly cat.

I'll wait another year, I decided, *and see how I feel about moving then.* Yes, things had gotten a bit uncomfortable recently, but I would not let a busybody like Mrs. Roor get the better of me. Besides, if I fled town now, so soon after these accusations, it would only make me look guilty. It was better to go about my business like normal and make myself useful. Apart from Mrs. Roor, nobody in Abbsville really wanted to get rid of the local veterinarian—I was far too valuable, in the grand scheme of things.

Besides, life wasn't really so bad here, was it? I had my cozy little house, clothes on my back, and enough food to keep my

belly full at night. What more did I need? Many people in the Federation had far less. Since my father's forebears had been among the first mages to settle in the southern state of Innarta and had received generous land grants, I'd grown up amongst opulent wealth. I had every intention of enjoying that wealth again once I reached my majority and could claim my inheritance. Two years wasn't that long to wait. Knowing it was only temporary, living modestly was fun in its own way.

You should be proud you've managed to make your way in the world all alone, I thought. *You left with hardly any magical training or money to your name, and yet you've managed to establish a career and identity for yourself. That's more than many can say, regardless of their race.*

The piercing whistle of a steam vehicle jarred me from my thoughts, and I peered out the window again, pressing my nose to the glass. A pair of headlights nearly blinded me as a massive steamtruck rumbled right up in front of my house. I was forced to throw my hand in front of my eyes to block the glare.

The kitten hissed at the noise, digging his claws into my leg.

"Ouch!" I lifted him off my lap, ignoring his protests. "You can't hog me forever," I told him as I sat him down on the floor. "This could be an emergency." For some reason, they tended to occur in the most beastly weather, but that was all part of my job.

I opened the door just as my unexpected visitor began to knock and blinked in surprise to see Fenris standing at my doorstep. What in Recca was he doing, coming for a visit in such awful weather? My heart beat a little faster at the sight of his yellow shifter eyes glowing from beneath his hat, slightly eerie in the gloom outside.

"Good evening," I said, stepping aside reflexively—he was dripping wet, and I was certain he did not want to stand out in the cold. "What are you doing out in all this rain?"

"Apologies for the intrusion, but it's urgent," he said as he came in. Rain dripped off his oilcloth coat, and he was careful to remain on the front door mat so that it would not get all over my floor.

"Urgent?" I echoed. "Has someone been hurt?"

Fenris nodded. "I was just over at Marris's farm, having dinner with his family, when their old mastiff had a fit." His yellow eyes were grave. "She was still half-comatose and shivering uncontrollably when I left to fetch you."

My heart leapt into my throat. "Oh no! They've had Tira ever since she was a pup," I said, familiar with Marris's dog. She was nearly thirteen now, and I'd already seen her several times in the past year for age-related ailments. I reached for my own coat, hanging from the rack, and slung it on. "I guess I'd better come," I said with a small sigh.

"Yes. They're quite distraught. Marris would have come himself if he had not been so loath to leave the dog."

I shoved my feet into my rainboots, grabbed my umbrella, and tucked the kitten back into his cage. "Don't give me that," I scolded as the kitten protested loudly. "You're not litter-box trained, and I can't trust you in the house by yourself yet. I'll be back before you know it."

The kitten glared balefully at me before raising one of his hind legs and embarking on the very important task of cleaning himself. "He's rebuffing you," Fenris said, his expression lightening briefly as he chuckled.

"Cats are cheeky animals," I said as I followed him out into the rain. I thought I heard him mutter, "Don't I know it," but it was hard to be sure with the deafening downpour. Even with my umbrella snapped open, I still got wet—the wind smacked me in the face with dozens of raindrops as Fenris and I hurried to the truck.

"Any idea what might have triggered the dog's sudden illness?" I asked as Fenris slammed his door shut. He started the engine, and we set off down the road with a lurch. Fenris drove carefully through the pouring rain, with the lights turned on full —he seemed competent enough, taking his time with the muddy road but calm despite the storm. I wondered if shifters usually drove vehicles—I'd seen a few on steambikes back home, but the ones I'd known in veterinary school preferred to travel on foot or paw, depending on which form they were in at the time.

"I'm afraid not," Fenris said. His knuckles tightened around the steering wheel. "There wasn't any way to examine the animal myself—they begged me to fetch you immediately. But given the dog's age, I am not optimistic about her chances. It could be a heart problem. If so, you might, at best, only be able to alleviate the symptoms with your magic."

I bristled at that. "And just how would you know what I can and cannot do with my magic?" He was right, unfortunately—I had yet to save any animal with a serious heart condition, but he didn't need to know that. I didn't like that he was making assumptions about my abilities after knowing me for such a brief time.

"I have spent a large portion of my life studying magic," he said quietly, keeping his eyes firmly on the road. He pressed down gently on the brake, and we slowed as the wheels navigated through a shallow ditch.

I gaped at him. "That's impossible," I sputtered. "Shifters are not allowed access to any of the texts mages study. Besides, as far as I know, magic is a wide, complicated field with many sub-disciplines and even its own special language."

"Indeed." Fenris arched an eyebrow, momentarily turning his gaze from the road. My shoulders tensed as those glowing yellow eyes met mine, speculation brewing in their depths. "And

just how much do *you* know about magic, since you are clearly the expert here?"

My cheeks flushed at that, and I looked out the front window. Thankfully, the gate to the Dolan Farm loomed right in front of us, sparing me from having to respond. The moment we rolled up to the house, I threw open the passenger door and rushed inside.

"Mina," Mrs. Dolan cried as I burst through the front door, Fenris on my heels. She was crouched in front of the fireplace where the dog lay on a rug, still shivering. Marris, Dana, Roglar, and Decrin, her children, were all crowded around the dog as well, and they jumped to their feet at my approach.

"Please," Dana said, grabbing my hand with both of hers. Her body trembled beneath the thin, floral-print dress she wore, and her heart-shaped face was stained with tears. "You must help her, Mina. She can't die yet. It's not her time to go."

"She is so much more than just one of our animals," Mrs. Dolan said, her voice raw. "She has always been a part of the family, and twice saved Decrin's life."

"I will do my best, but you all must give me space," I said gently. I gave Dana's hand a reassuring squeeze, then approached the dog. "Fenris, please take Mrs. Dolan and her family to the kitchen and get them to make some tea."

Normally, I wouldn't think to order around the matron of the house, but Mrs. Dolan wasn't in much better shape than her daughter, and I desperately needed them out of the way. Marris seemed to have a better handle on himself—he took his mother by the shoulders and began guiding her to the kitchen, murmuring soothing words. I nodded my thanks at Fenris as he herded the family out of the room, then focused my attention on the dog.

"There now," I said, stroking the trembling animal. "Come,

it's not so bad now. We'll have you back up to speed soon enough."

I continued to murmur soothing words as I stroked the dog, feeding her tendrils of healing magic with each touch. Minutes passed as I gradually lifted her suffering from her body and took it into my own. I gritted my teeth, bearing down on the acute pain. Eventually, her trembles ceased and her fur began to warm again. But I could tell it wasn't enough—the sickness was still deep inside her, and my limited skills were not able to penetrate or permanently heal it.

The door to the kitchen creaked open behind me, and I turned to see Fenris and Marris re-enter the room. "How is she?" Marris asked quietly, crouching next to me. Hope sparked in his eyes as he slipped his hand into the dog's fur and she turned her head to look at him. "She's stopped trembling."

I nodded. "I've eased her pain a bit with some medicine, but I'm afraid she won't survive more than a couple of days."

Marris stiffened. "But she's doing so much better already." His voice cracked on the word "better," and my stomach clenched as he turned pain-filled eyes toward me. "Are you sure there's nothing you can do?"

I swallowed against a sudden lump in my throat. "I think you may want to prepare your family for the inevitable."

Nodding, Marris stroked the dog one last time, then went back into the kitchen. I met Fenris's gaze. He had been standing just off to the side, watching. The lines in his face were taut, and he looked as though he was fighting some internal battle. I opened my mouth to ask him what he was thinking, then closed it again when he strode over and got down on his knees.

"What are you—" I began as he laid his hand on the dog's side.

"Shhh." Ignoring me, he began to lightly pat Tira down, his eyes scanning her body as if he was searching for something.

The sight stirred a familiar memory, and my mouth dropped open. I'd seen mage healers do this sort of thing—they used a special spell that allowed them to see inside the body and pinpoint injuries or sources of illness. I'd even attempted the technique a time or two myself, without success. It was beyond the scope of my abilities.

So then how is it that a shifter *is able to do it?*

"As I suspected, her heart is failing," Fenris murmured, jarring me from my startled thoughts. "I can mend it, but I will need to borrow some of your power to do it."

I stared at him. "You mean to tell me you can use my magic to heal her?"

Fenris merely held out a palm. "If you wish to save her, then take my hand."

I hesitated, staring down at his outstretched palm. It was much wider than my own, the skin roughened by outdoor work —there were some recent blisters that told me he'd been getting acquainted with the glamorous task of mucking out the stables with a rake. For some reason, the thought of Fenris doing such a normal, everyday task made me relax, and I placed my hand in his. He might be different from the rest of us, but from everything I'd seen, he had a good heart.

Besides, what is there to lose?

Fenris's fingers tightened around my hand, sending a zing of electricity up my arm. My breath caught in my throat as I felt a tug deep within my chest, and it was as though a dam had burst inside me, opening the floodgates to my magic. A gasp flew from my lips as power surged in my veins, and for a moment, I worried I might light Fenris on fire, just as I'd done to my lover's sheets years ago.

Fenris narrowed his gaze on our joined hands, his grip steady. Instead of exploding outward, my magic flowed smoothly into him at an even pace—enough for him to fuel the

spell, but not enough to drain me. Nodding in satisfaction, he turned back to Tira and placed a hand on her head, stroking her. The dog's eyes drifted shut, and her body relaxed into a deep sleep.

As I sat there, trying to process the fact that Fenris had just used a sleeping spell on Tira, he pressed his hand on her ribcage. The moment he did so, my vision altered. Suddenly, I could see past Tira's chest, through skin and bone and muscle, to the beating heart that lay beneath.

Torn blood vessels, I thought dumbly, staring down at them. These were the source of the heart trouble. Not only could I see them, I could also see my magic, guided expertly by Fenris. The glittering strands of power twined around the vessels, gently coaxing the fibers together with a deftness I could never have managed myself.

As the magic did its work, I heard Fenris's voice chanting strange words in my head, though his lips were not moving. *Is that Loranian?* I thought, nearly reeling in shock. Fenris's grip tightened on my hand, as if he sensed my distress, and I forced myself to calm down. The last thing I needed to do was distract him while he was performing a delicate operation.

But how *is he able to do this?* What I was seeing defied explanation. This level of healing was clearly the result of years, perhaps even decades, of practice. What shifter was able to do this? Even one who had studied magical texts would not be able to—studying was not the same thing as practical experience, and it was obvious Fenris had that in spades.

"There," Fenris finally said, pulling back. His face was taut with strain from the stress and pain of performing such a complicated healing, but satisfaction shone in his gaze. "It is mended."

I glanced down. Sure enough, the damaged blood vessels were like new again. "Amazing," I breathed, tracing the area with

my forefinger.

Fenris released my hand, and my magical vision subsided, the dog's chest returning to normal. A sense of loss filled me. I looked down at my hand, uncertain as to whether I missed Fenris's touch or the magical skill I'd briefly wielded because of joining my magic with him. Lifting my head, I met Fenris's yellow gaze, a dozen questions buzzing at my lips. His expression was completely unreadable, but his shoulders tensed. It was obvious he was not looking forward to the forthcoming interrogation.

Fortunately for him, the kitchen door swung open before I could ask the first question. Fenris and I both turned to see the Dolan family file in, identical expressions of composed grief on their faces.

"Thank you, Mina," Mrs. Dolan said as I rose to meet her. "We must come to terms that even the best vet cannot perform miracles. Please make her as comfortable as possible, give her something against the pain. Then we'll keep vigil with her for as long as she still has."

I smiled. "As it happens, I found on closer examination the case is not as desperate as all that," I announced. "She should fully recover once she wakes from her nap, and may live for several more months, perhaps even another year or two."

Marris's jaw dropped. "What?" Dana cried, tears of joy springing to her eyes. "But I thought you said we had days?"

"I was mistaken," I said, my smile growing wider at the looks of astonishment on their faces. "I gave her some sleeping medicine so she can finish resting up through the night, but in the morning, I think you'll find her to be full of energy."

"Oh, *thank you*, Mina!" Dana threw her arms around me and hugged me tight. Tears choked her voice as she squeezed my ribcage, and I held back a wince. Her younger brothers looked equally delighted, especially Decrin. "You've saved Tira's life!"

The Dolans spent the next few minutes rejoicing, crowding around the dog and petting her. Tira didn't wake from her magically-induced slumber, but her tail did wag a little, and that was enough to make them happy. They thanked me profusely for my help and offered to send me fresh strawberry pies in addition to the two coppers Mrs. Dolan pressed into my hand.

Fenris bid them goodnight, telling them he would take me home in the steamtruck and then fetch his horse from their stable to ride home. They offered him a bed for the evening upon his return—it was still raining outside, though not as heavily as before, but he politely declined, saying he needed to be at home to care for his own horses and make sure his new stallion had not been spooked during the storm.

A heavy silence fell between us as we walked toward the cab, and I found myself struggling to figure out how to respond to what had just happened. I was still in shock, my mind whirling as I tried to reconcile what I'd seen with what I knew about shifters and magic.

"I'm sorry I doubted you," I said once we were inside the cab, the doors closed firmly on either side. "It is very clear that you know much more about magic than I do, or at least about magical healing."

Fenris nodded as he started up the engine. "There is no need to apologize—you had no reason to believe that I had any skill with magic. The notion likely defies everything you have been taught."

"That's an understatement," I said as he eased us onto the road. "Try as I might, I can't understand how it is you were able to perform such advanced healing. Are you not truly a shifter then, but a mage in disguise?"

Fenris chuckled, a tinge of bitterness in his voice. "There is no easy way to explain what I am," he said, "but we certainly do need to talk. Perhaps over a glass of brandy."

Yes, I thought as we pulled up in front of my house. A glass of brandy sounded like just the thing right now. Fenris killed the engine, then hopped out of the truck. I reached for the handle to my own door, but he was already on the other side, opening it. He extended a hand to help me down, and as I took it, a current of warmth rippled up my arm. Our gazes locked as he gently eased me down to the drenched sidewalk, and my cheeks heated as his nostrils flared. Could he sense the way he affected me with these small touches?

Get a grip, Mina, I scolded myself as I turned away. I fished my keys out of my pocket and unlocked the door. *You're just shaken from all these recent upheavals.*

Fenris came in after me and shut the door behind him. As he shrugged his coat from his broad shoulders and hung it on the rack, my eyes were drawn to the play of muscles flexing beneath his damp tunic. Swallowing hard, I turned away and went to the kitchen to fetch the bottle of brandy tucked away in one of my cupboards. *Shifters couldn't scent butterflies in the stomach, could they?* I wondered anxiously as I crouched below the counter and opened the cabinet. The bottle beckoned, still over half-full, a welcome sight despite the layer of dust covering it. I rarely indulged, since the stuff was so expensive, but after the night we'd had, tea didn't seem like enough. Straightening, I pulled two glasses from one of the upper cabinets, then dusted off the brandy bottle and splashed a generous amount into each one.

"Thank you," Fenris said as I handed him the drink. He'd come to stand at the kitchen counter rather than sit on the couch. We both took a long sip, and I sighed a little as the liquid slid smoothly down my throat, leaving a trail of warmth in its wake. Some of the chill began to subside from my skin, and I was tempted to gulp down the rest. But not until I'd asked some questions.

"So," I said as Fenris took another sip. "How is it that a shifter knows Loranian?"

He froze, the glass halfway to his lips. It was the first time I'd seen him thrown off balance, his yellow eyes shimmering with shock, and for some reason, that filled me with satisfaction. *Not unflappable,* I thought as he slowly set his glass down.

"Loranian, eh?" he asked, arching a brow. "How is it that *you* recognize it?"

I blinked. "I'm a mage, of course. What else?"

He frowned. "As in, you were born to a mage family?"

The confusion in his voice was evident, and it suddenly dawned on me—he must think I was a wild talent, born to a human family, or perhaps even a half-breed like him.

"Yes," I explained, reaching for my brandy again. I took a long sip to steady myself before I spoke again—this conversation was about to steer into dangerous territory. My hands were already growing clammy as old memories threatened to rise to the surface. "I learned Loranian when I was quite young, as most mage children do, and had a special tutor for a year when I was fourteen. But that was over a decade ago, and I'm largely out of practice. I do still recognize when it is spoken, though," I said sternly, crossing my arms over my chest. "So let's not get distracted. How is it that you know it and are able to use it?"

Fenris hesitated, as if unsure of how much he should tell me. "My...ah...progenitor, shall we say, was a powerful mage, and I have learned at least as much as a normal mage apprentice, though for obvious reasons, I have never claimed official mage status. As you can imagine, it would be best if my possession of this knowledge remained hidden, which is why I prefer not to live among other shifters. Unlike humans, they would sniff me out the first time I used magic in their presence."

My eyes widened as realization suddenly dawned on me. "It

was you," I cried, pointing an accusing finger at him. "You're the one who made Roor stumble at the party!"

"Yes." To his credit, Fenris looked chagrined. "For which I am sorry, for as it turned out, my meddling did more harm than good. At the time, it merely seemed an easy way to defuse his aggression."

"I can't exactly blame you for immobilizing that lout when he was about to attack us," I admitted—as a matter of fact, had I known the sleeping spell, I might well have done the same at that moment, even if it had brought more trouble than it was worth. "But if you really feel guilty," I added with a grin, "you can stay for a while and answer my questions."

His eyebrows rose. "What questions?"

I rolled my eyes at the guarded look on his face and rounded the counter so I could sit down on the couch. Fenris trailed after me, and the weight of his regard pressed down between my shoulder blades. I expected him to sit down on the loveseat, but he joined me on the couch instead, leaning back into the cushions and spreading his free arm over the back. His tunic was still a bit damp, and the fabric clung to his powerful shoulders and chest as he regarded me steadily. *A mage with the strength and senses of a shifter,* I thought as I pressed myself into the cushions on the opposite end of the couch to give myself the illusion of space between us. He was more of an anomaly than I was.

The realization smoothed some of the nerves that had gathered tightly in my chest, and I loosened a breath I hadn't realized I'd been holding.

"How is it that you were able to heal the dog?" I asked as he took another sip of brandy. "You said that you've learned at least as much as a 'normal mage apprentice,' but I'm not a simpleton. That was an advanced healing technique, and you've clearly had plenty of practice with it."

"It was part of my training, a long time ago," he said. "More

recently, I had occasion to stay with one of my best friends, who specializes in healing magic." For a moment, I could have sworn that pain flashed in his eyes. "I used the opportunity to learn as much about it from him as I could."

I swallowed—his expression hadn't shifted, but I could sense that his mood had taken a darker turn. "Your best friend is a mage?" I echoed. "Does he know you've gone and moved to a tiny human town in the middle of nowhere?"

"I'd prefer not to discuss my friends, or lack thereof, at this very moment," Fenris said lightly. He drained his glass, then set it down on the table. "As much as I enjoy your company, I'm afraid I must be on my way. The Dolans will be expecting their tractor back, and I need to see to the horses on my farm."

"Right." My cheeks heated as we stood—of course he wasn't going to sit here for hours and let me grill him about magic. Why would he? He certainly had no obligation to satisfy my curiosity. In fact, he'd already shown me much more than he had likely been planning to reveal.

But even so, there was a tightness in my chest as I walked him to the door and handed him his coat from the rack. I didn't want him to leave, not when I had so many questions about magic. There had never been anyone around to talk about it with, not since I'd run away. Nobody that would be able to give me the answers I sought, or who I could trust to keep my secret—

"I didn't mean to snap at you earlier," Fenris said softly, pulling me from my thoughts. "I do not blame you for your curiosity, Mina, and believe me when I say I have questions, too. It is nothing short of remarkable that you have managed to survive so long on your own."

My cheeks warmed again, this time with pleasure instead of embarrassment. "Thank you for your help," I said, daring to reach out and brush a few droplets of water that had clung to

the front of his coat. "I could not have saved the dog without you."

He looked at me for a long moment. "Neither could I," he said softly, then disappeared out into the waiting night.

It took me a very, very long time to fall asleep that night.

12

FENRIS

As I trotted home in the rain on my gelding, Marris's steamtruck safely returned, a restless anxiety churned in my chest. It was almost as bad as when Garrett Toring had unexpectedly turned up at Solantha Palace all those months ago, coming so close to my secret I was forced to stage my own death. A line of sweat was working its way slowly down my spine, and it was all I could do not to urge the horse beneath me into a gallop.

But that would be a foolish thing to do on these muddy roads. Besides, there was nothing to run from. Mina would not betray my secret. Not when I knew hers. It seemed we had more in common than I'd realized—two magic-users in hiding, though I had no idea why Mina was skulking out here in this smudge of a town when she could be thriving under the skilled tutelage of a trained mage.

The power I'd felt when she'd given me access to her magic had been formidable, and had filled me with a heady buzz I had not experienced in a long time. Not since I'd been Polar ar'Tollis and had full access to my own powers. The magic in my veins was a fraction of what I'd wielded as Chief Mage, which was

why I'd borrowed some of Mina's to perform the healing. I probably could have managed it myself, but there was no point in depleting my resources when Mina was a full, eager well of magic next to me.

Imagine what you might be able to do if she was willing to let you borrow her magic again.

No. I stamped that thought out before it could fully take root in my treacherous mind. I would not start doing magical experiments out here, not in this small town full of busybodies. That would be the opposite of keeping a low profile. I had not brought any of my magical texts out here for this exact reason. The closest magical library would be near the Watawis Mages Guild in Willowdale, the state capital, several hours away. Visiting it was out of the question. It would only be available to registered mages and likely could not compare to what I had been used to in Canalo or Nebara.

The gates of my new home finally came into view, and my shoulders relaxed. The storm was finally beginning to dissipate, and a sliver of moonlight escaped from the clouds, illuminating the rooftop of the ranch house I was still getting used to living in. It was a far cry from Solantha Palace, but I was no stranger to living out in the wilderness—hunting had been a favorite pastime when I'd been a mage, and I'd often gone on wilderness retreats either by myself or with other mages.

Good night for hunting, the primal, wolfish part of me rumbled in the back of my mind as I guided the gelding toward the stables at the rear of the house. Indeed, I caught the faint scent of deer on the damp wind, within a ten-mile radius of my property. If I wanted, I could have venison for the next week. My fangs elongated at the thought of ripping into fresh deer meat, and I had to rein in my instincts as my horse let out a nervous snort and began prancing sideways.

"There now," I said, patting the side of his neck. I sent a bit of

calming magic into him, and the horse relaxed. My shifter instincts were getting harder to manage since I'd moved out into the country. It had been one thing to live as a shifter in Iannis's home, where there was no one to challenge my territorial instincts and no scents and sounds of the wilderness to coax my animal half to the forefront.

Indeed, it had been easy enough to master those animalistic urges, to the point I'd spent most of my time in wolf form, acting as Iannis's truth detector. The mages who came to see him routinely underestimated shifters and their ability to use their senses to detect a lie. Since it would be rude for a Chief Mage to use a truth wand every time he had a discussion with someone important, my presence had been the next best thing. Especially since we could communicate silently, in mindspeak, unbeknownst to the people he was officially talking to.

Things had changed when Sunaya came to live with us, I reflected as I removed the gelding's tack. Her presence had stirred my wolf, and had he been interested in her, perhaps I would have ended up as her mate instead of Iannis. But I'd scented the attraction between the two of them immediately, and from the start, my feelings toward her had been more along the lines of an older brother or uncle. Helping Sunaya and Iannis navigate the tumultuous waters that eventually brought them together had been the most fun I'd had in ages.

And now they are together, I thought as I rubbed down the gelding. *Happily engaged, accepted by most of society despite Sunaya's hybrid status, and...*

I felt a pang of regret. For once, I did not immediately shake it off. I should be standing at Iannis's side for their wedding, sharing in the joyous day when the two of them finally, against all odds, became one. Instead, I was stuck out here, without so much as a single magical text to while away the endless evenings, worrying about how my friends fared but unable to

risk any contact. Iannis and Sunaya would have their hands full rebuilding Solantha after that devastating quake had destroyed so much of their beloved city...but even so, I knew they would be thinking of me occasionally, wondering what had become of me.

Did they know I'd made it out alive, or did they presume I was dead? Hidden among the memories I had given Sunaya as a parting gift were clues that might lead them to suspect I had survived, but they could hardly be certain. I felt guilty about causing them to grieve unnecessarily, but it was for the best. Besides, they were too smart not to eventually figure out I was alive.

I'll send them a letter at some point, I decided as I finished brushing my gelding. I could not let them grieve longer than necessary. I'd done that to my parents when I'd fled Nebara four years ago. The circumstances were so damning that I could not give them any kind of explanation. They likely thought I was dead, too, and I could not console them without risking myself. But there was no reason to put Sunaya and Iannis through the same pain, not when they already knew my dangerous secrets.

After giving the gelding one last pat, I poured oats for both my horses, then returned to the house, still deep in thought. Was it any wonder I'd given in to temptation and used magic tonight, when I was still so utterly homesick? A wiser man, one more in control of his emotions, would have let the dog die tonight. She was old, and it had been her time to go. In the natural order of things, she would not live more than another year at most.

But Marris and his family had looked so stricken, and the sight of Mina crouching there on the ground, struggling to save the poor animal with the pitiful scraps of magic she knew, had been more than I could bear. I could not resist taking her hand and joining our magic to save the dog.

I would always remember the moment she realized I could use magic. The way the firelight had rippled over her, turning

her golden hair to flames and her eyes to molten silver. Eyes that had widened in shock and disbelief...and then gratitude. The relief in her expression, the joyful smile she'd given the Dolans as she'd delivered the good news...it had warmed something inside me that I'd long thought cold and dead.

In the privacy of my bedroom, I stripped off my damp clothes and changed into a thick bathrobe. A quick wave of my hand lit the fire in my living room hearth, and I perched on the edge of the horrid floral couch, staring into the flames. No, I did not regret helping Mina tonight. But doing so had altered my plans, perhaps irrevocably. Now, there was someone in this town who knew I could use magic. And even though what Mina knew was only the tip of the iceberg, it was still enough to break me if she chose to divulge it.

She won't, I told myself as my chilled hands began to warm. Her own position was precarious, and I could see, clear as day, that Mina was a good person. A gentle soul, but one with quiet steel in her spine, who spent her days easing the suffering of other creatures, and had somehow managed to deflect the town's curiosity and keep her heritage under wraps.

At least until you came along.

I paced back and forth in front of the window, reliving our first encounter. It had been my fault that Roor's mother had launched that silly inquisition into Mina's past. From the way she'd spoken of it, it was obvious Mina was greatly distressed. But her eyes had been brimming with hope when she'd talked to me tonight, with so many questions written all over her face. She saw me as a kind of lifeline, someone who could finally fill in the blanks for her about how magic worked and help her gain control. To help save more of her animal patients.

And instead of helping her, I'd run like a coward at the first question.

It was only natural that she would be curious about your past, I

told myself. Just as I was curious about hers. I should have deflected her question and turned the conversation back toward magic. Resinah knew I had plenty of experience at evading dangerous subjects. But as she'd sat across from me, the glow of the lamp highlighting the curve of her soft cheek and the rosy color of her lips, her gaze had roamed over my own body and I'd been struck by the insane urge to spill everything. To lean in and inhale that sweet scent of hers and confide my whole sordid history.

That was what had driven me from her cozy little house so soon after I'd arrived. And why I hadn't immediately extended an offer to help her with her abilities.

My attitude was irrational. I shouldn't let Mina's allure distract me from doing the right thing. There was no reason why I couldn't teach her a few things about magic and steer her away from trouble, while also keeping her ignorant of my past. As tempting as it would be to have a friend who really knew me, it would be selfish to put Mina at further risk. No, she would be far safer if she did not know the truth.

Tomorrow, I decided. *I will go to her house tomorrow.*

The prospect filled me with an absurd degree of excitement. In this state, I would never be able to settle down. Shrugging off my robe, I shifted into wolf form, exchanging bare skin for thick fur, blunt fingernails for claws. My sense of smell heightened as the glow faded from my vision, bringing me the charred scent of the logs still burning in the hearth, overlaying faint traces from the rich coffee I'd roasted this morning, the scent of horsehair, and the sweat that still clung to my skin.

I strove to ignore the perfume that lurked beneath, sweet lavender and warm golden sunrays, and slipped out into the night through the small swinging door I'd installed so I could come and go in beast form.

The scents of wind and rain, of churned soil and horse

manure, quickly cleared my nose of elusive memories. I lifted my muzzle to see what else I could sense as I stood on the back porch. Sure enough, the scent of deer was still here...mostly washed away by the rain, but present nonetheless. A small group had passed close to my garden, and they would not have gotten very far, not in this weather.

My blood thrummed in my veins as I let my inner wolf run free, galloping through the tall grass toward the thick woods that encroached on my lands. The wind whistled in my ears, ruffling my thick fur, and I savored the cool air and the scents it brought me—all ammunition for the hunt. Leaves and twigs crunched underfoot as I passed beneath the dark canopy of the forest, and my sensitive ears picked up the sounds of hedgehogs and rabbits scurrying away. Slowing to a trot, I focused on tracking the deer. The storm had muddied the scent, washing it clean in many places, but by now, I saw the hoofprints imprinted in the mud that the rain had not quite managed to wash away.

It was not too long before I found myself trotting through the grass at the edge of a meadow that cut through the forest. The deer had come here to graze. The grass was still tall, up to my shoulders, but there were traces of deer hooves and teeth, not hard to follow—

An explosion of gunfire cut through the stillness of the night, and I jumped forward instinctively. But my reaction came too late—a bullet had hit my left flank, ripping a howl of pain from my jaws as burning agony burrowed into my muscle. Suppressing the pain and the accompanying jolt of bone-chilling fear, I bolted for the other side of the meadow, where the forest beckoned. More gunfire exploded through the clearing, and another bullet singed my fur just half an inch from my skull. I was a sitting duck out here—I needed to take cover, fast.

My pulse thundered in my veins as I finally reached the shelter of the thick forest canopy. I pushed myself for another

half mile, despite my burning flank, until I was certain there were no other predators around, no humans wielding cowardly, illegal firearms. Fury burned hot and bright in my chest as I hunkered down behind a bush and took stock of the wound. To my relief, the bullet had gone clear through, but still...this should never have happened. Guns had been banned in the Federation. Farmers were supposed to use bow and arrow to chase off predators, not hunting rifles. And I had not threatened anybody's livestock.

Snarling, I shifted back into human form to heal the wound, then immediately back into a wolf. The burning in my flank vanished instantly, the wound reduced to nothing but a memory. But it was not a memory I would soon forget, and with anger still raging in my chest, I circled back around to find the hunter's hiding place. It was downwind, so I didn't catch the human's scent until I was nearly back at the meadow. My hackles rose at the familiar odor, and I slowed my pace as I slunk through the tall grass, headed straight for the cluster of bushes where the hunter had lurked.

Before I even reached them, I knew Roor had left, taking his illegal rifle with him. Thank Resinah the bastard had only shot me with lead bullets. I would have been in a world of trouble if he'd loaded silver instead.

But perhaps he wasn't hunting for me, specifically. I prowled around the area, trying to pick up any other scent clues. It was possible he'd just been shooting at random. But if so, why would he come out here alone on such a dark and rainy night?

Of course, he might not know that normal bullets did not usually kill shifters. And even if he did, it was unlikely that he could afford silver bullets. Few people in this town could.

Since Roor's scent was still fresh, barely a minute old, I decided to follow him back to his home and see what I could learn. I wanted to believe it had been a mistake, but it would be

foolish to dismiss a potential threat. It didn't take me very long to catch up to the young farmer. He was indeed walking through the forest with a rifle strapped across his back, making far too much noise for a man alone in the forest at night. It would be all too easy for me to attack him from behind, to pin him to the ground and snap his neck between my powerful jaws—

And that would make you no better than him, I thought as I reined in my vengeful instincts. My wolf side wanted blood for blood, wanted him on the ground screaming for mercy, but that would accomplish nothing, and very likely make things worse. If Roor was found dead in the woods with wolf bites all over him, his mother would be the first to point her finger in my direction.

Besides, judging from the slump of his shoulders and the sullen tinge to his scent, Roor knew he'd failed to kill me. This was not the march of a triumphant hunter. I could take satisfaction in that, if nothing else.

We reached the edge of the forest that bordered Roor's lands, and I stopped just inside the tree line, watching as Roor silently trudged toward his house. I waited until he'd stomped his boots on the mat outside and gone inside before slipping through the grass, close enough to the window that I could eavesdrop comfortably.

"Did you get him, then?" a stringent female voice asked— Roor's busybody mother, I could only assume. I spotted her through the window—a tall, spindly woman with brown hair knotted back into a severe bun.

"No, Ma." Roor's voice was surly. "I wounded him, but he got away."

"Wounded him?" She slapped her hand on the table. "Shifters heal from wounds faster than you can blink! You were supposed to shoot him in the head. You weren't trying hard enough, were you?"

"I'd like to see you try and shoot a wolf in the middle of the

night with almost no moonlight to see by," Roor growled, ripping the rifle from the holster on his back. He shoved it toward his mother. "Would you like to try, Ma, and see if you're a better shot than I am?"

"Don't you talk to me like that, Ilain Roor," she said in a voice of steel. Even though they were discussing my impending murder, I had to admire the way she faced down her son, who was a good foot taller and at least a hundred pounds heavier, without a trace of fear in her pinched face. "We cannot suffer a shifter to live among us as if he were our own. He might just be one, but if he stays here too long, it will attract others. Soon, they will overrun the whole community! We must put a stop to it right away."

"I'm trying, Ma." Roor gulped beer straight from the bottle, then wiped his mouth with the back of his hand. "He won't be able to touch any girls again when I'm through with him. I'm disgusted they allow it, but I guess they can't see that he's a filthy beast."

"Just make sure you get him next time," Mrs. Roor snapped. "I've ordered silver bullets for you, haven't I? I was simply hoping we didn't have to use them, since they are so expensive. But if that's what it comes down to..."

"The full moon is coming up soon," Roor said, sounding eager now. "He won't be able to avoid shifting then, and I'll have the proper bullets by that time. Don't worry, Ma. I'll take him out."

Having heard enough, I crept away quietly, my heart full of disgust. So they thought to take me down on the full moon, did they? Silver bullets were fatal to a shifter regardless of the form we were in, but I imagined they were waiting until I shifted again so they could pass it off as an accident and pretend they had mistaken me for a wild animal. Well, they were going to be sorely disappointed. I would find some excuse to be out of town,

or perhaps I just wouldn't leave my house that night. They couldn't very well pass it off as an accident if they came onto my property and killed me in cold blood.

I will definitely need to do something about them, I thought grimly as I returned home. Both hated shifters in general, and in the young man's case, that hatred was compounded with jealousy over Mina. I would not cower quietly while my neighbors plotted my demise.

MINA

The next morning dawned bright and sunny, the sky so clear and blue it was hard to believe it had unleashed a torrent of rain upon us yesterday. Even better, for once there were no urgent appointments waiting for me, so I lounged by the kitchen table in an old t-shirt and faded jeans, a cup of tea in one hand and a novel in the other.

It had taken me a while to fall asleep last night, with Fenris's yellow gaze haunting me, full of pain and secrets, and a tornado of questions whirling around in my mind. It had been obvious my questions about his past had pushed him away. Considering how skittish I was about my own secrets, I could hardly blame him. I had told him the bare minimum about my history, and I suspected he had done the same. I couldn't expect him to divulge more, especially since we hardly knew each other.

Still...the rejection had stung. As he'd walked to the door, I'd been afraid that was the last I'd see of the intriguing shifter. But his parting words had been kind, and he'd said he had questions, too. Perhaps he was just as curious about me as I was about him, and that curiosity would bring us back together again.

I had to believe that, because he was my only source of information about magic, and I couldn't bear to think that I had screwed up our budding friendship so early on.

The sound of the mailman opening the mailbox outside my door pulled me from my thoughts. Peering through the window, I was startled to see him drop a thick, cream-colored envelope into the box and then walk away. It didn't look anything like the flimsy envelopes containing bills I usually received... In fact, I thought, my heart sinking, it looked very official.

And I'd already received the letter from the tax collector this year.

Rising, I wiped my suddenly clammy palms on my pants before going to retrieve the letter. My stomach turned to lead as I pulled the thick envelope from the mailbox and stared at the Watawis Mages Guild seal imprinted on the back. On the front, the envelope was addressed to Mina Hollin, and on the return address, the words "Legal Secretary" stared at me, a silent but deadly threat.

I quickly retreated into the house, to the privacy of my bedroom, where busybody neighbors could not peer in through the windows. My hands shook as I tore open the envelope, and as I read the few but ominous lines, my chest tightened with every word.

Ms. Hollin,

As part of an official investigation into the possibility of illegal use of magic in Abbsville, I hereby summon you to the Watawis Mages Guild at your earliest convenience for an interview. Please respond within the next three working days.

Signed,

> *Janis Karadin*
> *Watawis Legal Secretary*

BY THE LADY. I scanned the brief letter over and over, until my vision blurred and I could no longer bear to look at it. I had always known I was at risk, had always known there was a possibility that someone might see too much and report me, but now that the day had actually come... I couldn't think straight. My mind was spinning, my chest constricted so tightly I could barely squeeze in a breath. The walls of my bedroom were far too close—I was trapped, a mouse in a cage, and it was only a matter of time before the cat's paw dropped down and grabbed me by the tail—

"Out," I gasped, lurching for the door. I had to get out before the panic suffocated me.

Shaking, I stumbled out the back door to my house, where my horse was tethered in the modest backyard, grazing at the new spring grass. She snorted, her ears flicking up as she noticed my obvious agitation, and I hurtled past her toward the small stable where I kept the tack. I knew my neighbors would notice my hasty retreat, but I didn't care. I quickly saddled and bridled her, then launched myself atop her back and urged her to take me far, far away.

As I clung tight to my horse, my body pressed so low that her mane whipped into my face, I barely saw the neighbors who pulled back their curtains to watch me canter down the street, or the ones who hastily dodged out of the way as I careened out of town, heading toward the empty dirt roads and the towering trees. My mind's eye was filled with the crumpled body of my cousin Vanley as he lay on the bottom of the long staircase,

immobile, perhaps dead at my hands... and nobody to take my side, to believe me.

I can't go back. No matter what it took, no matter what laws I broke, I could not go back to that house. To relatives who had left me to fend for myself against constant abuse, who might still want to mete out punishment for fighting back in the only way I could.

At first, I had no idea where I was going. All I knew was that I had to get out of the house, away from that blasted *letter*. But somehow, I found myself outside Ackleberry Farm's gates, left wide open for any visitors to come trotting down the road.

Or should it be Shelton Farm now? I wondered as I urged my mare to pass beneath the gate. The Ackleberry name was still there, wrought into the iron arch, but Fenris had only just bought the property. Lifting my head, I stared at the ranch house, wondering if he could see me coming through the windows.

Lady help me, I hope he's here. His stable was behind the house, and he didn't own a vehicle, so there was no way to know whether he was inside. My hands grew clammy again, and I had to wipe them on my pants lest the reins slip from my hands. I desperately needed someone to talk to right now, and Fenris was the only one who might understand and not toss me to the wolves.

I'm sure he'd appreciate that *pun.*

My lips twitched, and my anxiety lessened a little. Dismounting, I tied my horse to one of the posts near the front of the house, then climbed the porch stairs. I lifted my hand to knock on the door, but before my knuckles could connect with the wood, it opened.

Fenris took one look at me with that enigmatic yellow gaze and said, "What's wrong?"

I loosened a harsh laugh. "Is my distress that obvious?"

"I could smell your anxiety from a mile away."

My cheeks flushed with embarrassment. Of course he could. Suddenly I felt too exposed, too vulnerable in front of this shifter who saw so much more than he should. Heart hammering in my throat, I stepped back. "Maybe I'd better come back another time—"

"Mina." Lightning quick, Fenris grabbed my wrist before I could retreat. I jerked in surprise, my first instinct to pull my hand away, but his grip was gentle. "I didn't mean to make you uncomfortable." His expression softened. "Please, come in and have a cup of tea. It's obvious something is troubling you."

The sincerity in his voice allowed me to relax a bit, and I followed him into the house. The interior was sparse but clean, and Fenris led me into the kitchen, where a teapot and two cups already sat waiting.

I raised a brow. "A mile away, eh?"

Fenris coughed. "That may have been a slight exaggeration. But I was making tea anyway, and when I saw you coming down the road, I set out a second cup for you."

I smiled as I sat down at the table with him and allowed him to pour me a cup of the fragrant tea. It smelled of honey, orange, and linden blossoms, and the warm liquid slid over my frazzled nerves like a security blanket as I took a sip.

Fenris picked up his own cup, regarding me silently as he drank his tea. His expression was grave—no judgment, no annoyance, no eagerness for gossip. Just calm, quiet concern as he sat there and waited for me to collect myself and speak. It was a refreshing change from what I was used to. When Barrla sensed that I was distressed, she immediately smothered me with affection and concern and hounded me until I gave up and told her what was bothering me. Usually I didn't mind, but at times like these, when the secret terrors of my past were clawing

at my fragile defenses, her persistence was more of a burden than a help.

"I received a letter this morning," I finally said when my cup was half finished and my heart rate had returned to normal, "from the Watawis Mages Guild. They want to interview me, apparently because my name came up in an investigation into the use of illegal magic."

Fenris stiffened. "So Mrs. Roor has managed to get the Guild to take notice of her suspicions." He leaned forward a little in his chair, frowning. "Even so, I am surprised they are moving so quickly. Most guilds are covered in bureaucratic red tape—it takes weeks for them to get around to anything."

He sounded like he had considerable experience with Mages Guilds, but I wasn't going to risk alienating him again by pointing that out. "Bad luck, I suppose," I said, shrugging with a nonchalance I didn't feel. "Perhaps in such an underpopulated, poor state, they don't get much work otherwise."

Fenris's eyes narrowed. "You never mentioned why you chose this self-imposed exile," he said, leaning back in his chair as he studied me. "You told me you were a full-blooded mage, not a half-breed, nor born into a human family. Those would be trembling for their life now, but the law is biased in favor of legitimate mages. What would you risk by claiming your heritage?"

I swallowed hard as the ghosts of my past whispered insidiously in my ear. *Guilty, guilty, guilty.* "I...lived in an abusive home," I said carefully. I didn't want to delve too far into the details—not because I didn't trust Fenris, but because I didn't trust myself to maintain my composure if I started digging too deep. "My parents died when I was young, and after some years with my grandmother, she also passed away and left me the family fortune. I was taken in by my aunt and uncle, my only

living relatives at that point. I lived with them for nearly a year, and my cousin Vanley, their son, made my life hell. He taunted and molested me, and his parents refused to believe my complaints, so I stopped going to them for help." My hands fisted in my lap as anger flared in my chest. "On my last night there, I got into an altercation with Vanley that ended...that ended..."

My chest constricted as panic began to close in on me again, and I paused to take in a slow breath. Fenris said nothing, simply refilling my cup, but his jaw was clenched tight. I cradled the cup in my hands, letting the warmth seep into my skin as I inhaled the soothing fragrance. He waited patiently for me to collect myself despite his obvious anger, and gratitude swept through me—he didn't ask if I was okay, or try to burden me with meaningless expressions of sympathy that would only make me feel worse about my weakness.

"I'm worried that I might have killed him," I said quietly once the tightness had eased enough from my chest that I could speak again. "I lashed out with my magic and sent him flying down the stairs, then ran away without looking back. But even if I didn't, he would have been injured, and his family will hate me even more. Since I'm still technically a minor under mage law, I would be forced to return to their custody if I came forth to claim my identity. I won't go back to them." I clenched my hands into fists beneath the table. "I *won't*."

"I can't blame you," Fenris said softly, a look of under-standing in his gaze that loosened the knot in my chest further. "That bastard had it coming—I don't blame you at all for what you did to him." Anger flared briefly in his gaze, and my chest filled with warmth—it was good to know that there was someone out there who sided with me. "But as you already know, you cannot simply avoid the summons, or they will send someone to retrieve you. They will be assuming you are a wild

talent and may be rough with you until your true identity can be established. You would not enjoy that."

"No." I could just imagine Roor's mother standing in the street, watching as I was dragged kicking and screaming from my home into a waiting carriage with bars on the doors. The look of satisfaction on her smug, bony face...it was more than I could bear, even as a figment of my imagination. "But what can I do that won't compromise my identity? I need to stay away from my guardians until I am legally of age."

Fenris drummed his blunt fingers on the table, his narrowed gaze turning thoughtful. "The Guild is going to test you the moment you show up, so pretending you are not a mage is out of the question. As soon as they discover that you have magic, they will demand that you provide proof of your lineage and training, or you risk being subjected to the magic wipe." His handsome features twisted into disgust at that last part. Clearly, he didn't approve of that barbaric law any more than I did—just the thought of someone reaching into my soul and stripping me of my magic sent icy fingers of dread walking down my spine.

"How is it that *you* managed to avoid magical testing?" I asked, my curiosity getting the better of me. If I was to divulge my ugly past today, surely he could give me a few nuggets from his. "I imagine that if the Federation learned of your abilities, you would be subject to the magic wipe just like anyone else."

Fenris's grip on his cup tightened. "I have...friends in high places who helped me avoid scrutiny. But they cannot help me now—they have no influence in Watawis," he said, even as the question sprang to my lips. "If we are to figure out what to do about your predicament, we must do it on our own. We must use our wits to outsmart Roor's mother and the legal secretary who has summoned you."

We spent a few minutes deliberating various possibilities, such as persuading Barrla to go in my stead, disguised to look

like me. She would pass the test with flying colors since she had not a drop of magical blood in her veins, but though she probably would have volunteered and considered it a lark, I could not involve her in such a dangerous scheme. She was an innocent human, and I didn't want to bring trouble upon her head.

"The most promising option," Fenris advised, "is to confess to being a mage and pay a possible fine for not registering your name in the Watawis Mages Guild's guestbook, as all mages coming from out of state are required to do by law. You could give a different name and age so that you would not be forced to go back to your relatives."

I blinked. "That's not a bad idea... but my lack of experience is going to be an issue. It would not take much probing to figure out I am untrained, and then they might guess I was still a minor by mages' law." Attempting to deceive the mages would inevitably lead to punishment if I was found out.

"If that happens," Fenris said, "they would declare you a ward of the state and probably assign you to a master of the Chief Mage's choice. That might not be such a terrible fate, so long as he chooses someone suitable for you." He cocked his head.

"No." I pressed my lips together. "Even in hiding, I have far more control over my own life than I ever did while I was living with my relatives. I have heard horror stories about the way some masters treat their apprentices. I won't risk the Chief Mage handing me to some brute who knows little of healing magic and does not care about my feelings or desires."

Fenris nodded. "Regardless of how we deal with the summons, we should find out if there is a search warrant on your original identity, either as a missing person or a wanted criminal."

My stomach dropped—I hadn't considered that. "How can we find that out without drawing attention to me?"

Fenris shrugged. "I assume you have a family lawyer or trustee who looks after your property? I could write to him under an assumed name and ask about buying something from your estate. With any luck, we can deduce information about the absent owner's legal status from the answer."

"That might work," I said. "My grandmother's lawyer was Mr. Ransome, and I do believe he oversees my fortune. You could pretend to be interested in buying my grandmother's house in Haralis. It is a beautiful place."

"Good, and once we get a reply, we can take it from there. The other thing you should do is write back to the legal secretary and ask for an extension on the interview. You can claim professional duties—you are a veterinarian with patients to attend and cannot simply up and leave them at a moment's notice." He winked.

I smiled a little. "Well, there is a certain dog I should check up on."

Fenris was silent for a moment. "I am glad we were able to save her together," he said quietly. "I felt your power that night —you are strong and will be a formidable mage once you are properly trained."

A lump swelled in my throat at the pride in his gaze. "I...I've never had anybody say that to me," I whispered, looking down at my hands. "I've only ever been able to do small spells here and there, and though my grandmother believed in me, my aunt and uncle ...they made me feel weak, worthless. They tried to keep me from training for as long as possible. After all these years of using only the simplest spells, I'd begun to fear I might not be any good at it."

Fenris's eyes flashed. "That's nonsense. You have done extraordinarily well to teach yourself control and several useful techniques without the guidance of a master, or even so much as a magical text. Most of your peers would not have managed even a

quarter as well as you have left entirely on their own. With proper training, I suspect you will easily surpass these 'relatives' of yours." The way his tone changed told me exactly what he thought of my aunt and uncle, and the outrage blazing from him rendered me speechless. I'd never had someone in my life willing to stand up for me like this, and if I was honest, I wasn't sure how to handle it.

Fenris and I spent the next hour drafting a letter to Domich Ransome, my late grandmother's family lawyer and now the trustee of my estate. Under the name of the middleman who had helped Fenris buy his farm, the letter politely inquired whether my grandmother's mansion might be for sale and who was the owner of record. I was glad to leave the actual writing to Fenris. There would be no danger of his strong, masculine handwriting being in any way associated with me. The return address was that of a well-known tobacconist who lived in Willowdale, the state capital; according to Fenris, he often served as an informal and discreet post exchange for his customers.

"That will do," Fenris said as he tucked the letter into an envelope he'd conjured out of thin air and wrote the address in Haralis, halfway across the Federation, that I dictated from memory. "We can post it from the state capital as soon as one of us goes there. I need some painting and gardening supplies anyway."

I bit my lip. "I could use some medical supplies from the capital...but is it wise for me to go there when I'm about to tell the Mages Guild I can't make the trip due to business reasons? What if somebody sees me?"

"The Legal Secretary has no idea what you look like, and he will not have sentries hiding in the shadows waiting to see if you show up," Fenris said dryly. My cheeks flamed, and he added, "I understand your fears, but the Mages Guild is not nearly as

clever and all-seeing as most people would like to believe. We will be perfectly fine making a short visit."

I was just about to relax when he added, "Even so, we should probably prepare a disguise for you, ideally of an older man or woman, in case you do need to sneak away at some point. Do you have any experience with illusion magic?"

"No." The tips of my ears burned with shame, and I was glad my hair hid them. "I've tried changing forms, mostly to make my face a little older, but I can only hold it for an hour at most."

"That is better than I had hoped for," Fenris said, striding over to the wall. He plucked an old, rusty nail sticking out of the wooden paneling, then, with a casual twist of his fingers, changed it into a gold ring with a smooth, round blue stone. My heart began to beat a little faster as he offered it to me, holding out his hand in a silent invitation to give him mine.

"Is this a proposal?" I teased, trying to keep the mood light as I placed my right hand in his. His callouses scraped my skin gently, and the warmth from his flesh sent a zing of electricity straight up my arm. I had to resist the urge to bite my lip again, and prayed to the Lady he would attribute the heat in my cheeks to my earlier embarrassment.

Fenris chuckled softly, and the sound reverberated through me, awakening something I had long thought dormant. "Visualize a form you find familiar," he instructed as he slid the ring onto my finger. "Something you don't have to think too hard about."

"All right. I'll try for an image of my grandmother."

I closed my eyes, reaching for the core of power that pulsed within me. It reacted instantly to my touch, rushing into my veins with a surge that sent goose bumps rippling up my arms, and I had to push it back before it overwhelmed me. After a few minutes of struggle, I managed to take enough to spin it into the illusion of my late grandmother.

I held the image of her in my mind as I let the magic take hold—her silver-gray hair, her kind smile, the crow's feet around her gentle brown eyes. The wire-rimmed spectacles perched on her nose that were forever sliding off onto whatever book she was reading at the time. Her dove-gray robes that flowed elegantly around a willowy frame that had never bent despite her age. She had been very old, my grandmother—over five hundred when she passed away. Tears swelled beneath my eyelids at the familiar ache in my chest, and I had to force them back.

When I finally opened my eyes, I looked down to see that I had become several inches taller and now sported gray robes and old-fashioned, patent leather shoes.

"Excellent," Fenris said, still holding my hand. I looked down to see that my skin had become paler, blue veins running beneath the near-translucent skin that now bore faint wrinkles. "Your grandmother looks to have been a lovely woman," he said softly.

I blinked hard before more tears could come. "Thank you. She was...wonderful. She took me in when my parents died, and I lived with her until I was fourteen. It must have been difficult, since she was quite frail already, but she never made me feel unwanted for a single moment."

We both looked down at my hand again, and Fenris placed his thumb on the round blue stone. I felt the tingle of magic in the air, and the next thing I knew, Fenris's voice was in my head, chanting another spell. I nearly recoiled, but his hand tightened on mine, and the ring began to glow.

An anchoring spell, I realized as I focused on interpreting the words. *To bind the illusion to my ring.*

"There," he said, finally releasing my hand. "You can now turn the illusion off and on whenever you want, simply by

brushing your finger over the stone. Try it now," he said, gesturing to the ring.

I did as he ordered, and the gray robes flickered away, revealing my normal pants and sturdy work boots. "How...how is it that I am able to hear you speaking the spell in my mind?"

Fenris's eyes widened. "What do you mean?"

"I heard your voice in my head," I said, crossing my arms over my chest, "speaking the spell that you imbued in the ring."

A chagrined look flashed across Fenris's face. "I must have accidentally been using mindspeak," he said. "But that doesn't mean you should have been able to hear it, unless you have a natural inclination toward it."

"Mindspeak?" I echoed. Hadn't Barrla mentioned that concept when she was nattering on about her favorite series? I had thought it was just an invention of the author's.

Fenris nodded. "It's mostly a shifter ability, very useful since we can communicate with each other while in beast form, though the range is limited. I know of only one mage who can do it, but then he is extraordinary in many other ways." His eyes shone with curiosity. "Try sending me a thought."

I started. "What?"

"If you can hear me speaking into your mind, it stands to reason that you should be able to use mindspeak as well." Fenris folded his arms. "Come on, try it. Try to say something to me with your mind. Just focus on me, and imagine the thought beaming into my head."

Scowling, I planted my gaze on the spot between his eyes, then fired off the first thought that came to my head. *"This is stupid."*

Fenris grinned. *"Excellent."* I started as his voice echoed in my head again.

"I...this really works?" I pressed my hands to my cheeks,

wondering if I had suddenly become a different person. "How did I inherit this talent?" I asked aloud.

Fenris shrugged. "Perhaps you have a shifter ancestor hidden in your family tree or your natural affinity for animals inspired the ability. I don't believe that animals can use mind-speak, but they do have non-verbal cues for communicating," he continued, answering the question that sprang to my lips.

It was true I often seemed to know intuitively what animals were feeling, but this was different. I frowned suspiciously. "Can you also hear my thoughts when I'm not projecting them? You often seem to know what questions I'm about to ask before I even open my mouth."

Fenris grinned again. "Your face is like an open book, Mina —not much thought-reading required. At least when it comes to your curiosity about magic. Don't worry," he added when I opened my mouth to object. "I cannot spy on your private thoughts any more than you can on mine." My face flamed again, and he continued, "In any case, this discovery is most useful. It means we can talk to each other both when I'm in animal form and when we are in the presence of people who must not overhear us."

"Huh." I mulled that thought in my head for a moment. "If there is another shifter nearby, or a mage who can use mind-speak, will he hear us talking?"

"Not if you don't want him to," Fenris explained. "Mindspeak can be directed toward a specific person, like a telephone call on a single channel, or it can be broadcast, like a radio signal. It all depends on your intent. So long as you are not broadcasting your thoughts, only I should be able to hear them."

"I must be careful in that regard, then." By the Lady, there were so many rules!

"You'll catch up," Fenris said gently, once again reading me perfectly. "Do not be discouraged, Mina. One of my closest

friends did not start mastering her magic until her mid-twenties, but she caught up quickly under the guidance of a good teacher."

My eyebrows rose. "You know someone else like me?" I'd never considered that there might be other mages out there who had made it to adulthood without magical tutelage...but the Federation was a vast country. Among all those millions, it stood to reason there might be a few others with a similar experience to mine.

"Her situation was...unique, even compared to yours," Fenris said, sounding a little strained. "But yes, the basic issue was the same—she was far 'behind' in her studies compared to other mages her age and did not even know the rudiments of Loranian when she began her apprenticeship. But she did not let that hold her back, and neither should you, Mina." He placed a hand on my shoulder. "I will help you as much as I can. Once you are of age, you will find a master who can properly apprentice you and who will treat you well."

Fenris and I arranged to meet again at tea time tomorrow afternoon for my first magical lesson, and when I left the house to retrieve my mare, there was a distinct bounce in my step. I felt impossibly light compared to the panic that had driven me to seek help at Fenris's house, though perhaps my new optimism was foolish. I was far from out of the woods yet.

But the promise of *real* control over my magic eroded my fears of discovery, pushed out even the thought of my horrid relatives getting their clutches on me. And as I rode home at a much steadier pace than I had arrived at, I hoped that my time with Fenris would be enough that, should I ever have to face my aunt and uncle again, they would not find it so easy to push me around anymore.

MINA

Two days later, I was humming in my surgery, in a good mood after treating my latest patient—an elderly cat with arthritis in her hind legs. The magical lessons were going well enough that I had been able to ease her pain without too much difficulty—though as far as the owner knew, I had simply prescribed a tonic that had worked wonders—and I was using my magic right now to run a sponge over the table, cleaning it without having to lift a finger.

I was prepping the surgery for my next appointment at eleven when I heard a sharp knock at the front door. Frowning, I released the spell on the sponge and checked my watch. It was only 10:15, too early for my next patient.

It's probably Barrla, come to sneak away from the shop on her break, I thought as I went to answer the door.

"Good morning," a tall, wiry man in a set of green robes said in a cool voice, and my heart nearly stopped. The morning sunlight shone off the brown hair flowing around his shoulders. He had regular features—not particularly handsome, but not ugly either.

But none of those details registered beyond a split second,

because the only thing my mind was screaming was *Run, Run, Run.*

"Good morning," I managed, forcing my legs to stay ramrod straight even as they started to quiver like jelly. "How can I help you?"

"My name is Haltinas ar'Contir, and I am a representative from the Watawis Mages Guild's legal department," he said, eyeing me curiously. I was certain he was taking in the bits of cat hair that clung to my black top—my patient this morning had luxurious white fur that was impossible to get off. "You are Mina Hollin, the local veterinarian?"

"I am," I admitted, gripping the doorframe a little tighter than I should have. The mage seemed to notice that, too, and I forced myself to relax. "I did not expect someone to come all this way—I only just received the summons."

The mage nodded. "We normally give a week, but I happened to be passing through the area and told the Secretary I would stop by to save you the trouble of driving up. May I come in?"

The last sentence wasn't a request, not really, and I swallowed hard at his implacable gaze. Silently, I bowed my head and stepped back, allowing one of my worst nightmares to enter my home. His eagle eyes quickly swept over my surroundings, as if looking for any sign of magic, and I thanked the Lady that I had not been using any spells in my private quarters. I'd heard that mages could use a spell that would enable them to see if magic had been recently used, and the last thing I needed was for him to detect it.

You are an idiot, I told myself as I shut the door behind me. *Idiot, idiot, idiot.*

"Thank you," the mage told me as I handed him a cup of coffee, still fresh from the pot, and set a plate of cookies on the table. I'd already had two cups this morning and didn't dare

pour myself a third with my nerves so shaky, but I did snatch a cookie off the plate, mainly to have something to do with my hands instead of nervous fidgeting.

He stared at me intently. "I'd like to hear your account of the incident with Mr. Roor."

I pretended to nibble at my cookie, though my mouth was too dry to swallow even crumbs. "There isn't much to tell," I said after a second or two, pleased at the composure in my voice. "Mr. Roor and I were at a party, like most of the neighborhood, and he was making unwanted advances. A friend of mine stepped in to tell him to back off, and Mr. Roor threatened to attack him. The excitement, coupled with the many drinks he'd imbibed, was obviously too much for Roor, and he fainted."

The mage arched a brow. "I visited the Roor family before I came over here," he said, setting his mug down. "Mr. Roor is a large, strapping man. I am having some difficulty imagining that merely lurching toward someone would be enough to make him faint, not unless he drank an entire barrel full of ale."

I wrinkled my nose. "I wouldn't be surprised if he had. He's never been very good at controlling himself."

"Even so," the mage said, "I must insist that you allow me to gauge you for magic potential. If you are innocent," he said as a protest sprang to my lips, "then there should be nothing for you to fear. Protesting will only make you look guilty."

Panic began to claw at my mind, freezing my thoughts, making me want to crumble. But as the mage looked at me, I caught just a hint of smugness behind that bland expression. So, the bastard already thought he had this in the bag, did he? That he could make a quick arrest and toss me into prison without a single thought for the life he was ruining?

The very idea filled me with outrage, and the next thing I knew, I'd shot to my feet, a half-cocked idea forming in my mind.

"You want magic," I hissed, swiping a finger over the ring on my right hand, "I'll show you magic!"

The illusion of my grandmother quickly took the place of my own form, and the mage jerked back, his eyes widening in shock. "How dare a young whippersnapper like you presume to test me," I cried, using my magic to change my voice into that of an older woman. "I was already a mage long before you were a gleam in your father's eyes!"

"I—" the mage sputtered as he jumped to his feet. "What in Recca is the meaning of this?" he demanded, his face coloring. "Who are you?"

"My name is Tuala Harmon," I said imperiously, "and I insist that you leave my home at once."

"I will do no such thing," the mage snapped, going from astonished to angry. "I have never heard your name in my life, and it was certainly not in the registry, which I checked only the other day. Why are you living in this *hovel*, disguised as a human girl?"

As he spoke, I heard the back door softly open and close. I tensed, wondering if it was a neighbor, but no one stepped forth.

"It's just me," Fenris's voice whispered in my mind, so quietly I would have thought I'd imagined it if I hadn't been introduced to mindspeak.

I relaxed, focusing all my attention back on the mage before he'd realized my momentary lapse. "I am living in this *hovel*, as you say, because I bet a friend I could live amongst humans for three entire years without being discovered. I've already done two, and was doing a rather good job, before you came in and ruined everything." I glared at him, focusing all my earlier terror into perfectly genuine anger. "Thanks to you and that meddlesome Mrs. Roor, I've lost the bet. Why could you not leave well enough alone?"

"Your bet is none of my concern," the mage said stiffly. Skep-

ticism still lurked in his eyes, but I stared down my nose at him until he finally averted his gaze. "Your yearly allowance as a mage should be more than enough to cover it, unless you bet a truly outrageous sum. Besides, I can't see how any bet could be worth putting up with these tiresome humans for such an extended period."

"Three years is but the blink of an eye compared to my lifespan," I said archly. "You must be young indeed if you think that is such a long time." His face flushed at that, and I hid a grin. "Besides, I was getting bored, and I wanted a challenge in my life. Without occasional change, we tend to become stodgy and rigid."

"Is that why you chose to assume such a youthful appearance?" he asked, still sounding incredulous. "Because you wanted a 'change' in your life?"

I looked away at that, allowing my own cheeks to color faintly, as if in embarrassment. "I happen to be fond of young, handsome men," I told him. "Taking on a more youthful appearance makes it much easier to indulge."

A brief look of disgust flashed across the mage's face, but he masked it quickly. "And was Mr. Roor one of the men you found acceptable?"

I shrugged. "He is not worth keeping around, far too volatile. I admit, I slapped a sleeping spell on him when he was about to start a fight at a birthday party, and I'm not sorry either."

"Very well," he said, finally composing himself. "While your activities are certainly unusual, if you are in fact a trained mage, you have done nothing illegal aside from not signing the register. I must insist that you come to the Mages Guild at the first opportunity to do so."

"I suppose there is no reason not to," I said in a bored voice, "since you have already broken my cover."

"I'm certain you will find yourself much happier once you

start engaging in magical pursuits again," the mage said. "Speaking of which..." Haltinas switched to Loranian and asked who my master had been, and from which state I originally hailed. So he was still doubtful, double-checking my story.

I was going to reply in Northian, since my Loranian was no longer all that fluent, but before I could open my mouth, Fenris whispered the correct Loranian phrases right into my mind. I merely had to echo them out loud, claiming I had grown up in Osero and my master had been the late Maggals ar'Trud.

"Indeed?" Haltinas looked impressed. "I have read his book on offensive magic."

"*No!*" Fenris hissed in my mind. "*He wrote only one book, on weather spells.*"

I corrected Haltinas with an ironic smile. "Really, your memory must be very poor for such a young man. Maggals was a specialist on weather magic. That is the only subject he wrote about."

The mage shrugged, unapologetic. "Sorry, ma'am, but I had to be sure."

"If you're done with your inquisition, I do have other things to attend to," I said impatiently, flicking a hand toward the door.

To my surprise, a hard blast of air rippled toward the mage, tinged with red. I caught the flicker of runes along the edges of the magical shield as the mage stumbled toward the front door, which flew open of its own accord. "Good day, Mr. ar'Contir."

The shield pushed the mage right out the door, which slammed into his sputtering face before he could get another word in. I forced myself to remain standing, a frozen look of imperious rage on my face, until I heard the mage leave, his footsteps creaking as he descended the porch. I walked to the window as I heard the engine of a steamcar fire up, then let out a long, slow breath as I watched the shiny black vehicle rumble

up the street, no doubt headed straight back to the Guild so he could deliver his report.

Passing through indeed.

"That was an excellent performance," Fenris said, coming to stand beside me. He was close enough that I could feel the body heat radiating off him, and as I inhaled, his masculine scent filled my nostrils. His steady presence broke through the wall of ice and steel I'd encased myself in, and I began to shake like a leaf.

"There now," he said, taking me into his arms and drawing me away from the window. "You're safe. It's all right."

Tears—of fear, of relief—coursed down my cheeks as I pressed my face into his broad chest. They quickly soaked through his tunic, but he didn't seem to mind as he stroked my back, saying absolutely nothing as the pent-up emotion ripped through me. A sob tore from my throat, and the sound, raw and aching, startled me enough that I realized what I was doing.

"I—I'm sorry," I said, jerking back and wiping my face with my sleeve. "I didn't mean to fall apart on you like that."

"That's all right." Fenris conjured a handkerchief out of thin air and handed it to me to wipe my face. "You are quite the actress," he said as I dried my tears. "I heard the beginning from outside and came in through the back in case you needed assistance. But you held your own quite well."

"At least up until the end," I agreed, a cold shiver rippling down my spine. "I'm not sure what I would have done if I hadn't been able to evade his tricky test."

Fenris only smiled. "Somehow I think you would have found your way around that pitfall too, even if I were not here. If I had not known any better, you would certainly have fooled me—you sounded just like a grumpy, vain old lady mage."

The sincerity in his voice finally eased the knot in my stomach, and I even let out a shaky laugh. "I can't believe I actually

did that," I said, running a hand through my hair. "It was all so spur-of-the-moment." I shook my head as Fenris guided me to the couches. "My grandmother was dear to me, so it was easy to slide into her persona. The name I gave to that nosy mage belonged to one of my grandmother's friends, since my grandmother is deceased."

"Smart." Fenris picked up a cookie and bit down on it thoughtfully. "It might be possible for that inspector to discover your grandmother was not alive, or track your true origins through the family connection, so it was better not to use her name. I suppose we'll be taking that trip to the capital sooner rather than later, now that you've promised to sign the register."

"Yes." My stomach dropped at the thought. "I...I don't know if I can keep up this charade," I confessed, my skin growing clammy again. "It is one thing to fool one mage, but there will be mages everywhere at the Guild, and one of them is bound to trip me up at some point, especially if they test me again with trick questions." I scooped my hands through my hair again as the anxiety began to tighten my chest once more. "And let's not think about the fact that I'm about to commit another crime by signing the registry with a false name. What is the penalty for *that*?" I asked, bitterness creeping into my voice.

"It'll be all right," Fenris promised, his deep voice soothing my raw nerves. "I'll accompany you to the capital in disguise, just in case. That way, I can once again coach you through any difficult situations via mindspeak."

"I..." More questions bubbled to my lips at all that his offer implied. There was technically no need for him to go in disguise if he was going to communicate via mindspeak—he could simply come as my shifter companion. That he wanted to keep his identity hidden meant he had reason not to want other mages to see him.

Maybe he really is involved with the Resistance somehow. The

thought of being in cahoots with a rebel, or even a rebel sympathizer, made me uneasy, especially if I was bringing him into the Mages Guild. But how could he be, when the Resistance hated mages, and Fenris knew nearly as much, if not more, than a master mage? I suspected the average mage would not have been familiar with the writings of a deceased Osero mage. There was much more to Fenris than I had initially assumed.

It doesn't matter if he works for the Resistance. I could hardly judge Fenris for his loyalties, not while he was bending over backward to help me when it was obvious that he did not want to go anywhere near the Guild. So I forced my questions down and instead thanked him for his help.

And then prayed to whoever might be listening that this entire charade did not backfire horribly.

FENRIS

The next morning arrived far too swiftly, and I groaned as I rolled toward the sun slipping through the blinds. I had not gotten much sleep, my mind occupied with thoughts of Mina and our planned trip to Willowdale.

I'd been just up the street when I saw that shiny black steamcar roll up in front of her house, and genuine terror for her had seized me when I'd watched a mage get out of the car and knock on her door. My wolf's instincts had risen, demanding I charge forward and attack, and it had taken a supreme effort to rein in those primal instincts in and instead discreetly go around the back of Mina's house so I could assess the situation.

If necessary, I'd been fully prepared to disable the mage, scramble the encounter in his mind, and dump him out in the middle of nowhere to keep Mina safe. And just what did that say about my feelings toward her, if I was willing to put my rural sanctuary at risk so easily and without hesitation? Not to mention the damage I would have done to the mage's brain?

You are growing far too attached to her, I told myself sternly.

But it had felt damn good to take her into my arms yesterday,

to stroke and soothe her and tell her that she was safe. I'd felt fierce pride as I'd watched her handle the mage without falling apart. Despite her fear, she had kept up her quick-witted deception without flagging until it was safe to let go.

I hadn't realized, when I'd first met Mina at that party, that she suffered from a broken past. Most of the time, she acted as the calm, competent veterinarian who tended to the town's animals. But whatever had happened to her in her youth, whatever her family had done, had left deep scars, and this ordeal was bringing those painful memories back to the surface.

And it's your fault, a voice said in my mind. *Your fault for letting your territorial instincts take over and using your magic when it wasn't strictly necessary.*

I scrubbed a hand over my face. Yes, that was the crux of the matter, wasn't it? Living out here in the country, away from the confines of the Solantha Mages Guild, was forcing me to deal with those instincts. Iannis's home had been an ivory tower of sorts, and my wolf had retreated in the presence of so many mages. I had fooled myself into pretending I'd mastered both halves of myself, when, in reality, I'd only suppressed my beast, built a cage around him. It was only through my observation of Sunaya, a panther shifter at ease with that side of herself, that I realized I needed to hone my shifter abilities.

I still remembered the day she had looked down her nose at me when Iannis had given me that truth wand to interrogate the servants. *A real shifter wouldn't use a truth wand,* her gaze had said, and for a second, I'd felt ashamed. My lifelong habits had made me too reliant on magic, using it when there was no real need.

And I'd done it again at that party.

Perhaps Mina and I are two different sides of the same coin, I thought as I finally rose and dressed for the day. *She needs to master her magic, and I need to stop using mine as a crutch.*

Still pondering our similarities and differences, I went to the kitchen to make myself breakfast. To my chagrin, I found I was completely out of eggs and barely had enough coffee to last me through the next day. My stomach grumbled as I devoured a measly few pieces of buttered toast. At least this was a problem easily solved. I would go to the general store forthwith to replenish my supplies.

As I approached the store on horseback, the scent of eggs and bacon wafted from the inn pub just across the road, and I found myself altering course. While I knew the pub rented out a few guest rooms on the first floor, I had not been aware they served breakfast, but so much the better. As Polar ar'Tollis, I'd often skipped meals, but shifters needed to eat six times a day, so that was not an option now. Dismounting, I tied my horse to one of the posts outside, then headed into the dark, cool interior. My stomach rumbled again as I ducked inside.

I'd been there for the card games with Marris and his friends, and the scent of beer and stale cigarettes still hung in the air, though overlaid now with the more attractive odor of warm food. To my surprise, the place was completely packed despite the early hour. Most of the traffic seemed to be congregated to a recessed table toward the back.

I started when I noticed a mage in dark green robes at the back table, tucking into a breakfast of bacon and eggs and coffee. A large leather money purse sat open next to his plate, and a steady stream of people were waiting to see him, clutching forms in one hand and money purses in the other as they warily stood in line.

Right, I suddenly realized. *Today is tax day.*

Marris had told me over dinner last week that the tax collector held court at the inn every year and that the townsfolk would stop by throughout the morning to pay their dues. I suddenly became aware of the weight of my own purse hanging

from my waist. Luckily, I always carried some gold coins for emergencies, and there was enough in there to cover my yearly tax. I did not want to go back to the house to fetch more when I was already here and could not conjure fresh gold with so many witnesses around.

What Marris had not warned me about, however, was the shifter sitting right next to the tax inspector—a hyena, judging by the quick whiff I got of him. He was a young male with dark brown hair and a swarthy face, and though he did not look entirely pleased about having to do it, each time a citizen came up with coins, he ostentatiously sniffed them before allowing the money to drop into the waiting sack.

Sniffing for magic, I realized, my gut tightening. *For counterfeit gold.*

I debated getting into line and paying right then and there, but my stomach grumbled even louder, as if in protest. Right—taxes could wait. I found a seat at the bar and ordered a gigantic breakfast that would put even Sunaya to shame. A smile twitched at my lips, and I wondered what she would say if she were here. She'd probably make some snide comment about the tax inspector taking too much from people who had too little and then challenge me to see who could eat the most bacon within fifteen minutes.

A wave of homesickness filled me, and I forced it back as my food arrived. I needed to stop thinking of Solantha as home, or I would never get used to my new life out here. As I tucked into my food with gusto, I watched the tax inspector and his hyena sidekick out of the corner of my eye.

So the Federation was cracking down on illicit gold now that Thorgana's use of it had become public knowledge. The other shifter's eyes met mine for a moment as he hefted a small purse in his hand. I quickly turned back to my food—I didn't want his attention on me any longer than necessary. I routinely took

pains to mask the scent of magic from my body so that another shifter should not suspect anything amiss. But this shifter was allied with a mage, and I saw no point in courting trouble.

Just in case his nose was unusually acute, I pulled a small bottle of aftershave from the magical pocket in my tunic and surreptitiously dabbed a tiny bit just beneath my jawline on both sides of my neck. To a human, it wouldn't smell like much, but my eyes already watered from the strong cedar-and-mint fragrance. From the way the shifter's head suddenly came up, his nose wrinkling in distaste, I knew he scented it too. Now he certainly would not be able to detect any whiff of magic about me.

I waited until the crowd had thinned out a bit, then, on a hunch, waited some more. After a time, the tax inspector told the shifter he was going to take advantage of the break with a quick stroll, then secured the bag of gold with a magical lock that would not permit anyone to remove it or take out a single coin. Only prudent, under the circumstances.

The moment the tax inspector was out of sight, I slid off my stool and approached the booth. The shifter's eyes narrowed, and his nose began to redden as it twitched at my scent.

"Good morning," I said pleasantly, sliding into the booth. "I've come to pay my yearly dues. My name is Shelton."

"Why did you wait until the tax inspector was gone?" The shifter arched an eyebrow, suspicion lurking in his gaze.

I shrugged. "I do wonder how a shifter would consent to work for the Mages Guild," I said, reaching into my purse and pulling out three coins. "Mark them on the list as the tax for Ackleberry Farm." I slid them across the table to him, and he sniffed.

"Blast it," he growled, leaning over to open the window next to us. "That perfume you're wearing is killing my nose. Why in Recca are you wearing that disgusting stuff?"

I gave him a sheepish look. "I have a certain...lady friend... who gave it to me as a present, and she'd be hurt if I failed to use it. She was to meet me here at the inn for breakfast this morning."

"A human?" The shifter's eyebrows shot high up on his head. "I would consider that strange, if not for the fact that this is a human town. What's stranger is that *you're* living in it, well away from any other wolf shifters."

"I had a falling out with my clan," I said calmly, not willing to let him shift the conversation in my direction. "No doubt you have strained relations with yours, too, if you are so willing to throw your lot in with the mages."

The hyena let out a deep sigh. "There aren't that many jobs for shifters where I come from," he said, "and especially not hyenas. There are too few of us in the Federation to even have clans, and the other ones don't really like working with us. Can you blame me for doing whatever I have to, to make ends meet?" A tinge of bitterness seeped into his tone.

"Of course not," I said, filling my voice with sympathy even as I filed away this information about hyenas. I wondered if the average shifter knew this—the hyena didn't seem suspicious about my ignorance on the subject. "And I suppose you kill two birds with one stone—putting money in your pocket and helping the Guild weed out potential Resistance members in hiding."

The shifter snorted. "So you know why I'm here, then."

"It is easy enough for anyone with a modicum of sense to figure out," I said mildly. "I understand the need to put food on your table, but have you not considered how you might be ruining the lives of anyone who pays in illegal coin? With so much of it circulating these days, it is not as though everyone using it is actually guilty."

The hyena shrugged. "Doesn't bother me," he said, fingering

the coins I'd given to him. He placed them in the sack, marked the payment on the list, and slid a receipt and another form over to me from the stack on the table. "Says here Ackleberry Farm recently changed hands. If you have time to question me about my morals, then you have time to fill this out."

Hiding a scowl, I quickly filled out the form, then bid the shifter good day.

Leaving a few coins on the bar to cover my tab, I strode out of the inn, feeling irrationally guilty and apprehensive. Sunaya and I had first suggested using shifters to sniff out the illegal coins. At the time, when our sole focus had been hunting down Thorgana and stopping the Resistance, it had seemed like an excellent idea. But now that the lives of these harmless humans were at risk, I wished we had never brought it up. This day would only end in tragedy—the families Marris's little band of forgers had gifted their gold to would all fail the hyena's inspection, and they would be arrested. It was a miracle it had not happened yet, but then the day was still young.

By the Lady, I thought, my stomach churning. I could just imagine the shock and despair those poor people would go through—people who had been unable to pay their taxes despite all their hard work, who had thought their prayers had been miraculously answered, only to find out that the gold landed them into even deeper trouble than if they hadn't paid their taxes to begin with. It was one thing to be delinquent with taxes and forfeit one's farm, and quite another to be accused of being part of the Resistance. I could not see this ending well for anyone.

Warning Marris would do no good at this point. It wasn't as if he could go around and switch all that gold out for real coin. Yet any direct interference on my part might reveal I had magic. This disaster was not of my making; I owed these humans nothing. It would be more sensible, and far safer, to go home and

forget all about it. With any luck, the mages would not sweep up all the neighbors and associates of the culprits when the whole story came out.

But the tight clenching of my gut told me I could not simply step away without trying to help. I would never forgive myself for such cowardice. I left my horse tied to the post and walked through the town instead. I barely noticed my surroundings, and it was an effort to acknowledge the other townsfolk who greeted me with smiles and curious looks. Was keeping my secret, and saving my ancient hide, worth letting a dozen families be torn apart by the mage government? Marris and his friends had meant well; neither they nor their unwitting neighbors deserved the penalty they would suffer. I could not have foreseen that my suggestion to use shifters to authenticate money would lead to innocent humans paying the price. But if I stood by now and did nothing, then I would be guilty.

At bottom, the situation was not so dissimilar from the case over which I'd lost my career, my life as a powerful mage. I might be Fenris now, and a fugitive, but that did not mean I had to be craven. And deep down, I also felt an ignoble desire to thwart the mage officials any way I could, to make fools of the forces who hunted and condemned me.

Relieved to have resolved my doubts, I strode back into the inn. The mage had not yet come back, and the shifter was still seated toward the back of the dining hall, idly playing with his pen. He must have dispatched any other taxpayers in the interim, for the place was nearly empty.

With a flick of my hand, I hit him with a strong sleeping spell, and he slumped forward in his seat, already snoring. At the same moment, I caused a tray sitting on a serving table across the room to crash to the floor, sending bits of broken dishes everywhere. As the wait staff scrambled to clean up the mess and all the guests and taxpayers turned to see what was

going on, I hurried to the tax inspector's table. As fast as only a shifter could manage, I levitated the sleeping shifter up the nearby stairs that led to the guest rooms on the first floor. I kept my body in between the shifter and the staircase so that, hopefully, nobody could see us clearly for the few instants that mattered.

By the time I came back downstairs, unnoticed as far as I could tell, the hyena shifter was comfortably lying on an unused guest room in the inn, where he would sleep for a good three hours. If anybody came into the room, they would be unable to wake him until the sleeping spell ran its course.

I was about to take a seat at the bar again and order more coffee when the tax inspector strode back in, looking refreshed from his stroll in the spring sunshine. The relaxed expression on his face dissipated instantly when he laid eyes on the abandoned booth, and the sack of gold sitting there in full view, without anything guarding it other than his lock spell.

"What is the meaning of this?" He looked around angrily. "Where did my assistant go?"

I held in a snort—I doubted the hyena had been paid half as well as he would have been if he were a true "assistant." "I'm afraid he's run off," I said, drawing the mage's attention to me. "He probably decided the job wasn't worth the pittance you were paying him."

The mage rewarded me with a frosty glare. "Is that so? In that case, seeing as you are the only other shifter here, you shall have to take his place."

I stiffened, pretending outrage. "*Me?* I don't work for you, and certainly not for some paltry sum."

The tax mage clenched his jaw. "All taxpayers are obliged to help out if ordered to. And I'll double the fee, considering the short notice." He gestured to the booth. "Hurry up. There will be more people coming soon."

Hiding a smile, I did as the tax inspector ordered, taking the hyena's place. We sat in awkward silence for the next ten minutes, but gradually people began to drip in again, bearing their forms and purses of money. They seemed surprised, and even wary, to see me sitting next to the tax inspector, but they did not say anything and simply handed over their payment. I sniffed all the coins dutifully. To my relief, most of them were the genuine article.

"Good morning, sir," an elderly woman warbled as she approached the booth. She looked like a stiff wind could knock her over, and as she extended her gnarled hand, two shiny new gold coins in her palm, I didn't even have to lean in to know that the coins she held had not a trace of magic on them.

I took the coins from her. When she handed the tax inspector her form, I leaned close to sniff them. Under the cover of my hand and nose, I quickly changed the coins to copper, then back to gold, before putting them in the sack. The transformation would leave enough magical residue on the metal that they would pass for genuine mage-created coins, and with any luck, the tax inspector wouldn't notice what I was doing.

The woman moved on, and over the next two hours, I caught eight more townspeople paying with illegal gold. With each coin I changed, I grew more annoyed with Marris for putting these people at risk. He had not thought this plan through, and could have precipitated tragedies. By the time he came through the line, with a cocky grin on his face, it took an effort not to glare at him. Shock flashed in his eyes as he handed me his gold and saw me sniff it, but I kept my face inscrutable. I would not reveal, in front of the tax inspector, that the two of us were friends. And though questions burned in his gaze as his mind put two and two together, he was not stupid enough to ask them here.

"Well, well," the tax inspector said hours later, when the last name had been ticked off the list, leaning back in the booth.

There was a look of pleasant surprise on his face. "This is the best turnout we've had for Abbsville in years. There are usually at least five families who cannot pay up." He turned in his seat to face me. "I suppose you are relieved that none of the families came here empty-handed."

I kept my expression blank. "I don't have a particular allegiance to humans, but yes, I prefer not to watch my neighbors suffer."

Before the tax inspector could say more, the hyena shifter stormed down the stairs. I had to hide a grin at the thunderous expression on his face—his clothes were rumpled, and he was smoothing down his hair, which was sticking up every which way.

"Did you have a nice nap?" the tax inspector said in a deceptively soft voice as the shifter approached. It was obvious to anyone who looked that the hyena had been sleeping—there were lines on his cheek from where his face had been pressed into the pillow.

"That was no nap," the hyena hissed, his dark eyes gleaming with banked rage. "Someone put a sleeping spell on me!"

The inspector's eyes narrowed. "I find that hard to believe, considering I am the only mage in this inn. Are you suggesting *I* did such a thing?"

"Of course not," the hyena sputtered. "But..." His gaze landed on me, and he bared his teeth. "This wolf was preaching at me how I shouldn't help ruin the lives of innocent townsfolk. *He* must have done it."

I kept an icy grip on my composure as I held the shifter's gaze—even with the cedar aftershave, he would scent any fear or unease from me. "You are overestimating my abilities if you think that a shifter can cast sleep spells, *hyena*." My tone was scathing.

But the tax inspector's eyes were on me now, his gaze tight

with suspicion. "Double check these coins," he told the hyena, pushing the sack of gold toward him even as he continued to stare at me.

We sat quietly as he went through the entire sack, taking his time. I kept my gaze on the bag of coins while the mage watched me out of narrowed eyes. No doubt he was waiting to see if I did try to use magic—he had been too preoccupied to notice it earlier, and besides, he had not suspected me. But he could not dismiss the hyena's claims out of hand. Luckily, I had no reason to use magic again, so I made myself comfortable for the next twenty minutes.

Finally, the hyena put down the last coin, a deeply dissatisfied look on his face. "They are all authentic," he admitted, shoving them back into the bag. "Every last one of them reeks of magic."

"Good," the tax inspector said, taking the bag. "Then you have both done your job well."

"The coins are not the only things that reek of magic," the hyena snarled, turning that angry gaze toward me again. "Your new shifter employee stinks of it, too, even beneath that nasty perfume he poured all over himself." His gaze turned challenging, as if he now knew exactly why I'd put on the aftershave and was daring me to deny it.

I shrugged. "That must be because I've been sitting next to a powerful mage all day and handling all these magically created coins."

"Yes, I can see how that might confuse the scent," the mage said, sounding bored, while the hyena sputtered. Clearly, the mage had concluded the hyena was trying to get me in trouble out of spite. The mage stood up, pulled a quarter silver coin from the bag, and tossed it onto the table. "For your time, gentlemen," he said with a hateful smirk as he walked out.

I stared in disgust at the coin, impossible for either of us to

touch with bare hands. "Keep it," I told the still-snarling hyena as I left the booth. I had no need of the money, and it was the least I could do after ambushing him. He could pick it up with gloves or a folded handkerchief.

I can't blame the humans for being so resentful of the Mages Guild, I thought as I left the inn. The tax inspector had treated us all with barely veiled contempt, and the taxes were far too high compared to what simple farmers or artisans could earn each year. Since mages could produce as much gold as they wanted, the tax collection exercise was merely a means to keep humans under control. There was no reason not to lower the tax rate in years when the harvest was bad.

As I headed back home, I wondered what Mina would think about my good deed for the day. I had not seen her today, so she had likely handed her tax form in earlier in the morning, before I had arrived. With her knowledge of the area and my unusual abilities, she might have picked up on what I was doing, even with her scant training. Our lessons were going well—she was progressing faster than Sunaya had managed, because she already knew her Loranian and had tight control and a solid base to work from due to growing up in a mage family. She might be one of the rare prodigies who completed their apprenticeship in seven or eight years rather than the average ten.

It was too early to tell, though, and who knew where I would be when Mina completed her apprenticeship.

Speaking of Mina... I changed my mind about cooking a full meal for myself and quickly ate a sandwich instead. We had a lesson scheduled for the late afternoon, and I couldn't let this morning's excitement disrupt our schedule. Not if we were to be prepared for our visit to the Watawis Mages Guild.

FENRIS

I'd barely made it back into town before Marris and his friends waylaid me, all smiles and good cheer. They insisted on taking me to the pub for drinks, and while I wanted to refuse, I was reluctant to plead that I was on my way to see Mina. That would lead to a line of questioning I was not ready to deal with—the fewer eyes on our magical lessons, the better.

"You really didn't have to do this," I told them as I set down my near empty tankard. "Alcohol is wasted on me—shifters can't get drunk on human-style drinks."

Marris shrugged and poured me another glass from the large pitcher on the table. "At least it gives us the illusion that we're repaying you for what you did today," he said, lifting his tankard to me. "You saved our asses."

"Hear, hear," Cobil and Roth said, and they all drank deeply from their tankards.

I followed suit, then set down my beer and gave them all stern looks. "I'll admit, it was lucky I was here this morning," I told them gravely. "Your stunt with the gold coins, well-meant as it was, put a great many townsfolk in peril today." The young

men had the grace to look embarrassed. "The three of you must immediately exchange whatever coins you have left for genuine coins at the nearest city so that this does not happen again. I will not be able to intervene every time tax season comes around."

"Of course," Marris said, sounding abashed. "We should have thought of this earlier. Only, we had no idea the mages would suspect anything. They never checked the coins before."

"It's been...difficult," Roth said, an uncomfortable look crossing his face, "to shoulder this burden with just the three of us. We wanted to help the townsfolk, but in the end, we're simple soldiers, not strategists. We didn't have someone like you around who could look ahead and see the pitfalls."

"Well, I'm glad I was able to be of assistance." I smiled, ignoring the veiled invitation. Marris and his friends likely saw me as a potential ally, and were surprisingly inclined to trust me, merely on their suspicion that I had supported the Resistance. Though I did not want them to get in trouble, it would be foolish to get involved with their group. With any luck, I would find a way to deter them from other vigilante activities without actually joining their little band, and keep their activism confined to the illegal gold mining. I would set wards around the mine, careful spells that would keep other humans from accidentally stumbling upon the site so the secret was not revealed. They need never know about it, either.

If I had Iannis's abilities, I could simply wipe the location of the gold from their minds. But even he hesitated to interfere in others' minds without supreme need, and perhaps it was as well that I no longer had the power to perform such a complex spell. Anyway, the hidden mine's gold might yet serve a useful purpose. As an outcast myself, I did not feel obliged to uphold mages' privileges and the laws that underpinned their power.

I stayed with them for another hour, then prepared to take my leave—I was going to be late for my appointment with Mina.

Just as I was standing up, ignoring the protests from my new friends, the door to the pub slammed open and Roor came stomping in.

Along with three of his friends.

"There's the traitor," he crowed, his lip curling back in a sneer. "Did you have fun today gloating over us as you sat next to that filthy mage and took our money?"

I suppressed a sigh. Apparently, the bloodthirsty fool was no longer willing to wait for the full moon, only three days away.

"Shut up, Roor," Marris snapped, shoving out of his seat. Cobil and Roth silently rose as well, ready to step in with their fists if needed. "You have no idea what you're talking about."

Roor scoffed, stopping a bare foot away from me. "Oh, so I guess when I came up to the tax inspector, I just imagined this mongrel sitting there and sniffing at my coins like a well-trained dog?"

A look of disgust flashed in his eyes, but since he had no idea of my motives, his disdain left me indifferent. I shrugged. "Your opinion on the matter is hardly relevant, Roor. Or is it really your own opinion? Was it your mother, perhaps, who whipped up this ridiculous show of indignation? She does seem to be very busy these days." I wondered if the Roor family had received the silver bullets they planned to expend on me. Was there any point to bandying words with this young brute? Except that the moment we stopped, mayhem was likely to ensue.

Roor's cheeks burned like coals. "Don't you bring my mother into this," he growled, taking a step forward. "You're not welcome in this town anymore. Pack your things and go back to the mages, since it's so obvious you'd rather serve them." His two companions nodded at this but prudently kept hanging a step or two back, behind Roor's broad shoulders.

"On your word? Hardly," I retorted. "I've started making

friends here, and Miss Hollin is teaching me all about caring for horses." A lie—I was perfectly capable of caring for my animals. But trying to diffuse Roor's anger would get me nowhere—the lout was spoiling for a fight. It was best to get it over with.

"Don't you speak her name," Roor snarled, lunging forward. But I was fast—far faster than any human—and he crashed into the table behind me as I stepped aside. "I don't know what kind of lies or witchcraft you've spun into Mina's head, but I won't let you get away with it," he panted, whirling around again.

His cronies chose that moment to join in, and Marris and his friends surged forward to meet them. Grunts and snarls filled the air as fists flew, and there was a crash as someone decided to use a chair as a weapon. Roor lunged for me again, but this time, I ducked under his guard and grabbed him by the throat. My triceps flexed as I lifted him off the ground and stared into his eyes with lethal calm.

He barely had time to claw at my grip before I threw him across the room.

The bartender and the few patrons in the room all gasped as Roor went sailing a good fifteen feet, his body shooting straight through a cluster of chairs that clattered to the ground. He slammed into the far wall, and I could hear the crack of breaking ribs. Wincing inwardly, I watched as he slumped to the ground, his head lolling forward—had I gone too far? Was he still alive?

The rest of the pub had gone deathly quiet. Even the other brawlers had stopped fighting to gape at me. I turned my gaze toward them, and Roor's cronies blanched. One of them sported a broken nose already, the other a split lip from fighting with Marris and his friends, but it was the sight of their fallen leader that decided them. They took one look at me and fled, not even bothering to stop and collect Roor from his prone position on the ground.

"Sorry about that," I said to the owner as I knelt in front of Roor to see if he was still alive. The innkeeper was standing behind the bar, his eyes glassy with shock. After confirming that Roor was indeed breathing—though he would be in no condition to come hunt for me on the full moon—I set a gold piece on the counter. "This should be more than enough to cover damages—put the rest on my account."

I walked out of the pub without a backward glance.

"Damn," Marris breathed as he and the others followed me out into the afternoon sunshine. "That was some throw."

"Remind me to never pick a fight with you," Cobil said, his tone a combination of terror and reverence. "Ever."

I chuckled at that. "This has been fun, gentlemen, but I really ought to be going now. Until next time." I clapped Marris on the shoulder.

As I headed down the street to Mina's house, I felt lighter than I had in weeks, even with the weight of their stares on my back. Nothing like a fight now and then to lift the spirits. The weeks of sparring I'd done before my departure of Solantha had come in handy, and I forgot how good it had felt after a particularly intense match. Perhaps it was something I could indulge in more often...if I could find an opponent who didn't break so easily.

Or one who deserved breaking.

MINA

A week after Fenris had started our magic lessons, we found ourselves setting out for Willowdale. Waiting any longer, we agreed, could lead to renewed suspicion, while any less would not be in character for the grumpy old lady mage I was pretending to be.

Peering out the window of the rickety steambus that had direct service to the state capital, I pressed my hand against the cool glass pane and tried not to be too nervous. Fenris, in his wolf form, pressed against me—he sat in the aisle seat next to me, his large, furry body a comforting presence. He was too large to fit in the space between the seats, so I had bought an extra ticket so he could sit next to me.

The other passengers had glanced askance at Fenris—and some had looked downright alarmed—as we'd all piled onto the bus. Fenris didn't *really* look like a dog—his shifter form was large even by wolf standards, his paws nearly the size of my face. But I'd simply told them that he was a large breed and I was taking him to a new owner in the capital. It had seemed to settle them a bit. They all knew I was a veterinarian and very good

with animals, and that was enough to reassure them Fenris wouldn't try to maul them.

"Relax, Mina, you'll be fine," Fenris said in mindspeak, likely scenting my discomfort. *"We've practiced very hard these past few days."*

"I know." We'd done some magical training, but most of the past week had been focused on perfecting my role as the old lady mage. It had been harder than I'd expected, learning to slide into the skin of another person's identity. I'd used raw magic the day the inspector came calling to modulate my voice, and to save energy, Fenris had taught me the proper spell to do it. That spell had been a lifesaver, as my grandmother's deceased friend had possessed a northeastern accent very different from mine, but magic could do nothing about my woefully modern vocabulary. We'd spent hours conversing, perfecting older speech patterns, practicing how to carry myself, and discussing what a three-hundred-year-old female mage might say and do in certain situations.

It sounded very much like Fenris had personal experience with elderly mages. I wondered just how many older female mages he'd spent time with. And why.

As the steambus bumped and jostled along the road, groaning and creaking with every mile, I was glad that we were renting a steamcar for the return trip. Since everybody in Abbsville thought I was going into the city to pick up veterinary supplies, I couldn't very well return without them. Fenris, too, planned to do some shopping—he needed materials for refurbishing his home.

He'd been late the other day when he'd come for our lesson, reeking of ale, though he was clear-eyed and fresh-faced. When I'd demanded what had happened, he'd told me Marris and his friends had waylaid him for a drink at the pub, and he hadn't

been able to refuse them without giving away our semi-secret meetings.

I hadn't thought anything more of it—it was just the sort of thing Marris would do. But the next morning when I'd visited the general store, Barrla had been waiting, her eyes glowing with delight and her cheeks flushed with the gossip that was just *bursting* to come out of her. Apparently, Roor had stalked into the pub while Fenris was there, with a couple of his no-good friends, and had picked a fight. And Fenris had wiped the floor with him.

I don't know why you're so surprised, I scolded myself as I glanced sideways at Fenris. I wasn't an expert on shifters, but it was common knowledge they were stronger and faster than humans, and that even a small shifter female could best the average human male. But I was having a tough time reconciling the image of the calm, polite man who came to give me lessons with the feral beast who had lifted Roor off his feet and thrown him into a wall at the other end of the room.

Not that I was complaining. The bastard was cooped up in bed with broken ribs and a concussion, where hopefully he would remain for weeks.

"*What are you smiling about?*" Fenris asked as a grin tugged at the corners of my mouth.

I turned back to the window, hiding my expression from him. "*It's nice to know I have a gallant gentleman as my neighbor, one who is willing to break bones to defend my honor.*"

Fenris made a rumbling sound that might have been a laugh. "*It was my pleasure. Though you might have bestowed a favor upon me in return.*"

I was glad he couldn't see my grin. "*Perhaps I will, once we return from our little adventure.*"

The air between us seemed to heat several degrees, and a

blush stole across my cheeks as I realized what I was doing. It was a good thing Fenris was in his wolf form. When he shifted in his seat, his massive shoulder brushing up against my arm again, I realized I didn't know if I would be able to keep my composure if the bare skin of his arm were touching my skin, if the heady masculine scent of him were filling my head. My cheeks warmed at the thought, and I forced myself to think about other things, mundane things, lest Fenris scent my sudden change in mood.

We spent the rest of the three-hour ride in silence, and I was relieved when we finally stepped off the bus in the town's modest depot. Standing on the street corner, I took a moment to soak in the sights and sounds of the city. The air was hotter here in Willowdale, lacking the fresh scents of the open country, and somewhat stifled by the clouds of billowing steam from the various vehicles that rumbled up and down the white streets. But the buildings were quaint, made of glittering pale stone covered with red roofs, and the scent of sizzling meat and fresh bread wafted up the street from the open doors of restaurants and various food carts.

My grumbling stomach overtaking all other priorities, I grabbed two hot brisket sandwiches from a street vendor and fed one to Fenris. After wolfing down my own meal, I found a quiet, open-ended alley to duck into, then rubbed the ring on my finger.

By the time I emerged onto the other street, I was once more Tuala Harmon, straight-backed and regal, in a set of flowing gray robes shot through with silvery thread. They rippled and caught the light, and passersby turned to stare as I marched up the street. We were in the human section of town, and the sight of a gray-haired mage was likely just as exotic as the enormous wolf-like dog that strolled by my side as both companion and protector. I hailed the first steamcab I saw, and though the driver seemed nervous about letting Fenris climb in with me, he was

even more frightened of what a mage might do to him if he refused to obey.

"To the Mages Guild," I ordered imperiously.

The cab lurched forward, and I settled back for the ride. As in most other states, the Watawis Mages Guild and governmental offices were in the same building as the Chief Mage's residence. It stood in the center of the mages' section of town, a large, sprawling manor with green roofs a few shades darker than jade and a pale stacked-stone exterior. Balconies and verandas adorned the front, and spring flowers were bursting from the hedges and gardens.

If not for the patrolling guards and the state flag waving from the balconies, I might have thought it someone's grand home.

Had I grown up in Abbsville, I might have felt awe as Fenris and I descended the steamcar and glided up the path. But I had been born into wealth and luxury, and had spent most of my childhood in Haralis, a much larger and richer state capital.

It was only when I had run away and spent time living amongst human communities in several different states that I had begun to experience life among the middle class and the poor. Living without my creature comforts had bothered me at first, but my freedom was worth far more than the luxuries I had given up, and I'd soon grown used to making do with less.

Should I fail today, should my deceit be revealed, I might lose any kind of choice about my circumstances, where and with whom I lived, for several years. I could not bear that—*this had to work.*

Head held high, I boldly stepped into the building, my shoes a bare whisper on the stone tile. Chandeliers and stained glass gleamed above me. The broad windows were framed with heavy damask curtains and the floors were covered in thick rugs. Four guards stared at me and my unlikely companion, but I swept

past them, approaching the grand reception desk in the center of the foyer.

A female mage in teal-and-white robes beamed, her youthful face not yet hardened and emotionless, as so many mages tended to be by early middle age. "Welcome to the Watawis Capitol Building," she said cheerfully. "How can I help you?"

"My name is Tuala Harmon," I said coolly. "I have come to sign the guest book."

"Ah! Yes, Ms. Harmon." There was the slightest change of tone as she said the word "miss," as if she wasn't sure a lady of such an advanced age should be called that. If I wasn't only twenty-eight years old, I might have been offended, and as it was, I had to hold back a snort. "Mr. ar'Contir told me to expect you."

I refused to betray even a flicker of discomfort at the mention of the mage who had come so perilously close to revealing my secret.

"My name is Clostina ar'Mees, by the way," she continued as she pulled the guest book out of a drawer—the heavy red leather book's front was embossed with the Watawis state emblem in gold. She opened it to the most recent cream-colored page and placed a manicured fingernail to indicate where I should print, sign, and date before handing me a pen. "I was fascinated by your story when Mr. ar'Contir told us about you. Did you really choose to live amongst humans for three whole years simply because of a bet?" Her pretty brown eyes, long-lashed and the color of a fawn's hide, widened with unabashed curiosity as she looked up at me from her seat.

"The mages around here are bigger gossips than the towns-folk I've been living with," I groused, picking up the heavy pen. It was glossy red, like the guest book, with tiny etchings of leaves carved into the otherwise smooth surface.

Clostina's cheeks pinkened slightly, but she did not back down. "I take that as a yes, then," she said, leaning in and lowering her voice a bit. "Was it very difficult? Are you going to keep living there, now that you have lost your bet and are known as a mage?"

I decided to handle her impertinent questions the way my grandmother would have—by looking down my straight nose at her and giving her a withering stare. "I will depart on my own schedule," I said coldly. "Perhaps in a month, if I am so inclined. Perhaps longer."

The receptionist finally lowered her gaze, but I had a feeling she would not be quelled for long. As I signed the guest book, careful to disguise my handwriting, she produced a heavy, elegant envelope and handed it to me. I recoiled at the sight of the Chief Mage's personal seal stamped on the back and forced my hand not to tremble as I took it.

Fenris moved closer as I opened it, brushing up against my legs. *"What does it say?"*

I stared down at the meticulous handwriting on the glossy card. *"It's an invitation from the Chief Mage and his wife to attend a reception here at the Residence,"* I told him, stifling a groan of frustration. *"In three weeks' time."*

"Damn," Fenris said, dismay evident in his tone. *"It would have been wiser to announce that you planned to depart immediately."*

"And just how was I supposed to know this was going to happen?" I snapped.

"I didn't mean—"

"Is everything all right?" Clostina interrupted our silent conversation.

I lifted my gaze, suddenly aware I'd been glaring down at Fenris. "My new pet is still in the middle of training and has not yet learned the meaning of personal space," I said smoothly,

nudging Fenris away with my leg a little sharper than necessary.

"Oh. I thought perhaps it was the invitation that had upset you." Clostina's eyes sparkled, her words practically bubbling from her lips. "The Chief Mage is my grandfather, and he was telling me over dinner yesterday how interested he was in meeting you. It seems he has heard of the Harmon family—from the northeast, aren't they? I can tell by your accent. He thinks he met your cousin, or was it your nephew?"

My stomach dropped straight into the soles of my shoes.

"You're welcome to bring an escort," she continued, oblivious to the panic squeezing around my throat, "although I'm not certain if there is anyone suitable in your tiny human town."

"I daresay I can manage to rustle up someone," I said haughtily, closing the guestbook with a snap. "Good day to you, Miss ar'Mees."

I swept from the building with the letter clutched tightly in my fist, ignoring Clostina as she gaped after me, no doubt wondering what she'd done to offend me. Fenris trotted down the steps beside me, a silent, watchful presence, and we strode down the garden path and to the street, toward the row of steam cabs waiting for fares.

"I would strongly advise you to reject the invitation," Fenris said once we were settled into the back seat of the first cab and driving away. My heartbeat, which had been thundering in my ears, slowed with each rotation of the wheels, each foot of distance that was put between me and that cursed manor.

"And just how am I supposed to do that," I asked bitterly, *"without insulting the Chief Mage? I may not be as well-versed in mage protocol as I should be, but I do know that invitations like this are practically commands."*

"A refusal may indeed ruffle some feathers," Fenris said, unperturbed at my own ruffled feathers, *"but it is better than ruining*

*your disguise. Attending a gathering with so many mages is too
dangerous. They delight in comparing genealogies, finding out your
political views, and seeing if you have acquaintances in common. Not
to mention the degree of magical expertise they would expect from a
three-hundred-year-old mage."*

I gritted my teeth, a string of curses running through my
head, each one more profane than the last. Fenris was right. It
was one thing to fool a single inspector, or a naïve young mage,
like I had today. It was quite another to try to pass myself off as
an experienced mage to a crowd full of them. Besides, I had
never attended such a formal event in my life. I might slip up
over some stupid detail everyone else expected me to know.

The cab dropped us off on Main Street, and I ducked into
another alley to change back to my normal self. Fenris took the
opportunity to shift back to his human form, and we spent the
next several hours shopping. At first, it was hard to shake the
worries plaguing my mind, but Fenris distracted me with adventures from his past—he had traveled extensively when he was
young and had experienced many different cultures and
customs. The way his eyes sparkled as he regaled me with tales
of exotic dancers and acrobats, of strange foods, sprawling
vistas, and architectural marvels, had me wondering why he had
chosen to settle in a small, provincial town like Abbsville when
he could have gone anywhere.

But I was loath to break the easy flow of conversation by
reminding him of some painful secret, to watch those eyes
shutter and that smile dim. Fenris was more open, more relaxed,
than I'd ever seen him, and I found myself wanting to be
open too.

Except there wasn't anything all that interesting I could tell
him, I realized with dismay. His long life made it easy for him to
talk about his experiences without revealing his secrets, whereas
mine did not. Even so, encouraged by his evident interest in my

mundane experiences, I found myself telling him about various places I'd seen in my cross-country trek that eventually led me up to Watawis, and about the trials and tribulations of veterinary school.

"Oh," I said as we passed under the shingle of a bookshop. "I should pick up a new title for the book club while I'm here."

"That is an excellent idea," Fenris said, even though we were already laden with bags. Most of them were mine—his purchases were too big to carry, and we were going to pick them up from the supplier with our rented steamcar once we were ready to leave.

The bell tinkled as he pushed the door open and held it for me. The comforting smell of paper and ink enveloped me, and Fenris sucked in a deep breath next to me, as if he was enjoying the bookshop's scent as much as I was.

We spent a good half hour perusing the rows of shelves, and I ended up selecting a collection of memoirs from the time the western part of the Federation had been settled. *This would make for an interesting discussion*, I thought as I made my way up to the register.

Fenris joined me at the counter, and I was surprised to see he'd picked two books—an old classic novel and a history tome. He also bought a farmer's almanac and several magazines and newspapers covering a variety of subjects. Setting them before the clerk, he plucked my own book from my hands and paid for them all.

"It saves time," he said, ignoring my protests.

I gave up, taking the book back from him the moment we were done. "You certainly seem to read widely," I commented as we walked toward the car rental company.

Fenris shrugged. "I like to educate myself. Is that so strange?"

"It is in Abbsville," I said. "Roor and his ilk view reading as a

'feminine pastime.' I doubt they've opened a book since the day they left the schoolroom."

But Fenris wasn't from Abbsville, and neither was I. There were many learned men in the world, and from what I could observe, Fenris was one of them. I wondered if his natural super speed and strength as a shifter freed him of the need to appear "manly," or if perhaps he was simply too mature to bother worrying about that sort of thing.

I had known from the moment I met him that he was going to be the most eccentric man in Abbsville. But I didn't know that he was going to be so *intriguing.*

Fenris snorted. "I think I've made it very clear," he said mildly, "about what I think of Roor's opinions."

Definitely intriguing.

I winked at him. "You're far more of a man than he ever will be anyway," I said, flouncing ahead before he could respond. And though I didn't look back, I could have sworn he was grinning behind me.

MINA

In the weeks following our return home, Fenris and I settled into an easy rhythm. We continued our lessons every other day in the late afternoons, mostly focusing on spells that would help me heal animals, or make my life easier by saving time and effort, like a deep-cleaning spell for the household that I wished I had known years ago.

We discussed what magic should and should not be used for, and how it set mages apart from the general population, over tea and biscuits. I also made lemonade on warmer days, now that spring was nearly over and summer just around the corner.

These pleasant, informal sessions were quite unlike a regular mage apprenticeship, which would follow an established curriculum. Some of the spells he taught me were third- or fourth-year spells, but they did not strike me as that much harder. The main trick was to correctly remember and pronounce the Loranian words and visualize the desired effect as clearly as possible.

"I'm glad you already know Loranian," Fenris told me one day. "Your pronunciation is very good. If you had to start

learning it as an adult, it would be a real pain. All those declensions and tenses..."

"It must be almost impossible," I agreed. "Luckily, children pick up even the hardest languages with enough exposure. My parents would speak Loranian with me for at least an hour every day, and my grandmother sent me to a special tutor the year before her death in preparation for my apprenticeship." If I had to think about grammar at the same time as I memorized a new spell, it would have been a highly frustrating experience.

Although these new techniques were just a tiny part of a trained mage's repertoire, with each spell I mastered I found myself more confident in my identity as a mage and eager to grasp all the other intriguing abilities that still eluded me.

I had not realized, until now, just how removed I was from my own magic. For fear of discovery, I'd tried to use it as little as possible these past few years, mainly when medical means were not enough to save an animal and in situations where I felt safe enough to get away with it. But under Fenris's patient tutelage, I was learning to use my magic on purpose, to shape it to my will and make it do things not out of desperation, but because I *wanted* to. Magic could be fun, a concept I had all but forgotten over the years of my exile. Or was it that Fenris was such an excellent teacher?

At first, we'd kept the lessons to my house. But my quarters were cramped, and the cat did not care for the spells, so we eventually moved the lessons to Fenris's farm, where the wide-open spaces meant I could practice freely without worrying about damaging furniture or hurting any animals.

On a particularly sunny morning, I woke up with a bounce in my step...and a surprisingly clear calendar. I only had two patients to see, both routine check-ups, both quickly done in the morning. Such a lovely day should not be wasted lounging around at home. I saddled up my mare, and cantered over to

Fenris's farm. I saw no reason why we couldn't get in a little extra practice time if he was available.

I heard a horse snorting just as I was dismounting from my own mare in front of the house and frowned. After tying her up at the post, I went around the back of the house to see that the stallion and gelding were grazing in the backyard, untethered, their tails swishing lazily as their coats gleamed in the sun. Further off to the left, I could hear a rake scraping through hay and wood shavings.

The sound stopped, and Fenris walked out from the stalls, wiping sweat from his brow. "Mina," he said, blinking in surprise, and I blinked right back. He was completely shirtless, bits of hay clinging to his muscled stomach and broad chest. My mouth went dry at the sight of his tanned skin gleaming with sweat, and my fingers twitched as I wondered how it might feel to touch those bulging muscles.

His nostrils flared, eyes going dark, and my cheeks colored as I realized he might very likely be scenting my arousal. "S-sorry," I said, taking a step back. "I had a bit of spare time, and I thought maybe we could put in some extra time on magic lessons."

Fenris smiled, his face clearing. "Normally I would be happy to, but I'm afraid I've been neglecting the horses." He strolled over to where they were grazing and patted the stallion on his flank. I swallowed as I watched his back muscles ripple with the motion. "This one in particular needs to be exercised."

"I wouldn't mind helping you with that," I said, approaching the animals. The gelding lifted his head to look at me, and I stroked his velvety muzzle. "It's a lovely day for riding."

Fenris agreed, and we saddled up, leaving my own horse to graze in the orchard. "I guess I should put in a proper paddock, but for the time being, I have spelled a perimeter that makes the horses reluctant to go far from the stables by themselves," he

explained. "I would not want them to try and run back to their former home or get into the forest and meet a bear."

"Oh." It hadn't occurred to me that he could do that. "I suppose there are very few things that one can't do with magic, are there?"

Fenris shrugged. "I don't believe they've come up with a spell to bring the dead back to life, beyond necromancy." There was the briefest flicker of distaste on his face, and from my time spent with him, I knew that was the equivalent of a full-body shudder for anyone else. "And I haven't yet found a spell for eternal life, either. But yes, there are boundless possibilities for what can be done with magic, just by combining and refining what is already known. It is somewhat risky to try out new or less well-studied techniques, and most mages prefer not to try. You need the required amount of power, and have to be willing to pay the cost."

I raised an eyebrow at that. "The cost? Do you mean sacrifices?"

"Not precisely, though there are groups of magic users across Recca who do make sacrifice a part of many of their magical rituals." The look in Fenris's eyes grew distant as we trotted up the road—we would have to pass through the town to get to the hills that I had in mind. "For most spells, there is no cost beyond the drain of your own resources, but there are some that demand more. You are already familiar with the cost of healing magic, for example—taking in the pain and suffering of the victim in order to alleviate the wounds."

I nodded, wondering at the pensive expression on his face. "I gather that you have made some sacrifices?" I probed.

He was silent. "Yes," he finally said, so quiet his voice might have been the breeze itself, playing with the curling hairs that lay against the nape of my neck. "I sacrificed the man I used to be, most of my power, the love of my family, and the respect of

my peers. Sometimes, I wonder if it was truly the right thing to do."

The sadness in his voice filled me with compassion. "I'm sorry," I said, guiding my horse close enough to him so I could reach out and touch his hand. "That must have been hard."

Fenris curled his hand around mine briefly, then let go. "It was. But it is done, and life goes on."

We fell silent as we reached the town, unwilling to discuss magic where sharp ears might be listening. As we trotted through the streets, quite a few people turned to stare.

"Oh, is that a sapphire on her hand?" one woman cooed, and I blushed. "A present from her new suitor?"

"Figures it would take an exotic fellow like a shifter to catch Mina's eye," her companion said. "She's spurned even my son's advances, and he's quite a catch!"

I held in a snort at that—her son *was* good-looking, but like Roor, he did not have very much in the brains department. Thankfully, he wasn't a brute, and had left me alone when I'd made myself clear.

Fenris, who likely heard even more than I did with his sharp shifter ears, looked startled. "I have no idea why they are reading so much into our friendship," he said, lowering his voice and leaning in a little. A trio of young women twittered excitedly at that, and I held in a grin—Fenris was only reinforcing the impression, making us look like two lovers exchanging some delicious secret. "Surely nobody would think that we are romantically involved, not when you are so young and pretty, and considered human."

I shrugged, trying not to take the discomfort in his gaze personally. "Perhaps," I said lightly as we headed out of the town and onto the winding road that led to the trail. "But Roor's instant jealousy implies he considers you to be competition, and if he does, that means the other townsfolk do as well."

Fenris frowned. "Well, I am not his competition." He tightened the grip on his reins almost imperceptibly.

I flinched at the harsh tone, at the wall he'd suddenly slammed up between us. "Am I so repulsive," I said quietly, "that the mere notion of a romance with me is enough to make you recoil?"

Fenris started. "There is nothing about you that repulses me," he said, sounding instantly apologetic.

"And neither is there anything about *you* that repulses me," I said, suddenly struck by the notion that this might well be the reason Fenris was so keen to keep his distance. "I am not as young as I look, no matter what people might say, and..." My throat closed, and I forced the anxiety back. "I would not be averse to exploring something more than friendship with you." I blushed, but I wasn't sorry I had finally voiced my desires. The thought of something more between us had teased me for days, no, weeks. I had to know whether he felt the same.

Utter stillness filled the air around us. For a moment, I wasn't sure Fenris was even breathing. He'd turned in the saddle to face me, and that look in his dark eyes...it was as if he were seeing me for the first time. Gooseflesh rippled across my arms as he trailed his gaze up and down my body, and the unmistakable flash of hunger in his eyes had my core tightening with desire. Whatever he might say or pretend, he wanted me just as much as I wanted him.

"No." He ripped his gaze from me, turning it back to the road. "If you desire sexual release, it would be far safer to take a human lover than get yourself entangled with me."

I scowled. "I did not say I only wanted to take you to my bed," I snapped, urging the gelding forward as Fenris's stallion picked up the pace. "You aren't just some casual entertainment to me, no matter what the townsfolk might think. I like you for

who you are, not because you are a shifter, or a mage, or...or...
whatever you are!"

Fenris only shook his head. "It is dangerous to play with feelings," he said flatly. "Either mine or yours. And there is no point
in indulging in a dalliance, or anything more meaningful. I am
not a suitable partner for anyone, regardless of race. Why do you
think I came out here in the first place?"

A wave of sympathy swept through me at the note of anguish
in his voice, so faint I would not have detected it if I hadn't spent
so much time with him. But it wasn't enough to eclipse the
burning anger in my heart. "I don't know what happened to you,
Fenris, but you cannot simply live your days out here like a
hermit, cut off from the world. Everybody needs love, compan-
ionship. Family."

"Yes," he said quietly, "and you will find those things once
you reach your majority and resume your rightful place in society. You will find the man of your dreams, the man you deserve,
and then you shall forget all about me."

My throat burned with the desire to scold him for daring to
put himself down like that. I had never heard Fenris speak so
disparagingly of himself—he always exuded such quiet confidence, full of grace and strength. Today was the first time I'd
seen the crack in his armor, and it unsettled me deeply.

But I knew if I pushed him on this, it would only drive him
further away.

Time for a change of tack. "As you like," I said lightly, lifting
my chin. "It's your loss. By the way, I have decided to attend the
Chief Mage's party after all, and sent my acceptance. If I get into
trouble, I will simply pretend I am hard of hearing and play up
my role as an eccentric old lady." Sweat broke out along my
spine at the very thought, and I yanked back on the emotion,
hard, before Fenris could scent my nerves. It would just be for
an hour or two, and if I could pull it off, I would be safe until I

came of age. It would mean I could stay here in Abbsville in the meantime.

An alarmed look flashed across Fenris's face. "Please reconsider, Mina," he implored, all traces of our previous argument wiped from his gaze, leaving only frank concern. "You do not have the knowledge to pass yourself off as a mage in such a setting, where the others will be watching you like a hawk since you are a newcomer. I cannot possibly help you," he said as I opened my mouth to ask him to do just that, "as it would be suicide for me to mingle with the Chief Mage and his entourage. I chose my rural retreat precisely because it is so far away from mage society."

Disappointment filled me at his outright refusal, but I really had no right to expect him to risk himself further for my tangled affairs.

"Fine," I said, pointedly turning my gaze from him. "I shall do well enough on my own, whatever you may think of my acting skills. I would appreciate if you helped me practice for the role, but I quite understand if you don't have the time for that either."

With that parting shot, I turned the horse around and rode back to town, urging the gelding into a gallop. As I clung to the horse, I channeled my annoyance into the powerful hooves thundering beneath me, the wind whipping my hair from its ponytail so it flew around my face like a wild banner. It was only when I was nearly back to town, slowing the horse down again, that I realized I was on Fenris's horse, not my own.

Well, he can come back to my house if he wants to retrieve him, I told myself, trying not to feel too silly. But embarrassment heated my cheeks all the same. Fenris must think me a flighty, immature girl, too hotheaded to respond rationally instead of with catty words.

No wonder he's not interested in you.

Not ready to go back home, I went to the general store to visit with Barrla. To my relief, she was completely alone, sitting behind the counter reading one of her shifter romances.

"Mina!" Barrla hopped off the seat. "It's been an age since you last visited. How was your trip to the capital?"

Casting my argument with Fenris from my mind, I leaned my hip against the counter and told her an embellished version of my trip, emphasizing the bookshop and omitting the visit to the Mages Guild. "I'm afraid I'm going to have to miss the next book club meeting, as I'll be quite busy this week."

Barrla raised an eyebrow. "I can only imagine," she said, crossing her arms beneath her ample chest. "You've been entertaining Mr. Shelton quite a lot." She didn't sound entirely pleased.

I sat up straight at the tone in her voice. "We're just friends, Barrla."

She snorted. "Friends don't look at each other the way he looks at you," she said. "I suppose I can't be angry he's turned his gaze your way, but I thought you would at least have the decency to tell me that the two of you are seeing each other since you knew how interested I was." She pouted.

I winced, feeling incredibly guilty. "I'm sorry. I didn't think to tell you, because there isn't much to tell. Fenris and I really haven't done anything more than talk—he likes to discuss literature, and we get along quite well, so he comes around a lot. We really are just friends."

Barrla laughed. "Friends? I wasn't aware that men gave presents like that to women who are 'only friends.'" She gazed pointedly at the ring on my finger.

"I did get the ring from him, but it's not what it looks like," I admitted, my cheeks flushing. I knew Barrla would spread news of this to all corners of the world if she could, and that any hope

Fenris had of convincing the townsfolk that our relationship was platonic would be crushed.

Let him deal with the fallout, the part of me that still smarted at his rejection sneered. *It would serve him right for trying to decide what kind of men you should and shouldn't be looking at.*

"So there," Barrla declared, looking triumphant. "That settles it. He's your new beau. And I will forgive you for stealing him out from under my nose, if you tell me what you two are *really* doing when he comes over." She waggled her eyebrows at me.

I had to laugh at that. "I do like him," I admitted, my lips still twitching, "but he is a gentleman to the core, and has not taken any liberties so far." That sense of honor he clung to would not permit him to act on the desire I'd seen in his eyes. And as I remembered the charged look he'd given me earlier in the day, and the heated glances he'd given me over the past few weeks when he thought I hadn't been looking, something in me relaxed. Maybe Fenris didn't think we should be together, but there was no doubt in my mind that he did want me.

"Well then, you'll just have to take matters into your own hands," Barrla decided, putting her hands on her curvy hips. "Seducing him won't be hard, Mina—with the way he looks at you, I'm surprised he hasn't taken you to bed already."

I sighed. "I've broached the subject, and he seems determined to resist. But I'll think about it." I wasn't about to make another move on Fenris, especially not so soon. I'd already declared my feelings—the rest was up to him.

I bid Barrla farewell with the promise to have tea later in the week. And as I rode the gelding back to my house, I wondered if Fenris was going to come and pick him up, and if so, how I could face him again after that humiliating scene.

MINA

I spent the rest of the week religiously practicing my role every chance I got—which was less often than I'd hoped due to a highly contagious cough that had spread amongst the cattle at various farms. I'd been called out to deal with the infection several times. Fenris had not come to my house again, except to collect the gelding, and that he had done while I was out, leaving only a note behind as evidence he'd been there. My heart ached at the abrupt severance of our friendship, but I did my best not to think about him too much.

He was not obligated to help me, and I certainly could not force him to act on the attraction between us. If he did not think helping me was worth the risk...then he was not worth pining over.

As I waited at the bus station for the steambus to arrive, I kept glancing over my shoulder, in the absurd hope he would change his mind and show up at the last moment. It was only when I'd finally settled into my seat, the town of Abbsville disappearing behind us, that I accepted he really, truly wasn't going to come help me.

How had I come to depend on Fenris so quickly, in just a few

weeks, when I had lived alone quite well for all those years? Cross with myself, I folded my arms and scowled at the passing scenery. It had been a mistake to let myself get so attached, and at the rate things were going, I'd better get used to depending solely on myself again.

With no one to keep me company but my gloomy thoughts, I spent the three-hour ride working myself into a nervous wreck as I contemplated everything that could go wrong. *Why in Recca had I thought this was a good idea?* I wondered as the steambus hurtled past towns and villages that grew progressively larger and more advanced the closer we got to our destination. After all these years hiding out as a human, I had nearly forgotten what it was to be a mage. These past weeks of training myself to act like one had challenged me to the limits. Under the scrutiny of real mages, I might very well crack. Any small detail could expose my lies, my inexperience.

A vision of my cousin Vanley cornering me in the hall late at night, leering at me with his cruelly handsome features, sent my gut roiling with nausea. My skin went clammy as I recalled what came before my escape—months of lewd comments and threats when nobody else could hear, unwanted touches in sensitive places whenever he caught me alone, even bruises on my arm from his violent grip. Worst of all was the feeling of helplessness. *That* was why I had to do this, no matter the risk.

I would never subject myself to those horrors again. Never submit to those callous relatives who did not care about me and brushed off my complaints about their darling son. Relatives who only saw me as a welcome source of money, instead of a person with needs and feelings.

Descending into fresh air at the Willowdale terminal, free of the sweat and bodily odors of the other passengers, went a long way toward clearing my head and diluting the anxiety that was crawling beneath my skin. I hailed a cab and directed the driver

to take me to the hotel I'd booked just a few blocks from the manor. It was far too opulent for someone of my income level, as was the classically cut purple robe that waited in a white box on my bed. I'd nearly cleaned out my savings to purchase both. But a mage of my pretended status could not be seen staying at a hostel, and I knew enough about the sort of clothes expected at a formal function that I could not show up in anything currently hanging in my closet.

With hours left until the party, I ordered room service—another luxury I could ill afford —and tried to subdue my worries by indulging in a delicious salmon fillet and a slice of cheesecake. But though I did my best to savor each bite of the rich food, it was not enough to fill the time. I showered and donned the robe, but since I was using the ring's illusion to disguise myself as the old lady, there was not much else to do to get ready aside from fixing a set of earrings into my lobes and sticking some faux jeweled pins in my upswept gray hair.

Eventually, the time came to leave, and I called down to the front desk and asked them to call a car for me. I could easily have walked over, but that would not do—I needed to arrive in style. As I paced back and forth, wearing a hole into the carpet with my fancy shoes, a knock came at the door, startling me out of my wits.

"Coming," I called, hurrying to the door. I hadn't expected the driver to come up and collect me, but maybe—

"Good evening." A stunningly handsome man with thick, wavy blond hair, who was dressed in neatly pressed apprentice robes, stood at my door. He bowed, a devilish smile on his full lips. "Are you ready to depart, Mistress?"

I stared at him. "Mistress?" I asked, just barely remembering to use my haughty tone. "And just who do you think you are, young man?"

The stranger was not easy to intimidate—his grin broadened

as I looked down my nose at him, and he took my pale hands in his large ones and kissed them with an elegant bow. "Fennias ar'Lutis...and your date," he said, his voice a melodious baritone that slid down my spine like a sensual caress. Heat bloomed on my cheeks as his thumbs brushed the backs of my hands, lingering longer than necessary, and as he looked up, his form flickered, revealing—

"Fenris!" I gasped.

"Shhh." Grasping me by the shoulders, he pushed me into the room before anybody could come down the hall and see us. My heart thundered as he closed the door behind us, and we were suddenly alone together for the first time in nearly a week. "A lady of your distinction should not attend a party without escort," he murmured, cupping my face with both hands. A magical tingle rushed across my skin, telling me he'd stripped my illusion away, and I suddenly found myself short of breath. "And since you have let it be known that you have a taste for younger men, who would be more fitting at your side than an apprentice?"

A surprised laugh escaped me, forcing past the questions scalding my tongue. "I thought you weren't coming, that it was too much of a risk—"

He pressed his finger against my lips to silence me. "Never mind the risk," he said quietly. "I was being foolish. Since then, I have had a long time to regret my hasty refusal when you so bravely indicated what you wanted. I may not be worthy of you, but if it is me that you want, Mina, I would be an idiot not to take full advantage before you come to your senses."

He silenced my next laugh with a kiss, fierce and full of joy. The dam of fear and anxiety in my chest burst, and a floodgate of exhilaration burst through me, making me giddy and light-headed as I wrapped my arms around his muscular neck and kissed him back. His broad hands slid around my waist, pressing

me close until I could feel his heart galloping beneath his strong chest, just as mine was doing.

This was real, I told myself as he finally pulled back to stare into my eyes. But even as my gaze roamed over his flushed cheeks and dark eyes, which had gone molten with desire, disbelief filled me.

"If you truly felt this way," I breathed, brushing the back of my hand along the scruff covering his jaw, "then why wait until now to tell me? Why didn't you come to me after our fight? I missed you, Fenris."

"Because," he said, leaning in to nip at my lower lip, "I can think of little else more romantic than gallantly charging in at the last moment to save my lady from disaster."

I snorted at that, shoving him away. "I hardly need saving," I said, rubbing the stone on my finger to reactivate the illusion. "But even so, I will gladly accept your assistance for the evening."

Fenris's eyes twinkled in amusement as he changed back into the handsome apprentice. "Then allow me to escort you to your carriage, my lady."

I took his arm, and he led me down to the foyer, where I could see a gleaming black steamcar waiting outside through the sparkling glass doors. Despite my old lady guise, I felt like a princess going to a ball, especially when the uniformed driver opened the door and Fenris helped me into the vehicle.

"Is 'Fennias' a real person, or did you make him up?" I asked as we sped off around the corner.

"He did exist—a young mage, long dead, from a distinguished family in the central continent. You can say I am a sixth-year apprentice, if anyone asks. And if the worst should happen, you can simply tell them the truth, which a truth wand can verify—you never knew my real identity."

A shiver crawled down my spine at the way he so casually

spoke about the disaster we flirted with. The central continent was an ocean away—there was little to no chance of the Chief Mage knowing the family of the mage Fenris was impersonating. But still... *"You really didn't have to do this."*

"Yes, I did," Fenris said simply, squeezing my hand.

I had to fight to keep the blush out of my cheeks.

By the time we pulled up in front of the manor, I'd regained my haughty composure. A red carpet had been rolled out across the garden path, leading straight to the front doors that had been thrown wide open. Music and light spilled out from the open doors and through the window panes, and as Fenris and I passed through the entrance, I could hear tinkling laughter and the buzz of conversation.

A guard dressed in fine livery greeted us with a bow, then escorted us to the ballroom down the hall. My anxiety rose as I beheld the room full of people—among over a hundred persons, there had to be at least eighty mages, maybe even more, decked out in colorful robes and jewels as they swirled about the dance floor or stood in groups, talking and drinking champagne. I grabbed my fear by the throat and shoved it down as a tall, regal-looking mage dressed in deep red robes stepped forward, a stunningly beautiful woman on his arm.

"Zander ar'Mees, the Chief Mage, and his wife, Marilla," Fenris said in my head.

"Good evening, Lord Zander," I said, bowing. "Thank you for your kind invitation. I am Tuala Harmon, currently residing in Abbsville."

"It's a pleasure to have you," Lord Zander said smoothly, his dark blue eyes bright with curiosity. He had a narrow but handsome face framed by a mane of silver-streaked black hair. "This is my wife, Marilla," he said, and I bowed to her as well.

"Zander says he has met your family," Marilla purred,

"during his travels on the East Coast about a century ago. But you were not amongst them when he visited."

"I have lived all over the Federation," I said coolly, turning my attention to the Chief Mage again. "But I am pleased we have had occasion to finally meet."

"And who is your handsome friend?" Clostina, resplendent in pink and gold, gushed as she glided up alongside her grandparents. Those doe-colored eyes gleamed with frank interest as she sized up Fenris, who had been standing patiently by my side the entire time.

"Oh, how rude of me." I turned to Fenris. "This is my apprentice, Fennias ar'Lutis. He is rather accomplished for his age, and already in his sixth year."

"A pleasure to meet you," Fenris said in that melodious baritone, bowing to the ladies. He kissed both Marilla and Clostina's hands, and the latter blushed, even though, as a full mage, she was higher ranked than him.

The Chief Mage and his family made polite conversation with us for a few minutes, then went to greet the next guest. It was a relief to see them go, especially since Clostina spent the entire time flirting madly with Fenris. But just as soon as we moved into the crowd to find refreshments, another mage couple came up to us, wanting introductions and peppering me with questions about my famous bet to try to pass for human. With whom had I made it, and why? For how much? Where had I come from? What had I done before I moved here? Did I have a family waiting back home? And how did I manage to continue Fennias's apprenticeship this entire time?

I'd prepared for all of these questions except the last one, but Fenris managed to coach me into giving a plausible response involving correspondence and occasional meetings. As the hours dragged on, I grew increasingly grateful for his presence, especially when the conversation turned to mage politics and

high-society gossip. I knew nothing about any of these subjects, but mysteriously, Fenris did, and he helped me navigate the treacherous waters so well I impressed the others with my knowledge and insights. Was there anything he *didn't* know?

"You are doing splendidly," Fenris assured me as we sat in one of the side rooms off the ballroom, drinking from glasses of sparkling wine. He had magically removed the alcohol from mine. We'd determined it would be best if I didn't allow myself to become inebriated under these circumstances. Around us, sitting on various stuffed couches and chaises, older ladies were taking a break from the festivities to play cribbage and other card games. They'd invited me to join, but I didn't have patience for those games, and I merely perched on a chaise and told them I'd prefer to watch.

Eventually, we were called back into the ballroom for an elaborate five-course dinner. The Chief Mage had placed me at his table, and had an extra chair brought for my "apprentice," whom they had not been expecting. I endured another hour of talk about politics as we dined. Fenris seemed particularly interested when talk of the Resistance came up.

"Happily, the Resistance seems to be on the retreat ever since the Benefactor was unmasked and caught last year," Fenris said. "Have you been experiencing trouble with the rebels here in Watawis?"

"None," the Chief Mage said easily, cutting off another bite of his steak. "Watawis is quite secure in its loyalty to the Federation. We did recently catch a jeweler who was producing counterfeit coin, after the Chief Mage of Canalo sent out a general warning to be on the lookout. It turned out the fellow acted from greed and had no political motive at all. He'll be punished anyway, of course—we must set an example."

"Of course," Fenris said smoothly, but there was a flash of something in his eyes, gone almost too quickly for me to notice.

He seemed more interested in gossip about the Resistance than anything else we'd discussed tonight, and I wondered again if he had any involvement with the rebels. He knew a lot about mages...but he had also taken great pains to stay as far away from them as possible.

Which is completely understandable, given they would likely strip him of his powers if they found out about his true nature.

Right. I cast the thought out of my head. Of course Fenris wasn't a rebel. He was simply doing what he had to do to survive.

After the meal was over, the Chief Mage invited other mages onto a small stage to demonstrate their latest techniques. A reed-thin woman with brilliant gold hair sashayed onto the stage and spun an enchanting vision of ballerinas dancing, crafted of red, blue, and gold flames. It was not the flames that were stunning, or the fact they did not burn the stage, but rather how carefully crafted they were, spun into such lifelike renderings that the lacy tulle of the gowns, the gleaming skeins of hair, the curve of calves and cheeks, seemed amazingly real. But the heat emanating from the stage...if I tried to dance with them, I would surely roast.

Another mage turned a simple jade necklace into a legendary bird with teal and gold feathers, whose every movement charged the air and crackled with lightning. The next, with seemingly little effort, changed the entire ballroom's ceiling into a starry night sky and made us feel as if we were all floating in the middle of space, far beyond Recca's atmosphere. As more mages paraded up to the stage to show off their accomplishments, my stomach sank lower and lower. The feats were spectacular, but they only drove home how little I knew of magic. Less than the rawest apprentice, I realized, as even a few of them came up to the stage to show off.

Finally, the Chief Mage turned to me. "Miss Harmon, would you like to show the room what you can do?"

Panic tried to grip me again, but I gave the Chief Mage a lazy smile. "I am far too old for such games," I said, waving an indulgent hand toward Fenris, "but my apprentice would be more than happy to demonstrate something he recently learned."

"It would be my pleasure," Fenris said. He inclined his head with a wink at me, but instead of pushing back his chair and heading up to the stage, he simply picked up an empty wine bottle from the table and held it in his palm, turning it slowly between deft fingers. Tendrils of hazy magic began to rise from his skin as he worked whatever spell he'd thought of, and I heard Clostina gasp from the other end of the table as the green glass gradually began to change shape, forming into a ball. The magical mist swirled around it, hiding it from view, and when it parted...

"Beautiful," the Chief Mage murmured as Fenris handed his creation over to him.

It was a glass globe of Recca, the size of a grapefruit, but crafted to scale, right down to the last detail. I leaned in slightly, forcing an expression of boredom on my face as I watched the clouds drifting across the surface, passing over the various continents, green and brown and white where the ice was. The oceans rippled between the land masses, lazily following the major currents I knew were accurate from my childhood geography lessons.

"This is very advanced for a sixth-year apprentice," the Chief Mage's wife said, looking thoroughly impressed. "You must train him very hard."

"He is a gifted student, but yes, I am quite a taskmaster." I allowed a small smile to flit across my lips as I sat back in my chair.

The rest of the demonstrations went by quickly after that,

and the tables were cleared away so the dancing could begin again. As Fenris and I made to move away, the Chief Mage's wife said, "There is one thing I meant to ask you about."

Slowly, I turned around. "And what is that?"

Her gaze narrowed on Fenris. "Why is it that your apprentice wears a disguise? Is his real face not handsome enough?"

Fear tightened my gut, but Fenris smoothly stepped in. "I change appearances quite frequently—it is the whim of my mistress," he declared grandly, a broad smile on his face. Before everyone's eyes, he quickly began shifting through a variety of forms, each one more handsome than the last. The crowd gasped—several of them were even shifters—and the Chief Mage and his family watched, their gazes wide with shock. "It is also excellent practice," he said, reverting to his original disguise with a flourish.

As one, everybody turned speculating gazes to me. There were scandalized looks on many of their faces, especially the women, and Clostina's mouth stood open. It was obvious they were wondering just what other "preferences" my young apprentice catered to...so I decided to go for broke.

"At my age," I drawled, laying a frail arm over Fenris's broad shoulders, "surely I have the right to surround myself with pretty objects to look upon. It makes the training so much more enjoyable."

They all looked at Fenris, whose smile only widened. "I am always happy to fulfill any order from my mistress."

The Chief Mage, realizing the sensation this was causing, ordered the music to resume. Everyone else took that as a cue to stop gawking, and the dance floor began to fill once more. But as Fenris and I took our leave, thanking our hosts once more, I had to hold in giggles at the expressions of those around us as we passed. Fenris's own face remained placid, as far as I could tell,

but I did not dare to look too closely—if I caught his eye, I might very well break down.

It was only when we finally got into the cab and were safely driving away that we began snickering like idiots. The driver glanced in his rearview mirror, no doubt thinking we were either inebriated or insane, but we completely ignored him.

"That was some performance," I said in mindspeak, my mental voice still rife with laughter.

Fenris chuckled. *"You're one to talk,"* he said, twining his fingers with mine. *"I've never had a woman treat me like a boy-toy before. It was quite an enlightening experience."*

I grinned. *"If you don't want to be a boy-toy, then perhaps you shouldn't dress up to look like eye candy."*

"I don't mind," he said, leaning in to press a kiss against my temple. *"So long as it's for you."*

FENRIS

Since I'd already reserved a steamcar for the evening, I directed the driver to drop us off at the rental company, then took the wheel for the long drive back to Abbsville. We made a very brief stop at the hotel to get Mina's belongings, then headed straight home—as much as I would have preferred to spend the night, I had not arranged for anyone to care for my horses, and I was loath to leave my farm unattended.

A few miles out of town, I changed us back to our natural shapes and hid Mina's purple robes with an illusion. They were too long for her real size but could probably be shortened. Not that she would have the right to wear them openly for many years yet.

Mina didn't notice the change. She had fallen sound asleep within minutes of our departure, her head tilted back in the seat as she snored softly. With the illusion no longer hiding her features, she looked adorable, her pretty features relaxed, her full lips slightly parted. More than once, I found myself reaching out to brush back a strand of the blonde hair tumbling down her shoulders or trace the curve of her soft cheek highlighted by the moonlight streaming in through the window.

But I did not want to wake her, so I contented myself with the memory of her lips against mine, how soft and sweet they had felt when I'd finally kissed her back at the hotel room. Her sweet lavender and sunshine scent that filled the car brought the scene to life in my mind's eye—the sensation of her soft curves pressed against me, the pounding of her heart beneath those shimmering purple robes, the sleepy desire in her eyes as I'd finally forced myself to pull back.

Negotiating a sharp bend, I pushed the seductive images out of my mind before I drove off the road. *That* would certainly kill any blossoming romance between us.

By the time we rolled into Abbsville, the entire town was asleep, with only one or two lights flickering in the windows of the houses we passed. I pulled up in front of Mina's house, then leaned in and pressed a kiss against her brow, as I'd been itching to do for the past three hours.

"Time to wake up, Mina," I murmured against her skin.

She responded with a sleepy moan, her lashes fluttering. "Home already?" she murmured, her breath warm against my face.

I nodded, then reached across to unbuckle her seatbelt. The cab was spacious enough that it took little effort to lift her from the seat, and I ignored her sleepy protests as I carried her inside. A simple spell had the door opening without having to touch it, and I used another spell to close and lock it behind us as I brought her to her room.

"Thank you..." she murmured, her eyelids still closed as I laid her down on the bed. "For...for everything..."

"You're more than welcome." I pulled her slippers off her feet, then gently tucked her beneath the covers.

"Please...stay..." Her hand lifted to brush against my face, and her eyelids opened to half-mast. Heavy with sleep...but also desire. I'd scented it on her more than once during these past

few weeks, and had chosen to ignore it, but the way she was lying in front of me now, warm and open and relaxed...it would be so easy to take her now. To strip that lovely robe off her willowy curves and worship her body, as my own was aching to do.

But I did not want our first time to be like this, with Mina half-delirious from exhaustion. I wanted her awake and alert, ready to experience our joining to the fullest. So I merely brushed a kiss against her soft, rosy lips and left before I could give in to the urges that called to me just as surely as the moon overhead.

THE NEXT MORNING, I rose with the sun, unwilling to waste any more hours in sleep. Thoughts of Mina, of what I had refused when I'd left her house the night before, plagued me both waking and in my dreams. Since she was not here, there was nothing I could do but get away from my fantasies and get on with the day.

But as I stood in my kitchen in my pajama pants, frying an omelet, my thoughts drifted to Mina once more. She was the kind of girl I should have married when I was younger, a respectable mage with a brilliant future ahead of me. But I had never met someone like her in those days, a mage full of kindness and grace but with a spine of steel beneath that gentle exterior.

Even if you had met someone like her, would you have been able to truly appreciate her? a voice in my head asked. I had been so wrapped up in my career, I likely would have thought her too unsophisticated, too innocent, to be a politician's wife.

What a fool Polar ar'Tollis had been.

But I was not Polar anymore. I was Fenris, and as Fenris...if

Mina invited me to her bed again, I would not refuse. In fact, I planned to coax her into mine at the first opportunity.

The sound of a horse trotting down my drive interrupted my daydreams. I shut off the stove and went to the window to see who it could be. My heart leapt in my chest—my very bare chest, I belatedly remembered—at the sight of Mina, looking entirely too fresh and lovely for someone who had stayed up as late as she did.

But then again, she had slept in the car. And what did I care? She was here, and that was all that mattered.

I turned toward my bedroom to put on a shirt as she dismounted from her horse...then thought better of it. I'd liked the way she'd looked at me when I'd come out from the stables that day, slick with sweat. Even with hay plastered on my chest, she'd looked ready to tackle me right then and there, the horses be damned. It had been very difficult to hide my reaction to her every time her desire was stirred—my predatory instincts had risen every time, eager to claim what her body was offering.

But I didn't just want her body. I wanted *all* of her—body, mind, and soul. And I knew in the back of my mind, even while hiding behind my own denial, that she had not been ready either.

"Good morning," I said as I opened the door, giving her a lazy smile. Her eyes went wide at the sight of me, that kissable mouth falling open, just the way I'd hoped. My smile widened, and I leaned against the doorjamb, crossing my arms over my chest. "Couldn't stay away, could you?"

Mina snorted a laugh, her eyes sparkling. "Your performance of the seductive rogue is not half-bad," she said teasingly, running her finger along my bare bicep. The sensation of her skin against mine ignited the hunger that had been simmering low in my chest, and a growl slipped from my throat. "But beneath all these muscles, you are the same gentleman who

gave me a chaste kiss and tucked me in rather than taking advantage of my invitation to ravish me."

"A mistake I shall not repeat," I said, grabbing her by the wrist and yanking her inside. The door had barely slammed shut before I pulled her into my arms and kissed her, greedily drinking in the scent of her, the feel of her tempting curves pressed up against my half-naked body. She was wearing a simple white dress, and the fabric was quite thin—a joke of a barrier between our heated flesh.

"Oh good," she breathed against my mouth. "I was wondering when you were finally going to get serious."

Laughing, I tangled my fingers in her silken hair, then slid my tongue between her lips to taste her fully. The moan she made reverberated through my entire body, and it responded, growing harder than I ever had in my life. It had been so long since I'd last had a woman, so long since I'd experienced the pleasures that could be had tumbling between the sheets...

But I would not take things too fast. Not when it had been even longer for Mina...and not when, as I suspected, she had little experience to begin with.

"I'm going to make you make that sound again..." I kissed her chin. "And again..." I licked a path along the edge of her jawline. "And again..." I bit down lightly on her earlobe, and she moaned again. "Until you've forgotten how to speak anything but my name on your lips."

Her knees gave out from beneath her, and I swept her up into my arms and carried her to the bedroom.

MINA

My heart pounded hard in my chest as Fenris laid me gently down atop his cloud-soft bedspread. His mouth was still fused to mine as he crawled atop the mattress with me, his beard scraping my cheeks in a way that sent tingles down my spine and into...other places. I was alive, burning with need, my core molten and throbbing.

And when his hands slid beneath my dress, pushing the fabric up, I was filled with breathless anticipation.

"No underwear?" he asked, and I might have blushed if his tone hadn't been of surprised pleasure.

"I've fallen behind on my laundry," I gasped as he glided his hands up my bare skin, bare skin that he revealed inch by excruciating inch. His broad palms and calloused fingers left trails of fire in their wake, and the insides of my thighs grew even damper, if that was possible.

Fenris only chuckled as he lifted the dress higher, pulling it over my head and tossing it to the side. He sucked in a sharp breath as he took in my fully naked body, and I held perfectly still as his yellow gaze, bright with lust, roamed over my bare skin. His hands skimmed down my ribs, then came up to cup my

breasts. Pleasure shot through me as he gently scraped his rough thumbs over my nipples, and I arched my back.

"More," I gasped.

Happy to oblige, he ducked his head and took one of my nipples into his mouth. I moaned as pleasure filled me, threading my hands in his thick, dark hair. One of his arms slid around my lower back, dragging me closer until I was sitting in his lap. I hooked my legs around him and clung tightly as he feasted on me, my mind spinning. I didn't remember things feeling this good with my last lover—my skin tingled, and my core was pulsing, aching for more.

"You are the most gorgeous creature I've ever seen," he said, lifting his head to look at me. And his yellow eyes blazed with such sincerity that my own began to burn with tears.

Wordlessly, I reached out to splay my palms against his chest. Crisp, dark hairs teased my hands as I explored the firm muscles, and when my fingers brushed over his nipples, he hissed. Emboldened, I let my hands trail lower, across the ridges of his muscled stomach, toward the hem of his pajamas, where I could see the evidence of his arousal straining.

He caught my wrist just before I could slip my hand beneath and shook his head. "Not yet," he said, leaning in to kiss me again. "Right now, this is all about you."

Those tears burned at my eyes again, and this time, one escaped. Fenris noticed, but he said nothing, just tenderly licked it away. The touch made me completely forget about everything else in the world, especially when he began to kiss a path down the center of my body. I squirmed when he dipped a tongue into my navel, swirling it around, then arched my hips when he slid his hands beneath them, using his shoulders to nudge my legs apart.

"Absolutely beautiful," he breathed as he lowered his head between my legs, staring at me with those molten eyes.

He licked my center, and my hips came straight off the bed. His answering chuckle vibrated through me, and I fisted my hands on the sheets as he teased me with that clever mouth of his. My core pulsed with each stroke of his tongue, spearing me with pleasure, until I was a writhing, panting mass of need.

"Please," I begged.

"Please what?" He licked me again, hitting my sweet spot, and I groaned.

"Yes, like that!" I fisted my hands in his hair, holding him fast, and he laughed again and did as I asked. And just like that, I came, a blinding wave of pleasure overtaking me as I cried his name.

FOR THE NEXT FEW HOURS, Fenris refused to let me out of bed. He pleasured me over and over again, bringing me to climax more times than I could count. I tried reaching for him more than once, but every time I did, he would only push me back and lower his head between my legs until I'd forgotten everything but the feel of his mouth and hands on my skin, and the blissful sensations he created.

He made love to me until I was limp with exhaustion, then coaxed me into a state of such relaxation that I fell asleep, curling into his strong arms as he spooned me from behind.

I fell into such a deep sleep that by the time I woke, shades of orange and vermillion were spilling in through the slats of the blinds. Sunset. Blinking, I pushed myself upright as alarm spiked through me. By the Lady, had I slept the day away? I racked my brain, frantic that I might have missed out on some patients...but no. I'd had no appointments scheduled for today.

As soon as I relaxed, I noticed Fenris was no longer curled up in the bed with me. Frowning, I wrapped the bedsheet

around me and quietly crept to the door. A moment of listening assured me that no guests were outside, or, if they were, they weren't speaking, so I ventured into the rest of the house.

I found Fenris sitting at the kitchen table, his thick, dark brown hair delightfully mussed from the hours I'd spent with my fingers in it. He still only wore his pajama pants, and I grinned a little at the sight of the score marks on his broad shoulders from my nails. But my smile faded as I saw his expression—his brows were drawn into a pensive frown, and in his hand...

"That's an awfully official-looking letter," I said quietly, coming up beside the table. The paper was thick, expensive-looking stock, and the stationary bore a complicated engraved design that looked faintly familiar.

"It's the reply from your family lawyer, regarding my interest in buying your grandmother's house." Fenris set the letter down on the table and looked up at me. "Would you like to read it?"

My chest began to tighten as anxiety banded around me, as it always did when I had to think back to my old life in Haralis. But I forced myself to take in a deep breath, to remind myself I wasn't alone anymore—Fenris was here with me now.

Even if the news was bad, I could get through this with him.

"Yes, I would." I took the chair across from him and picked up the letter.

In neat, flowing script, the lawyer informed Fenris's fictional buyer that the childhood home I'd grown up in, part of my inheritance, might be on the market within a matter of weeks. Horror filled me as he explained that the heiress it belonged to would shortly be declared legally dead. As soon as these proceedings were completed, he would consult the new owners about whether they would entertain offers. He would write again once he'd had a chance to talk to them.

"Dead?" I sputtered, utterly taken aback. My hands were

shaking so hard I was forced to set the letter down before I accidentally tore it. "Why are they going to declare me dead? Why now? And it doesn't say if my cousin Vanley is still alive, or if I killed him!" My voice rose at the memory of that awful night when I'd fled that awful house. Perhaps I deserved to be declared dead for killing him... But no. It had been self-defense, and whatever had happened, it was time I found out the truth.

Fenris met my gaze, his own as rock-steady as I'd ever seen it. "There is usually a waiting period of some years before a missing person is declared dead, and no proof is necessary. The heirs can then take over the estate. Waiting for so long will already have irked them a great deal."

"I can only imagine," I said bitterly, my voice rife with sarcasm.

"What would you like to do?" he asked quietly. There was not a hint of judgment in his voice, nothing to indicate whether any choice I made was right or wrong.

I looked down at the paper again. "I'm not sure," I murmured, staring at the flowing script, though I wasn't really seeing it. "If I go back, I'll have to explain my actions on that last night, and perhaps be punished. And I risk being forced to live with my aunt and uncle again."

"You may not have to," Fenris said. "If we present a convincing enough case, we might be able to get the Chief Mage of your home state to assign you a different guardian for the remaining period. With luck, given your age, it will be a mere formality."

"We?" I lifted an eyebrow. "I don't see how you can help me without...blowing your cover," I said, though I wasn't certain if that was an accurate term for his situation. We had grown so close now, yet there still so much I did not know about him...

Fenris gave me a crooked smile. "Don't worry about me,

Mina. I have my ways, and after everything we've been through, I'm developing a taste for adventure. I wouldn't let you face this on your own."

Sheer gratitude swept through me, and I blinked as my eyes burned once more. "Thank you," I said hoarsely, then looked down at the letter once more. The lawyer's words on the cream paper taunted me—how could he speak so casually of selling off my childhood home, my family heirlooms? Of allowing my abusers to profit off my inheritance? Mr. Ransome had been a regular guest at my grandmother's dinner table, had known me since I was a child. Did he not care at all?

"I cannot stand by and allow them to do this," I finally said, folding up the letter. "It isn't so much the wealth—it's the principle of the thing. My parents, my grandmother, would expect me to stand up for my rights and own up to my actions. Whatever the risk, whatever I might have to face...I have to stop them."

Pride gleamed in Fenris's eyes, warming me from the inside out. But his expression remained grave. "It will not be easy, this undertaking," he warned, even as he reached across the table to lace his fingers with mine. "We will have to prove your identity beyond reasonable doubt, and with a fortune at stake, you might find yourself in danger."

I stiffened at the underlying meaning of his words—that my relatives might very well try to kill me. "I don't think they are quite that callous, except perhaps my cousin Vanley, if he is still around. Regardless of the danger, I must try," I said firmly. "I have run from my past long enough."

And as Fenris and I sat talking long into the night, planning our strategy, the shaky, scared part of me that had fled from home all those years ago began to harden into firm resolve. No longer would I be a cowering victim, skulking around in poverty because nobody believed me when I needed help. I would *make*

them believe, and to hell with anyone who dared stand in my way.

To be continued...

Fenris and Mia will return in CLAIMED BY MAGIC, Book 2 in The Baine Chronicles: Fenris's story. If you'd like to be notified when the next book comes out, make sure you're subscribed to Jasmine's newsletter!

CLICK HERE TO SIGN UP

GLOSSARY

Abbsville: a small town in the state of Watawis, population ca. 800 including the surrounding farms.

Apprenticeship: all mages are expected to complete an apprenticeship with some master mage, that usually lasts from age fifteen to about twenty-five. Only after the final exam may they use colorful robes, and are considered legally of age. Otherwise they only attain their majority at age thirty.

ar': suffix in mages' family names, that denotes they are of noble birth, and can trace their descent to one of Resinah's twelve disciples.

Baine, Sunaya: a half-panther shifter, half-mage who used to hate mages and has a passion for justice. Because magic is forbidden to all but the mage families, Sunaya was forced to keep her abilities a secret until she accidentally used them to defend herself in front of witnesses. Rather than condemn her to death, the Chief Mage, Iannis ar'Sannin, chose to take her on as his apprentice, and eventually his fiancée. She struggles to balance her shifter and mage heritage.

Baine, Rylan: Sunaya Baine's cousin, and like her, a panther shifter. An active member of the Resistance, with the rank of

Captain, he was captured and imprisoned during the uprising in Solantha, but ultimately pardoned.

Benefactor: the anonymous, principal source of financial support to the Resistance, who was eventually unmasked as the socialite Thorgana Mills (now deceased).

Canalo: one of the fifty states making up the Northia Federation, located on the West Coast of the Northia Continent.

Central Continent: the largest of the continents on Recca, spanning from Garai in the east to Castalis in the west.

Creator, the: the ultimate deity, worshipped by all three races under different names.

Haralis: a port city on the east coast and capital of Innarta, one of the most prosperous states in the Northia Federation.

Iannis ar'Sannin: Chief Mage of Canalo. He resides in the capital city of Solantha, from which he runs Canalo as well as the Mages Guild with the help of his deputy and Secretaries. Originally a native of Manuc, a country located across the Eastern Sea.

Innarta: one of the fifty states of the Northia Federation, where Mina's family hails from.

Lady, the: mages refer to the First Mage, Resinah, as the Lady, most often in the phrase "by the Lady!"

Loranian: the difficult, secret language of magic that all mages are required to master.

Mages Guild: the governmental organization that rules the mages in each state, and supervises the other races. The headquarters are usually in the same building as the Palace of the local Chief Mage, to whom the Guild is subordinate.

Magorah: the god of the shifters, associated with the moon.

Mills, Thorgana: socialite and former owner of a news media conglomerate as well as numerous other companies. After being exposed as the Benefactor she was imprisoned. She

managed to escape, but died around the time of the Solantha earthquake.

Nebara:, one of the fifty states making up the Northia Federation, located north of Canalo, and Fenris's home state.

Northia Federation: a federation consisting of fifty states that cover almost the entire northern half and middle of the Western Continent.

Northian: the main language spoken in the Northia Federation.

Osero: one of the fifty states of the Northia Federation, located north of Canalo on the continent's west coast.

Pandanum: a base metal used, inter alia, for less valuable coins.

Polar ar'Tollis: former Chief Mage of Nebara, who vanished after being condemned to death by the Convention.

Recca: the world of humans, mages and shifters.

Resinah: the first mage, whose teachings are of paramount spiritual importance for the mages. Her statue can be found in the mage temples, which are off-limits to non-mages and magically hidden from outsiders.

Resistance: a movement of revolutionaries planning to overthrow the mages and take control of the Northia Federation, financially backed by the Benefactor. Over time they became bolder and more aggressive, using terrorist attacks with civilian casualties, as well as assassination. The discovery that the Benefactor and the human leaders of the Resistance were planning to turn on the shifters once the mages were defeated dealt a blow to the unity of the movement, but its human component is far from completely defeated.

Rylan: see under Baine, Rylan.

Shifter: a human who can change into animal form and back by magic; they originally resulted from illegal experiments by mages on ordinary humans.

Silver: the metal is toxic to shifters, and burns their skin when they touch it. It is nevertheless used for coins in the Federation.

Solantha: the capital of Canalo State, a port city on the west coast of the Northia continent. Seat of Chief Mage Iannis ar'Sannin and the Canalo Mages Guild, and home of Sunaya Baine.

Testing: human and shifter schoolchildren in the Northia Federation are tested for magic at least twice during their schoolyears, and a positive result will normally lead to the magic wipe (often with permanent mental damage.)

Thorgana: see under Mills, Thorgana

Toring, Garrett: mage, Federal Director of Security, former Federal Secretary of Justice; an ambitious high official in the Federal government.

Ur-God: the name the humans call the Creator by.

Uton: one of the fifty states of the Northia Federation.

Watawis: one of the fifty states of the Northia Federation, landlocked, in the mountainous northwest. It is one of the least populated and poorest of the fifty states.

Willowdale: capital of the state of Watawis, seat of its Chief Mage and government.

ABOUT THE AUTHOR

JASMINE WALT is obsessed with books, chocolate, and sharp objects. Somehow, those three things melded together in her head and transformed into a desire to write, usually fantastical stuff with a healthy dose of action and romance. Her characters are a little (okay, a lot) on the snarky side, and they swear, but they mean well. Even the villains sometimes.

When Jasmine isn't chained to her keyboard, you can find her practicing her triangle choke on the jujitsu mat, spending time with her family, or binge-watching superhero shows on Netflix.

Want to connect with Jasmine? You can find her on Instagram at @jasmine.walt, on Facebook, or at www.jasminewalt.com.